ONE
WRONG
MOVE

"Another fantastic suspense by Dani Pettrey! I fell in love with Christian and Andi's sweet romance, and the plot kept me on the edge of my seat all the way to the end. Excellent!"

—Susan May Warren, *USA Today* bestselling author

Praise for Dani Pettrey

"This action-packed thriller is sure to please."

—Irene Hannon, bestselling and award-winning author
of *The Deadly Shallows*

"Pettrey delivers another outstanding novel filled with romance, mystery, and suspense. Fans of DiAnn Mills, Lynette Eason, and Dee Henderson will be drawn to this book."

—*Library Journal* starred review of *The Killing Tide*

"I love Dani's writing, and *The Deadly Shallows* is one of her best! Tightly written and dripping with tension. I couldn't turn the pages fast enough."

—Carrie Stuart Parks, bestselling and award-winning author
of *Relative Silence*

"Pulse-pounding. . . . Pettrey masterfully balances Noah and Brooke's burgeoning relationship with the unraveling of the tightly plotted mystery. Fans of Lynette Eason and DiAnn Mills will enjoy this."

—*Publishers Weekly* on *The Deadly Shallows*

"Pettrey kicks off her new COASTAL GUARDIANS series with an intense blend of suspense, love, and faith. *The Killing Tide* features romance that's as thrilling as the action, and faithful characters integrated seamlessly into a complex web of crime. Fans of Susan May Warren's MONTANA RESCUE series and of Dee Henderson's novels will enjoy this exhilarating read and delight in the tantalizing clues dropped throughout the book hinting at what promises to be an entertaining sequel."

—*Booklist*

ONE WRONG MOVE

DANI PETTREY

BETHANYHOUSE
a division of Baker Publishing Group
Minneapolis, Minnesota

© 2024 by Grace and Johnny, Inc.

Published by Bethany House Publishers
Minneapolis, Minnesota
BethanyHouse.com

Bethany House Publishers is a division of
Baker Publishing Group, Grand Rapids, Michigan

Printed in the United States of America

Library of Congress Cataloging-in-Publication Data
Names: Pettrey, Dani, author.
Title: One wrong move / Dani Pettrey.
Description: Minneapolis, Minnesota : Bethany House Publishers, a division of Baker Publishing Group, 2024. | Series: Jeopardy falls ; 1
Identifiers: LCCN 2023045253 | ISBN 9780764238482 (paper) | ISBN 9781493445264 (casebound) | ISBN 9781493443666 (eBook)
Subjects: LCGFT: Thrillers (Fiction) | Novels.
Classification: LCC PS3616.E89 O54 2024 | DDC 813/.6—dc23/eng/20231003
LC record available at https://lccn.loc.gov/2023045253

This book is a work of fiction. Names, characters, places, and incidents are the product of the author's imagination or are used fictitiously. Any resemblance to actual events, locales, or persons, living or dead, is coincidental.

Published in association with Books & Such Literary Management, www.books andsuch.com.

Baker Publishing Group publications use paper produced from sustainable forestry practices and post-consumer waste whenever possible.

24 25 26 27 28 29 30   7 6 5 4 3 2 1

To Calvin and Brenn

For all the laughter and joy you bring into my life
and for all our wild adventures—
crazy car rides, holding alligators,
petting stingrays, and nonstop days on the beach.
I love you and our adventures together so much!

PROLOGUE

HE INHALED THE STIFF RESOLUTION of her death. She'd seen Cyrus. Remembered him. Now he'd need to silence her before she could mention Cyrus to anyone at the gallery. The imbecile should have been more careful, but that's why *he* was in play. To assure things went according to plan, to remove anyone who stood in their way, and when it was done, to take out Cyrus and Casey. That he would delight in. Cyrus had been a pain in his rear as far back as he could recall. Casey. He was just a lamb to the slaughter, unfortunate fool.

Enrique released a smooth exhale, then inhaled the spicy scent of the girl's perfume wafting on the stiff October breeze—whistling through the wind tunnel the long row of downtown businesses made.

Killing her would alert Cyrus to his presence in the States, but, perhaps it would keep him on his toes. Someone needed to.

Maintaining a good distance from his prey, Enrique followed as she meandered through the shops, wearing one of those recyclable grocery bags slung over her shoulder. A baguette and fresh flowers peeked out of the top. She made another stop, this time popping into a coffee shop. He kept walking, stopping a handful of stores down on the opposite side of the street, and waited, letting the other shoppers meld him into the crowd.

A cup of coffee in hand, the girl emerged.

He turned back to look in the storefront before him, waiting until she was far enough ahead for him to resume following. Nearly a fifteen-minute walk out of town, in an isolated patch of wind-stirred mesa, sat a two-story adobe building. Four exterior doors, each with a letter on it. Apartments.

Watching from behind a copse of trees, he waited while she retrieved her keys from her pocket, opened the bottom exterior door on the right, and disappeared inside. He held back, awaiting nightfall. He glanced at his watch. Not long. He surveyed the building, using binoculars to peer through the sheer curtains of her unit. A light in the bedroom shone, and slips of it spilled from what he could only assume was the adjacent bathroom.

He smiled.

The sun dipped below the horizon, and soon darkness shrouded the land. Time to move. Heading around to the back of the building, he found a sliding door to her unit. Easy enough. He jimmied the lock and eased inside.

Water ran in the bathroom, but a voice carried in song from the other side of the apartment. "Carry on Wayward Son." Interesting choice.

He moved with stealth, approaching what he discerned was the kitchen. A teakettle whistled as steam from the open bathroom door filled the space. The girl turned the corner, dressed in a robe, a teacup in her hand. Her eyes locked on his, and panic flashed across her face as the teacup fell and shattered on the floor.

He smiled. Time to have some fun.

ONE

"WAIT HERE," Cyrus ordered.

"Why?" Casey asked—though pawn suited him better. As much as it galled him, Cyrus needed the insipid man. Needed his skills. For now. But when they were done, so was he. "Why?" he asked again.

Cyrus gritted his teeth. So incessant. He shook out his fists. Only a handful of locations to go and the questions would cease. *He* would cease. "It doesn't take two of us to get what we came for," he said, hoping Casey would accept the answer and let it drop, but he doubted it. "I've got this. Two of us will only draw more attention."

"Fine." Casey slumped back against the van's passenger seat.

The imbecile was pouting like a girl. And, that knee. Cyrus wanted to break it. Always bouncing in that annoying, jittery way. The seat squeaked with the rapid, persistent motion. He shook his head on a grunted exhale. If Casey didn't settle . . . if he blew their plans. Cyrus squeezed his fists tight, blood throbbing through his fingers. Too much was at stake. His own neck was on the line.

He turned his attention to the task at hand. "I won't be long," he said, surveying the space one last time before opening the van door. The lot behind them was dead, the building still. He climbed out, his breath a vapor in the cold night air. He glanced back at their van, barely visible in the pitch-black alley.

Shockingly, Casey remained in the passenger seat, his knee still bouncing high.

He shut the van door as eagerness coursed through him. The

thrill and rush of the score mere minutes away. Just one quick job and then it was finally time.

He slipped his gloved hands into his pockets. A deeper rush nestled hot inside him, adrenaline searing his limbs. His fervency was for the kill.

He moved toward the rear of the restaurant, where the rental rooms' entrance sat. His gloved fingers brushed the garrote in his right pocket, and he shifted his other hand to rest on the hilt of his gun. Which way would it go? Garrote or gun? Anticipation shot through him. Rounding the back of the building, he hung in the shadows and then stepped to the door and picked the lock—so simple a child could have done it. But what had he expected of a rent-by-the-hour-or-day establishment?

Opening the door, he stepped inside the minuscule foyer and studied the two doors on the ground level. Nothing but silence. He found the light switch and flipped off the ceiling bulb illuminating the stairwell, then crept up the stairs, pausing as one creaked. He held still, his back flush with the wall, once again shadowed in darkness. Nothing stirred.

Reaching her room, he picked the lock, stepped inside, and shut the door, locking it behind him.

She was asleep on the shoddy sofa, a ratty blanket draped across her. Getting rid of her now might be easier, but what fun was it killing someone while they slept? And he needed to make sure she had the items.

He stood a moment, watching her chest rise and fall with what would be her final breaths, then he knocked her feet with his elbow.

Her eyes flashed open as she lurched to a seated position. She rubbed her eyes. "You're late."

Less chance of witnesses.

"You have the items?"

She nodded.

"Get them. We're in a hurry."

She got to her feet and headed for the bedroom.

He followed.

To his surprise, she climbed up on the dresser and reached for the heating vent.

Huh. She was smarter than he'd expected, yet not bright enough to know what was coming.

Pulling the dingy grate back, she retrieved a black velvet pouch and a bundle of letters held in place by a thick rubber band.

"Hand them over," he said.

She hopped down and hesitated. "I get my cut, right?" She clutched the items to her pale chest.

"You'll get your cut," he said, wrapping his hands around the garrote.

She released her hold. Taking the bag first, he slid it into his upper jacket pocket, then slipped the letters into his pant pocket. "Good job."

She brushed a strand of hair behind her ear, revealing her creamy neck. "Thanks."

Restless energy pulsed through him.

"Are we done here?" she asked, shifting her stance, her arms wrapped around her slender waist.

"Just about."

"What's left to do?" she asked, her head cocked, and then she stilled. She took a step back. So she'd finally figured it out.

"No." She shook her head, backing into the paneled wall. In one movement, left hand to right shoulder, he spun her around and slipped the garrote over her head.

He'd intended to give her the option—the easy way with a gunshot to the head or the hard way with the garrote. But the hard way was far more pleasurable, giving him the best elated high.

It really was a shame. She was a pretty thing.

Five minutes later, he was back in the van, leaving the body behind.

"You got everything?" Casey asked as they pulled onto the street, their headlights off.

Cyrus smiled and handed both items to him. They were a go. The appetite for what was to come gnawed at Cyrus's gut, but in a good way. It was time to feed the anticipation that had been growing in him for nigh on a year. It was time to scratch that itch.

TWO

CHRISTIAN'S HANDS gripped the rock face. Granules abraded the tender flesh beneath his nails, leaving them raw. Pushing up on the ball of his foot, he strained, his fingers searching for the crag. Finally, his hand landed on the cold surface—only three inches deep. On a sharp inhale and slow exhale, he lunged upward—only the slightest hold kept him from the hundred-foot drop to the forest below. His foot landed on the next hold, and he settled, his muscles hot in the brisk dawn air. Blood throbbing through his fingers, he shifted the weight onto the balls of his feet.

Mapping the next route in his head, he leaped for the next hold. Air replaced the solid rock for the breath of a second, and searing adrenaline crashed through him as the hold slipped away. His pulse whooshing in his ears, he slid down, finally grabbing hold of a crag on his rapid descent. His fingers gripped hard—the only thing holding his body weight and keeping him from the ground far below.

He examined the cliff, looking for a foothold. Something. Anything. Adrenaline raked through him, quivering his arms. *Not good.* Time held motionless until he anchored his foot on a narrow ledge, small rocks shifting under the soles of his climbing shoes. He kept his weight on the ball of his foot while scanning for a new route up. He exhaled as he found it, but it was going to require another leap of faith.

Releasing his hold, he lunged for a more solid handhold. Gripping it, he worked his way up to another ledge—this one deep enough to settle comfortably onto.

His breathing quickened by the climb, he turned and pressed his back against the volcanic rock—cool against his heated and perspiring skin—and exhaled in a whoosh. Talk about a close one. He smiled. One more adventure down.

He held for a moment, taking in the morning light spreading across what seemed an endless sky. Man, he loved this view. Narrow shafts of sunlight streamed down through the early morning fog, lighting the yellow-and-orange foliage ablaze. Everyone talked about the beautiful fall colors in New England, but for him nothing beat fall in New Mexico, and it was peak season.

He sank into the silence. Only the occasional chirping of birds in the trees below rushed by his ears on the stiff, mounting breeze.

The brilliant orange sun rose higher above the horizon, its rays glinting off the rushing water of the swift creek at the bottom of the valley—chasing away the fading chill of night and replacing it with renewed warmth of the coming day.

"Ain't Worried About It" broke the silence with its melody. Who on earth was calling so early? He prayed nothing was wrong. It was the only reason he kept his cell on him while climbing—in case there was an emergency and his family needed him.

He shimmied the phone from the Velcro pocket on his right thigh and maneuvered it to his ear without bothering to look at who was calling. "O'Brady."

"I need you here now!" Tad Gaiman's voice shook with rage.

Why on earth was Tad calling him so early? Why was he calling him, period?

Tad's heated words tumbled out. "My gallery's been robbed!"

"What?" Christian blinked. There was no way. The security system upgrades he'd installed made it impenetrable, or so he'd thought.

"Do you hear me? My gallery has been robbed!"

"I do." He kept his voice level. Tad was frantic enough for the both of them. "Which gallery?" The man owned three.

"Jeopardy Falls."

15

The one in their hometown? Crime was nearly nonexistent in their small ranching, lately turned tourist, town of five hundred. "Take a deep breath and calm down so you can focus."

"Calm down?" Tad shrieked, and Christian held the phone away from his ear. Even his sister Riley couldn't hit that high of a pitch. "Did you not hear me? My gallery's been robbed."

"I hear you. Let me call you back."

"Call me back? You cannot be serious!"

"I'm balanced on a ledge on Manzano."

"Of course you are." Tad scoffed.

"I'll call you when I'm on the road."

"And how long will it take you to get here? This is a DEFCON 5 situation."

Christian shook his head. Clearly, Tad had no idea what he was talking about. DEFCON 5 meant peacetime.

"Christian! How soon?"

"I need to climb down and make the drive back to town. I'll see you in an hour."

"An hour!"

"We'll talk through it on my way in."

Scaling down the rock face as fast as he could, Christian reached his vintage Bronco.

Climbing inside, he clicked on the Bluetooth he'd installed. It'd cost a lot, but in his line of work, he needed to be able to talk while on the road chasing down a case. He shook his head, still baffled that anyone had beat the security system.

He dialed Tad.

Normally his drive along the winding dirt roads through the mountains was calming, but not today.

Tad picked up on the third ring.

"Okay," Christian said, swiping the chalk from his hands onto his pants—the climbing towel too far to reach. "Walk me through it. Did the alarm go off?"

"The one on the security system you said couldn't be beat? No!"

Christian took a stiff inhale. How on earth had someone gotten through the door without the key fob? *The fob* . . . "Tad, do you have your key fob?"

Silence hung thick in the air as Christian's Bronco bumped over the ruts in the dirt road, the drop-off only inches from his tires. He rounded the bend, and the road—if it could be deemed one— widened. "Tad?" he pressed.

"Okay, fine. I don't have it."

"Where is it?" Christian asked as he headed for the main road that led back to Jeopardy Falls.

Tad swallowed, the slippery, gulping sound echoing over the line. "I think the woman I spent last night with after the gala took it."

"Riley mentioned she might attend the gala, but she couldn't make it."

"It was well attended."

"And the woman you mentioned?"

"I met her at the gala."

"She's not local?"

"I've never seen her before last night."

"So she just strolled into the gala?"

"Yes. It was a semiprivate affair. I sent out invites but welcomed anyone, given it was Friday Night on the Town."

Their small town had instituted the night on the town for one Friday a month about a year ago, and it had really drummed up business for the eclectic downtown shops.

"Let's shift back to the gallery," Christian said. "I'm assuming you used Alex's fob to get into the building?"

"No. I can't get in."

"Why not?" Christian pulled out onto the paved road.

"I can't reach Alex, despite the fact she's supposed to open this morning."

"Okay . . . so walk me through what happened with the fob."

"I woke up and that . . . woman was gone, and the fob wasn't where I'd left it. I searched my place, but it's not there, so I rushed to the gallery. I stopped at Alex's place on the way, but no answer. She is so—"

"Settle down, Tad. Let's think this through. Do you think Martha would let you into Alex's place if you explained the situation?" Maybe the landlady would understand. Jeopardy Falls was a small enough town where everyone knew everyone, which was still taking time for him to get used to. To be known. Well, known at what he was willing to show, which wasn't much.

"I'm not leaving my gallery. Not until I get inside and see what damage is done. You get the fob from Martha."

Christian furrowed his brows. "If you can't get in the gallery and the alarm didn't go off, how do you know it's been robbed?"

"Because I can see the three front cases through the porthole windows in the door. They're open and empty." A sob escaped Tad's throat, though he tried to cover it with a cough.

Christian exhaled. "All right. I'll call Martha, but she might not feel comfortable letting us in." It was a lot to ask. "Actually, I think in this case, it's best to have Sheriff Brunswick to reach out to Martha."

"That's a good idea," Tad said. "Give him a call."

"Wait?" Christian tapped the wheel. "He's not there yet?"

"No."

"Did he give you an ETA?" Maybe Joel was on another call. Their county was large, and with only him and one undersheriff, they had a lot of ground to cover.

"I haven't called him yet."

Christian's brows hiked. "You called me before the sheriff?" Where was the sense in that?

"You put the supposedly impenetrable system in. I want to know what went wrong. And I need you to get me inside if we can't get Alex's fob."

"Me?" Christian tapped the wheel.

"You installed the system, so surely you know how to beat it. And, regardless, you're the one the sheriff calls when they need a locksmith or safecracker on a case. Though you're quite more than a simple locksmith, aren't you?"

Christian stiffened. "Meaning?"

"Whoever did this obviously had knowledge of the system."

"And . . . ?" Christian tightened his grip on the wheel, his knuckles turning white.

"As far as I'm concerned, you're to blame."

Christian swallowed the sharp retort ready to fly and took a settling breath instead. "I'll be there in twenty."

He disconnected the call before Tad could throw another barb in his direction. He knew all too well how those stinging barbs felt, but this time he was innocent.

THREE

THE THRILL of working another heist surged through Andi's limbs as she raced down her dirt drive, heading for Jeopardy Falls.

Her boss said he'd call to apprise her of the details he'd received once she was on the way to the quaint town situated in the Sangre de Cristo Mountains roughly halfway between Santa Fe and Taos. He'd also informed her that Tad Gaiman's catalog of his collections was already being shipped next-day delivery from FedEx.

As she quickly accelerated, a coyote raced into the road, its eyes glistening in the rays of the rising sun. She slammed her brakes, and dust clouds swirled and billowed as her truck rocked to a halt—her heart pounding in her chest.

The animal froze, its kill dangling from its mouth.

Her cell trilled, jolting her just as the animal shook out of its stupor and took off on gangly legs, vanishing into the tumbleweeds and brush.

The trilling continued. She fished her phone out of her purse. "Hi, boss." Her breathing came in tight, short spurts as she switched it to Bluetooth.

"You sound spooked. Is something wrong?"

"No. A coyote in the road just startled me."

"You good now?"

Regaining her composure, she once again pressed her foot on the accelerator, only not quite as fast this time. "Yep. Ready to fill me in?" She pulled onto the road leading her north toward Jeopardy Falls. It was a cool, artsy town with several galleries, cute restaurants, and shops with beautiful Native American jewelry and arts. But it was also a ranching town, which made for an interesting dichotomy. Good thing she liked dichotomy.

"I just got more details from Mr. Gaiman."

"Are the cops on site yet?"

"No. The sheriff and his undersheriff were on a call up by someplace called Truchas, but they're on the way now."

"Okay." She wasn't looking forward to dealing with law enforcement. They rarely viewed what she did as an investigation. But that's what separated her from the adjusters. She worked the case just like a detective would. "So what do we know?" she asked, tapping the toe of her left foot on the floorboard.

"Only that Mr. Gaiman can see three cases are open and empty."

"Can see?"

"Apparently, he's stuck outside the gallery, but the lock technician is on the way. Sounds like you'll all arrive about the same time."

All of them at the same time . . . *great*. She swallowed a deep inhale, her nerves already frayed at the thought of what was supposed to have happened last night, but that deserved no place in her mind. *He* deserved no place in her mind. While she felt bad that Mr. Gaiman had been robbed, the case would be a nice distraction for her. Even if it meant dealing with law enforcement.

"Gaiman says the jewels in those three cases are worth close to a million."

Andi's mouth slackened. "A million in three cases? In a Jeopardy Falls gallery?" The town held several high-end galleries, but she hadn't expected that high-end.

Papers rustled on the other end, followed by the tapping of fingers on a keyboard. "Tad Gaiman is insured for ten million dollars."

"Seriously?"

"Yes, but that includes his Albuquerque and Taos galleries too," Grant said.

She increased her speed after the car in front of her turned off and the road ahead opened up. "I'll call you with all the details when I wrap up the initial assessment."

"Or you could debrief me in person. Say . . . tonight in Albuquerque?" Grant said.

Please, no. She gripped the steering wheel tighter. *Not this again.*

"Natalie really wants you home for the balloon fiesta. We're all going to be there through the weekend. It's less than a two-hour ride down, Bells."

She couldn't help but smile at the nickname he'd given her when she had to have been no more than five, wearing little bells on her shiny red shoes. But . . .

"It really weirds me out when you call my mom Natalie." Despite Grant basically being family—her big brother's best friend as far back as she could recall.

"I'm thirty-two. I think it's okay to drop the *Miss* part. But back on topic, your mom insisted you come home."

Her mom could insist all she liked, but she wasn't going home. It stopped being a safe haven the minute her life fell apart.

FOUR

ANDI SLOWED as she entered Jeopardy Falls and the speed limit on Juan Tabo dropped to thirty. She cruised along the two-lane road running through the center of town. Last time she'd been here, it was with her bestie, Harper. After a day of perusing the fun and quirky shops, they'd shared dinner on the outdoor patio of a cozy restaurant with white twinkly lights strung overhead. Good memories. At least she had a few post-devastation, and that was one of them.

Shifting her gaze down a half dozen or so blocks, she kept an eye out for Gaiman's business. If she recalled correctly, the four art galleries in town each straddled a different corner at the intersection of Juan Tabo and Comanche Street, which the locals had dubbed "gallery corner."

Passing the feed store, she spotted cowboys heading in and out. She halted at the crosswalk, letting one strapping, handsome cowboy pass by. He thanked her with a tip of his hat and a wink. She smiled despite herself. Continuing on, she passed the lone Italian restaurant in town, along with a slew of Mexican restaurants serving New Mexican–style cuisine. Sadie's was her favorite, and their green chile stew was to die for.

Her stomach grumbled just thinking about it. She'd rushed out without breakfast, but food would have to wait. She had a job to do, thanks to Grant's pity or compassion. Either way, she owed him everything. He'd given her purpose when hers had died.

Banking right at "gallery corner," she noted the steady stream of folks heading into Frannie's Diner. Rumor had it she made the best biscuits west of Charleston.

Glancing catty-corner, Andi spotted the Gaiman Gallery. But how could she not? It had the most ostentatious exterior. The building was painted a textured cobalt blue, but it was the mirrors in random shapes plastered about the gallery that gave it that "blingy" feeling. Not to mention the murals—all done artistically in a Picasso-esque style with vibrant colors. For housing such an expensive gallery collection, it was quite the odd exterior.

Pulling into the parking lot, she spotted a silver Porsche Panamera and a sheriff's vehicle.

Taking what she hoped would be a calming breath, she whispered a prayer and stepped outside. The warmth of the rising sun swarmed around her, enveloping her in its beautiful heat after such a chilly night.

Halfway across the lot, she paused, the hair on the nape of her neck tingling. *Odd.* She ignored it and continued across the newly paved lot, but within a handful of steps forward, a shiver brushed across her skin. She stopped and surveyed her surroundings. The only people visible were those heading in or out of Frannie's, and none seemed particularly interested in her. Chalking it up to nerves, she strode toward the building, rounded a brick wall . . . and nearly plowed into the sheriff.

"Oops. Sorry. I wasn't expecting . . ."

The sheriff tipped his hat. "All good."

Her gaze darted to the other man present, outfitted in genie-style striped pants and a purple satin shirt sprinkled with colorful geometric shapes. He paced the terracotta-tile entryway much like a coyote did when searching for its next kill.

The sun glinted off the man's bleached-blond hair feathered back in '70s style. Or was it the '80s? Whichever it was, it certainly wasn't this century. She'd place him in his early to mid-forties, so it seemed a fitting style for his growing-up years.

"Sheriff Brunswick." The six-foot-tall man with blue eyes, weathered skin, and a crinkly smile extended his hand.

"Andi Forester. It's a pleasure." At least she hoped it would be. Law enforcement either treated her with professional courtesy or they ridiculed her, but she had a good feeling about Brunswick—though that odd uneasiness of being watched burrowed deep in her gut and wouldn't let go. She tried to shake it off but to no avail. She turned to the other man. "Mr. Gaiman, I presume."

He stared at her, green eyes blinking.

"I'm the insurance investigator with Ambrose Global."

"Investigator?" His brow furrowed. "I thought they were sending an adjuster."

"Not in these types of cases."

His brows hiked. "*These* types?"

"Heists. I work like a detective to get to the bottom of the case. To find the perpetrators."

"I thought that was my job," Sheriff Brunswick said.

"It is, but it's also mine," she said, bracing herself for the sheriff's reaction. But none came, so she continued. "It's my job to determine who pulled off the heist." She turned back to Sheriff Brunswick. "I hope we can keep each other in the loop."

The man lifted his Stetson off his head and raked a hand through his dark hair. "I don't see why that would be a problem, as long as boundaries are kept."

She released her pent-up breath. "Of course." Then, going for broke, she said, "I'd love a copy of the police report when it's ready, and I'm more than happy to share any of my notes." Her words rushed out in a harried fashion, hoping to get the last point in before he had a chance to say no to her request.

Brunswick settled his hat back in place. "I don't see that being a problem." He looked up at the sound of a car engine.

"Finally," Tad said, his tight shoulders drooping.

Brunswick moved for the lot. Andi stuck her head around the entrance wall to see a green Bronco pulling into a parking spot.

"Who's that?" Andi asked.

"The man who's going to get us in the building," Tad said. "He installed the system, so only he can beat it to get in."

Prime suspect number two. Installation guy. Tad was number one. The gallery owner always was. It was crazy how many robbed their own gallery, or had it robbed, to collect on the insurance money—at least based on Grant's worldwide cases. One had even been stupid enough to hide the "stolen" pieces in his home.

She shook her thoughts back to the present. "So why aren't you able to get into your own gallery?"

"Well, I . . ." He broke off as Sheriff Brunswick rounded the wall, followed by another man.

"There's the responsible party," Tad said.

"I'd hardly say I'm responsible." Sunlight continued to stream down, and it took a moment for the installation man to step out of the bright beams far enough for her to lay eyes on him. When she did . . . wow! Rugged build, at least six-three . . . maybe six-four, with brown hair cresting his broad shoulders. He was decked out in hiking—no, climbing—clothes, given the chalk swipes on his pants. An embarrassing heat rushed her cheeks.

"Who's this?" the man asked Tad, lifting his chin in her direction.

"Andi . . . something or other," Tad said. "She's with the insurance agency."

"Ah. The adjuster." He stretched out his muscular right arm and extended his hand, still dabbed with a hint of chalk. "Christian O'Brady."

"Andi Forester," she replied. "And I'm not an adjuster."

Christian arched a dark brown brow. "No?"

"I'm an insurance investigator."

"Investigator. Really?"

"Yep."

He smiled. "That's very cool."

"Yes. Yes," Tad said, waving his arm, his shirt sleeve billowing in the breeze. "It's cool. Now can you let us into my gallery so I can see what else was taken?" He shook his head, bewilderment flashing across his tan face.

"You okay there?" Brunswick asked.

"Just hoping that nothing else was taken."

"I doubt that's the case," Christian said.

"Why not?" Andi asked.

"They beat a nearly unbeatable system. I'm sorry to say, they probably had all the time they needed to take whatever they wanted."

"Wonderful!" Tad snorted. "Now, can you please get us in?"

Christian looked at Brunswick. "Were you able to talk to Martha about letting us into Alex's place?"

"She said she would after she tried to get ahold of Alex—but only if it's just me in a law-enforcement capacity."

Tad rested his hands on his hips, bangles jingling on both wrists. "Then why were we waiting on him?" He practically sneered in Christian's direction.

"Because Martha's on her way down to Albuquerque for some medical appointment. She said she'd let me know when she's back in town and I can go take a look. So for now, we need you"—he looked at Christian—"to work your magic."

"I don't understand," Andi said. "Who is Alex, and what does he have to do with getting in the building?"

"Alex is a she," Brunswick said. "And she has the other fob."

She furrowed her brow. "Fob?"

"It's how you enter the building." Tad gestured to Christian. "He can fill you in later, but for now, can we please just get in my gallery?"

"I have my kit in the Bronco," Christian said.

Andi's attention locked in as he strode to and from the car and dropped his kit in front of the door. Sheriff Brunswick and Tad took several steps back to let him work, but she stayed in place. The man was either extremely cocky or exceedingly good—or maybe both. She no longer trusted her gut, but if she did, she'd have wagered he was going to pull this off.

He knelt in front of the door and pulled out what looked to be two intricate skeleton keys. "I have to insert them into both sides of the slot simultaneously without pressing anything else down accidentally." He did so. "Now . . . I push up with equal force until they disconnect from each other, and . . ." A click sounded. "*Voilà!*"

"That's it?"

He stood and brushed off his hands. "That's one piece of the map."

"Excuse me?"

"There are several actions necessary to get in." Christian placed his hand on the knob. "There's usually a shrill alarm." He looked to the sheriff. "I called the alarm company to let them know it might go off."

"Wait," Andi said. "The alarm never went off?"

"Apparently not," Christian said. "Which means they somehow avoided triggering the motion sensors and made it to the keypad in time."

"The keypad?" she asked.

"You have two minutes from the time you use the fob to get to Tad's office at the back of the gallery, open the safe, and key in the code before the alarm goes off."

"You put the keypad in a safe?" she asked.

He nodded.

Ingenious. "And the chances that someone without prior knowledge could figure out all the steps of the map, as you called it, are what?"

"One in a million," Christian said.

"Right." So it had to be someone on the inside or someone with contacts on the inside. She looked between him and Tad, wondering who the guilty party was.

FIVE

CHRISTIAN O'BRADY held the heavy cobalt blue door open, and Andi stepped inside the Gaiman Gallery. It was, in a word, exquisite. Terracotta walls, glass display cases with gold-rimmed bases, and on the far wall, two Georgia O'Keefe paintings of the New Mexico landscape in shades of orange and rust that immediately drew her in.

Even the lighting was superb—a combination of track and up-lighting. Whoever designed the space was very talented, and the collections echoed the high-priced insurance policy Tad Gaiman possessed.

Andi's gaze pinned on the empty cases—each one standing six inches higher as they moved to the right. "What items did these cases hold?" she asked while Christian and Sheriff Brunswick strode to the back of the gallery to check on the alarm keypad and the safe that was supposed to keep it just that. Then Christian would need to reset the system.

"They . . ." Tad finally sobbed. He pulled a clumped-up tissue from his pocket, dabbing it at his tearing eyes. "They were my pride-and-joy collection."

That was a first. She'd never seen an owner moved to tears over their loss. Anger, outrage—that she saw a lot—but tears and sniffles, never.

"Let's begin with you telling me about them," she said, wasting no time. Brunswick held the primary investigative role, but it made no sense to stand around waiting. She'd be sure to fill him in on anything she learned and would give him the leeway to conduct his investigation first. It was frustrating at times being in the second seat when she'd been the golden child at the Bureau, but that had been a lifetime ago.

Tad sniffed, this time dabbing the scrunched-up tissue to his nose. "There are nine missing pieces, all necklaces."

"I'm going to need you to go into more detail."

"They were my five Mexican fire opals and four artistically designed Mayan jade jewelry."

That was serious money.

She looked around the gallery. "What else is missing?"

His gaze followed hers around the open space with industrial-style, open ceilings.

"I'll have to do a walk-through," he said.

"Agreed." It was a necessary part of the process.

They'd barely moved into the next gallery room of miniature Mayan statues when Sheriff Brunswick and Christian O'Brady returned.

"So?" Tad asked, his leg bouncing, his boot tapping against the tile floor.

Christian exhaled. "They knew what they were doing. They left the safe open and dismantled the keypad with great precision."

"Like someone knew where it was located and how to dismantle it?" Andi posed.

Tad looked like a deer in the headlights, then blinked. "Surely you aren't suggesting me, my child."

She'd opened her mouth to answer when "Welcome to the Jungle" played from Tad's pants. He held up a finger to pause her, then retrieved his phone from his right pants pocket.

"Hello . . . I can't talk, Cara. My Jeopardy Falls gallery has been robbed. . . . What?" The blood drained from Tad's face. "It can't . . . Are you . . . Okay." Tad hung up the phone while the woman was still talking.

"What is it?" Christian asked.

"Cara called. My Albuquerque gallery was robbed too."

Andi's eyes widened. "What?"

Back-to-back heists. That was practically unheard of. A set hadn't been pulled off since those teens managed to a solid decade ago. She'd read about the case while prepping for the job Grant had so graciously offered when her world imploded. She'd taken time to review every major art heist in the last twenty years. He'd given her a job she didn't deserve, the least she could do was excel at it.

"And Cara is?" Sheriff Brunswick asked.

"My assistant in Albuquerque. She runs the place while I'm here," Tad managed to say in his dazed state, his eyes glassy, his movements oddly pronounced, as if he were moving in slow motion.

"I'll call Albuquerque PD. Give them a heads-up that we're likely looking at connected cases. If you'll excuse me." Brunswick grabbed his phone and stepped away.

Andi bit her bottom lip, hard. It was the last thing she wanted to utter, but she had to say it. "Based on what my boss briefed me on, your Albuquerque gallery has—"

"Hold that thought," Tad said, cutting her off. "I need to make one more call." He dialed then paced. "Jessica," he said, his voice a frenzy of syllables. "Is everything okay at the gallery? Yes, I know it's early, but I need you to check on the gallery. Why? Because my other two have been hit. Okay. Call me back."

"Your Taos gallery?" Andi asked.

Tad's face, now splotched with patches of deep red, was stricken with panic.

"They've already sent a team out to your Albuquerque gallery," Brunswick said, striding back over.

Christian looked to Andi. "What were you trying to say to Tad earlier?"

She swallowed, praying the words didn't get caught in her throat. "While this gallery is focused on art pieces, Mr. Gaiman's Albuquerque gallery contains ancient artifacts of cultural significance."

"And?" Tad frowned.

"Cultural artifacts are the FBI's jurisdiction." There, she'd said it. Mentioned *them*. "You'll need to call the Bureau's art theft team." She took a steadying inhale that did anything but steady her.

"You okay?" Christian asked.

"Fine," she said, trying to convince herself of that.

"You just look a little faint," he said.

"Oh. I skipped breakfast," she blurted out. It was true. Not the reason for the discomfort sifting through her, but true all the same.

"Then we better grab something on the way out of town," Christian said.

"Wait. *We*? What?"

"We both need to go to the Albuquerque gallery. No sense driving separately."

"I . . . uh . . . I'm fine driving," she said.

"Okay, I can ride with you then."

"I . . ." She could insist she drive alone, but while she prayed the man wasn't involved in the case for only heaven knew why, he was still a high-priority suspect, and the ninety-minute ride would give her plenty of time to question him. "Okay," she said. "But I'm good with you driving." Her head was still swirling at the thought of the Feds. She just prayed Adam wouldn't be there. Anyone but Adam . . . and Jeremy, of course, but if he'd stuck to his plans, he and his new bride were off on their honeymoon.

Heat rushed her limbs. He'd kept the same wedding day, same honeymoon location—just got a different bride. Could she be a worse judge of men?

The list of the stolen items from Tad's Jeopardy Falls gallery complete, Andi and Christian headed for the door and Gaiman's Albuquerque gallery.

"I'll continue working the scene here," Brunswick said, "and then I'll swing by Alex's." He lifted his chin at them as Christian held the heavy gallery door open for Andi. "Keep me in the loop."

"Will do," she said.

Christian nodded. "Always."

Tad scampered after them and climbed into his silver Porsche. "I'll meet you two down there."

"You think he's okay to drive?" she asked Christian as he held the passenger door of his Bronco open for her.

"I'm sure he'll be fine."

She started to climb into the Bronco, then paused.

"What's wrong?" Christian asked.

"I need to get my work satchel. It's in my truck." She lowered her foot. "I'll just be a sec."

"No problem." He smiled. "Take your time."

He was so calm, level, as if this were an everyday occurrence. It threw her. The thrill of working a case pulsed through her. But Christian O'Brady was as solid as a rock.

She strode across the lot, her heels wobbling on a loose piece of asphalt.

Unlocking her truck, she moved for the door, then paused at the paper stuck under her windshield wipers.

"What's up?" he asked, his hand still on the passenger door.

"Must be a flyer," she said, pulling the cream paper out from under the wipers. Odd. It was an envelope. She cocked her head and flipped it over. Her name was scrawled across the front.

Curiosity raking through her with an air of unease, she opened it and pulled out a tri-folded paper. Her gaze had been so intent on the envelope, she'd missed Christian striding to her side.

"A letter?" he asked, his brow arched.

"Yeah. With my name across it." She unfolded the paper.

"From someone you know?" he asked, stepping beside her.

She cast her attention to the cursive handwriting, and her gaze fixed on the signature. "It's signed Penn and Teller."

"What?" His broad shoulders went taut.

"I don't know anyone named Penn or Teller," she continued, then cocked her head at Christian's clenched jaw. "Do you?"

He cleared his throat, his fists releasing, his fingers shaking out. "They're famous magicians." He tilted his head. "You've never heard of them?"

"No." She shook her head. "Magicians never really were my thing."

He held out his hand. "Do you mind?" he asked, stepping closer still, his six-four frame dwarfing her five-four one, despite her two-inch heels.

"No." She handed him the paper.

He gripped it, his eyes scanning the page as hers did the same. *My friend Stan never loses at the poker table. How come?*

"I don't understand," she said.

"It's an old poker riddle," Christian explained.

"But why would someone leave a poker riddle for me on my car?" It made zero sense.

"Are you sure it was left for you?" Why was his voice so tight?

"It has my name on the envelope." She shrugged but couldn't fathom who'd leave her such a message. She held it up for him to see, and his shoulders slackened. *Odd.* "Does it make sense to you?" Curiosity pricked in her. Did he think it'd been left for him? And if so, why?

"The answer is—"

"Stan never plays," she said.

A soft smile curled on his lips. "Right."

"So, the question stands—why would anyone leave a riddle on my car? Let alone one signed by magicians."

"I think the thieves left it."

"Wait. Why?" She narrowed her eyes.

"The message," he said. "I think they're saying this is a game."

"A game?"

He nodded. "I'm afraid so. And, I think they just invited us to play."

SIX

"BUT," SHE SAID, "if they left the letter on my car after we entered the gallery, then . . ."

"Then they're close by," he said, scrutinizing their surroundings, fixing on the diner patrons across the street. He scanned each face, looking for one out of place. Or . . . He stilled. Was it someone he knew?

"But that means they broke in here, rushed down to Albuquerque, then circled back?" she said.

"Weirder things have happened." He knew by experience. "I'm going to run this in to Joel. I'll be right back."

"Joel? I'm assuming you mean Sheriff Brunswick?"

Christian nodded.

"I didn't realize you were on a first-name basis."

"We play baseball together. And . . ." He shrugged. "It's a small town."

"Right," she said, her piercing gaze still scanning the diner scene.

Twenty minutes later, they were heading south on Highway 14—aka the Turquoise Trail—for Albuquerque. Andi kept her hands, damp with cold perspiration, at her side. Something about the note had spooked Christian, and returning to Albuquerque—likely to see the FBI art theft team, no less—had completely upended her. They made quite a pair.

"You okay?" he asked, one arm draped across the wheel.

"Mmm-hmm." She wasn't asking why he asked. She already knew the answer. Instead, she'd focus on him.

"How often have you seen back-to-back heists?" he asked before she could do just that.

"None since I started in this line of work, but I do recall reading about one while I was researching for the job."

"This line of work?" he asked. "Is it a newer occupation for you?"

The guy was too intuitive for his own good. "Yes." Which led to the question she didn't want to answer.

"What'd you do before?"

"I worked in an office." It was true. The FBI crime lab was in an office building. Before he could prod, she shifted the focus. "So what about you? How'd you get into the security business?"

He tapped the wheel. The sun fanned out across the windshield, spilling in to warm her. "It's not my main profession," he said, his tone once again casual. Unaffected.

"Oh?" What else did a security consultant do? Security officer, perhaps? Which would give him even more time inside a gallery to rob it. She pinched her lip with her teeth. *Don't assume.* But . . . She exhaled, shifting to face the man better. *Don't trust.* "What is your main profession?"

He glanced over at her with a sideways smile. "I'm a private investigator."

"Really?"

He chuckled. "You don't have to sound so shocked."

"Sorry." She offered an apologetic smile. "I just hadn't anticipated that."

He dipped his head. The man was entirely too handsome for his own good. "And what did you anticipate?"

"I don't know." She smoothed her skirt. "Maybe a security guard."

He chuckled again, the sound warm and inviting.

Whoa, girl. He's a suspect, remember? "So . . . private investigator? How'd you get into that line of work?"

He straightened and swiped his nose. "Just fell into it."

"And the combo of the two?"

He rubbed his hand along his thigh. "While investigating cases, I noted that a lot of thefts, break-ins, and intrusions could have been prevented with a more sophisticated security system."

"And you knew how to make them?"

He glanced in the rearview mirror and then over to her. "I studied it enough that I started consulting. After some time, I installed the upgrades myself. But that's only a small portion of what I do." He glanced in the mirror again.

She turned to look over her shoulder. "What is it?"

"Nothing. I just thought I . . ."

"You . . . ?"

"It's nothing," he said, but his lingering attention in the mirror said otherwise.

She glanced back one more time, then turned toward him, her attention back on the case. "I didn't get a chance to ask Tad about his missing fob before the call about his other gallery came in. That's first on my list when we arrive."

"No need." He glanced in the mirror again.

She shifted. Seriously? What was up? "Is something wrong? Someone following us?" That would be a first.

"There's a white SUV about a half mile back. I can only see it on the straightaways, which are few and far between."

"This is a two-lane road," she said, curious at the intensity in his eyes. "I imagine it could look like anyone is following us."

"True." He clamped the wheel. "But I noticed the vehicle in the diner lot as we drove past."

She squinted as the sun beamed off the windshield. She pulled her sunglasses out of her bag. "You're quite observant."

"PI." He shrugged.

She wondered what the profession was like. What he was like. There was something enticing about him that made her curious, but she wasn't following that inclination, period.

"Do you really think he or they are following us?" she asked, turning and resting her weight against the back of the seat.

"We'll find out."

Before she could ask what he meant, he banked hard right. Now, instead of running parallel to the trees and lush forests, he pulled into the midst of them.

Reaching a small dirt road, he once again banked hard right . . . pulled up about ten yards, then made a U-turn. The Bronco rocked to a stop as her heart thudded. Anticipation roiled through her limbs, her hands no longer clammy—now everything was hot.

Dust billowed on the road. Someone was coming.

SEVEN

THE SOUND OF AN ENGINE GROWLED, and then a blue minivan bumped across the rutted dirt road that crossed by theirs.

Andi looked over at Christian. Nervous laughter, yearning to be released, bubbled in her throat, but she kept the pressure inside.

"Huh," he said. "I guess I was wrong." Again, with the casual reaction.

Christian shifted the vehicle in gear, pulled back onto the road, and followed it out to the highway.

She couldn't help looking back, but there was no white SUV in sight. "So," she said, resituating herself, "you were saying something about Tad and his missing fob."

"Right. . . . Mind if I crack the window some? It's so nice out."

"Not at all." In fact, she did the same. Warm wind whistled through the Bronco, fluffing wisps of hair from her intricately woven bun.

"Tad filled me in on my ride into town," Christian explained.

"And?"

"He knows who took the fob."

"Great. Who is it?"

Christian tapped the wheel. "That's the problem, he doesn't know."

She frowned. "I don't follow."

"Tad went home with a woman from a gala he hosted last night.

He met her at the end of the night. She's not local. They were both three sheets to the wind. They went to his place. They . . ." He tilted his head. "Gracefully sidestepping that one. Several hours later, he woke, and the woman and the fob were gone."

"He doesn't know the woman he went home with? I realize, not the point to focus on, but ewww."

"Agreed. We'll have to question the rest of the gala guests. See if someone there knew her. I highly doubt some unknown person just waltzed into town, happened to be dressed for an art gala, and randomly ended up with Tad."

"So, you're thinking she was part of the heist plans?"

Christian tapped his nose. Adorable as it was. Seriously! What was up with her? Of course, she noticed handsome men, but only in a passing glance. Christian was sticking in her mind, and that was not acceptable. "You think she set Tad up?"

"Absolutely. She played him."

"Played him?" she asked.

"Like in a con . . ." His gaze flashed to the rearview mirror, and she turned, this time seeing a white SUV barreling down the winding road behind them. "Hold on."

The pulsing of unrestrained fear seared her limbs as she braced for impact. This wasn't happening.

"Hang on to the roll bar!" Christian hollered.

She scrambled to curl her fingers around the silver bar overhead.

Christian gunned the gas, but it made no difference. The SUV rammed into the rear driver-side door, the collision whipping Andi's head forward, her body jarring, pain radiating down her legs.

They rocked to a stop, mere inches from the guardrail but still on the pavement.

Christian looked over, his gaze slipping over her. "You okay? Are you hurt?"

"I'm okay," she started, and then her eyes widened as a white flash of movement swept across the back window. "He's backing up!"

Christian revved the engine. The Bronco lurched forward, but the SUV rammed into the rear, thrusting them skidding sideways, the odor of burning rubber and burning brakes filling her nostrils as the SUV plowed them into the guardrail.

He hit the gas, but the wheels just spun out. "Come on." He pumped the gas, the wheels kicking up smoke, but he couldn't gain traction.

The SUV backed up and came barreling at them again.

Without thinking, Andi reached over and took his hand. He intertwined his fingers with hers. The SUV collided, whipping them sideways, crashing them over the guardrail.

A scream burst from her throat as the ground dipped away.

Please, Lord. I'm not ready to die. But if it's my time, fly me home to you.

They landed with a slamming lurch. She opened her eyes and looked at Christian—confusion passing between them.

He ever-so-carefully moved toward the window, looking out. His shoulders drooped on an exhale. "We landed on a ledge."

"Oh, thank you, Lord."

"Amen," he said.

"What now?" she asked.

"Well, the good news is the ledge is holding us for now."

Her chest squeezed. "And the bad?"

"We're at a precarious angle, and—"

The Bronco slid.

"Aaaaah!" She braced herself with one hand on the doorframe, the other with a flattened palm on the roof.

EIGHT

ROCKS GROUND BENEATH the Bronco's tires, and Andi's throat squeezed shut.

The Bronco slid to a gravel-crunching stop.

"That's the bad news," Christian said, his hands braced on the dash.

Her breath hitched. "Any good news? Will help come?"

"If anyone witnessed what happened, they'll call it in, but . . ."

"We don't have time for that."

"Right."

"So what's the plan?"

"Yep," he said.

Yep was not an answer.

"Christian?"

"Okay," he said, assessing their situation. "We need to get out of here."

"Agreed." She nodded, unbuckled, and shifted.

And so did the Bronco.

She froze as it slid again before rocking to a lurching stop.

He held his hands out in a steadying signal. "We need to get out of here *very* carefully and climb up."

"Climb up?" Was he kidding?

"We've got this." His voice remained calm. How could he always be so calm?

She took a shallow breath, trying not to full-out panic.

"Okay," he said. "I want you to *very slowly* try and open your door."

She shifted, and the Bronco rocked. She held her breath until it stopped.

"Try again. Nice and slow," he whispered.

With as little movement as possible, she eased back the door handle. Crunching metal sounded as the door stopped hard.

"What's wrong?"

"It won't open. Something's blocking it."

"Okay," Christian said, looking behind them. "My door won't open either. We're going to have to climb out the back hatch."

"The hatch?" Was he crazy?

"You go first," he said. "Just crawl back to the back hatch. You can do this."

She prayed he knew what he was talking about.

"Take a deep breath for me. . . ."

She gulped in a shallow breath.

"Try a bit deeper. . . ."

She inhaled, the air reaching her lungs this time.

"Now, nice and steady."

She nodded, eased off her heels, and inched across the flipped-down back seat.

The Bronco rocked.

"Go fast!" he shouted, scrambling after her.

NINE

SHE BOLTED FORWARD, gripped the handle, thrust the hatch open, and lunged out. She collided with the rock face, her knees taking the brunt of the motion, the rock scraping the soles of her bare feet. As she struggled for breath and purchase, a powerful weight slammed into her, pressing her against the cliff.

"Sorr—" A loud growl rent the air, cutting him off.

She sneaked a look beneath his arm. The Bronco teetered and then, with crumbling rocks spilling, tumbled over the edge.

Christian released an exhale. "That was too close."

She nodded, the words not forming.

He shifted his full weight off her, both hands flattened on the rock on either side of her. "You ready?" he asked.

"Ready for what?"

"Climbing up."

"What?"

"I don't hear any sirens yet. I think we're on our own for now. We need to get topside."

"How do you propose we do that?" she asked, looking at the ridge a solid twenty feet up.

His hand clamped over her right one. "Just like this grip," he said of the hold she'd found. "You find handholds and footholds and work your way up."

"Aren't we supposed to have ropes of some kind before attempting that?" She looked down at her bare feet. "Or climbing shoes."

"I free-climb all the time, and you'll be okay without shoes. At least it's fall, and the rock face is cool."

She swallowed, staring again at the drop. "I don't think I can do this."

"Sure, you can. . . . Wait, are you afraid of heights?"

"Bingo."

"Sorry."

It wasn't something to be sorry for. Just a fact, but she appreciated his compassion.

"I'll spot you all the way up," he said, his tone assuring.

She swallowed. "What does that mean, exactly?"

"I'll follow right behind you. Keep my hand on your back as much as I'm able. You can do this. I promise."

"That's a hefty promise, mister."

He chuckled. "There. That humor, that strength you clearly possess. That's why I know you can do this."

Rocks shifted beneath his foot when he moved it.

Yikes! It was impossible to push herself closer to the mountainside. She was already flush against it.

"Okay," he said, his right hand still cupped over hers. "And put it here." With strength and tenderness, he lifted her hand up and rested it on a narrow ledge in the rock. "Good," he said. "Now, your foot is going to wedge on that opening six inches to your right."

She looked. A protruding crag no more than a handful of inches deep. "Seriously?" Her breath spurted . . . so shallow.

"You've got this, and I've got you." Oddly, she actually believed him—a man she'd met just hours ago.

"Okay," she said, pulling on the ledge above, stretching her bare foot over to the opening, and surprisingly finding purchase. She released a quivering exhale. Maybe she could do this.

"Good." His hand remained splayed on her lower back. "But push up on the balls of your feet. Use your legs' momentum instead of your arms. They tire faster."

She nodded. "Where next?"

He instructed the movements, and she followed.

His hand slipped off her back.

"Hey." She made the mistake of looking back. Her head swirled.

"Easy," he said, his hand resting against her back once again. "Just had to make the move. I've got you. Deep breath and let's go."

She tried. She really did, but her breath only came in shallow gasps. Where was a brown paper bag when she needed one?

Two more holds and Christian was nearly against her again—his warmth radiating through her. His strong muscles keeping her steady.

"Okay, last move. I want you to stretch your leg as far as you can and place it on that ledge out to your left, then push up on the ball of your foot and grab the top edge. See that rock there . . ." He indicated up.

She looked and nodded, fear trickling through her.

"You can wrap your hand around it."

Her chest tight, her hands throbbing with the abrasions, and scrapes on the soles of her bare feet, she squeezed her eyes shut.

Please, Father, let us make it up. Be with me. Wrap your arms around me and carry me up.

"You okay?" he asked.

"Just saying a prayer," she whispered.

"Same."

So Christian was a Christian.

"You've got this," he said.

She nodded and slid her now tattered skirt up over her knees. Heat pulsed through her quivering leg, but her foot settled on the crag. She pushed up, perspiration sliding down her face as she stretched her hand out. *Come on!* Finally, her hand caught the crag and closed around it. She pulled at the same time she pushed up off her foot. With blissful relief she lifted over the edge and onto solid ground.

A man and a woman rushed forward. "Oh, my goodness. Are you okay?" The man knelt by her side, and the woman stood, covering her mouth. "We were higher up the road but saw that SUV push you over. Gail called the police," the man said, indicating the woman, whose eyes were wide, her jaw slack now that she'd moved her hand away.

Andi looked over to see Christian, but he wasn't over the edge yet.

Her heart thudding, she looked back down, ignoring the swirling of the world below, and spotted him dangling on a handhold ten inches down.

"What's wrong?"

"The foothold cracked. I'll get it. I just need a little momentum." *Please, Lord.*

The crazy man shifted his weight, swinging his body to the side and then up in a swoop, his leg landing on the ridge. A breath of a moment later, he rolled over the ledge and lowered his head on a swift puff of air.

The man scooted back as sirens blared in the distance.

Christian locked his gaze on her, his eyes and smile soft . . . tender. "You did good."

"Thanks." It'd been his help. Otherwise . . . she hated to think what would have happened otherwise.

Sirens rent the air. Christian got to his feet, and Andi fixed her gaze on the blue and red swirling lights rounding the bend, then up the switchback at a flash of movement. She frowned and zeroed in.

"What is it?" Christian asked.

She stilled. A man moved on an upper ridge, headed for a white SUV.

Christian bolted forward.

"What are you doing?" she called after him, watching his hand shift to rest on the grip of his gun in his holster. Unfortunately, her gun was still in the Bronco, along with her purse.

"Going for him," Christian hollered back as he raced for the switchback.

"Are you serious? You can't catch him."

"I've gotta try."

TEN

HIS LUNGS BURNING, Christian rounded the bend as the white SUV disappeared into the distance. He bent at the waist, planting his hands on his knees while he settled his breath, frustration pulsating through him.

If only he'd been faster, had seen the SUV's plate. Something to go on other than the nondescript vehicle.

He glanced back at the scene, the twisted guardrail. So close to death. If the Bronco hadn't landed just right on the ledge . . .

Thank you, Lord, for saving us.

God had protected them, preserved them. He knew it in his bones. Sirens blared, soon followed by red and blue lights swirling below. The emergency vehicles pooled at the side of the drop-off.

Making his way back down the road, he passed several cars cut off by the fire truck, ambulance, and police car. The people inside stared at him, wide-eyed, as he passed.

"Christian," his friend Axle said as he reached his side. "I should have known it was you causing trouble."

Andi looked up from her place on the back of the ambulance as a paramedic examined her.

"This climbing feat was definitely not by choice," he said, clasping his baseball buddy's hand.

"Axle, this is Andi Forester," he said.

"We already exchanged pleasantries," she said with a smile.

"Good." He shifted his gaze to Axle as he examined her, queasiness welling inside. "Is she okay?"

Axle looked up at him. "Some serious bumps and bruises, but she's going to be fine."

Phew. "Great."

"Christian, this is my partner, Cass," Axle said, lifting his chin as a second man rounded the back of the ambulance. "This is Christian O'Brady. We're on the Los Lobos regional baseball team together."

"Cool," Cass said. "Nice to meet you, man. Why don't you have a seat next to her . . ." He indicated Andi. "And I'll check you out."

"Appreciate it, but other than a few scrapes and bruises, I'm good."

"Humor me," Cass said.

Christian exhaled. He was only doing his job. "Okay," Christian said, sitting down on the back edge of the ambulance beside Andi.

"Great," Cass said, moving to examine him. "When we wrap up here, we'll take you to the hospital."

"No need," Andi said.

Axle looked at up her, pausing from cleaning out the wound on her right knee.

"Just bumps and bruises, like you said." Andi smiled at Axle.

"It wouldn't hurt to be checked out," Cass chimed in.

"I appreciate it," Andi said as Axle resumed cleaning out her wounds.

Christian winced. They were seriously bruised, swelling, and scraped up. "Maybe a good look wouldn't hurt," he said.

"Really, I'm fine."

Christian smiled at her persistence. The lady wasn't budging.

"All right." Axle smiled with a shake of his head.

Cass looked up and lifted his chin at the approaching policeman. "I'm sure Jim has plenty of questions for you."

"Jim?" Andi asked.

"Santa Fe police," Christian said.

"Do you know everyone around here?" she asked, curiosity tickling her tone.

"It's a small enough area. In my line of work, you get to know local law enforcement. Besides, our baseball team that Axle mentioned? It's a regional law enforcement and emergency service league."

Andi stood, wincing in the process.

"You sure you're okay?" he asked her again.

"Christian," Jim said, greeting him, then shifted his gaze to Andi.

"Andi Forester," she said.

"Officer Sandez, Santa Fe police, but you can call me Jim."

"Jim." She nodded.

He looked to the guardrail then back to them. "What on earth happened here?"

An hour and a half later, they sat at the Santa Fe police station on Camino Entrada, both a little worse for the wear, but at least they'd convinced Axle and Cass they didn't need to be seen at the hospital. What they needed was a vehicle to get to Albuquerque. They still had a heist scene to get to. Andi rubbed her hand along the pebbled leather surface of her purse.

"I'm glad the retrieval team was able to retrieve and return your purse and handgun so quickly," Christian said.

"Me too."

"I'm going to call my brother to run us a car and give me some fresh clothes," he said. "I can either ask my sister to bring you an outfit, as you look about the same size, or I'm more than happy to drive you to your house to get changed." Her poor skirt was torn up all along the hem. "Where do you live?"

"Down in Lamy. I feel strange asking a total stranger, but if you're sure your sister wouldn't mind lending me an outfit, that would be great. I'd hate to waste time by diverting to my place."

"I'm sure she won't mind at all." He got to his feet. "I'll be right back." She nodded, and he headed to the nearest available phone.

"Hey, bro. What's up?" Deckard said, answering on the fourth ring. "What's the deal in Albuquerque?"

"We haven't made it yet." Christian stepped out of an officer's way, moving to stand by the side of the vacant desk.

"You left hours ago," Deckard said.

50

"We kinda had an accident. Could you and Riley run me a car?"

"Sure," Deckard said. "Where are you at?"

"The Santa Fe police department."

"Not a problem. I'm at the office. I'll grab Riley. But what kind of accident?" Deckard asked.

"Who had an accident?" Riley asked in the background loud enough to hear.

"Let me put you on speaker so I don't have to repeat everything," Deck said. "Okay, go."

"What happened?" Riley asked. "Are you okay?"

"We're fine."

"Who's we?" she asked.

"Him and the insurance investigator," Deckard said.

"Guys, focus," Christian said. "I need . . . we need a car and a set of clothes for Andi—the insurance investigator. Riley, she's about your size. Will you have to swing home to grab an outfit?"

"Nah, you know I keep outfits at the office—just in case."

"Where's your Bronco?" Deckard asked. "You total it or something?"

"Totaled it?" Riley asked. "Just how bad was your accident?"

"I can help run a car over," Greyson offered.

"Hey, Grey," Christian said. "I didn't realize I was on with everyone."

"You should know the man is always listening." Deckard chuckled.

Wasn't that the truth. Greyson Chadwick was a man of many talents—somehow always seeming to know everything, but then again, he'd taught them everything they knew about the PI business.

"The Bronco is done for." He tried to leave it at that, but as anticipated, Riley wouldn't allow it.

"So what happened?" she pressed.

He exhaled. They were going to freak. "We were run off the road."

Cyrus's phone rang. He took a sharp inhale and gripped his cell, debating whether or not to answer. But Teresa would just keep calling. She always did until he answered. He couldn't even take a shower without her incessant calls at times.

He looked at Casey. "I'm going to take this outside."

His partner frowned. "Why?"

Again with the questions. "Because it's private. I'll be back."

The call dropped, and within a breath she was calling back.

"What?" he answered through gritted teeth.

"I haven't heard back from Enrique. I can't reach him. Did he take them out?"

So she'd told Enrique to keep tabs on him. He knew someone was there. Knew the outcome of the job from his source but didn't know which one of Teresa's thugs it was until now.

"Cyrus?" Impatience saturated her high-pitched voice.

He smiled with satisfaction at the disappointment this news would fill her with. "Probably because he botched the job."

"What?" Hesitation hung heavy in her now Mexican-laced accent. It was ridiculous how quickly she took on the persona, became the person her husband believed she was, but he knew better. Knew her cruelty.

"Enrique failed." *He* wouldn't have. He leaned against the siding of the dilapidated mobile home that was base—at least until they'd wrapped up the last heist in the state. Then they'd move on. "My source confirmed they survived." He lit a cigarette, and satisfaction filled him with the first blissful inhale.

"Can your source be trusted?" Her tone sharpened.

"Clearly more so than Enrique. He blew it." He took another drag and moved under the somewhat remaining porch as rain pounded down. He hunched his shoulders against the burgeoning wind. "I don't even know why you sent him here. . . ." He knew exactly why, but he wanted to hear her say it. "Unless you're trying to keep tabs on me."

"I want to make sure *you* don't blow it," she said.

He gripped his cell harder, his hand cramping with the tight hold. "I'm not the one who did." Orange glowed on the tip of the cigarette as he inhaled again.

"Yes, you did, and Enrique covered your rear."

He straightened. "What are you talking about?" He had this. Everything was in place.

"You let the girl see you."

"What girl?"

"That girl from the gallery you cased."

His muscles coiled. "How do you know that?" He didn't even know that.

"Enrique was *keeping tabs on you,* as you say. He saw her recognize you on the street the day of the gala."

His muscles grew taut. "What did he do?" If he screwed this up . . . drew more attention to them . . . he'd take Enrique out himself. "I doubt your thug was discreet in killing her." Cyrus would have been. He could have handled it.

"He got rid of her. That's all that matters."

"If they find her body, it'll only draw more attention to the case."

"And killing Julia won't?"

He inhaled, fury raking through him. He loathed being watched. "She won't tie back to us. I made sure of it. She's a nobody. The only place that investigation will land is a dead end. I doubt you can say the same of Enrique." They would just have to wait and see, but the girl was someone. People knew her, and clearly knew she tied to the gallery. This was bad.

"It'll be fine."

They'd see. Now to the matter at hand. "Call your thug off."

"No. I have every right to keep an eye on my investment."

"There'll be no investment unless you call him off." He flicked the ashes on the porch. The stupid place could burn down for all he cared. They could have stayed someplace decent, but his partner insisted no one would find them here. He was tired of listening to people—his partner, his sister . . . "I mean it. Call him off or I walk."

"You walk and you're dead." Her voice went cold—that cruel frigidness he'd dealt with all his life.

"Your threats don't scare me. I can take Enrique." *In the blink of an eye.*

Silence.

"You know I'm right." His voice deepened as his boldness grew. He wasn't the little kid she'd bullied for years. He was no longer under her thumb, even if she didn't realize it yet. This was his show, and he'd run it any way he pleased.

"There are plenty of others I can send," she said.

He smiled.

She was grasping at straws.

"It's your choice," he said. "I can get the job done or I can spend time taking out whoever you send after me."

"That's big talk for little Cyrus."

He gripped his cell harder still, his fingers numbing. The rain shifted, coming in the porch sideways. "I'm not a kid anymore. Don't test me."

Silence.

He smiled. He had her—at least on this round, but it wouldn't surprise him in the least if she ordered Enrique to take him out after it was over. That's why he had plan B. She'd never see it coming.

ELEVEN

TWENTY-FIVE MINUTES LATER, Christian waved as his brother pulled into the lot in his black Chevy Equinox, followed by his sister in her red Miata convertible. He shook his head every time he saw her drive on or off their ranch in the vehicle. It looked like a windup car, but she loved it.

"Your family, I take it?" Andi asked.

He'd offered for her to rest inside the station while he got the SUV from Deckard, but like him, she was antsy to get to Gaiman's Albuquerque gallery, so she joined him outside. At least by now, he hoped they'd have the gallery to themselves. Surely local police were gone. But given the cultural objects, they weren't just talking local law enforcement. The cultural artifacts meant the Bureau's art theft team would be involved. He groaned inwardly, praying it wouldn't be Agent Hopkins who showed. But he still was based in Cali, last Christian heard. Just the idea of the Bureau's art theft team set his nerves on edge—the fear he'd be unmasked.

And Andi . . . They'd just met, but somehow the thought of it happening in front of her dropped his stomach.

Deckard climbed out of the SUV, sunglasses on. It was sunny for the moment, but glancing at the sheets of rain coming from the south, they'd soon be driving in a deluge.

"Hey, man," his brother said, pulling off his sunglasses and sticking them atop his tousled blond hair. He took two steps forward, then his gaze shifted to Andi, and he stopped dead in his tracks.

"Oh, you've got to be kidding me," Andi said.

Christian's gaze bounced between them. Both of their jaws clamped, their faces flushed red. He frowned. "Do you two know each other?"

"You bet we do," Deckard said.

Andi turned to Christian, her breath labored, her words coming out in spurts. "Deckard MacLeod is *your* . . . brother?"

Riley hopped out of her Miata with a colorful woven bag. "I brought clothes for you," Riley said, stepping to Andi, no doubt attempting to defuse the tension. Always the peacemaker. At least when it didn't pertain to her bold and wild side. "Hi." She extended a hand. "I'm Riley."

Andi struggled for composure. "Thank you," she managed, her jaw still tight as she shook Riley's hand. "I appreciate the change of clothes."

"I can only imagine what you two went through," Riley said, linking her arms over her chest. "If I get my hands on whoever did this . . ."

"You and me both," Andi said, and then her gaze flicked to Deckard—holding there, her shoulders growing taut.

Christian studied their body language, expressions, and tight gazes on one another. What was up between them, and how did they know each other? From a past heist investigation? No. That didn't make sense. He worked the heist cases. Deckard handled the cons and scams.

Deckard's shoulders broadened, his stance poised for a fight.

Confusion shifted through Christian. What was happening?

Andi turned her pointed gaze back on him. "Your name?" she said, shaking her head. "I don't understand. You said your last name was O'Brady?"

"It is," he said without elaborating, but he doubted she'd leave it there.

"How do you know each other?" Riley asked, echoing Christian's exact sentiments.

Moisture welled in Andi's eyes, taking Christian aback. What on earth?

"Your brother—" She cleared her throat, her fierce gaze fixed on Deckard—"ruined my career."

The words barely left her mouth before Deckard retorted, "She destroyed Mitch Abrams's life."

"Mitch Abrams?" Christian said, perplexed. He was the innocent man Deckard helped set free from prison. "What on earth does Mitch Abrams have to do with Andi?"

"Andi?" Deckard dipped his chin. "This is Miranda Forester. The FBI crime lab agent who botched the DNA results that sent Mitch to jail."

Christian's gaze bounced back to Andi. She'd been FBI?

"I was set up," she lobbed back. "Which I told your brother. But that didn't matter to him."

Before Christian could respond, Andi turned heel and strode into the station, Riley's clothes in hand. He stood rooted in place, trying to wrap his head around what had just happened. She was the one who botched the evidence? Somehow it didn't fit in his mind. Not based on his first impression, and summing a person up fast was his gift. He prayed he wasn't wrong this time, despite Deckard's words.

Why it mattered so much for a woman he just met, he couldn't say, but something inside him wanted her to be innocent. He needed to hear her side. Had she really been set up? And if so, why hadn't his brother discovered that?

Deckard stepped forward and dropped his car keys in Christian's open palm.

"Thanks."

"Why didn't you tell me you were working with Miranda Forester of all people?" Deckard said.

"Settle down, Deck," Riley said, moving to stand by her brothers.

"How was I supposed to know?" Christian shrugged.

"Her name for one," Deckard grunted.

"I was working that case in Germany at the time of Abrams's

case, so the particulars are fuzzy. And when you spoke of the FBI lady, you usually referred to her as 'that agent.'"

Deckard raked a hand through his blond hair. "So now she's going by Andi and has found a new occupation."

"Because you got me fired from the Bureau," Andi said, striding back out wearing Riley's clothes.

Christian tried to stay on point, but for a moment he took in how beautiful she was—how Riley's Wrangler jeans fit her curves, and how the black silk blouse brought out the blonde highlights in her light brown hair.

"Because you botched the DNA evidence and then lost the shirt—or took it," Deckard said, his gravelly voice rising in volume, pulling Christian back to the conversation at hand.

"I told you," she ground out. "I was set up."

"Okay," Riley said, positioning herself between Deckard and Andi. Deckard shifted to move to the side, and she turned and rested a hand on his chest to still him. "These two have a job to do," she said. "And we should get going."

Deckard stood fixed.

Andi did the same.

"Deck," Riley said, "let's go."

"Fine," Deckard said, his gaze flashing to Andi one last time as he moved to the side.

"I'll wait in the car," Andi said. She looked at Riley and smiled. "Thank you for the clothes."

"Anytime." Riley smiled back.

"I'll be right there," Christian said.

Deckard strode to his side and clamped a hand on his shoulder. "A little advice, baby brother. I'd stay as far away from Miranda Forester as you can. She's already destroyed one man's life."

TWELVE

HER BODY RIGID, Andi sat stone still as Christian climbed into the driver's seat of Deckard MacLeod's SUV and buckled in, waiting for what was to come.

He glanced at her as he started the engine. "You were set up?"

She blinked. That was the last place she thought this conversation would start. She'd braced for a condemnation ride. "It's a long story," she said. No doubt Deckard had taken the opportunity to warn Christian before he left. She'd seen them talking through the glass door, Deckard's movements heated.

Her chest squeezed, making breathing a strain. Not this again. Would she ever be able to leave this behind?

"We've got plenty of time," he said, indicating the long stretch of road before them. Storm clouds brewed on the horizon, and the sheets of rain fell like streaks of gray in the distance. She loved watching the storms move across the mesa, but there was more than one storm coming. Her past was ready to rear its ugly head again and wash over her in a brutal downpour. She stiffened. She wasn't ready to drown again.

"Andi," he said, his voice tender, nudging.

They had an hour-long ride before them. Did she open herself up for ridicule or judgment by sharing her side of the story, or did she refuse to talk about it and let Deckard's false claims stand?

She wavered, her chest squeezing tighter, pain stabbing her right rib.

"You okay?" He glanced over for a moment, before returning his gaze to the black pavement ahead.

She nodded, feeling anything but, and wishing with all her might that she had her own vehicle. But taking time to grab an Uber back to Tad's gallery in Jeopardy Falls would have killed nearly an hour. She couldn't, in good conscience, give up that time. She needed to be onsite ASAP, and as painful as this ride and conversation was going to be, she was a professional. She wouldn't let her feelings override her duty.

"Andi?" he asked again, his voice even softer this time.

Her defense mechanism kicked in. "I'm sure your brother will fill you all in."

"I'd like to hear what happened from you," he said, flipping on his blinker and switching lanes. "You said you were set up?"

She forced a sharp breath into her lungs. She didn't know why she felt Christian might actually believe her. It made no sense. He didn't know her from Adam. No doubt when it came down to it, he'd side with his brother. But she was tired of not being bold in the truth of what had really happened. Deckard never gave her the space to explain—just cut her off, telling her to hire her own PI—but his tone and stature was one of disbelief. He believed her guilty, and apparently nothing was going to change that.

Praying she wouldn't get pummeled, she went for it. "Okay," she said, shifting in her seat to better face him. "But before I share, why do you have a different last name?"

"Fair enough." He tapped the wheel as dark gray clouds blanketed the sky overhead, the threatening rain pelting the windshield like tiny daggers. Christian switched on the wiper blades. "O'Brady is my middle name. I thought it suited me better."

"Uh-huh . . . Somehow I feel there's more to that story."

"It was just the right fit for me," he said, not elaborating.

She understood the power of a name. After everything that went down, she'd considered changing her last name, but she'd done nothing wrong, and despite running from Albuquerque to the boonies outside of Santa Fe, she refused to let the past cower her into being someone she was not.

"Now, your turn," Christian said.

She hesitated.

He glanced at her out of the corner of his eye. "I'm not here to judge you."

"Funny." She fidgeted with the lowest button on her blouse. "Everyone else does."

"I'm not everybody else."

She studied him, his steadfast profile, the kindness in his eyes when he glanced at her. His kindness was throwing her off . . . like being on a Tilt-A-Whirl with the world spinning around her. Her breath came in spurts.

"It's okay," he said. "Focus your breath."

Embarrassment swarmed hot up her neck, flashing across her cheeks. She focused, and after a moment of utter, breathless panic, she got it to still . . . some.

He dipped his head to look her in the eye. "You okay?"

She nodded.

"I'm sorry I upset you. I'd just really like to hear what happened." He kicked the wipers on high to keep up with the dousing rain as thunder rumbled in the distance. Why was he being so nice?

Streaming out a somewhat settled breath, she spoke before she chickened out. "I never mishandled or misplaced anything. I was set up, and no one other than my brother; my best friend, Harper; and Grant believed me."

"Grant?" he asked.

"Grant Harrison, my boss, who's an old family friend."

"Speaking of family," Christian said. "Surely the rest of your family believed you."

"They remained silent. I told them what happened. They said okay, and that was it, but every time it came up, they gave each other looks that were painfully clear. They didn't believe me."

"I'm so sorry. Family, of all people, should have your back. Unfortunately, that doesn't always happen."

She eyed him. "It sounds like you're speaking from experience."

He shrugged a shoulder. "I've been there."

Lightning sizzled through the blackened sky, followed a breath of a second later with the roaring growl of thunder.

They were driving into the heart of the storm.

"But . . ." he said, "that's a story for another day. Let's get back to you." He redirected the conversation. He had a knack for doing that. "Do you know who set you up?"

"You say that like you believe me." She tried to keep her tone from slipping into defensive sarcasm.

"I don't see a reason not to."

She narrowed her eyes. "You'd take my word over your brother's?"

"I'm not saying that, but it sounds like Deckard doesn't know the whole story."

She linked her arms across her chest. "He wouldn't listen to me. Just cut me off. Told me to hire a different PI if I had concerns."

"He was working for Mitch. It would have been a conflict of interest to look into your case."

She furrowed her brow. "You said my case, not my claims."

"Yeah."

"I don't understand why you're not assuming the worst." Everyone else did. Well, nearly everyone else. Gratitude for the three who believed her welled inside.

Christian tapped the wheel. "I don't judge people at first glance. I look at all the information before making a determination."

Lightning struck the ground on her side of the vehicle, the thunder rattling her window. She liked storms, just, perhaps, not that close.

"What happened with Mitch's case?" he asked.

She swallowed and fought the panic rising in her throat as horrid memories flooded back. She shook it off as best she could manage. "I was in the lab the night of the murder—Anne Marlowe's. Evidence came in, and I worked the DNA. I found Mitch's DNA on the one recovered item that didn't belong to the victim."

"Which was?"

"A man's red polo-style shirt."

"I remember Deckard telling me it belonged to some judge, I think."

"Yes, Judge Simmons. The detectives on the case tracked it to him."

"How?"

"The shirt was stitched with Eagle's Nest Country Club, where the judge was a member."

"But surely all members have a shirt like that."

"Yes, but they stitch the member's first name on the shirt, and given Judge Simmons was having an affair with Anne Marlowe, they—"

"Wait. Deckard told me *Mitch* was having an affair with Anne."

"According to the detectives, he was. Anne had broken off her affair with the judge when she met Mitch."

"Okay . . ." He shook his head, then glanced back at her. "So . . . back to the lab that night, to your work."

"I found the blood on the shirt belonged to the victim. I then started looking for any trace of second-party DNA. I swabbed the inside of the shirt and found several epithelial skin cells in the sleeve. I then amplified the cells using polymerase-chain-reaction technology, known as PCR, to create identical copies that are large enough for proper analysis. I ran the sample, and it came back a match for Mitch Abrams. Since it was trace evidence and only a limited number of cells, I testified it was a partial DNA match, but the estimated chance of obtaining matching DNA components to someone else unrelated to Mitch Abrams is approximately one in one billion."

"Was any of Judge Simmons's DNA found?"

"No."

"How is that possible?" he asked.

"I believe they said the shirt was stolen from the cleaners, but your brother—since he worked for Mitch—might know more than me."

"Okay. I'll ask him. So . . . you tested the sample and then . . ?"

"I stored it properly and put the shirt in the evidence locker."

"And then?"

"The investigation ruled out Judge Simmons based on the shirt having gone missing from the dry cleaners, no DNA matching his, and an airtight alibi. So they switched the investigation to Mitch based on my findings, and he was convicted and went to prison.

"His parents immediately hired your brother to work his case." She swallowed, the pain of false judgment sinking in her gut. "They found the shirt missing from the evidence locker and the DNA sample compromised. Having no other physical evidence and no way to retest the DNA sample for an appeal, the judge vacated Mitch's sentence. I got labeled as botching my job so bad that I sent an innocent man to jail and was immediately let go from the Bureau."

"But you believe it was Mitch's DNA—that he was guilty?"

"I know the work I did and the match it made. Though partial, as I said, it belonged to Mitch Abrams. I'm sure of it. And I preserved the sample properly and never took the shirt back out of the evidence locker."

"With all of that, when Deck told you to hire another PI . . . why didn't you?"

"Whoever set me up did a good job of it. With the exception of the three people I mentioned, no one else believed me, and, to be honest, by that point I was just worn down. So instead of fighting, like I should have, I ran." And regretted it ever since, but she was done with that life.

"Maybe you shouldn't run anymore," he said with a soft smile.

She narrowed her eyes. "Meaning?"

"Meaning now that Deckard no longer works for Mitch Abrams, maybe he could look into your case. He's the best."

She laughed.

He arched a brow.

"Oh," she squeaked. "You're serious."

"Why not? What's the worst that could happen?"

Rain still gushed as they pulled up to Tad's gallery in Albuquerque, puddles splashing up in thick surges in the wake of the Equinox's tires.

Andi's jaw slackened as she took in the building. The exterior was reminiscent of Incan ruins. Tad really went big or went home.

Her heart still fluttered at Christian's apparent belief in her, though the idea of asking Deckard MacLeod to look into her case was ludicrous. No matter how sincere Christian was, Deckard would never agree.

Christian's cell rang, making her jump.

"Okay there?" he asked, his brown hair ruffled, his deep brown eyes full of amusement.

"Yep." She swallowed. She needed to settle down so she could do her job effectively.

He answered on the fifth ring. "O'Brady."

"Christian," Joel said, a hard edge to his voice.

That didn't bode well. He straightened. "What's wrong?" he asked, exchanging a concerned look with Andi as they both listened.

"Martha let me in Alex's apartment when I explained what was going on," Joel said.

"And?" Christian asked, bracing for whatever bad news was about to come.

"She wasn't there, but there are signs of a struggle."

Christian raked a hand through his hair. "Ah, man. That's not good. Have any idea where she is?"

"I wish I did."

THIRTEEN

ENTERING THE GAIMAN GALLERY in Albuquerque was like entering another world.

Faux-rock caves filled with fog and mist surrounded them. It was rather like being in the T-Rex Cafe in Downtown Disney when the show was on. But instead of dinosaurs roaring, the jungle sounds of monkeys permeated the space.

"This is incredible," Andi said. "But I'm surprised he has all these effects going during an investigation."

"It's all tied together. You turn the lights on, this all comes with it. It's the most convoluted system I've ever seen."

"You designed the security system here too?" she asked, knowing that, too, upped him on the suspect list.

He nodded. "Yes, but Tad insisted on ignoring several of my suggestions, so I refused to fully guarantee my work for this gallery."

"Interesting."

Christian shrugged. "I think he just got cheap on this one."

"Bet he's regretting that now," she said, noting Tad's ignoring the security consultant's suggestions. Having a solid security system was a requirement for insurance with Ambrose Global.

"The primary exhibition area is through the main tunnel." Christian indicated for her to go first, and she led the way, her curiosity piqued with each cave-like structure they passed, wanting to know what each nook and cranny held.

Jungle vines arched across the stone façade. She touched it, amazed by how real it looked. "Oh, my word," she said. "It is *real* stone."

"I know. Tad spared no expense on the display."

"But cheaped out on the security system," she said. "Nice." She rolled her eyes. Why did she have the feeling Tad would still try to blame this on Christian's poor work? "Does this one have a key fob system too?" she asked as a chill of cold air washed over them. A shiver raced along her limbs.

Christian slipped off the windbreaker Deckard had brought him and held it out to her. "Take this."

"Oh, thanks, but I'm okay."

"You're shivering, and your lips are turning blue."

She touched her mouth. That had to look really attractive.

"Please," he said, extending his arm with the jacket clutched in his hand.

"Okay." She took hold of it. "Thanks." She slipped it on—the material had wicked the rain away, and the lined interior was warm, cozy, and smelled like Christian—pine and the wild outdoors, if the fresh outdoors could be encapsulated into a scent.

"Oh," he said. "To answer your earlier question about whether or not Tad used the key fob system here, no he did not. I strongly recommended it, but he wanted all three galleries to have different security systems, so if a thief were ever to crack one system and commit a heist, he wouldn't automatically know how to get into the other two undetected."

"That clearly didn't work," she said, then exhaled. "So how is this one set up?"

"With motion sensors and a silent alarm. I did the best I could with what he'd allow me to do. Figured it was better than what he had, which was like kiddie play."

The tunnel ended, and they entered an Incan-style ruin—the facade of the exterior and interior meshing seamlessly to display the Incan, Mayan, and Aztec artifacts he sold. How he had legal provenance she couldn't imagine, but he must have all his ducks in a row, because governments—both domestic and international— were cracking down on the sale of cultural objects.

"I'm curious," she said as they moved toward the sound of Tad's voice drifting down the corridor. "Mesoamerican jewelry at the Jeopardy Falls gallery, Incan and Mesoamerican artifacts here . . . Does he sell the same at his Taos gallery?" she asked. "I haven't had opportunity to look at that one yet."

"Nope," he said as they neared Tad's voice. "Wine."

"I'm sorry. Did you say . . ."

"Yep. Wine. Very old, refined, and wildly expensive."

The man's tastes ran eclectic across the board, it seemed. "Okay," she said. "I would have never called that one."

Tad stopped talking but then picked up again, and it took her a moment to pin down the direction his nasally voice was coming from through the winding passageways. "This way," she said, heading for the far side of the re-created pyramid—the jungle overtaking it as if it were the ruins in Peru she'd visited during college. Reaching the far edge of the pyramid, they rounded the corner, and her heart leapt into her throat.

Adam.

FOURTEEN

A SMUG GRIN spread on Adam's face.

She straightened her shoulders, fighting the urge to flee.

"Well, if it isn't Agent Forester," Adam said, nudging the agent beside him.

Tad stood in the distance, deep in conversation with a young woman—probably Alex's equivalent for the Albuquerque gallery. At least she was safe. Her heart cracked for what might have happened to Alex—a young woman she didn't even know.

"Aren't you going to say hi?" Adam prodded at her silence.

"Hello, Adam."

Christian stood stalwart beside her, his six-four frame dwarfing Adam's five-ten. His gaze bouncing between her and Jeremy's best bud was evidence of him trying to determine what was happening. No doubt he heard the mocking in Adam's gruff tone. It was readily apparent, and she braced herself for the next wave.

"Jared," he said to the agent standing beside him. "This here is Miranda Forester, formally with the Bureau."

And there it was. Of course, he couldn't leave it. Always so brash. She'd often wondered why Jeremy was friends with the rude, crass, ex-frat boy, but once Jeremy's true colors came out—it was readily apparent.

Jared's brown eyes narrowed, and she wanted to melt into the ground.

Don't let this happen, Lord. Not in front of Christian. Not in front of anyone.

"Why is that name familiar . . . ?" Jared said, then recognition dawned on his face, his eyes widening. "You're the one who botched the evidence in that murder case. . . ." He snapped his fingers, clearly trying to place it. "Adams . . . No, Abrams. I remember now."

Adam rocked back on his heels, his grin morphing to cockiness. *Say something. Walk away. Do something besides stand here.*

At least she was managing to keep her shoulders straight, her head high despite the hot shame of embarrassment threatening to engulf her once more.

"Nah," Adam said. "Not just botched. Outright destroyed and stole evidence."

"I did not," she said, finding her voice.

"Oh." Adam chuckled. "So you're still sticking to that story."

She leaned forward, finding an ounce of boldness. It'd been long enough that she couldn't let this creep knock her down. "It's not a story. It's the truth."

"Right . . ." Adam drawled. "Well, at least Jeremy was bright enough to call off the engagement."

Christian's gaze didn't waver, but the slight flicker of the muscle in his jaw spoke of suppressed questions.

Great. Not only did she have to more fully explain what happened with Abrams's case, but now she had to suffer the humiliation of Christian learning her fiancé dumped her because he believed her guilty.

Christian took a marked step forward. "I think this conversation has run its course, gentlemen."

Adam arched his brows. "And who are you?"

"A colleague . . . and friend," he said.

Friend? That was kind of him, considering they were just getting to know each other.

"Well, I'd watch your back, friend," Adam said.

Christian's shoulders broadened wider still.

Adam opened his mouth to speak, but Tad rushed over in a flustered flurry.

"My rarest artifacts are gone." Tad's tone bordered on shrill whininess. "They might as well have taken my home and my car, and I don't know . . . a thousand other things from me to equal their worth. And you . . ." He pointed his finger at Christian and poked him in the chest.

Christian stiffened, his hands balling into fists. "Don't. Do. That. Again."

Tad's face paled, and he backed off. "The point is, your fancy security system failed again."

"Oh, so I see you two make a great pair," Adam said with a chuckle. "On that note, I'd say we're done here." He looked to his partner, and Jared nodded.

"Here's my card," Adam said, handing it to Tad. "And a word of advice?"

Tad waited.

"Watch your back with these two." He glanced back at Andi. "Bye, Miranda."

She gave a clipped nod, and the burn of adrenaline releasing its hold sizzled through her as the lightning had the sky on their way into town.

She swallowed, an ounce of relief loosening her rock-hard shoulders. But the mortification remained. The reminder of Jeremy's betrayal. And the brutal fact he had married another on their wedding day. It was the blade that cut to the marrow despite her lack of any loving feelings for him for months.

"What was that all about?" Tad asked as the young lady, whom she could only assume was his assistant, came to stand beside him. "Is there something I should know"—he pinned his gaze on Christian—"other than the fact that your fancy security system failed again?"

"You'll recall," Christian said, "that you rejected my recommendations and left several points of entry vulnerable. So I'm going to take a wild guess and say the thieves used one of the weaknesses to break in."

Tad shifted his stance, planting his hands on his hips—his genie-style purple pants crimped beneath his hold. "We'll see about that, but first we're going to go over the items taken." He gestured to Andi, his multipatterned silk shirt sleeve sliding down his arm, along with his bangles.

"Can I go now, Mr. Gaiman?" the young woman asked beside him.

"Actually," Christian said, "it would be helpful if we could ask you a few questions."

"More?" the woman said, little color in her face.

Andi studied her. Had the FBI raked her over the coals? Adam doing so would hardly surprise her.

"Excuse me," Tad said. "I'm the one who had close to a million stolen. I think the focus should be on me."

Andi tried not to roll her eyes. Of course he did. "Why don't we divide and conquer," Andi said to Christian, "and then we can compare notes." They were already many hours out from the discovery of the heist, so for the sake of time, it made sense for Christian to talk with Tad's assistant while she got to the heart of things with Tad.

"Sounds good," Christian said, looking at the young woman. "Cara, how about we head to your break room?"

Cara nodded, and the two headed down the back corridor, the high-pitched call of monkeys echoing around them as a fresh waft of fog poured forth.

"Don't be long," Tad called after them, then turned his attention to Andi. "What did the agents mean about watching my back with you two?"

"It was old business between me and Adam," she said, praying he'd leave it there, but most people wouldn't.

"Fine." Tad waved it off. "Let's get to what matters—the fact that my second gallery has been robbed."

"Let's go over what was taken," she said.

He exhaled. "Finally. This way . . ." Tad power-walked to a series of six open glass cases—all staggered in height—then he gestured to the dozen hollows carved into the stone surrounding them, all with empty cases nestled inside. "They . . ." He swallowed a sob and tried again. "They took my rarest and most expensive items."

"Which ones, specifically?" she asked, moving around the cases, a pencil over her ear, a notebook in hand.

"Where to start." Tad held his balled-up hand to his mouth, pacing from one case to the next. "Let's start here," he said, indicating the smallest case in one of the hollows of the wall.

She struggled to focus on Tad's words, her mind drifting to the young woman with Christian. The news about a sign of a struggle at Alex's rattled her, and she prayed Cara wasn't in any danger.

FIFTEEN

CHRISTIAN HELD THE BREAK ROOM DOOR open for Cara. She moved past him into the sterile white galley-style kitchen and took a seat at one of the white plastic chairs.

Not Tad's style at all. Had his ex-wife, Veronica, decorated this room? The galleries had been half hers at one time, or at least that's how she always saw it and was never shy to let folks know.

Cara kicked one ballet flat over her opposite knee, her arms wrapped snug against her chest. "I had nothing to do with this, and that's not going to change if you bully me. Got it?"

Christian held up his hands. "Got it." He pulled a chair out, spun it around, and straddled it. "Is that what the Feds did?"

"And the local police, and Tad. He was the worst of it."

"Lovely." Christian shook his head, and Cara cocked hers.

"Look," he continued, "I have no intention of bullying you. I just want to ask you a few questions. Okay?"

"Okay, but that's how they started out too." She shifted her jaw, and it popped.

Christian winced. *Ouch.* "Okay, let's just start at the beginning. You came here this morning?"

"Yeah. I like to come in early. Home ain't that great, ya know?"

"I get that." More than she knew.

She tilted her head, leeriness in her eyes. She didn't trust easily, and he didn't blame her. He'd never trusted easily either.

"So you came in early . . ."

"Which Tad swore meant I'd been involved in the heist."

"He said that?"

"Yeah. Threw me under the bus with the cops and the Feds, but I just come in early to get away from it all." She shrugged a shoulder. "That's all."

"Okay." He kept his tone soft, feeling awful the girl felt safer sitting in an empty gallery in the early morning hours than in her own home. At least she had a home. A set one. Or so he presumed. He shook off the painful tangent and refocused. "So you came in, and what was the first thing you noticed?"

"The alarm didn't go off."

"Not at all? No lights, sounds, any of it?"

"Nada," she said.

"Okay, and about what time was this?"

"Maybe eight."

"Was there a sign of anyone here?"

"Nah." She leaned forward, planting her left foot back on the ground beside her right, the toes of her navy ballet flats polished in a shade that didn't quite match. "But I felt something, and it spooked me. So I took my pepper spray out and took my time working my way through the gallery. No one was here, but Tad's stuff was gone, so I called him."

"I'm glad you're safe."

Her already arched brows hiked higher, a dramatic edge to them. "Why wouldn't I be?"

"I just mean I'm glad no one was still here." He didn't want to freak the girl out about Alex missing and her home indicating a struggle. His gut clenched at the thought. Alex was a sweet girl. But, without going into too much detail, he'd warn Cara to watch her back before she left.

"Me too," she finally said with a shiver.

"I'm not going to go through all the stuff I imagine the cops and Feds already did, except . . ."

She narrowed her green eyes. "Except?"

"I'm sure you get a lot of people in and out of here . . ." He led her into the flow of questioning.

"Yeah." She shrugged.

"Was there anyone who stood out to you as lingering too long, being evasive, keeping eyes averted . . . that sort of thing?"

"I don't know." Cara tapped her foot, her face pensive. "There was this one guy."

"Yeah?"

"Well, he didn't do nothing wrong, but I remember him because there was just something about him that gave me the creeps. You know how you can get those feelings?"

"Yeah." His instinct for summing people up was a fine-tuned gift.

"So this guy gave me a weird vibe."

"Do you remember about how long ago this was?" he asked, leaning against the chair back.

"Not long after Tad redid the statue room," she said, her stiff shoulders easing a little.

He cocked his head. "The room of artifacts that were stolen?"

She nodded.

Got 'em. At least a little more than they had a second ago. "That just happened a few months ago?" He'd updated the security system after the redo.

"Yeah. Midsummer. I remember because the AC went out for a few days, and it was sweltering."

So they'd cased the place months ago. "What did this guy look like?" He prayed she remembered. After letting them know about Alex's apartment, Joel said he'd watched the gala footage along with what heist footage they had before the thieves nixed the video. They were dealing with two men in all-black outfits, zero feature details.

"That's the thing. I didn't really see him."

His shoulders tightened, his hope of a description dwindling. "I don't understand."

"He had sunglasses on . . . or those lenses that change with the light."

"Transition lenses."

"Right. I assumed that's what they were—otherwise why would someone keep sunglasses on in a building."

Unless he was trying to hide his eyes. "What about the rest of him? His hair? Build?"

"He wore a baseball hat. His hair was cut short, so I didn't really see much of that either. If I had to guess, just based on the small amount visible in the back, I'd say brown."

"What kind of baseball hat was it?" Sometimes it was the littlest of details that broke a case wide open.

She shrugged her right shoulder. "Just your average sports team one."

"You don't happen to remember which sports team?" he asked, praying she did. At least it would be something tangible.

"Yeah. Houston Astros," she said, crossing her legs and swinging her foot. "My loathsome ex of a boyfriend loved them."

"That is super helpful," Christian said.

The hint of a smile curled on her lips. "It is?"

"Yeah." He nodded. "What about his height? His build?"

"He wasn't as tall as you." She chuckled. It was awkward but endearing. She was a good kid. A little messed up, but a good kid. He prayed she found her way. Maybe he'd get the chance to talk with her another day about unhappy homes and Jesus.

"So about . . . ?" Christian stood and held out his hand, moving it down a few inches from his head.

"Uh-uh." She shook her head, her dark hair with one pink stripe grazing her shoulders.

He lowered his hands a couple more inches.

"Yes. About there," she said.

"Great. So about six feet." Exactly how Joel had described one of the thieves from the heist footage.

"What about weight . . . was he skinny, heavy, muscular?"

"Not like you . . ." She smiled. "I'd say he was average. You know, not super skinny, but not heavy. Right in the middle."

"Gotcha, so average build. This is great."

"Yeah?" Her smile widened.

"Yeah."

Ten minutes later, they finished up, and he thanked Cara for her help.

"Can I go now?" she asked, standing.

"Yeah . . ." He rubbed the back of his neck. "Cara . . ."

"Yeah?" She turned before reaching the break room door.

"Do you have any place you can go to get away?"

She narrowed her eyes. "Why?"

He didn't want to tell her about Alex's place or the fact someone had tried to take them out, but he wanted to keep her safe. The fact she was still alive said she might not be in the thieves' crosshairs, but he wasn't going to risk it.

She rested her hands on her hips. "What's up? Is this about that creepy guy?"

"I'm concerned. We need to get you someplace safe." And he and Andi had to watch their backs, because he doubted today's attempt on their lives would be the last.

SIXTEEN

"WHERE'S CARA?" Tad asked as Christian rejoined him and Andi.

"I sent her someplace safe."

"As in home?" Tad asked. "She's still on the clock."

"Not for a few days," Christian said.

"Excuse me?" Tad flicked his head, shaking the clump of hair from his brow. That man flipped his head more than anyone Christian knew. He was surprised Tad didn't have whiplash.

"I sent her someplace safe," he reiterated.

"That's not your call," Tad scoffed.

"I made it my call." He looked at Andi, and she nodded her unspoken agreement. "Look, Tad, Alex's place showed signs of a struggle."

Tad blinked, his long lashes flickering like a daddy longlegs struggling in a spider's web. "What do you mean *struggle*?"

"Exactly how it sounds," Christian said. "We don't know any more . . . but I wasn't going to chance it by letting Cara go home."

Tad's cheeks flushed. "Do—" He cleared his throat. "Do you think *I'm* in danger? I mean as the owner . . . ?"

Christian paused, then responded, "I don't believe so."

"If you think the girls are in danger, then why not me?" Tad asked.

Andi inclined her head.

"Maybe they didn't come after Cara because the guy assumed she hadn't noticed him surveilling the gallery or had forgotten him.

They might have broken into Alex's place to get information about the security system, or because they had reason to believe Alex noticed something or saw him someplace shortly before the heist and couldn't risk her mentioning it."

Tad blanched. "Wh-what do you think he did with her . . . with Alex?"

"I'm praying nothing." Though he feared otherwise.

"But . . . ?" Tad swallowed, his Adam's apple bobbing on the gulp.

Christian stiffened. Something uneasy anchored inside.

"This isn't good," Tad muttered. "I never thought . . ."

Christian's curious gaze met Andi's, then they both looked to Tad.

"You never thought *what*?" Christian asked.

Tad froze in place for a flicker of a moment, then shook himself out of it. "That I could be robbed like this." He looked to Andi, puffing his chest out like some preening peacock. "Your company must reimburse me for my losses. Jeopardy Falls was bad enough, but this . . ." He glared at Andi. "They got my Aztec eagle whistle, all my jade and gold necklaces. Along with my statuettes, and . . . my masterpiece, my—"

He mimicked a sob, but Christian wasn't buying it. Tad was putting on theatrics. The question was, why? Did Tad know more than he was admitting? Clearly, he wasn't bright enough to pull off a heist like this, but he could be dumb enough to hire someone to do it. Someone who went off-leash.

Fear for Alex bit at him. Why couldn't he shake that gnawing in the pit of his stomach?

"And your masterpiece was?" he asked a pacing Tad.

"My Aztec carved obsidian jar representing the monkey—the god of dance, play, and love." Tad waved his arm, his bangles clanging over the hoots of the near-incessant monkey calls piping through the speakers.

Of course that would be Tad's favorite piece.

"It was the only large item they took, but it was my most expensive piece. It alone was worth well over a hundred thousand."

"They were smart," Andi said.

"Smart?" Tad huffed. "Now we're complimenting the thieves?"

"They took highly valuable but small objects that are easy to move and hide. The only large item was the jar, and even that was only . . . I'm guessing maybe eight inches tall," she said.

Tad's thin, arched eyebrows lifted. "How do you know that?"

"Based on the time period of this collection and what Aztec jars typically look like, eight inches is a relatively safe call." She clearly knew her artifacts.

"You're correct." Tad exhaled.

"I'm curious," she said, striding toward him. "How did you come to have so many cultural artifacts?"

Tad straightened, his lashes flickering again. "I bought them from a private collector."

"All from the same collector?" Andi asked.

"Yes," Tad said, offering no more.

"That's quite a private collection for one person to have," she remarked.

Tad lengthened his neck. "It was a recent acquisition," he said haughtily.

"How recent?" Andi asked.

"Three months," Tad and Christian said.

Andi's questioning gaze flicked to him. "How . . . ?"

"Tad redid the room when he got the new collection," Christian said.

"A new collection necessitated a new space," Tad added.

Christian smiled at the concrete timing.

Tad narrowed his eyes. "Why on earth are you smiling?"

He wasn't telling Tad that Cara recalled the man, but what she said had just been confirmed by Tad. The space had been renovated when the man came in, but it wasn't to see the renovated space. He was casing the new collection. "It means the thieves had to have cased the place within the last three months, which gives us a window of video footage to watch. It'll take a while, scrolling through for a single man. . . ." He'd fill Andi in when it was just them. He didn't trust Tad, and his distrust was growing as the case proceeded.

"I thought there were two men," Tad said, then rose rushed his cheeks. "I called Joel, and he said the video showed two of them in Jeopardy Falls."

"He was talking about the heist. You only need one to case the place," Christian said. "No sense sending two when one will do."

"Okay. Well, now what?" Tad asked.

"We watch the video footage of this heist." Christian stretched. He doubted it lasted more than an hour. Whoever the men were, they were good. Good enough to obtain Tad's fob, break into his Jeopardy Falls safe, and turn the alarm off. And they were brash—hitting a second gallery in the same night. "Then I'll stake out your Taos gallery."

"*We'll* stake out your gallery," Andi added.

"Is that really necessary?" Tad asked, swiping his nose.

Christian narrowed his eyes. That little liar. He *did* know something. "I think we're going to need to have a chat before we go."

"About?" A clueless expression filled Tad's fake-tan face.

Christian linked his arms over his chest. "Your involvement with the heists."

"My—" Tad squeaked. "My involvement," he tried again, but only managed one octave lower.

SEVENTEEN

AN HOUR LATER, Christian held the gallery door open for Andi, and they darted through the still-pouring rain to Deckard's Equinox. Every time she saw the man's car, she pictured his condemning face. That he and Christian were brothers seemed surreal. From her short interactions with each, there were more differences than just their last names.

"I don't think I've ever seen a grown man squirm like Tad did," she said as Christian climbed into the driver's side. "I'm sure he knows more than he's saying."

"Agreed." Christian raked a hand through his wet hair, pushing it back from his face. She warmed despite being drenched in the cold rain. He had the most handsome profile.

He moved to start the ignition, then froze.

"What's wrong?" Then she saw it. The envelope on the dash—on the inside of the car. They'd been there again, and this time it was even more intrusive. They were growing bolder.

"Hang on," Christian said. "I've got gloves in the back. We're going to need to give this to the Feds."

Which meant more interaction with Adam. Just what she needed, and on this weekend of all weekends. She no longer loved Jeremy. That love had ceased long ago, but the sting of his marrying another on what was to be their wedding day still burnt her heart. "Couldn't

83

we just give it to Joel?" she asked, knowing that's not how things worked.

"Nope. We're out of Joel's jurisdiction, and they're on the case now." A kindness filled his eyes.

Great. He could pity her now. But his expression wasn't one of pity, but of . . . *compassion*? "I'm gonna have to crawl to the back to get the case if I don't want to get drenched again." He shimmied sideways between the seats. "Sorry," he said as his legs brushed her.

"All good," she said as an unexpected warmth shot through her. She scooched back against the door, so he had more room, but he'd already tumbled into the backseat and was leaning over it to the rear of the vehicle. It took him a rustling moment, but he sat back up with two pairs of gloves and a plastic evidence bag in hand.

"You come prepared," she said.

"PI gig," he said. "Never know when you're going to come across something."

She scooched her back flat against the passenger door as he climbed back over and landed in his seat with an oomph.

Sliding the gloves on, he handed her the second pair and the evidence bag and then reached for the envelope, flipped on the interior vehicle light, and held the envelope between them.

Andi was scrawled across the front of the envelope—in what looked like a woman's handwriting. Her chest squeezed. "I don't understand why it's addressed to me."

"Could it be someone you busted in the past?" he asked, rain pelting off the steamed-up windshield.

"It's possible." She swallowed as Christian started the SUV and kicked on the defrost.

"How many thieves have you busted?" he asked.

"Four."

"All from heists?"

"Yes. Two heists, each with two thieves."

"Impressive." He smiled. "Who were they?"

"In the first case, both had prior arrests for art theft, and they are in prison for a good while. The other two were gallery owners trying to cash in their insurance policy."

The whir of the defroster filled the space, and Christian knocked the fan down one as the fog slipped from the windshield bottom to top.

"And the gallery owners . . . did they go to jail?"

"No. Since we never paid out, they had no restitution to make, but they both got fines, probation, and community service."

"So it could easily be one of them. Fill me in on the way to Taos. I'll call the office and ask Greyson to run the men. I'm assuming it was two men?"

"Actually, one man. The other was a woman."

"Really?" He arched a brow. "You don't see women involved in heists too often, but there is the mystery woman Todd met at the gala, who apparently conned him."

"And stole his fob?"

He nodded. "Could she be the female gallery owner you busted?"

Andi shifted in her seat. "I suppose so. Tad couldn't remember much about her, right?"

"Right." He nodded. "Other than the fact that she had long, wavy brown hair, which Joel confirmed seeing in the gala footage he watched. He said she came in near the end of the night and managed to keep her face off camera."

"That's intriguing. You think she cased the place too?"

"She did, or someone else did and gave her the rundown of the place."

"And Tad can't give any more of a description? Anything about her face?" she asked. How could a man be with a woman and not be able to describe her? The notion sloshed her stomach.

"Unbelievably, no."

"Do you think he's lying?" Was he somehow involved? They'd pressed him hard before leaving, and he didn't incriminate himself in any manner other than the murmured comment, but he'd grown stronger as a suspect in her mind. Probably not on-the-ground involved, but that didn't mean he hadn't hired someone to rob his gallery and given them the information to bypass the system Christian had installed.

"I don't know for sure, but I'm certainly not counting him out."

"So he could be in it with the woman?" she asked.

"Yes. It could be a total setup. I mean, this handwriting seems to indicate a woman's involvement in at least some regard. I'm sure the Feds will run it through their handwriting experts. Maybe we'll get something helpful from that."

"Maybe." She shifted in her seat. "Let's open it."

"Right." He flipped back the unsealed flap and pulled out a cream tri-folded sheet of paper.

What does this say? Or nothing. Or nothing. Again, in what appeared to be a woman's handwriting.

"Double or nothing," he said. "And signed by Chris Angel and Houdini."

"Another gambling riddle signed by two magicians," she said.

"Illusionists," he said.

Her brow quirked. "What's the difference?"

"Magicians work on a smaller scale. Illusionists perform grand illusions like disappearing people, or in both Chris Angel's and Houdini's cases, their most famous—or one of their most famous acts—was Metamorphosis."

"Which is?"

"Two magicians appeared to transform into each other."

"Wow, that's quite the illusion." She narrowed her eyes. "You seem to know a lot about magicians and illusionists." She'd never paid attention to any, but he easily recalled who they were by their names.

He shrugged. "I liked watching them as a kid."

"Interesting. Did you ever try to pull off tricks?"

The muscle in his jaw flickered.

"I used to play ballerina," she started, sharing first. "I had my pink leotard and bedazzled tiara."

He smiled, and his clamped jaw loosened. "You have a tutu too?"

"Absolutely, a bright pink one."

He chuckled.

"It's funny what we want to be when we're kids."

"I suppose so."

"What did you want to be when you were a kid? A magician?"

He shrugged. "Just a kid."

She held his gaze a moment, and he seemed utterly sincere, but what kind of a kid didn't have a dream? She turned her attention back to the letter. "May I?" she asked, holding out her hand, wanting to examine it more closely.

"Sure." He handed it to her.

She held it in her gloved hands. "Why gambling riddles?"

"I think they're still telling us it's a game," he said, holding the evidence bag for her to place the note in when she was finished.

"And there'll be more?" she asked, studying the scroll.

"Double or nothing means another one is coming."

She agreed. This wasn't over, and with Alex missing and them run off the road, this "game," as the thieves appeared to view it, was growing extremely dangerous. She exhaled, praying it stopped before it became deadly, but the worst feeling about Alex gripped her chest tight.

Father, please don't let her be . . . She didn't want to even voice it, but she needed to pray what was on her heart. *Please don't let her be dead.*

EIGHTEEN

CHRISTIAN SWERVED as a tumbleweed toppled across the road, his headlights illuminating it as it danced in a flurry of blustering wind. He glanced at the GPS. Nearly there. They hadn't wanted to wait around for the Feds to take the letter, so they'd dropped it off with the Albuquerque police detective who Tad said had been on site before the Feds showed. He could get it to them. Or they could duke out jurisdiction, for all he cared. Right now, he was focused on the task at hand. And—he sighed—growing enthralled with the beautiful woman sitting beside him. She kept him on his toes in the best possible way.

What would it be like to get to know Andi Forester better? He definitely wanted to find out. They were both tied to the case, which he prayed would end tonight. He'd alerted the local sheriff, Harold Brookes, about their plan—explained they were hoping to catch the men in the act. Harold had a pressing case and couldn't commit to being with them but said he was only a phone call away.

Pulling up to Tad's Taos wine gallery, Christian cut the ignition and pulled out the keys.

"Excuse me," he said, leaning toward her. "I need to grab my gun."

Andi scooched back into the seat as he pulled the Glock from the glove box, then shut it and straightened.

"I'm going to grab an extra mag, and then I say we run for it." Of course, Deck didn't have an umbrella.

She nodded.

He grabbed the mag from the rear lockbox—the back of his shirt soaked and suctioned to his skin in a matter of moments—and then grabbed her door for her. Taking her hand, they bolted for the front entrance, squishing under the narrow overhang.

"How do we get in this gallery?" she asked, her arms wrapped about her.

A triple set of keypads. Christian plugged the first code into the exterior pad. The door buzzed, and he held it open for her.

"Thanks," she said, stepping inside, water dripping to the floor and puddling around them.

"I'll take care of the next two alarms and see if we can't find something to dry off with. Or . . ." He winced at the sight of her shivering. "At least warm up somehow."

She nodded and followed him as he disarmed the system.

"If they come and see the alarm is off, won't they know we're here?"

"I'm going to reset them."

"Then won't we set them off?" she asked as he opened the back-office door—only the emergency lighting on.

"No motion sensors here. Another of Tad's brilliant choices."

"But you installed the system," she said, her teeth chattering.

"I suggested upgrades to what he had in place, and he took two of my recommendations and blatantly ignored the rest, so I refused to back my work here too."

She rubbed her arms beside him, and he fought the urge to tug her in his arms and warm her up.

He swallowed at the thoughts of her pulling at his mind. He hadn't felt anything for a woman in a long time. How had Andi Forester managed to invade his mind in such a short amount of time? He shook off the thoughts of her dancing through his head and moved for the light switch.

"It's almost like Tad wanted to get robbed," she said. "The way he handled the systems . . ."

"I'm starting to wonder," he said, flipping the lights on in the

89

windowless office. They bathed the room in a warm glow. He took in their surroundings, and his gaze locked on the closet. "I bet Tad keeps a jacket or something in here," he said, striding for it.

"Here we go," he said, opening the door to find a jacket, dress shirt, tie, and even a pair of loafers. "This should help," he said, pulling the jacket off the hanger, which clanged against the metal bar behind him as he strode to Andi. He draped it across her shoulders and tugged it together, reaching for the zipper.

"What about you?" she asked as he zipped her up, still wanting to pull her into his arms.

"I'm fine." But he needed to focus on the case rather than how intriguing she'd become to him.

"You're soaked to the bone," she said, shivering. If she didn't warm up soon, he *was* going to pull her into his arms.

He glanced back at the closet. "I'll change my shirt. That'll help." He was taller and broader than Tad, but it would work well enough for the night.

Andi's cheeks burned red at the sight of Christian O'Brady without a shirt. Struggling to hide her smile, she turned her glance away.

"Sorry," he said. "I could have stepped outside if that made you uncomfortable."

"No. It's fine. No different than seeing you or any man in a swimsuit." Though she doubted any man was ripped like he was. *Wow.* She looked upward and mouthed, *Good job.*

"It's a little short," he said, and she flashed her gaze back on him, and unbridled laughter spilled from her lips. The cuffs hit several inches from his wrists, the fabric straining.

He looked down and grabbed the hem of the shirt, it also landing several inches above his waist. "Yeah, not sure this is going to work." He chuckled.

"It's better than staying soaked. Besides, if you . . ." She strode over, unbuttoned the sleeves, and rolled them up his sinewy forearms one at a time. How did he have muscles like that for forearms? *Sheesh.* "There you go," she said, finishing up.

"And this?" He grinned and pointed to his exposed waistline.

"That you're just going to have to deal with." She chuckled.

"Glad you find this so amusing."

"Sorry." She pressed her lips together, trying to stem her laughter, but it was no use.

The fact that she was supposed to have been married and off on her honeymoon by now was a harsh contrast to standing in a windowless office with a man who somehow disarmed her guard. And he was making her laugh. Belly laugh for the first time in a year.

"It's okay." He chuckled. "I know it's ridiculous, but like you said, it's better than being soaked." He draped his wet shirt over the chair. "I can only hope this dries by morning, because I'm not wearing this home. I'd never hear the end of the ribbing."

She shuffled her foot. "You and your brother . . . are close?"

"Yes."

"But you believe he's wrong about Mitch's case?" At least he'd said he was inclined to believe she'd been set up, which went right in the face of Deckard's judgment of her.

"I believe what Deckard found happened."

Her stomach dropped, and she braced for what was coming.

NINETEEN

"BUT I ALSO DON'T BUY that you messed up," Christian continued, stunning her. "Or, at least, I think your case should be investigated."

"Wait." She squinted. "So are you saying you believe both of us?" How was that possible?

"I believe Deckard found what he did. However, it doesn't negate the fact that you could very well have been set up." He rolled one of the two computer chairs over, spun it around, and straddled it, draping his hands over the back, gesturing with them as he spoke.

"So Deckard found the DNA was compromised and the evidence missing. We can consider that a fact. The sample was deteriorated beyond retesting, and the shirt is missing. But neither of those things means you did anything wrong. Especially if you believe you were set up."

"I don't *believe* I was set up. I *was* set up." She bit her lip to keep from screaming.

He held his hand up. "I get it. Why don't you walk me through more of the case."

She shuffled her leg, pulled the jacket tight around herself.

"You could go in the ladies' room, take your shirt off to dry, and wear the jacket zipped," he suggested.

"That's not a bad idea." Her blouse was plastered to her. "How far is the bathroom? I don't want to risk the thieves seeing me through one of the windows or doors. Actually, why don't you just turn around and I'll change here."

He arched a brow. "You sure?"

"I trust you not to look."

"Really? Don't you know the hero always sneaks a peek?"

A bemused smile twitched on her lips. "So you're the hero now? Does that make me the damsel in distress?"

"Hardly. I feel certain you can hold your own."

She smiled. "All right, mister. Turn around." She waited until he did so, then swapped out the shirt for just the jacket. "Okay," she said as she'd finished zipping it up.

He turned around. "Feel better?"

"Much." She draped it on one of the conference table chairs. "It's interesting—"

"What's that?"

"Tad's galleries are primarily fine jewels, ancient artifacts, and exorbitantly priced wines, according to the dossier my boss just emailed over." She wiggled the phone.

"But?"

"But he has all these modern, neo-minimalist areas within the galleries."

"The exorbitant world is Tad. The Zen-minimalist is his ex or soon-to-be ex-wife, Veronica Gaiman."

Andi arched her brow. "That's a new one. What on earth is Zen-minimalism?"

"It's defined as an 'extension of simplicity,' according to Veronica," he said, using air quotes. "She says it's where you take complex things to simple, getting rid of anything that's unnecessary."

"So the plain white tables and chairs, the lack of artwork in the break room or the offices," she said.

"Exactly."

"They sound like an interesting pair."

Christian's eyes widened on an inhale, then he streamed it out. "You don't know the half of it. We probably could add Veronica to our suspect list too. I pray after tonight we'll have caught the thieves and we can track down who all might be involved."

"Tad's on the suspect list, the mystery woman he supposedly can't remember . . ."

"Me . . ." He moved to take a seat on the floor, propping his back against the wall and stretching out his legs.

She moved to sit beside him. "You kinda have to be on the list, given your knowledge of the security systems. It would be unprofessional of me to just assume your innocence."

"I get it."

"But my gut says you're far from involved."

"Why's that?"

"You've been with me when both letters were left. The one is in a woman's script. You said Joel . . . Sheriff Brunswick ran through the heist footage, and he would have noticed if one of the thieves was your size."

"A perk of being tall, I suppose."

"So who else should we have on the list?"

"Besides Veronica, Tad's ex–business partner, Brad Melling."

"So he's got two exes."

He chuckled. "In a manner of speaking, yes."

"So what happened with Tad and Veronica's split?"

"It was public and ugly. Both accusing the other of cheating."

"Any merit to the accusations?" She relaxed, letting the solid wall hold her full weight. As soon as tonight was over, she was crashing out—at least for a handful of hours. She was going on fumes.

"Knowing both of them . . . it wouldn't surprise me on either end. Neither did their splitting up."

"Oh?" She arched a brow as he bent a knee, draping his right arm over it.

"They were a flash-in-the-pan couple. Whirlwind romance and then a crash and burn."

"I'm looking forward to meeting her," she said. Veronica Gaiman was high on her list of suspects. She had to be, given the situation. A scorned ex and all that.

Christian chuckled. "She's certainly entertaining."

She bent her legs, hugging her knees to her chest.

He bumped her leg with his, warming her. "Can I ask?"

"I wondered how long that would take." She swallowed.

"We don't have to talk about it if you'd rather not." His deep brown eyes held kindness—something she hadn't seen a lot of since her fall from grace at the FBI.

"It's okay." Other than with her bestie, Harper, it'd be the first she'd spoken of it since he'd dropped her—faster than a burning match. "I met Jeremy at a pub the Bureau hangs out at."

"He's on the art theft team?" Christian asked, his hand brushing hers as he shifted. And warmth permeated her again, his sturdy hand surprisingly soft.

He wrapped his hands around his knee, his solid presence strong beside her.

"Yep," she finally said, struggling to focus on the conversation at hand and not the handsome man sitting beside her.

"And you were engaged?" he asked, his voice gentle. It was amazing how tender such a rugged man could be.

"Yes. We dated for a year, then got engaged."

"But . . . I hope I'm wrong and you dumped him, but it sounded like . . ."

"He dumped me as soon as the accusations I'd messed up flew."

"I'm sorry." He reached over and laid his hand atop hers, giving her hand a gentle squeeze before draping his hand back over his knee.

She wanted to grab it back, hold tight, but reason dictated otherwise. What was it about this man that drew her in so easily? After what happened with Jeremy, she'd kept a strong guard in place, and Christian had managed to somehow dissolve it—or nearly so. That both delighted and terrified her.

"I'm guessing he didn't believe you?" he said, his voice still tender.

She shook her head.

"What a scuzzball."

She laughed. "That's a new one."

He shrugged. "Seems like it fits."

She smiled, despite the topic, and she attributed it to the man beside her. "I most definitely agree."

"And that agent . . ."

"Adam." She released an exasperated exhale. "Jeremy's best bud."

"He seemed like a winner."

"You have no idea."

"I think you can tell a lot about a person by who they hang out with. Bad company corrupts good morals and all that."

Was he quoting Scripture and mentioned prayer? "You're a believer?"

"Yes," he said with a smile. "You are too?" His gaze fixed on her.

She turned to look him in the eyes. "Yes. He's how I got through losing a job I loved, was good at, and . . ."

"Getting over Jeremy?" he asked.

She leaned her head against the wall, facing him. "That happened so fast. His actions showed who he was, and I'm thankful I found out before I married him." That would have been horrible.

"I can imagine."

"What about you?" She slipped her legs into a cross-legged position, thankful for Riley's jeans so she could stretch out. Her body still ached from the jarring accident.

"What about me?"

"Anyone special in your life?" *Please say no.* Seriously, what was up with her? Why was she praying his answer was no? She'd just met the man. Usually it took her time to build interest in someone, but there was something contagious about Christian O'Brady. Crazy as that was.

He shifted sideways to face her. "Nope. No one," he finally said.

"For how long?" The question slipped out before it'd even registered in her brain. She wanted to know, but she wouldn't have asked such a personal question if her brain had remained logical rather than her emotions driving her questions and fueling her feelings.

"It's been a long time since anyone grabbed my attention . . . until now."

She blinked. Had he just said . . . ?

"I . . ." His gaze flashed to the door.

"You . . ." she pushed, dying to hear what he was about to say.

"Hang on." He stilled.

Hang on? Following his gaze to the door, she spotted smoke floating in underneath it.

The sooty smell of something burning carried in with the thickening smoke. She looked at Christian, her eyes wide.

"Fire," they said in unison.

TWENTY

CHRISTIAN STRODE to the closed office door and dabbed his hand against it with a quick swipe. He yanked it back as fast as he'd touched it and shook his fingers out. "Hot."

She scoured the room for another way out. Not finding any, panic bubbled up her throat.

"We need to get out of here."

Her chest squeezed the breath from her lungs.

"Here," he said, handing her his cell. "Call Harold. His number is in the contacts under his first name," he said, while searching through cabinets.

"Hello," Harold answered.

"This is Andi Forester. There's a fire at Tad Gaiman's Taos gallery. Christian O'Brady and I are inside."

"I'm on my way. Will get paramedics and the fire team en route."

"Thank you." She looked up to see Christian holding a fire extinguisher. *Oh, thank you, Lord.*

"This might buy us enough space to make it to the back, emergency door."

"Might?"

Christian gave a curt nod.

She swallowed, smoke burning her throat.

"Drape your wet shirt over you like this." He laid his over his head.

She did so.

"There's going to be a blast when we open the door."

Stabbing pierced her chest, knocking the air from her lungs. She needed to calm down, conserve her oxygen.

"Come stand behind the door. Crouch down low and put your hands over your head." He demonstrated.

"And you?"

"I'm going to use my shirt to open the door and bump back behind the door low, just like you. Now this next part is crucial. After the blast, we crawl on our hands and knees with our shirts over our heads. I'll try to clear enough of a path to make it to that emergency door."

"Got it. And if they stayed after starting the fire . . . What if they're waiting to see if we make it out?"

"One threat at a time." He took his belt off. "Wrap your finger around the buckle. I'll hold the other end. Don't let go. If the smoke is too thick, we'll have to lay face down on the ground and army crawl our way out. Just follow my lead."

Tears burned her eyes as smoke swirled around her in spiraling wisps.

He clutched her hand. "We've got this."

She nodded.

"Get behind the door."

She did as instructed.

He pulled the door open, and a wave of unbelievable heat roared in, consuming the air they'd just been breathing.

He tugged the belt, and she followed. Crawling on hands and knees with her head down, the shirt draped over her, all she could see was smoke. It engulfed the air. The high-pressure air from the fire extinguisher spurted out in a strong whir. The heat of the flames danced close, and she prayed as she followed Christian, her fingers gripping the belt buckle tight.

Please, Lord, let us get out of this, and don't let anyone be waiting to take us out if we make it outside.

She blinked, trying to see . . . something, anything, through the welling tears, but it was no use. It was a hazy blur, except for the sparks landing by her feet.

Her chest heaved. Her lungs felt like an overinflated balloon ready to burst.

Suddenly hot met cold, and they tumbled outside.

Thank you, Lord.

"Let's move," Christian said, helping her to her feet.

"What's wrong?"

He held the gun, scanning their surroundings. "I heard something. We need to get away from the building. You stay still, and—"

"You die." She knew the concept well from her Bureau training, though that had been years ago, and she'd never been a field agent. Her burning lungs stifled her breath and she fought for air.

"Deep breath," he said without looking back. "Stay on my six. I've got you."

Sprinting across the parking lot for the trees on the other side, she couldn't help wondering—were they running from danger or toward it?

TWENTY-ONE

ANDI HUNG TIGHT on Christian's six, finally managing to take a deep inhale of the fresh night air, and the spasm in her lungs began to settle as they hit the edge of the trees.

Sirens whirred, growing closer and closer still.

Thank you, Jesus.

Swirling red lights danced across the pavement as a fire truck rounded the corner, followed by an ambulance and a sheriff's vehicle.

Firemen jumped out, rushing to pull the hose.

Andi stared, taking in the devastation surrounding them. The building ablaze.

Firefighters held the hose, the spray arching up in the air before landing down on the flames.

The sheriff pulled into the lot, his lights swirling. He angled his vehicle to block the parking lot from the road.

"You two okay?" a paramedic asked.

Christian looked at her.

"I'm fine." Embarrassed she'd freaked out. Yes, it was a fire, but she was no longer that little girl in that four-alarm fire that scourged her childhood neighborhood. She'd been a federal agent, for goodness' sake.

"I'll need to take a look at you all the same," the paramedic said. "I'm Josh, and you are?"

"Andi."

"Well, Andi, why don't we head over to the ambulance? Let me check you out." He turned his attention on Christian. "You too, sir."

Sir? The guy could only be a handful of years younger than Christian, but she supposed the southern twang in his voice indicated he'd been raised to overdo the politeness.

At least he knew better than to call her *ma'am*.

They strode for the ambulance as the sheriff stepped over to meet them.

"Glad you're okay, brother," he said, clapping Christian's hand.

"Me too." Christian looked back at the building. The light spilling out from the open bay of the ambulance revealed the ash covering his handsome face.

She touched hers. Did it look the same? Marred by soot? She coughed.

"Right here, miss." Josh patted the back of the open ambulance doors.

"I'll be right back," Christian said. "I want to talk to Harold."

She nodded.

"Okay, let's listen to those lungs," Josh said.

An hour later, she sat on a cot in an ER bay, waiting for the doc to "observe" her.

The cool liquid from the IV chilled the vein in her hand where the needle was secured with white tape that pulled the skin.

Christian was somewhere in the ER, but it was frustrating not knowing where. They needed to talk about the fact someone had tried to kill them twice in less than twenty-four hours.

Cyrus tapped his foot, waiting for Teresa to answer. She owed him well over a hundred thousand. The '89 Chateau Haut-Brion collection was nearly thirty thousand per lot—of that he was certain. He'd invested so much time researching the heist locations and the items cataloged in each, spent equal time planning them out.

That's why he couldn't lose his partner yet. Unfortunately, Casey possessed skills he needed to see their plan through, but when it was done, he was as dead as Julia.

"Yes, Cyrus," Teresa finally answered, her voice belabored.

Yap. Yap. Yap.

Great. She had that stupid dog close. On her lap, he'd bet. Insipid ball of hair had bitten him multiple times. If Teresa or one of her husband's goons wouldn't have shot him for doing so, he'd have killed that stupid animal years ago.

"What is it?" she asked, the connection blipping in and out.

"I thought you were calling off Enrique."

"What?"

"I thought you were pulling Enrique back," he said again. Not being able to hear everything she said was a bonus, but she needed to hear what *he* was saying.

"I called him off you," she said, boredom ripe in her voice.

"But not them," he ground out.

"I told you I'm protecting my investment."

"I see. So, the fact that Enrique set the wine gallery on fire and destroyed our haul makes no difference to you? Oh, and the investigators survived."

"What?" Her voice rose to that ear-splitting octave.

"He burned the place down." The imbecile possessed no self-control. Enrique could never wait for the opportune moment, and he was sloppy as all get out. He needed to take Enrique out before he cost them anything more.

"How do you know?" she snapped.

Good. She was upset. She should be. "I followed him there. You had him tracking me. I decided to track him in turn."

"That's not your job. Your job is to focus on the heists."

"Call him off and I will." Until Cyrus had the chance to take him out, he needed Enrique to cease and desist.

"I don't trust those two," she said. "Your toying with them has gone on too long."

He reclined against the van's front seat. "You're just lucky that

Casey wasn't with me when it happened, or he would have walked then and there."

"You think you can keep him from hearing about it?"

"Considering we're supposed to hit it later tonight, he's going to know. But I've got it covered."

"How?"

"I'll tell him Julia did it."

"Doesn't he know she's dead?"

"No. As long as he doesn't see her face on the news, which he never watches, he won't find out."

"And he'll believe she did it because . . . ?"

"She wasn't happy with her cut and got vindictive. If she wasn't making money, neither would we . . . or something along those lines."

"You'll think he'll buy it?"

"Trust me," he said, shifting in his seat. "I know how to sell it. Besides, he's dependent on me to finish this out." Casey might possess skills he didn't have, but he possessed equally needed skills. They were in this together . . . right up until they'd completed the final heist.

Yap. Yap. Yap.

His muscles coiled. "Shut that thing up."

"Don't talk about my precious like that."

"Don't push me." Now he was the one with the cold edge to his voice. He wasn't playing, and if she was wise, she'd realize that. She was dependent on *him,* and it was time she remembered that.

"Or what?" She released a mocking chuckle.

"Or I'll stop and you'll have to find someone else to finish, but good luck making that happen. This has been in the works for two years. It's been fine-tuned—until you unleashed your thug. Success lies in the balance."

"Fine. I'll tell him to hold . . . for now. But he's still going to watch them, and if I think for one second they are a threat, I'll give the order."

TWENTY-TWO

CHRISTIAN APPRECIATED the hospital staff, but he wasn't spending the rest of the night in the frigid ER pit with an IV strapped just below the hollow of his elbow. Someone had tried to take them out twice. It made no sense. They were leaving them messages, asking them to play some twisted game, all the while trying to kill them. What kind of sicko were they dealing with?

This time there'd been no message left. He figured it was due to one of two options. Either the thieves assumed they'd be dead and there was no use leaving one, or someone else was involved. Oddly enough, he was leaning toward the latter. He couldn't see any reason the thieves would purposely destroy their intended heist. Most thieves didn't have it in them to destroy something so valuable. Even if they'd seen them there, they could easily have come back another night. It wasn't like he and Andi could watch the gallery nonstop. It didn't make sense. But he hadn't had time to chat with Andi about it.

They'd whisked her away in the first ambulance before he'd even been looked at by the second. He didn't care about being looked at second. What he did care about was her being out of his sight while they were in a killer's.

His muscles tensed, and the BP sleeve inflated like clockwork, squeezing his arm. 140 over 80. That would flag the nurse's concern, but he wasn't staying.

Thankfully, Harold had his undersheriff run Deckard's SUV to the hospital for when they were discharged. But Christian wasn't waiting around for an official discharge. They'd want to observe them for hours, possibly a day. And they didn't have that kind of time. They had thieves to track, and they were just killing time sitting around.

If Andi was good enough to leave, then they'd go. And if she agreed, he was bringing her to the ranch. She'd no doubt balk, but until they caught the thieves, he wasn't letting her out of his sight. With no note left, the belief someone else was in play only dug deeper into his gut. The thieves were intelligent, very precise in their work. It didn't match the rash attempts on their lives.

Thirty minutes later, he'd had enough of sitting around, listening to beeping machines and the click of the IV machine as it fed liquid into his system. It had been long enough. He loosened the tape around the IV needle, and with one swift yank, tugged it from his arm.

Swinging his legs over the bed, he snagged his clothes from the yellow plastic bag, pulled the curtain closed, and changed.

His clothes reeked of smoke, but they were all he had. He'd shower and change once back at the ranch.

Seeing no signs of his nurse, he headed down the corridor, looking for Andi. He caught sight of her through a curtain opening and smiled. She looked just as thrilled about their surroundings as he was.

"Hey," he said, clutching the curtain in one hand. "Okay to come in?"

"Of course." She waved him in. "Hey, how come you got discharged and I didn't?"

"I just left."

"Exactly what I'm going to do."

"Are you sure you're okay?"

"Yes, I'm fine. We gotta go."

"Okay, I'll be in the hall."

Within two minutes—if that—she stood by his side. "What about our ride?"

"In the lot. Keys under the mat, thanks to Harold's undersheriff."

He stepped out first, then gave her the go-ahead. He only relaxed—slightly—once they were in the SUV. He started the ignition, and they were out of the lot before Andi had even buckled in.

"Sorry," he said as her belt clicked in place.

"All good. I was ready to be out of there too."

"We should stay at the ranch tonight."

"We? The ranch?"

"Don't worry. We have three houses on the property. You can stay with my sister Riley or wherever you're most comfortable. We need to stick together until we get whoever's behind this, okay?"

She bit her bottom lip and shifted in her seat. "Okay," she finally said.

Relief sifted through him.

"So you live on a ranch?" she asked, swiping a hand through her hair, which now tumbled down her shoulders.

"Yeah." He tapped the wheel. "It's a ways north of Jeopardy Falls. Secluded. And we're all armed. We'll be safe there." He prayed.

TWENTY-THREE

"WE'LL GET TO THE RANCH so you can get some sleep," Christian said as they drove through the lifting darkness.

"Can we get my truck on the way?" she asked. "It's still at Tad's gallery."

"Sure." He tapped the wheel. "We go through Jeopardy Falls to get to our ranch."

"I appreciate you offering to let me stay." She wanted to stay near Christian, but the thought of being at Deckard MacLeod's place . . . Her heart palpitated, clamminess clinging to her palms. *Great.* If she wasn't enough of a mess, she was about to have a panic attack in front of Christian. "But . . ." She took a moment to calm her voice. Well, as much as possible.

"But?" he asked, his tone resolute.

"But I'll be fine at my house," she said. "I'm armed, thanks to the retrieval team getting my gun, and my place is so out of the way, I think they'd have a hard time finding me."

"It's not worth the risk," he said, concern thick in his voice. "You can take my room, and I'll take the couch, or you can bunk with Riley."

She finally managed a deep inhale and then released it slowly, trying to quell the anxiety pulsing through her. He wasn't going to take no for an answer, was he?

Dawn broke right as they pulled into Tad's Jeopardy Falls gallery lot, the promise of light after a long dark night soothing.

"Thanks," she said as he hopped out and opened her door.

"I'll wait, so you can follow," he said, his arm draped over the still-open door.

"Probably a good idea for me to put your address in my GPS . . . just in case." That way she could pull back, drive slower, put off facing Deckard MacLeod a little longer.

Christian nodded and gave her the address.

"Thanks. I'll see you there," she said, trying to push her fears of seeing Deckard at some point down to the pit of her gut and praying they wouldn't rise to the surface—raw and painful.

"I'll see you to your truck," Christian said.

She smiled—as much as she could manage with the heightened frenzy of panic swarming her ears in a fast-pitched whirring and clutching her chest in a squeezing sensation. "Such the gentleman," she said as they walked to her truck door. She used the fob to unlock it, and it beeped, its lights flashing on cue.

"You know . . . you act like no man's ever seen you to your car or even opened your door first."

"Rarely at best."

"Now, that's a sad commentary on men these days."

He opened her door, and she climbed into the truck.

"Thanks," she said, her gaze pinning on the windshield. Relief slid over her at finding it empty. Devoid of another note.

"My pleasure," Christian said with a smile.

She started the ignition.

"I'll wait until you're ready and you can follow me out."

"You know, I should probably grab clothes and toiletries."

"I'm sure Riley has plenty to share."

"That's nice of her, but—"

"She won't mind in the least. I know it might not be comfortable, but the ranch is fortified. We'll be safer there. We can run and get your clothes later in the day if we determine we're not in the killers' crosshairs."

"Killers?" They'd survived.

"I should say *attempted*."

"Okay." She bit her bottom lip.

He reached over and squeezed her hand. "We'll be safe there."

She nodded, unsure which worried her more—the possibility of the men still coming after them or the thought of facing Deckard MacLeod again. It should be no contest. Logically, she knew that. Emotion-wise, it was a whole different story.

Christian closed her door and tapped the hood before heading the few empty spots over to Deckard's SUV.

Christian pulled out of the lot, and as she moved behind him, the crushing weight of the last twenty-four hours suffocated her. The sun crept higher over the horizon, and she prayed for the constricting force to dissipate, but it only pressed harder against her rib cage.

In addition to knowing she was about to face Deckard MacLeod for the second time in twenty-four hours, seeing Adam . . . hearing his harsh, mocking words brought all the memories and emotion of the fallout roaring back like a lion.

Tears that had been waiting to fall since she first saw Deckard, and then Adam, dashed her resolve and burst forth in a flurry. It was the first private moment she'd had since, and frustration consumed her. She'd let Deckard—and Adam—get to her in a matter of seconds. Felt knocked back a year in an instant. Everything awful oozed around her. Memories of unheard claims of innocence and hot shame sifted through her.

She prayed Christian couldn't tell she was crying if he looked in the rearview mirror, but best to get them out and done before they reached the ranch. She refused to cry in front of Deckard MacLeod.

Her cell rang. Who was calling so early? It could go to voicemail. But if it was about the case somehow . . . ?

Sniffing, she swiped the tears from her eyes and glanced at the number. Harper.

Before she could answer, her voicemail kicked in and the call dropped. Probably for the best. If they talked, Harper would know something was wrong, even if she managed somehow to keep her voice level. Harper just had a way to get to the bone and marrow of a person.

Her cell rang again.

She straightened her shoulders and took a stiff breath. *You've got this.* She'd mastered pretending she was okay and that nothing was wrong. "Hey, Harp," she said as happily as she could muster, but it was a pitiful attempt.

"What's wrong?"

She dropped her head, her hair spilling across her shoulders. Of course, Harper would see right through her. "It's just been a day. . . ."

"I know, honey. And that's why I'm surprising you."

"Surprising me?" She straightened and caught a glance at herself in the rearview mirror. *Lovely.* Black mascara lines tracked down her cheeks in dark rivulets. She attempted to swipe them away but only managed to make wide, inky smudges across her cheeks.

"I'm on the way to you now. I got a call from ICRC yesterday. They've delayed my trip for at least a week, so I have time to burn. I should be there in forty-five . . . an hour at most," Harper said, as if her driving up from Albuquerque for a visit was already planned.

"It's sweet of you, but—"

"I'm already on the way."

Of course she'd waited to call until she was on the way, so Andi would feel like a heel telling her to go back home. "Look, I appreciate it, but—"

"I know this is a difficult time for you, so I say we have some girl time. Maybe hit a spa for some pampering. Take a hike."

"I'd love to, but I'm in the thick of a case."

"No worries. I'll stay out of your way."

Andi nearly chuckled. With Harper, that was impossible. "I'll just feel bad leaving you alone while I work."

"Alone doesn't bother me."

It never had. Harper's independence was fierce, her boldness unparalleled, but she supposed that's what made her best friend the perfect volunteer for the International Committee of the Red Cross.

"You know me. I can find plenty of things to do. And we can hang out when you're not working."

"With this case, I don't know if that'll happen."

"Oooh. Sounds intriguing. You'll have to fill me in."

"I have way more than the case to fill you in on." Just hearing Harper's voice burned the desire to spill it all. It was her bestie's brilliant and extremely annoying gift.

"I'll be there soon."

"I'm not at home. . . ."

"Okay. You gave me a key last time. I can let myself in."

"No. It's not safe."

TWENTY-FOUR

"WHAT DO YOU MEAN it's not safe?"

As much as she didn't want to admit they were in danger, and how much she didn't want to stay on a ranch with Deckard MacLeod, based on the last twenty-four hours and two attempts on their lives, it couldn't be denied.

"I'll explain it when you get here. Let me make a call, and I'll call you right back."

She dialed Christian.

"Hey," he answered. "You okay?"

"Yeah," she said, clearing any trace of sorrow from her voice. "My friend Harper is surprising me, and she'll be here in an hour. I hate to tell her to turn around."

"Tell her to come to the ranch."

"Are you sure we won't be imposing?"

"Not at all."

"Okay. Thanks. I'll let her know."

Calling Harper back, she gave the address and the promise she'd explain when she arrived. She wouldn't have to explain Deckard. Harper knew it all.

Andi followed Christian up a steep incline, leaving the town in the distance. They continued climbing until finally they turned down a narrow dirt drive winding around the mountain's top rim, where they reached a plateau, and the driveway grew straight. Shale cliffs stood in the distance, pinions and evergreens dotting the land-scape. Soon cattle paddocks came into view, and horses galloped in the distance.

It was beautiful.

A few minutes later, they drove under a sign with *Second Chances Ranch* in large black letters against silver metal.

Unique name choice, one that hit a strong chord. She'd gotten a second chance thanks to Grant, but unless she discovered who'd set her up, she couldn't truly move on. Seeing Deckard and Adam again had drilled that home.

Soon a sprawling adobe house came into view. Its large front porch with exposed wooden beams standing every five feet joined the adobe slab to the stucco roof, windchimes dangling from it. A large horse pen stood to their right, and at least a half dozen horses appeared over the rise, galloping for the fence.

She pulled to a stop parallel to Christian in the oversized dirt driveway and had barely shifted to climb out when Christian opened the door for her.

"Thanks." She smiled.

He offered his hand, and she took hold of it, stepping down to the running board and then the hard-packed earth below, her hand tingling at his touch.

"Beautiful place you have here," she said, taking a wide sweep of the pastures and the large ranch house nestled against the mountainside and trying to shake the tingling from continuing up her arm. Man, how did he do it?

"That's Deck's house," he said, pulling her back to the hard present of being at Deckard MacLeod's home. "Mine's down this way," he continued and pointed down the lane. Her gaze followed. In the distance, past a metal barn and a wooden white one, stood what looked like something about the size of the guesthouse she lived in. Windchimes clanged in the morning breeze.

"That's yours?" she asked, of the quaint dwelling.

"That's Riley's. Mine's beyond that. I'll give you a tour after we check in with Deck and Riley."

The odor of smoke filled her nose as wind streamed over her. She desperately needed a shower and a change of clothes.

———

Christian led the way to Deck's door, praying he'd be nice to Andi. Or at least cordial, especially after all they'd been through. He didn't want her hurt. She'd brought a protectiveness out in him. Not that she needed it. She was clearly strong and a fighter—after all she'd been through. Her resilience was amazing, even if she didn't see it that way.

He reached for the doorknob, but it opened before he could turn it.

"Hey," Riley said. "Andi, so good to see you again." She engulfed Andi with a hug.

Andi looked overwhelmed, but a smile graced her lips.

Thank you, he mouthed to Riley.

"Come on in," she said, stepping back. "We've got breakfast going."

He looked to Andi, at the vulnerability in her eyes, but she held her head high.

"Whoa," Deckard said, rounding the corner. "You reek of smoke, dude. . . ." His words cut off at the sight of Andi. "Sorry," he said, giving Andi a nod.

"No problem," she said. And then they all stood there, awkwardness filling the room.

"Why don't you show Andi to my house," Riley said to Christian, then shifted her attention to Andi. "Feel free to use any of my clothes."

"Thanks," she said, smoothing Tad's jacket, nearly forgetting that's what she still had on.

"We'll get cleaned up and then come grab breakfast and fill you in on the case," Christian said.

A moment later, he led the way down the winding dirt path to Riley's house. Opening the door, he stepped in behind Andi.

"Nice place," she said, gazing about the room until she fixed on the shelf unit to the right of the kiva fireplace. "Are those belt buckles?" she asked.

"Yep. Barrel racing."

"Your sister's in the rodeo?"

"Yep. The local circuit."

"That's awesome." She indicated the buckles. "May I?"

"Sure."

She strode over to the hewn pinewood bookcase, and he moved to her side.

Her gaze danced along the rows of buckles. "So many. She must be really good."

"She was offered a spot in the PRCA, but she preferred to stay close to home."

"Wow." Andi slipped a strand of hair behind her ear, exposing the gentle slope of her neck, and the image of him trailing kisses down it flashed through his mind.

Whoa! Get a grip, dude.

"How about you or Deckard?" she asked in the midst of his muddled thoughts. "Do either of you ride in the rodeo?"

"Deck rides saddle bronc, but I prefer just free riding. How about you? You been riding?"

She nodded. "My brother is a ranch manager, and we used to go a lot before I moved up here."

He nodded, not questioning her move from Albuquerque. That was her business, but he was happy since it had brought her into his life. "We'll have to take a ride one day."

She smiled. "I'd like that. When all of this is over."

He prayed it ended soon with no more surprises, but something said there were far more headed their way. The question was, how deadly would it get?

TWENTY-FIVE

ANDI EMERGED from Riley's home feeling a thousand times better. A hot shower and a fresh pair of clothes, even if not her own, made a huge difference. She glanced at her watch. Harper should be arriving any minute. Actually, she might have already arrived. If so, Andi had no doubt she'd get a warm welcome from Riley.

Christian's sister was a sweetheart, and it was touching seeing the three siblings interact. There was a bond there that had been apparent from the start. She and her brother, Tracey, shared an equal one. She smiled as a thought occurred. Tracey was a ranch manager, had several of his own horses, was single . . . She'd have to introduce him and Riley when this was all over. And she prayed that would be sooner rather than later. They could only dodge death for so long.

She knocked on the front door of the main house, where Christian said he'd meet her, but heard voices carrying from around the east side of the house. She stood still, listening. One voice was Christian's, then Deckard's. Not sure what to do, she was about to knock on the door again when Harper's voice joined in.

She glanced past Deckard's SUV and her truck to see a glimmer of the blue hood of Harper's Rogue, the paint sparkling in the sunlight.

Weaving around the back path toward the voices, she passed cacti, potted agave, and autumn sage—the latter's fuchsia flowers gorgeous against the white stone landscaping.

117

"Answer this," Christian said, his voice carrying on the wind. "When Andi came to you claiming she'd been set up, did you believe her?"

She froze in place. Here's where Deckard said no.

"I believe *she* believed she'd been set up," Deckard responded.

Hmm. Wasn't the flat-out *no* she'd anticipated.

"That's not what I asked," Christian said.

"Look," Deckard said, his gravelly voice deep. "It wasn't my job to determine that. It would have been a huge conflict of interest while I was working for Mitch's family."

"So she could have been set up," Christian pressed.

"Anything's possible," Deckard relented. "But look at it from my perspective. Mitch's family hired me. The evidence, and by that, I mean the lack of evidence—being it was basically destroyed or missing—pointed directly at Miranda Forester."

"Because she was set up," Harper cut in.

Of course Harper would jump in the conversation after just meeting the siblings. *Shy* was the last word to describe Harper.

"You don't work for Mitch's family anymore," Harper continued.

"Where are you going with that?" Deckard asked.

"I want you to look into Andi's case," Christian responded.

"Ditto," Harper said.

Deckard released a stunned laugh. "You couldn't possibly want me," he said. "Either of you."

"On the contrary, you're the perfect guy for the job," Christian said.

"Why on earth is that?" Deckard asked.

A bug zinged by Andi's ear, and she swatted it away.

"Why on earth would you want me?" Deckard asked.

"Because I trust you'd be impartial. You'll look at and study the evidence for what it is, and when you discover she was set up, you'll find a way to prove it," Christian said.

"You're assuming she was set up," Deckard said.

Andi shooed another bug away from her ear. She shouldn't be eavesdropping, but she needed to hear how this conversation would end. Though she feared she knew. No way Deckard MacLeod would take her case.

"You will too," Harper said, her tone imploring and impassioned.

"How can you be so certain?" Deckard asked.

"Because I know Andi, and I know she's telling the truth."

She smiled at Harper having her back—always.

"That's what you think too?" Deckard asked.

No doubt talking to Christian.

She continued on the path, moving to join them, anxious and nervous to hear Christian's response.

"Yes," he said.

"How can *you* be so certain?" Deckard echoed his earlier question to Harper, only this time to Christian. "You just met her."

"You know I can sum a person up within—"

"A few minutes of meeting them. I know, and usually it's helpful. . . ."

"Usually?" Christian asked.

"Right now, it's a pain in my rear."

Around back, the stone path spilled into a beautiful, sprawling flagstone patio complete with a stone grill, a fire table, a smattering of comfy chairs, and an oversized patio sofa. Everyone had their back or side to her. All focused on the conversation at hand.

"How so?" Christian asked.

"Because between the two of you, I either work Andi's case or I never hear the end of it."

Andi held at the edge of the patio. What was he saying?

"So you're going to work her case?" Christian asked, leaning forward, resting his forearms on his knees.

"Yeah. I'll take it, but you know I work the facts, and the chance exists you might not like what I find."

Her eyes widened as her jaw slackened. Had Deckard MacLeod just said . . . ?

Christian's gaze flickered up to her. "Deckard's taking your case," he said, beaming with a smile.

Harper stood. "And I'm going to help him."

Deckard flickered his hands up in a questioning maneuver. "I'm sorry—what?"

"I'm going to help you," Harper said with a wide smile of her own.

Andi remained frozen on the edge of the patio, trying to absorb what was happening.

"Look, lady, I appreciate your offer, but—"

"It's Harper," she reiterated.

"I'm sorry." Deckard inclined his head. "Harper. I appreciate that she's your friend and that you want to help, but I work alone."

"I can see that about you, but as I was there when this happened, and considering I still work in the lab you're going to need access to, I think it'd be a good idea if we paired up." Harper linked her arms across her chest.

Deckard's brows arched. "You're FBI?"

"Yes." Harper nodded with a smile brimming with her usual confidence. Always so strong.

"And you work in the same lab Miranda did?" Deckard asked.

"Yes." She gave another nod.

"You're a crime-scene analyst?" he asked.

Andi took a seat beside Christian, her gaze bouncing between Deckard and Harper as they lobbed responses back and forth.

"Yes," Harper said, "but in a specific area. Andi's the expert in DNA analysis."

She paused long enough for Andi to study Deckard's face in relation to the comment. He shifted his lips but didn't say anything.

Harper continued, "I'm a forensic botanist."

"A forensic botanist. Wow. That sounds interesting."

"It can be," she responded, "but the main point is that I worked at the lab when everything went down, so I have some firsthand knowledge."

"You worked in the lab that night with Miranda?" Deckard asked, taking a glass of lemonade from his sister. "Thanks, Cool Whip."

Cool Whip? Andi mouthed to Christian.

Later, he mouthed back.

She nodded, forcing her gaze off his lips—Where was her mind?—

and back on Harper and Deckard duking it out in what would have been a very entertaining conversation if it wasn't her reputation in the balance. She prayed Harper won, and knowing her friend's diehard persistence, Andi had strong belief she would. Andi had witnessed her relentless pursuit firsthand in everything from how she approached her work to how she played games. She'd played poker with the woman once and hadn't been foolish enough to do so again.

Harper finished sipping her drink and set her glass on the side table. "Where were we?"

"I was asking if you saw Andi's work in the lab that night first-hand?"

"No."

"No." Was that disappointment echoing in Deckard MacLeod's tone?

"I was in the field," she explained.

"In the field?" He sat forward, propping his elbows on his thighs. "You worked Anne Marlowe's crime scene?"

"Yes."

He swallowed, his pronounced Adam's apple bobbing. He rubbed the scruff on his face. "I'm sorry. That had to be tough. Given the nature of the murder . . ."

"Sadly, it wasn't one of the worst I've worked."

"That's saying a lot."

"It's not a job for the squeamish, that's for sure."

"Okay, let's go back to that night. You're working Anne's murder. Walk me through what happened on your end, and then we'll shift to Andi. I'd like to hear as much about that night as possible."

Deckard had seen a copy of the case file from the defense attorney, just words on a page, and some copies of photos—those nearly turned his stomach. But even that wasn't the same as being on the scene. Mitch hadn't been there that night, despite what the initial evidence indicated. So he hadn't been able to fill anything in, and the prosecutor was clearly stonewalling him, along with the homicide detectives who had worked Anne's case. All believed Mitch was where he deserved to be—guilty and behind bars. None of them wanted to help him prove otherwise.

"Okay," Harper said, setting her glass of orange juice on the blue side table. "I was called to the scene after the initial walk-through was completed by homicide. I joined the CSI team in progress. For whatever reason, they always call in botanists and entomologists last."

"So you arrived on scene . . ." He led her like a witness, because that's what she was.

Andi had sat beside Christian, and he hadn't missed his brother resting his hand over hers. Just how friendly were they? Until this was sorted out and Andi found innocent—if she ever was—he had to warn his brother off.

"Right," Harper said, popping one more strawberry in her mouth from the plate Riley had placed beside her.

His sister always played the generous host, but he needed everyone to focus.

Harper took a sharp inhale, then released it. "It was an awful sight. She'd been stabbed half a dozen times. Poor girl."

"And what else did you see?"

"She was lying on a pile of rocks, blood on the rocks. The detective's theory was that the stab thrusts knocked her down on the rocks, she hit her head, and blood spilled out, the wound adding blood to the scene."

"You hitched when you said *theory*," Deckard said, her pause indicative of a different opinion.

"I think her assailant . . ." Harper began, emphasizing the word *assailant*, no doubt for his benefit.

He tried not to chuckle. Andi's friend was a spitfire, and a gorgeous one at that.

"I think he . . . or let's just go with *assailant*," Harper said.

"You're not suggesting it could have been a woman?"

"Women, as a rule, don't stab other women," Christian said. Occasionally men did, if they were in a heat-of-the-moment fight and a knife was readily available.

"No. I'm just saying Andi believes, based on her evidence, that Mitch Abrams killed Anne Marlowe. Deckard believes he didn't," Harper said. "If you're going to work her case, you both have to set your conclusions aside and just study the evidence, or you're going to be at constant odds."

He looked at Andi, and they both indicated their agreement with a quick nod. He'd work the evidence, like he always did. Evidence was black-and-white. He'd base his investigation on the facts, and the dominos would fall where they may. He just prayed they didn't knock his brother over in the process.

TWENTY-SIX

CYRUS LAY on the sloped ground of the foothills, trying to ignore the rocks prodding him. They sat on the stone patio, all around the fire table. He noted each one by the names they spoke and the way they interacted. He tightened his grip on the long-range microphone and video recorder—the long stick fitting easily in his hand.

Pleasure rippled through him. The chick's case would distract them, even if they weren't the ones working it. Now he hoped they'd discuss the heist case. He needed to know how much they knew so he could make an educated decision. If they got any closer to him, they'd have to go, regardless of the trouble it would cause. If they were still working clues that didn't lead anywhere close, he'd let them live—for now. Hopefully, Teresa listened to him and hadn't sent another order to undermine him, to prematurely take out Andi and Christian. But he wouldn't put it past her.

"Okay, let's focus," Deckard said. "You started to say you think the assailant . . ." He inclined his head toward Harper. Getting first-hand information about the crime scene would be super helpful in understanding the full case.

"Right." She crossed her legs—long, shapely legs. Shorts and a long-sleeve shirt with Docksiders spoke of Cali or the East Coast, but not typically New Mexico. He'd have to ask where she came from, but later. Right now, his job was to keep her on track.

He glanced at Christian and Andi whispering to each other, their gazes locked, very in tune with one another. *Not good, baby brother.* He prayed God would guard his brother's heart until the truth came to light.

"So," Harper finally said, "I think the killer was someone she knew. Someone who told her to meet him there for a midnight picnic or some romantic nonsense."

He smiled.

She narrowed her eyes. "What?"

"You don't hear many women calling a romantic gesture nonsense."

Harper shrugged. "I'm just a more practical person, I guess. . . . Anyway, there was a bench at the crime scene and a string of fabric from Anne's skirt was found on it. I think she waited on the bench. The killer approached from behind, knocked Anne unconscious, threw her on the rocks, and stabbed her there."

"That's quite the theory."

"There was no blood on the grass, only the rocks, and she'd have to nail those rocks with her head amazingly hard to have the deep head wound she had."

"But the rocks had blood on them by her head, right?" He'd read that in one report or another.

"Yes. I think the killer dropped the rock he'd knocked her out with in the pile, then threw her on top of it and finished the job."

"Why?" he asked.

She narrowed her eyes. "Are you asking me why I think it happened that way or why he killed her?"

"Why you think he killed her that way?" He got to his feet to demonstrate. "Come here, Riley."

"Great. I get to play the victim again," she said.

"Stabbings are typically personal, sick as that is. They're crimes of passion and often by someone the victim knows, often intimately," he explained.

"It's horrifying to think so, but yes, that's my understanding as well," Harper said, standing.

He turned Riley to face him.

Christian and Andi stood and shuffled to get a clear view as well.

"Most men—and stabbings are predominately by men—will overtake the woman, push her against a solid object if one is available. If not, they'll grasp hold with one hand"—he demonstrated by gripping Riley's left upper arm—"and stab with the other." He simulated a handful of stab wounds as had occurred with Anne Marlowe. "If it's a crime of passion, it doesn't make sense to stab an unconscious victim. What's the point? If she's knocked out, why not slit her throat or strangle her?"

"Deckard!" Riley said.

"I'm not saying anyone should. Just trying to approach it from the killer's perspective."

"My theory?" Harper said.

"Sure."

"It wasn't a crime of passion. It was premeditated, staged as a crime of passion, and the shirt left behind was left on purpose. And to top it off, apparently Judge Simmons and Anne Marlowe used to meet up at the hiking area she was found adjacent to."

"So you're suggesting it was premeditated to look like a crime of passion?" Deckard asked.

"Correct," she said. "And set up to make Judge Simmons take the fall."

Andi leaned forward. "Mitch Abrams had an alibi. He was at a conference in Las Cruces. But when the prosecution submitted the DNA evidence I processed, they argued that the three-hour trip to and from Albuquerque fit within the parameters of his committing the murder."

"Judge Simmons's alibi was easier to prove," Deckard said. "Clint, the defense attorney, said he had last-minute judicial company, a Judge Sawyer and his wife, who decided to stay for the night, as it was late."

"So whoever intended to set him up was unaware of the alibi he had," Andi said.

"Any way Judge Simmons could have snuck out?" Riley asked.

"The visiting judge's wife has awful insomnia," Deckard said, the facts of the investigation seared into his mind. "She said she was up until well past four a.m. Simmons would have had to walk right past her to get out of the house."

He ran it all through his mind, then fixed his gaze on Harper. "So you not only think Andi was set up but that the murder was a setup too?"

"Most definitely."

Deckard tilted his head. *This should prove an interesting investigation.* He looked at Harper. *And an interesting woman to work it with.* Most people he could easily categorize, but not Harper Grace. He couldn't pin her down, and something about that was appealing.

Cyrus smiled. So they were preoccupied with Andi's case. He'd done his homework. Found who Ambrose Global would send out when Tad Gaiman's galleries were robbed. She had an interesting past, to be sure. And, as long as that kept their attention divided, the better. Knowing Enrique, his brutish force, and sick perversion for killing people in dramatic ways, it wouldn't be long before they found the girl's body. It was coming. He could feel it. As long as it didn't draw them to him or get in the way of what lay ahead . . .

Andi returned to her seat beside the giant, averting his attention.

His muscles coiled, the odd heat of jealousy rippling through him. *Not again.* Last time he fell for a woman, it'd landed him in jail.

He gripped the microphone scope harder. *No.* He'd admire the beautiful woman from a distance and that was it. Unless she got close to catching him, and then she'd meet him face-to-face.

TWENTY-SEVEN

"WE SHOULD HEAD into the office," Deckard said to Harper. "Run the case with Greyson."

"Sure, but who's Greyson?"

"He's our Alfred," Deckard said. "And our Lucius."

A smile curled on Harper's lips. "So runs everything to support you guys and is brilliant?"

"Yeah," he said, surprised and impressed she'd gotten the Batman reference. But it still wasn't enough to describe the pivotal role Greyson played daily. The man had taken him under his wing when he was a young kid in Tucson, trained him to be a PI, then sold the company to him after moving it to Santa Fe, but thankfully remained on to help in a supporting role. It was odd and awkward having him in that role, but that's the life Greyson wanted. Said he'd been in the field too long; he was getting jaded. He wanted to work on the backend, and, of course, he did an amazing job of it. They would struggle to function without him and his expertise that ranged from knowledge of exquisite wines to being able to recall case details at a moment's notice. Something called hyperthymesia, he'd explained. So rare less than one hundred people in the world had it, but it made Greyson's gift nearly unmatchable.

"Shall we go?" Harper asked, standing.

"Just a sec." He looked at Christian and Andi sitting leg-to-leg cozy on the love seat. "I'd like an update on their case."

Christian looked at Deckard and then to Andi. "Where to begin?"

"Starting at the top usually helps," Deckard offered, sitting back and linking his fingers on his lap. He wanted a better read on the two. If they were beginning to exist as a *two*. Would they finish each other's sentences, pick up on each other's cues?

"All right," Andi said. "So we started at Tad's Jeopardy Falls gallery. . . ."

A half hour later, Andi and Christian wrapped up.

Deckard sat forward. "Sounds like Tad might be involved," he said, having learned the fact and gained confirmation that his brother and Andi were working very in sync with each other. Until he finished investigating her claim, he feared for his brother. He didn't fall easy, normally, but the way Christian looked at Andi . . . it concerned him.

"That's what we're thinking," Christian said, pulling him back to the conversation, "but surprisingly, he didn't crack."

Deckard dipped his chin, intertwining his fingers together. "Maybe you have to push harder."

Christian exhaled. "You're probably right."

"Or . . ." Deckard said, looking at Andi. "You could outsmart him." She had that in her. Hopefully only for good, but it was there all the same.

"I've been thinking of ways to do that," she said, then looked at Christian. "*We've* been thinking."

There was another use of the word *we* with the deepened inflection in her voice. "Any other suspects stand out?" he asked.

"Tad's ex, Veronica, and Brad Melling. Either could want revenge. Veronica for him cheating on her. A woman scorned and all that," Christian said.

"And this Brad guy?" Harper asked.

"His ex-business partner," Riley said, speaking for the first time in the last hour. She'd just sat back and taken it all in. She liked to observe. It was her gift. That and her ability to find anyone anywhere. Or help someone get lost—particularly abused women, but she'd also worked with eyewitnesses to crimes who weren't put in

WITSEC for one reason or another. Thus far, all she'd hidden had remained safely so.

"Oh," Harper said, crossing her legs.

"After we get some shut-eye," Christian said, indicating himself and Andi, "we plan on starting our interviews."

"You think they'll hit again?" Deckard asked, fearing he already knew the answer.

Christian stretched out his legs and rested his arm on the side of the outdoor sofa. "Unfortunately, my gut says this is far from over."

"Agreed," Andi said.

"They're very brash to pull off multiple heists," he said, intentionally not looking at Christian. His comment wasn't about Christian or his past. It was simply about the thieves they were after.

"It's not easily done," Christian said, leaning forward and resting his forearms on his thighs. "They're really good, whoever they are."

"Catchable?" Deckard asked as Christian's cell rang.

Christian shimmied the phone out of his pocket and glanced at the screen. "It's Joel. I better take this." He lifted the phone to his ear. "Hey, Joel. What's up?" A few seconds in and Christian's face paled.

Deckard's muscles stiffened. Whatever Joel was telling his brother, it wasn't good.

"Okay. Thanks for letting me know. And keep me posted." Christian hung up, a dazed look in his eyes.

"What's wrong?" Riley asked.

"Alex is dead."

Harper cocked her head. "Alex?"

"Tad's assistant at the Jeopardy Falls gallery," Andi said.

Christian nodded. "They found her body at the bottom of Barrows Point."

"What's that?" Harper asked.

"It's a BASE-jumping spot not far from here," Christian said, shock still registering in his eyes. "A group of teens were partying in the caves at the bottom of the canyon and found her."

"Did her parachute not open?" Harper asked.

"She wasn't wearing one."

TWENTY-EIGHT

ENRIQUE HAD PROVED just as stupid as he'd always been. Cyrus exhaled. And, he'd been right just as he always was—at least for a very long time. Of course Enrique would kill the girl in some over-the-top way. Tossing her over a BASE-jumping cliff? What a showboat. The man lacked all precision, but he was one of Teresa's thugs after all, so what did Cyrus expect. Luckily, he had no involvement. That was all Enrique. Even if the cops managed to find anything, it couldn't be tied to him.

Anxious to get going, he fought the restless urge to move. But he waited to get to his feet until the group split off and headed in different directions. Deckard, Harper, and the sister, Riley, were going into the office—wherever that was—to work Andi's case. Christian and Andi were heading to grab some sleep before conducting interviews. He stiffened in the good way, warmth swelling in his tight limbs.

The beautiful Andi Forester asleep mere yards from his lookout point. Dare he creep in . . . take a closer look? He inhaled the pleasure the mere idea filled him with. His gaze tracked to the Neanderthal. How tall was that guy? It mattered not. If he wanted in, he'd get in, *period*. And right now, he wanted in or as close to it as possible. There was something about her that tugged a part of him he thought long-lost.

Andi followed Christian down the path that led to Riley's place. They paused outside.

"Riley said to grab any clothes you wanted. Need something comfier to sleep in?" Christian asked.

"That'd be great."

"All right, but since we're the only ones on the ranch, I'd feel better if we slept at my house. It's my home base. I know where the weapons are . . . that sort of thing."

"You think another attempt is coming?"

"At this point, I'd be surprised if it didn't."

That was a lovely feeling—waiting for an attack and not having a clue when it would come.

"You can sleep in my room," he said.

She frowned. "Where will you sleep?"

"On the couch."

"You don't have to do that." It was super kind, just like the man she was getting to know. "I can stay at Riley's so you can have your room."

"I don't want you there alone. Besides, I'll feel better being out in the front room. I'll be better able to make sure no one enters."

"Okay." She nodded, letting the threat hanging over them wrap around her mind. It was tenuous walking a tightrope where she couldn't see more than a few feet in front of her. What awaited her ahead in the dark was unknown, and she hated not being in control.

After grabbing a pair of yoga pants and a T-shirt from Riley's place, she and Christian headed down the winding dirt road toward his place.

"Here we go," he said, leading the way up a brick walkway past cacti, succulents, and a vast array of bird feeders.

She arched a brow with a smile. "I hadn't pictured you as the bird-feeder type."

"Yeah . . ." He rubbed the back of his neck. "I've always liked the sound of birds. For some reason, it's soothing to me. What about you?"

"What about me?" she asked as he opened the brown arched door.

"What do you find soothing?"

"You're going to laugh." Everyone did.

"I won't laugh," he said with all sincerity, but she doubted he'd be able to help it.

"The carnival music ice cream trucks play."

A wide smile broke on his face, mirth filling his eyes.

"Go ahead and laugh. Most people do."

"Nah." He pressed his lips together and smirked.

"I have good memories of them in the summer. I'd get excited whenever I heard them coming."

"That makes sense." He ushered her inside.

The interior of his house was gorgeous. Roughhewn beams ran in parallel lines across the ceiling. A beautiful kiva fireplace rose to the ceiling with brown leather couches angled around it and the large flat-screen TV. Even the floors were beautiful. "Pine?" she asked, gesturing to the floor.

"Yep. Deckard built the main house, then helped me and Riley build ours."

"Really. That's impressive you all did this yourselves."

He raked a hand through his hair. "It was kind of cool putting everything together the way we each wanted. It makes it actually feel like home."

As opposed to? What else would a house feel like, she wondered, but didn't push.

"And I love your courtyard," she said, moving toward it. It was similar to hers. Square, in the center of his home, sliding doors on all four sides, the space open to the sky above. Two swing rope chairs hung from a wooden beam that anchored on either side of the courtyard, and a loveseat patio sofa sat opposite them, a fire pit in the middle. "The swings are great," she said.

"Riley's idea."

She'd have to take a sit in one later, after she rested. Her mind, body, and soul were bone-tired.

"Oh," she said, her eyes catching the metal pink flamingos standing one-legged outside in the distance nestled by a lit palm tree. "I love the tropical touch."

He smiled. "Also Riley. She went on vacation to Florida last year and has been fixated on items like that ever since."

"You think she wants to move there?"

"Nah. She loves it here. This is home to her. But she said she wouldn't mind a small beach escape place there."

"Have you been?"

"No, but she keeps trying to drag us there." He pushed off the wall he'd been leaning against. "If you want to follow me, I'll show you the bedroom."

"Sounds good. Thanks."

He led the way down the back hall, and she got a sneak peek of the kitchen—which looked rustic and gourmet at the same time.

"Here's the bathroom." He opened the second door on the right. It was stunning. White marble tiles covered the floor, matching marble lined the walk-in shower with a rainwater showerhead. And cool frosted-glass bowls topped the vanity. The man had good taste.

"The bedroom," he said, leading her to the next and last door on the left, "is here." He opened the door to reveal what looked like a ski chalet. Warm earthy tones of cream, brown, and hunter green made up the color palette, rustic wooden beams lined the ceiling, and a stone fireplace sat opposite the pine bed.

Her eyes danced to the green comforter, then the cream chair with a rich brown woolen blanket draped over it. Bookcases lined one wall, a dresser stood on the other, and on the far side was a sliding door. She stepped to it, gazing at the deep crest of the mountain full of aspens and junipers. Then she lowered her gaze to the flagstone patio, complete with a hot tub. The thought of sharing time in it with Christian flashed through her mind. She blinked. Where had that come from?

"Well, we need to get some shut-eye. I'll be in the front room if you need anything," he said. "I'm just going to grab a pillow and a blanket."

"Of course." She stood to the side.

He grabbed one of a plethora of fluffy pillows off the bed and retrieved the blanket from the reading chair—or at least what looked like it would be a great one.

He stepped to the doorway and leaned against the frame. "Sweet dreams."

She hadn't heard that in ages. Not since she was a little kid and her dad tucked her in bed at night after reading her a story or three. She'd always asked for another one and another one, but he maxed out at three. She missed those times when he'd shown deep affection for her. Now it was limited interaction. And the fact they remained "neutral" on what went down with Mitch's case showed her parents didn't believe her. They just didn't want to say it outright.

"You okay?" Christian asked, still leaning against the doorjamb, staring at her in a way he hadn't before. There was affection there. And that, while it felt innately good, unsettled her, because she was beginning to feel affection for him too. But they had to stay focused on the case, and the fact was, she was scared to trust anyone with her heart. Even a man as kind as Christian.

"Yeah," she finally managed, slipping her hair over her shoulders. "Just spacing out . . ."

"I'll let you get your rest." He pushed off the doorjamb and stepped fully out of the room. "I'm right out there if you need me," he reminded her. He needn't have. She felt innately safe with him there.

He pulled the door closed, and she looked back to the bed. It was hard taking time to sleep when they had so much work ahead of them on the case, but if she didn't sleep, she'd be ineffective.

Climbing into the luxurious, plump bed in comfy clothes, she sunk into the mattress. It felt like lying on a cloud. She fluffed one of the top pillows and fashioned it under her head just so, then rolled on her side to face the sliding door. It was beautiful outside, but she couldn't shake the sudden feeling that someone was out there—watching.

TWENTY-NINE

DECKARD PULLED HIS SUV to a stop in front of the two-story brick building in downtown Santa Fe.

Harper had used the ride over to fill Deckard in on the particulars of the case that she knew like the back of her hand. She'd waited so long for Andi to hire someone to look into who had set her up. Now she was beyond thankful. The fact that it was Deckard MacLeod was, in a word, unique. But after watching him interact with Andi and the questions he asked, he was the right man for the job. The fact she'd get to spend the duration of the case with such a handsome man was just a bonus.

She glanced up at the big silver letters on the top-right corner of the building. MIS.

Sun glinted off them—its rays blinding. She shielded her eyes with her hand. "MIS? MacLeod Investigative Services, I'm guessing."

"Close. It's MacLeod Investigations and Security."

"Oh, because Christian does security system analysis." She'd gotten that much from Andi, though the two had barely had a moment alone to speak. She couldn't wait until they had time for Andi to fully dish on the hunk that was Christian MacLeod. Not that Deckard was any slacker, with his chiseled jaw, rugged build, and ice-blue eyes she could get lost in. They were certainly a beautiful family, but any attachment to the man—even a casual date—was out of the question. As soon as the new itinerary for her ICRC mission came through, she'd be leaving for two months. No sense starting something she'd just have to leave.

The borderline flirtatious comments on the ride over were fun, but dangerous. Even if he was showing interest, which she believed he was, it didn't mean he wanted to take it any further by asking her out on a date. She needed to chill and focus on Andi's case.

Joy filled her that the truth would finally come out. For whatever reason, she believed Deckard could get to the bottom of it. And she'd be right there to help. Her friend had suffered enough. It was time to set her free.

Deckard climbed out of the SUV and moved around to open her door, then paused near the hood.

"What's wrong?" she asked.

"I've nearly got a flat," he said, sinking down out of sight.

She eased the door open, not wanting to hit him while he no doubt examined the wheel well. She climbed out and shielded her eyes with her hand. The sun was bright and hot today—the dry heat like a sauna. Too long in it and she withered. "Flat?" she said, glancing at Deckard hunched down in front of the tire in question.

"Yeah." He tapped the nail in it. "Must have just run over it, but it's leaking steady."

And fast. "Bummer."

"It's okay. It's got enough in it, I can run it over to Leroy."

"Leroy?" she asked.

"Runs a garage about four blocks west. I'll run it over and walk back."

"I'll go with you," she offered.

"Thanks. I appreciate the offer, but—"

"No buts." She cocked her head.

He held up his hand with a chuckle. "Yes, ma'am."

Fifteen minutes later, Deckard led the way across the newly paved parking lot, the spaces closest to the door still roped off. They both turned and waved to Riley as she roared into the parking lot in her red Miata.

Warm air swirled around them as she waited while he punched a code into the keypad.

The door buzzed open.

"Morning, Deckard" sounded over the intercom.

"Greyson," he said, holding the door open for Harper. She stepped inside the office building's foyer, and he followed.

"We're on the second floor. Are the stairs okay?"

"Sure." She started up, and he once again followed her.

Reaching the office suite door, Deckard placed his index finger on a fingerprint scanner. The door buzzed open, and they entered. Elation filled her that someone, and someone with the reputation Deckard had, would be working Andi's case. She had no doubt that the Bureau wouldn't be happy with them digging around a case that had been closed. But someone had set Andi up; she knew it in her bones. Which meant, they had a criminal to catch. One who, no doubt, wouldn't be happy with their digging. Whoever set Andi up had higher-ups in their pocket, had power, and certainly wouldn't relinquish it easily. Andi and Christian were in danger with their case; she felt strangely confident the same would be true of her and Deckard.

THIRTY

ENTERING, DECKARD FOUND GREYSON at his desk, wearing his pressed pink shirt—which he insisted was salmon every time they teased him about it—a gray tie, and what Deckard assumed but couldn't see were matching gray dress pants.

"Who do we have here?" Greyson asked, standing and stepping around his desk to greet Harper.

"This is Harper Grace," Deckard said. "She's a good friend of Andi's." He'd caught him up about Miranda's . . . *Andi's* case. He shook his head. That would take a while to get used to.

"Greyson Chadwick. Nice to meet you, Harper."

"Same," she said with a smile.

That smile. It could render a man speechless. Shaking himself out of it, Deckard continued with her full introduction. "Harper's an FBI agent—a forensic botanist in the Albuquerque crime lab."

"Impressive," Greyson said.

"Not any more so than being a PI, I imagine," she said. "It seems like a fascinating profession."

"It's definitely interesting," Greyson said. "Will you be joining us at the round table?"

Her nose crinkled. "Round table?"

"You'll see." Greyson smiled. "But first, coffee. Would you like a cup, or I can make a latte or a cappuccino?"

"I'd love a cappuccino," Harper said. "Thanks so much."

"My pleasure." Greyson dipped forward slightly at the waist.

Deckard sighed. Greyson had one of those espresso machines in the lounge, along with accessories to whip up any number of drinks and a full row of syrups in pump bottles. The counter mimicked that of Starbucks.

"Let me guess . . ." Harper said, studying Deckard.

Great, the lady was analyzing him. He was curious where this was going.

"You're a black cup of coffee, right?"

"Only way to go," he replied.

"And, Greyson . . . I'm guessing you're a double espresso kind of guy."

"Very good." Greyson smiled and strode through the doorway.

"But he puts that whipped cream gunk on top," Deckard added.

"Gunk?" Harper said, brows arched. "Did you just call whipped cream gunk?"

"Yes, ma'am." He smiled and winked.

"Then you're going to have a hard time staying at my place."

Deck frowned. "Your place?"

"I assume we'll be investigating in Albuquerque, where everything took place."

"Yes."

"Well, then you're staying at my place."

"I appreciate the offer," he said, "but I don't want to put you out." Though the thought warmed him. She was beautiful, clearly intelligent, and a bundle of enthusiasm, but he wasn't looking for a romantic connection. He liked his life as-is. Maybe someday he'd feel different, but for now, he was content, though a woman as vivacious as Harper Grace just might make him change his mind if she was hanging around longer. But, according to Andi, Harper had a two-month humanitarian service trip just around the corner.

"You're not putting me out," she countered. "It's the least I can do for you working Andi's case. I have an empty guest room."

He didn't see how to get out of that one gracefully. "All right. Thanks."

"You're welcome." She winked as she smiled. Not a flirtatious wink. Just the friendly sort, but it did set his insides spinning. She was trouble. He bit his bottom lip, then restructured his thoughts. "While we're in Albuquerque, Greyson can be working the case with us, just headquartered here. He's a whiz at all things research."

"Awesome," she said.

"Well, let's get started. I just need to grab something out of my office."

"I'll show her the way to the round table," Greyson said, returning with fancy mugs in hand. "Your cappuccino, madame."

"Thank you." She smirked at Deckard. "I'll take your bitter black coffee with me, if you'd like."

Determined not to give her the satisfaction of a reaction, he just said, "Thanks. I'll just be a minute."

In his office, he spun the file cabinet lock, stopping on the numbers that made up his combination, and the A drawer unlocked. He pulled it open, fingered through the files, and found *Mitch Abrams*, along with a copy of the case file, courtesy of Mitch's defense lawyer, Clint James. He was old-fashioned, but he didn't trust keeping everything on a computer that could crash. He liked the hard copy of everything. Greyson, on the other hand, input everything into their computer systems, which gave them a backup should anything happen to his files or vice versa.

Stepping out of his office with files he never thought he'd need again tucked under his arms, he headed for the round table.

He found Riley and Harper chatting up a storm, but no Greyson. He set the files on the literal round conference table. "Where's Grey?"

"He said he had to grab something, but he'd be right back," Riley said.

Deckard took his seat and swallowed a swig of his coffee just as Greyson returned.

"Harper's drink looks scrumptious," Riley said, shooting Greyson a glare, or at least an attempted one. She was too sweet to pull off angry. Unless it was dealing with a case or offense—then look out. She became a wildebeest. "I would have loved a drink, should someone have asked."

Still standing, Greyson pulled a cup from behind his back. "Madame."

Riley smiled, her freckles spreading across her cheeks. "Thanks, Greyson. I don't care what Deck says about you and your drinks—you rock!"

Deck shook his head on a sideways grin. "So easily bought."

She took a sip, then smiled, foam covering her upper lip. "For this . . . you bet."

"My pleasure." Greyson dipped at the waist and gave Riley that smile he only gave her.

Deckard took another sip of his coffee, eyeing them over the rim of his cup. If he didn't know better . . . He shook off the thought and took a prolonged sip of his coffee. "Mmm-mmm." He smiled at Harper. "Great sludge." He held his mug in salute to Greyson.

"Hopeless." Greyson shook his head, then strode to the wall of glass panels framed with white beams where he always stood while they ran a case. "Shall we begin?" he asked.

"Let's do it," Deckard said with a nod at Harper.

She nodded back with a deep expression of gratitude.

"What do we know?" Greyson asked, a black dry erase marker in hand.

"We know Andi worked the night of Anne Marlowe's murder," Deckard said. "She was in the lab with a tech and another analyst." According to what Harper said on the way over.

"Our supervisor, Kevin Gaines, was out sick," Harper continued. "And our forensics manager, Todd Phillips, covered for Kevin, which he never did."

"Why not?" Greyson asked, having written the supervisor's and manager's names each on a separate glass panel.

"Protocol was to call another shift supervisor in," she explained.

"Did Todd say why he made the shift from protocol?" Greyson asked.

"Andi said he told her that he was available, so he jumped in."

"But it hadn't ever happened before?" Deckard asked again, just to be sure.

Harper shook her head.

"What about since that night?" Greyson asked. "Has it ever happened again?"

"Todd's no longer with the FBI," she said. "He got a huge job upgrade not long after Anne Marlowe's murder."

Greyson's brows arched. "Interesting timing, I think we can all agree." He tapped Todd's name written in black marker on the glass panel.

"Agreed," Riley said, chiming in.

"Okay . . ." Greyson said. "What are the tech's and analyst's names from that night?"

"Marshall Palmer was the tech, and Pam Whitmore the analyst."

"Do they still work in the lab?" Greyson asked, adding their names to the board in perfect penmanship.

Deck reached for a sip of coffee. Not that good penmanship was something he aspired to by any means, but Greyson's scrolled handwriting made his look like a kindergartner with crayons.

"Yes," Harper said to Greyson's question. "They do."

"And the new job Todd Phillips got?"

"He was appointed to chair of the Arizona Forensic Science Academy."

"That does sound like a big jump," Greyson said.

"It was." Harper nodded, then took a sip of her drink—foam clinging to her lips. She reached for the cocktail napkin Greyson had brought with the cup and dabbed it away.

Deckard smiled. She looked adorable. *Adorable*? What was up with him? He needed to focus. Needed to be at his best to maneuver the change from what he'd known during his investigation for Mitch to seeing the other side of the coin.

"Any other job changes . . . promotions?" Greyson asked.

"Our supervisor who was out sick the night of Anne Marlowe's murder, Kevin Gaines, slid into Todd's role, and we got a new supervisor, Doug Jones."

"That's a lot of changes," Riley said.

"That was my thought." Harper nodded.

"Let's look at the idea of Andi being set up in relation to all these personnel changes," Greyson said, smoothing his jacket.

"Either the changes are directly related to something going down in the lab that night . . ." Riley looked at Harper for confirmation, and Harper nodded. "Or it's a huge coincidence. But I, for one, am skeptical of coincidences."

"What we need to figure out is who gained the most from what went down," Deckard said, a raw sensation gnawing at his gut.

"Kevin's and Doug's promotions were big, but Todd's was a huge leap, and he surpassed our forensics director, Greg Dunkirk, for the position."

"So Greg was up for the position?" Riley asked.

"I only heard a few rumors, but if the forensic science academy was looking to fill the position with someone from our lab, Greg had the superior position and knowledge. He has his PhD in forensic science while Todd just has his bachelor's. It doesn't make sense."

"We should start our investigation by interviewing Todd Phillips," Deckard said.

"Okay, I'll get his number," Harper said. "I imagine he still has the same cell number."

"In person is always better," Deckard said. "That way you can read a person's body language, their expressions. We'll pay him a visit tomorrow." It was surreal looking at things from a different perspective, but he'd promised Christian he'd investigate for Andi, and he'd keep that promise. But he couldn't control the outcome. He prayed it wasn't one that crushed his brother.

THIRTY-ONE

ANDI ROUSED FROM SLEEP and blinked at the vaulted ceiling with wooden beams overhead. She rubbed her eyes. *Where . . . ?* Her sleepy mind started to wake. *Christian's.* Blinking, she rolled over and gazed out at the beautiful mountains, the sun's rays lighting the yellow aspen leaves. Her gaze tracked down to the jutted sandstone crags layered with shale. A light flashed across the top.

She blinked again, wondering what the sun was illuminating. The light flashed again, its shaft skipping across a section of the blanket covering her.

Curious, she moved toward the sliding door, opened it, and stepped to the edge of the stone patio. The light ceased as she searched the ridge. A shiver snaked up her spine—the sensation of being watched raked back over her again.

"Hey, Andi," Christian said from the other side of the patio. "I didn't know you were awake."

"Yeah." She turned to face him, but out of the corner of her eye she caught a swift shift of movement. She spun back, and the silhouette of a man ducked into the trees. "Christian!"

"Go inside," he said, running past her with his gun in hand, dust kicking up behind him.

No way was she letting Christian chase the man on his own. She raced back in the house, slipped on the shoes she'd borrowed from Riley, and grabbed her gun from her purse.

Darting back outside, she scrambled up the sloping hill and moved into the trees. Shafts of light illuminated small pockets in the forest, but shade dimmed the remainder. "I'm in," she hollered, giving Christian a heads-up so they didn't accidentally shoot one another.

Rounding a steep, angled bend in the slope, she made out two figures weaving around trees, flitting in and out of her line of sight.

She increased her pace, breaking into an all-out sprint. Her lungs burning in the cool air, she wasn't making up time fast enough.

Please, Lord, let Christian get him.

She was tired of looking over her shoulder, waiting for the next attack to come.

Struggling to fasten her gaze on the two men and not focusing on the ground before her, she stumbled over a rock, tumbled forward, unable to correct herself fast enough. She landed hard, her knees taking the brunt of the fall—knees still bruised and scabbed from the first attempt on their lives.

Pop. Pop. Pop. Three gunshots reverberated through her chest. Birds squawked, surging toward the sky in a dark swirl about fifty yards due west.

She scrambled to her feet and plowed forward.

Pop. Pop.

Her chest squeezed, blood whooshing in her ears. *Please, Lord, let Christian be safe.*

She swallowed the bout of nausea sloshing in her gut.

A bullet whirred by, and she ducked.

A shattering *thwack* exploded ten feet to her right—the bark of the tree it hit flying in shards about the forest floor.

She scrambled to a boulder twenty feet in the opposite direction, pressing her back against the cold rock, her gun tight in her hand.

Another shot whirred by, shattering another tree ten feet away.

Had the man backtracked?

Footsteps sounded—nearing her. She prayed her thudding heart didn't give her position away.

She pressed her back harder against the boulder as the heavy footfalls approached. Closer. Closer still. She could hear his breathing.

Dear Lord, help. Securing her gun in her grip, she waited, ready to fire.

A shot nailed the boulder mere inches from her head. A second shot followed, closer still.

She leaned around the side of the boulder and pulled the trigger before the man could get his next shot off.

The Glock recoiled in her grip. *Crack. Thwack.*

The man's torso flung as the bullet collided with his shoulder. A cursed moan escaped his lips. Cussing a string of obscenities, he returned fire. She dropped low, and the bullet nailed the boulder across from her. Then, with a groan, he turned and ran.

Pop. Pop. Pop. At her nine. Fifty yards and closing fast.

Christian.

Rising, she broke into a full-out run, trying to locate Christian's position. She bounded out of the tree cover, the sun blinding. A hand grasped hard around her upper arm, yanking her back so swiftly, her feet went out from under her. Adrenaline seared through her, and she swung.

"Whoa!" Christian said, taking the punch in his jaw.

Her eyes flashed wide. "Sorry. I thought you were him."

He settled her back on the ground but didn't let go. "He's headed for the creek." He pointed, and she looked, her head swirling on the steep drop-off she'd nearly run over.

Thank you, Lord, for Christian. That would have been a deadly drop.

"There," Christian said, pointing at the figure sliding toward the creek, the forest floor skidding like sand in his wake.

"This way." Christian pointed to his three o'clock. "If we hurry, we can probably cut him off at the road."

"Don't wait for me." It was amazing how fast he ran.

She followed, but he disappeared into the distance again. Light and shade vacillated in moving shadows before her, dizzying her head, but she pressed on. She tramped over damp moss, her feet sliding across the slick surface, but she managed to maintain her balance this time.

Christian's silhouette flashed into her line of sight, then disappeared over what had to be another ridge.

Air burning her lungs, it seemed to take forever, but she finally reached the ridge. Christian was already down it.

She shifted sideways, moving along the natural slope of the hill, trying to avoid rocks and moss. Thick brush and brambles covered her path. She shimmied through as fast as she could, thistles sticking to her yoga pants.

Reaching the creek, she looked up and down, and finally spotted Christian climbing the ridge on the opposite side.

A gun retorted.

Please, Lord, keep Christian safe.

Two more shots fired.

She splashed into the free-flowing creek, having to slow enough to balance on slippery rocks. *Come on. Come on.* How many rocks did this creek bed have?

Finally, on the other side of the creek, she started up the ridge. Halfway up, two more shots fired. She slipped, sliding partway back down the ridge.

She scrambled her way up, finally reaching the top. She spotted Christian walking back toward her.

Her shoulders drooped. "He got away?"

Christian nodded. "He made it to the road and drove off in the white SUV that's been dogging us."

THIRTY-TWO

SWEATY AND GRIMY from the chase, Christian padded back across the stone patio with Andi at his side. He'd come on *their* property, to his family's homes. Knowing Deckard and the fighting Irish in him, he wouldn't sit around and wait. He'd go on the offensive. And the cowboy in him would protect his ranch with his life. Just as Christian would do. He refused to sit around waiting for someone to strike again. They'd not only work the investigation; it was time to go on the hunt. No doubt it was the same man who ran them off the road in the white SUV he'd just exited in.

"I'll call Joel. Let him know what happened. He'll want to know," Christian said.

Andi nodded. "Good idea."

About two minutes later, he ended the call. "Joel's on his way over. Wants to check things out and take an official police report."

"That makes sense."

"He's also bringing the gala footage and that of the heist. He's cleared it for us to watch."

"That's great."

He looked over with a smile to catch her gingerly rolling her shoulder. "You okay?"

"Yeah. Took a tumble . . . or two," she said with an embarrassed smile.

"But you nailed him."

"Yeah." Her smile widened.

"Which means he's going to need medical attention or supplies, at the very least." They were lucky *they* didn't need serious medical attention. The guy was a good shot. He'd very narrowly missed Christian, and Christian had the flesh wound to show it. But they were safe now, at least for the moment, he hoped. Adrenaline still seared his limbs, his fight mechanism still at full throttle.

"How'd you know he was here?" she asked as they reached the living room sliding door.

"I was standing here and saw light reflecting off his . . . binoculars, I'm guessing."

"Yeah. I saw the flash too." She looked up at him. "I'm sorry about the punch."

He rubbed his jaw, knowing there was red on his face. "I'm impressed," he said with a crooked smile. "It was a good one."

"There was this bully in fifth grade, and my older brother taught me how to fight." She smiled.

Her face lit up so cute. "What?"

"He always told me, if it looked like a fight was coming, go in swinging. Pop the guy before he could even swing."

"Good advice." He chuckled. "And did you?"

"Yep. That guy never bullied me again."

"You punched a guy in school?"

"Yep. On the playground at recess. I got sent to the principal's office, but he never bothered me again."

He prayed, thanks to Andi's shot, the man would never bother them again, but he knew better. They'd just stirred up the hornet's nest.

"You've got blood on your sleeve. . . ." She stepped forward to examine it. "Are you okay?"

"Just a flesh wound."

"He got you?"

"Barely brushed me."

"Let's get you cleaned up. Where do you keep your first-aid kit?"

"In the hall bathroom."

"Okay, come on, mister." She waggled her fingers, and he followed. He would have argued, but with Andi Forester, he knew it would be a lost cause.

She flipped on the light switch, and he directed her to the kit under the sink.

"Okay, take a seat." She patted the counter.

He leaned back and sat on the edge, taking in the sight of her as she fished through the red plastic box.

A sliver of bark clung to her right cheek, pine needles in her hair, and were those brambles or thorns on her yoga pants?

"Here we go," she said, pulling out several alcohol wipes, a gauze patch, and tape. She blew a stray hair from her face, revealing a small twig stuck at her temple.

"Hang on," he said, and with tenderness pulled the twig from her hair.

"Lovely," she said, when she saw what it was.

"Yes, you are." He swallowed. Had he just said that out loud?

Red flushed her cheeks, but she didn't look away.

Something moved inside of him, and his focus dropped to her lips. Sweet and full. "Don't hit me again," he whispered, reaching up to cup her cheek.

"Why would I—"

He swallowed her words. He moved tentatively at first, but as she returned the heated kiss, he deepened it, snaking his arm around her waist and pulling her tighter to him.

Time disappeared until the chiming of the doorbell interrupted what was the best kiss of his life.

She inched back, her lips pink from his kiss.

He feared she'd pull back farther, make an apology for giving in to the kiss, but she did neither.

The doorbell rang again.

He fought the nearly consuming urge to pull her back in his arms and ignore the world.

Thoughts raked through his mind. When exactly had he completely fallen for Andi Forester?

THIRTY-THREE

"HEY, JOEL. Thanks for coming out," Christian said, joining him outside while Andi ran in to grab a sweatshirt—the chill in the fall air nipping now that they'd cooled off from the chase.

"Of course," Joel said. "I've always got your back."

"I appreciate it, man." He clamped Joel on the shoulder.

"I'm sorry you guys are having such trouble. Hard to believe two art thieves are taking it this far."

"Yeah. Definitely not a normal heist situation. Rarely do they get violent other than when the thieves go in with guns and take out security guards at the bigger museums, but even then, murdering anyone is nearly unheard of." He rubbed the back of his neck, still trying to put the puzzle pieces together and coming up at a loss as to why they had found themselves in the midst of such a dangerous game—a deadly game. Poor Alex.

Joel nodded. "Three heists in a row, or two plus an ambush, definitely isn't the norm either." He tucked his hands in his tan pants pockets. "You think they'll hit another gallery?"

"I hate to say it, but, yeah, I'd bet money on it." He shifted his stance, keeping his footing firm—something he hadn't felt since this case began—stability. "I doubt they'll go back for more from Tad, but I have a bad feeling this is far from over."

Joel rocked back on his heels. "Unfortunately, I agree."

"Poor Alex," he said, "I still can't believe she's dead. And for what?"

"What's your guess?" Joel asked.

"I'm not sure. Maybe she saw someone or something she shouldn't have, recognized one of the thieves from them casing the joint."

"Her folks are all tore up about it," Joel said, taking off his Stetson and clutching the tan felt cowboy hat in his hands. "Her mom said the funeral will be next week out in Tucumcari, where they live, where Alex is from."

"Any leads on that front?" Christian asked.

"Herman Samuels said he was out doing his after-work nighttime walk the day of the heist and saw Alex pass by him in the passenger's seat of a white SUV that was pretty banged up along the grill."

"Exactly where the SUV that smashed into us would be banged up."

"I'll add that description to the BOLO," Joel said.

Christian nodded, then shifted his thoughts to Alex. They'd survived the hit. She hadn't. He exhaled his burgeoning anger. "Did Herman see who was driving?" The feedstore owner walked after closing up the store like clockwork, which at least helpfully established a solid timeline for them.

"He said it was a man, but he only caught a glimpse of him in the glow of the streetlights lining Main Street."

Christian grimaced. They needed more. Alex deserved more. Anger chewed at him. During his stint in juvie, there'd been two killers in there. Two . . . kids, now that he looked back, who would get off at eighteen just because they'd committed the crime as juveniles. It didn't always go that way, but it did for Ricardo and Timothy. Murdered a woman, and they were out in three years. It was straight-out injustice. He'd paid his time, too, but that guilt still clung to him. Kept him from moving forward.

As much as he was falling for Andi Forester—and given the kiss, she was falling for him as well—things couldn't go any further until he told her. He preferred to leave his past in the past, but now that feelings were involved, and the possibility of things growing deeper existed, he had to tell her. He should have told her before kissing her, but he'd been so consumed in the moment.

He shifted his stance. Fear she'd want nothing to do with him settled deep in the pit of his gut, but he had no choice. This was why he'd avoided relationships. Baring his soul, his ugly past—just the thought was painful and filled him with shame.

"Did you hear me, Christian?" Joel asked.

"What . . . ?" He raked a hand through his hair. "Sorry . . ."

"All good, man. I was just saying that Herman said, after they passed by, they hung a right onto Comanche, and he didn't see Alex in the car anymore."

Christian's muscles coiled. "He probably held her down once he caught sight of Herman."

"My assumption as well." Joel put his hat back on and tugged the brim in place.

"Herman notice anything about the man? Anything at all?"

"He said he got a better look with Alex not between him and the man. He said the man was on the taller side based on how high his head was in relation to the SUV roof and said he looked broad."

"Anything else?"

"He said he had dark hair and, from what he could tell, dark skin."

————————————■ ■————————————

Andi slipped her hands into the sweatshirt pockets as she approached Christian and Joel talking beside the cars. The sun was warm and beautiful, but the fall air was crisp. "I thought I'd join you," she said. "If that's okay."

"Of course," Joel said, catching her up to speed.

"The SUV Herman saw sounds like the one that ran us off the road," she said, looking at Christian, who nodded.

"And," she continued, "the basic description of his height, build, and dark hair sounds rather like our intruder today."

"You get a good look at the intruder's face?" Joel asked, a hopeful glimmer in his crisp blue eyes.

"I wish, but no," Christian said.

"Nope." Andi nodded, wishing she had.

"He ambushed Andi," Christian said, "but she shot him." He looked at her with a smile . . . a proud one?

She hadn't had anyone look at her like that in a long time, and it felt good. "I . . . um, got him in the shoulder," she said, managing to shift her attention off Christian and back on Joel.

A sideways smile curled on Joel's lips. "Is that right?"

"It was a great shot," Christian said.

She shrugged. It had been a solid shot. It was good to know she still had the skills. It'd been too long since she'd been to a gun range. "We chased him, but he got away."

"So, you know you're looking for a man probably five-eleven. . . ." Christian looked down at her. When would she get used to him being a foot taller? She felt like a dwarf beside him at times. "Would you agree?" he asked.

"Yep." She nodded. "And he had broad shoulders, which gave me a good target."

"And dark hair," Christian said. "It was hard to get a solid look, given the circumstances, but I think it was wavy."

"Mind if I take a look where all this occurred?" Joel asked.

"Of course," Christian said. He looked back at Andi. "You good coming?" he asked.

"Absolutely. Let's go."

"Much appreciated," Joel said, before rolling a piece of gum in his mouth. The fresh scent of mint swirled in the air.

"Would either of you like a piece?" he asked.

"I'd like one," Andi said, and Christian followed suit as they trekked across the backyard and started climbing the slope.

An hour and a half later, they returned to the driveway. Joel had collected casings. "I'll need to clear the nine-millimeter casings from your two guns, then I can run his. See if we can pull any information from it. What kind of handgun make and model we're dealing with. You said it was maybe a SIG Sauer?"

"I can't be certain, but that would be my guess," Christian said. "No idea on the make."

"Certain SIG models take the .357 like I pulled from the tree," Joel said, slipping his thumbs through his belt loop. "I'll send this to the CSI lab in Santa Fe to run ballistics, and I'll get someone up here to take a tire tread impression from where he was parked."

"Thanks, Joel." Christian clamped him on the shoulder.

"Oh. I almost forgot," Joel said. "I've got that gala and heist footage for you in the patrol vehicle. I'll be right back."

"I'll walk you to the car," Christian said.

Joel turned to Andi and tipped his hat. "Ma'am."

"Sheriff Brunswick." She smiled. Normally, she detested the use of *ma'am* as she didn't feel old enough for people to be calling her that yet, but in his western drawn-out drawl, it was endearing.

"I thought I told you to call me Joel," he said, dipping his chin.

"Right." She smiled. "Bye, Joel, and thank you."

"Better, and you are most welcome." He smiled, then turned heel and walked with Christian toward his SUV.

She took a seat on the edge of the stone patio. . . . Well, she didn't know exactly what to call it, with its large fireplace and chimney standing at least twelve feet high, along with the side wings—one with an oversized grill, the other a prep station. She supposed it was an outdoor kitchen of sorts.

Not much later, Christian strolled back down the dirt path. He caught sight of her, and they both smiled. Man, he was handsome. But more important, he made her feel safe and strong and vulnerable and such a clumsy mix of emotions. It was crucial for her to not get tangled up in those feelings.

Tangled up. Warmth flushed her cheeks. The image of her and him tangled up in white sheets reading the paper on a Sunday morning flashed through her mind.

Whoa! *What* was she thinking? *Get it together, girl.*

Christian tilted his head. "Everything okay?"

"Yep. Why?" She smoothed the sweatshirt.

"You looked really happy, then your expression rapidly shifted."

"Oh?" She tried to will her cheeks to stop flushing.

"Yeah. Like shock or surprise washed over your face."

"Hmm." She shrugged.

"So what are you thinking?"

"What do you mean?" she blurted out with something akin to a snap.

"Whoa." He held his hands up.

"Sorry," she said. "Just all stirred up . . . from the chase and all."

"I get it," he said.

She smiled and nodded. She needed to settle.

"I think we should watch the footage today. It'll take hours, but it's important to watch before we conduct our interviews," he said.

"Agreed." She nodded. "It may prompt questions we wouldn't think of otherwise."

"Or alert us if anyone tries to lie to us."

THIRTY-FOUR

ANDI SETTLED IN on the sofa and got comfy as Christian headed to the kitchen.

"I'm going to make some popcorn," he said. "Do you want some? It's amazing."

"A*maz*ing?" She smiled. "Pun intended?"

"Actually, happy accident." He shrugged on a smile.

"You like puns?" she asked, sitting cross-legged.

"I love them," he said. "As kids, we moved a lot, so Riley and I spent hours in the back of the car seeing who could come up with the better pun. It drove Deckard and . . ." He cleared his throat. "It drove Deckard nuts."

She was about to press him on what he was going to say before he cut himself off, but he hadn't pushed her, so she wouldn't push him. As kind and relaxed as his manner was, his countenance spoke of a weight he carried. One of shame, perhaps. Deckard's countenance spoke of pain and anger, Riley's of fear and vulnerability. What had their parents done? No way three siblings struggled like that without something happening growing up. At least, that'd been her experience.

"I won't be long," he said, disappearing into the kitchen. "Make yourself comfortable."

"Thanks," she said.

He returned a moment later, catching her with her arms tangled in the sweatshirt yanked over her head. She composed herself and pulled her arms out of it, setting it aside.

Christian leaned against the doorjamb, his arms crossed, a bemused smile on his lips.

She was afraid to ask. "What?"

He lifted his chin. "Static cling."

Oh sheesh. She smoothed her hair. "Lovely."

"Yes, you are."

She gulped down a swallow, and despite her best efforts to will her gaze away, it remained locked on him and his on her.

At some point the microwave beeped, breaking the spell, and she hopped to her feet. "Let me help you."

"Thanks, but I think I'm good with the popcorn."

"Right. How about I get us something to drink?"

"That'd be great. There's a bunch of drinks in the fridge. Help yourself."

A bowl of popcorn on Christian's lap and two glasses of cider on the end tables later, they started the footage. It was a four-hour gala, plus a heist, so they had their work cut out for them.

"I'll point out who everyone is as we go," Christian said before popping a handful of popcorn in his mouth.

"That'll be great. Let me grab my notebook and pen."

Christian paused the footage. "Take your time."

She hopped up, ran into his bedroom and grabbed her stuff, then paused. *Dear Lord, guard my heart, because I feel it thudding outside of my chest, and I don't know what to do about it.*

After Jeremy, she'd convinced herself she wasn't a good judge of character when it came to men. But he'd fooled everyone. A wolf in sheep's clothing.

Christian wasn't Jeremy. Maybe she could trust him. *I'm scared, Lord, please hold my heart and direct me by your Spirit.*

Returning to the family room, she sank down on the couch beside Christian.

He smiled. "You're fast."

"Thanks. I ran track in school." Why had that come out? It was like her mouth was set on "share" more and more around him.

"I can see that."

"Oh, really?"

"Yes, really." His smile widened.

"How's that?" She loved how his smile lit his eyes—deep brown eyes.

"You're always on the go."

"Is that right?"

"Yes. Either physically or mentally."

She arched her brows. "Mentally, huh?"

"Something's always going on in that head of yours." He smirked.

So he'd pegged her well. Curiosity rippled through her, wondering if she knew him as well. "Hmm. Well, let's see what I know about you."

"Okay." He angled to face her better. "Take your best shot."

"Let's see. You're pensive."

He ducked his chin in. "Pensive. That doesn't sound so good."

"Thoughtful," she said. "Is that better?"

"Much. I like the idea of being thoughtful. Anything else?" He shifted to face her better still.

"You love and are loyal to your family, you excel at what you do . . ." This was just going to go to his head, but he'd asked. "And you take things in stride, for the most part."

He straightened, curiosity dancing in his eyes. "For the most part?"

She bit her lip, trying to think how to best phrase it. "You carry something around with you."

He didn't argue, which spoke volumes. "Why do you think that?"

"Because I know what it's like to carry something." She carried the weight and stigma of who they'd painted her to be. Her colleagues. Her then fiancé. Nearly everyone in her life. "But yours is different than mine. . . ."

"Oh?" His shoulders grew taut.

She wasn't trying to upset him. She just hated seeing him hurting—

and he was. The question was why. She reached out and brushed the hair from his brow.

He jolted a little at her touch.

"Sorry." She moved her hand back.

"No," he said, his deep voice low. "It felt good."

She swallowed. "I can just see you're hurting," she said, deciding to be bold. "It's like you're . . ."

"I'm . . ." He furrowed his brow, inching closer to her.

Her breath slipped from her lungs as his deep gaze fixed on her.

"It's like you're punishing yourself for something."

He stiffened and looked down.

"I'm sorry. . . ." She bit her lip. "I didn't mean to . . ."

He looked back up—the weight of emotion heavy in his deep, brown eyes. "It's okay." He cleared his throat. "Let's get back to the footage. We've got a lot before us."

"Okay . . ." she said, biting her bottom lip.

She should have been quiet. Not pushed. She didn't like when people pushed her, but the ache he wore hurt her.

THIRTY-FIVE

HARPER ROLLED the paper wrapper from her sub into a ball and tossed it in the trash can across the room.

"Nice shot," Deckard said. Quite the distance.

"Thanks." She shrugged.

He did the same with his wrapper.

Greyson, of course, ever the dapper and distinguished man, simply stood and placed his wrapper in.

"Chickened out again," Riley said, tossing hers in too.

Greyson straightened, holding his tie against his chest. "I think we both know better, Riley dear."

"Again with the *dear* stuff." Riley frowned.

"It's a term of politeness," Greyson said with that quirk of a smile on his lips.

Deckard shook his head. *Those two.*

"It might be polite, but it makes me sound like a kid sister," she said.

Greyson arched a brow and gave her that look—the one he reserved for her and only her. Was it brotherly affection or did more linger there?

"I'm a decade your senior," Greyson said as Deckard retrieved his notepad and pen from the table behind them. Time for another round.

"That makes you an old man." Riley smirked. "Not me a child."

Greyson shook his head with that sigh of exasperation that only Riley could elicit.

Deckard chuckled.

Harper glanced over at him. "Am I missing something?"

"Nah. Just these two."

The pair didn't hear them, or simply didn't acknowledge them because they just kept going.

■ ■

Four hours of gala footage later, Andi was about to doze off when Christian nudged her arm.

"I think we have our mystery woman," he said.

She sat up and straightened as he backtracked the video. Sure enough, it was a woman with the long, wavy black hair that Tad had described—all he'd been able to describe of the woman he spent the night with.

The woman made her way in during the last half hour of the gala. She beelined for a drink and then straight to Tad, while somehow managing to keep her face off camera. The most they saw was one instance when they got a peek at her chin.

"She clearly knew where the cameras were," Andi said.

"So we can with near certainty connect her to the thieves. She was sent in to get the fob."

She and Tad left the gala together, the entire party remaining at the end leaving in mass exodus.

"Most of them probably went down into Santa Fe for the nightlife. Jeopardy Falls, other than events like the gala, closes down by ten," Christian explained.

She smiled. Yet another aspect of Jeopardy Falls that felt cozy. Rugged and cozy at the same time. She'd shirked away from community, but the town was definitely growing on her.

"All right," Christian said, sitting forward. "Let's see how long until the heist." He fast-forwarded through the footage.

"There," she said at the movement by the front door.

"Here we go." He scooted farther forward, nearly tumbling off the edge of the sofa.

Two men dressed in all black entered the gallery. One signaled toward the back of the gallery with a swipe of two fingers, and the other proceeded out of the main camera's line of sight.

"Joel said it was all on this." The footage of the back office popped up.

A man entered, moved straight for the picture covering the safe, took it down, and opened the safe within a breath. Then he defused the alarm with ease.

"Wow!" Christian sat back, his elbows propped on his knees, his head propped in his hands.

"If that isn't an inside job, I don't know what is," she said.

"If it's not an inside job, they nailed it," he said.

"We need to have another talk with Tad."

"Okay, so we've gone through what Andi did the night of Anne Marlowe's murder," Deckard said, pacing the conference room. "What did you do the night of her murder?" he asked, looking at her.

Harper's muscles tensed. That night still haunted her. She'd worked many gruesome scenes, but this one stuck with her well before she knew it would tear her friend's life apart.

"Perhaps what we should do is go through the night from Anne's perspective," Greyson suggested.

Harper tilted her head, curious how they approached that.

"What does the police report say?" he asked Deckard.

"I don't have the police file," he said, moving for the pile he had going on the side table. "All I have is the mini–case file Mitch's defense attorney, Clint James, assembled for me. It had the basics but certainly was not the full report."

"Knowing you, I'm sure you asked for it," Greyson said, sitting back and steepling his fingers.

"Yep. But the detectives on the case wanted nothing to do with me. Neither did the prosecutor. They believed they had their man and had zero time for me."

"Okay." Greyson sat back. "Let's go through what you do know."

"Okay." Deckard opened a file with colorful paperclips sticking out.

Harper smiled. Riley's touch, she was betting.

"I'll start with what I know about Anne," Deckard said, clearing his throat before continuing. "Anne worked in Councilman David Markowitz's office. She'd met Mitch about two months prior to her death, and the two began an affair."

"And Mitch was married, right?" Riley asked. "Between him and the judge, it's clear she had a thing for married guys." She shook her head. "I don't get that."

Greyson looked over at her, and it was as quick as a blink of an eye, but Harper caught a soft smile before it disappeared. He thought highly of Riley, despite the banter about her being the "kid" of the group.

"Anne broke off her relationship with Judge Simmons once she started up with Mitch. Both Simmons and Mitch confirmed this," Deckard said as Greyson shifted back to the glass boards and uncapped a marker.

"What about Mitch's wife?" Riley asked.

"Kim," Deckard said.

"Did she know about the affair?" Harper asked.

"Not until after the murder."

"And?" Harper asked.

"She kicked him to the curb. Refused to speak on his behalf," Deckard said. "Or so Clint told me."

"Surely they summoned her," Riley said.

"I'm sure, but she wouldn't have anything glowing to say about Mitch."

"So who was Anne going out to the isolated hiking park to see that night?" Riley asked. "It was late, right?"

"The call came into the lab at about one," Harper said.

"So . . . she broke off the affair with Simmons, and he has an alibi. Mitch is at a conference in Las Cruces." Riley sat forward, resting her hands on the table. "Who did she think she was going to see?"

Deckard sat back, dropping his pen on his notebook. "That is the million-dollar question. Let's make some calls."

"I thought you wanted to talk to people in person," Harper said.

"Most definitely Todd Phillips, given his promotion, or upgrade as you said, and we'll hit the lab tomorrow, but I think placing a few well-directed calls would give us a head start."

"Great." Harper lifted her pen. "Shall we divide up the list?"

"I think calling on speaker would be best. I'll lead, but if something crops up you want to jump on, go for it."

She smiled. "Sounds like a plan."

"I'll run some records for you," Greyson said.

"I'll help," Riley added, getting to her feet as Greyson did. Excusing themselves, they shut the conference room door behind them.

"Who's first up?" Harper asked.

"Let's start with Kevin Gaines. He was the one out sick?"

"Yes." Her brow furrowed. "But he wasn't there."

"Exactly." Deckard smiled.

THIRTY-SIX

DECKARD SANK BACK against the office chair and swung back and forth with the rotating seat. He looked over at Harper, a pen behind her ear, her blond hair wrapped up in some topsy-turvy bun. He smiled. It looked adorable. He might not be interested in having a relationship now, *period*. But, if he did, he supposed it would be with someone very much like Harper. Intelligent, funny, vivacious, but what he loved most of all was her quirkiness. She was confident in who she was, and that was extremely sexy. But . . . he tapped his pen against the legal pad covered with his chicken scratch . . . he wasn't interested in a relationship. Romantic connections meant commitment, and while he had no problem being committed to family, faith, or work, to a person he would one day love like God loved the church? That he couldn't do. It could bring his demons along for the ride. Until they went away, he stayed away from romance. That was, if they ever went away.

"I don't know about you, but things are starting to blur," he said, arching his back.

"Yeah." She sat back and swiveled too. "I'm starting to confuse facts."

He glanced at the clock. *1930*. "Shoot. Riley is going to kill us."

"Hmm." She followed his line of sight to the clock. "Yikes. She said seven sharp."

His sister had left a couple of hours ago to prepare dinner for everyone, and they'd only gotten Greyson out at a decent hour for once by convincing him Riley needed his help making enough grub to feed the slew of them.

They'd only remained behind because his tire wasn't ready, then time slipped away. No doubt Leroy had left it fixed with the key under the mat.

He exhaled and glanced around at the dark office—only the conference room light shining down on them and the muted glow from Greyson's small desk lamp. He liked the silence. Stillness.

Stretching, he kinked his neck, then closed the folder in front of him. They'd spent hours upon hours on the phone, interviewing lab tech Marshall Palmer, forensic manager Kevin Gaines, and everyone they could get ahold of save Todd Phillips and Pam Whitmore. Harper had even taken the initiative and placed a call to Councilman Markowitz. While he was focusing on the lab, she was focusing on those who knew Anne.

"We should probably wrap up." He tapped the legal pad scribbled with notes with his pen.

"I agree, and I'm pretty sure your sister is going to read us the riot act when we get to your house."

"Yeah. Not going to lie. I'd face a man with a gun before going up against Ri."

Harper laughed, really laughed, and a crooked smile curled on his lips, her laughter bringing him an unexpected joy.

"Well," she said, collecting her things into a pile, "I think we made good progress."

"You can brief me on your call to Markowitz, and I can update you on the items Greyson flagged."

"Sounds like a plan."

"You know . . ."

She looked up with those beautiful blue eyes. "Yes?"

He rolled his bottom lip slightly in his mouth, then released it. "Before we go—"

The lights cut out.

He frowned. "That's odd. The backup generator should kick on the emergency lighting."

A breath of a minute later, it did. The two exit signs illuminated—one for the main door, one for the rear that led to the stairwell. The emergency lights mounted over the rear sign illuminated, but the rest of the office remained shrouded in shadows.

Deckard stood and pulled his SIG, sliding one into the chamber.

Harper stood in sync, pulling her Glock—her big blue eyes wide in the dim light sweeping in through the crack in the door.

He held a finger to his lips.

Footsteps.

Deckard indicated for her to move to his six behind the slit in the nearly closed door.

She moved in place, and he positioned himself to look through the crack. Two figures in black cut a swath across the light's beam.

"Remember," the one man said. "Don't leave a trace. Just see what they have and put it back in place. Boss's orders."

"I got it," the other replied.

Deckard waited until they passed toward the back offices, then lifted his chin. They'd come out behind the men and have a clear shot. "Ready?" he mouthed.

She nodded.

He opened the door, and everything went black.

THIRTY-SEVEN

HIS HEAD FEELING like he'd been run over by a semi, Deckard blinked. Weight lay crisscross over his legs. What in the blazes was happening? He stared up at the dark ceiling. He lifted his head, and the world spun. Wet stuck to the back of his neck. He reached back and pulled his fingers back to reveal sticky blood. What on earth? With a stiff breath, he glanced down at Harper laying at a forty-five-degree angle across his legs, unconscious.

"Harp . . ." With gentle force, he shook her arm, his voice low. "Harp."

He glanced around, his hand reaching for his SIG. *Gone.* He reached down and with tenderness moved Harper off his legs, rolling her easily to the floor, pushing the hair from her face. Darkness engulfed them as he reached for his knife, cool along his left calf. He remained still, listening. No one was moving, but it didn't mean they were gone.

He reached over and rubbed Harper's arm. "Harp," he whispered. "Harp." He tried again. He looked and saw her weapon was gone too. *Great.*

"Hmmm," she murmured, rolling her head.

"We gotta go," he said, his voice hushed, his gaze sweeping what he could see of the office from his vantage point.

Her eyes fluttered open, then widened.

He pressed his finger to his lips.

She nodded.

He pointed toward the door, and she nodded again, then winced. Blood drizzled along her already swelling temple. He ground his teeth. Whoever did this . . . He couldn't focus on them right now. He had to get Harper out of the building as fast as possible and somewhere safe.

"Back stairwell," he said, pointing to the adjacent exit sign as he retrieved his cell.

She gave a flash of a nod.

He punched in a code to his friend Sam and hit Send.

Helping Harper to her feet, they strode toward the edge of the hall and looked around the corner.

Sam texted back in the affirmative.

Seeing no one, they bolted for the door, opened it. Deckard cleared the space.

They moved in unison down the three flights of stairs, making sure each flight was clear before proceeding down it.

Walking four open blocks to his vehicle was untenable. Hence Sam.

They exited into the night but hung against the building in the shadows until Sam's blue pickup roared to a stop in front of them.

The question registered on Harper's face, but she didn't ask, just moved with him behind her to the truck and climbed in.

"Hi," she said to Sam.

He returned the quick greeting as Deckard climbed inside and shut the door.

Sam peeled off. "What happened and where to?"

"Drop me a couple blocks from Leroy's and take Harper to Frannie's diner." It was knowable ground with lots of people always sifting in and out. She'd be safe there.

"Roger that."

"What's happening?" Harper said.

Deckard kept his gaze in the side mirror. "Getting us someplace safe and making sure no one is following us in the process."

"Right here is good," Deckard said to his friend, thankful for the backup measures they'd put in place should an emergency like this—or any for that matter—arise.

"I'll wait with her at the diner," Sam said.

"Thanks, man." He clasped his friend's hand, then turned to Harper, her temple swollen and marred with splotches of black and blue in the light of the moon. "I'll be to the diner a matter of minutes after you. Go in, grab a seat. Stay with people until I pull up."

She nodded then winced again.

Climbing out, he made his way to the garage, moving fast and in the darkness of night, making sure he wasn't being tracked. Reaching the SUV, he climbed in and grabbed the key from under the mat, then started the engine. There must have been a third man who'd come around the other side of the conference room. It was the only thing that made sense, but he couldn't dwell on that. His mission was to get Harper and get to the safety of the ranch.

Pulling up outside of the diner, Harper caught sight of him, lifted her chin, and headed out with Sam at her side. She climbed into the Equinox, and Sam's hand braced on the open door. "You two be safe."

"Thanks for being there," Deck said.

"I'm just glad I was home to help."

"Me too." Though they had three friends in play should the need arise.

Sam shut the door, and they were on the way to the ranch, Deck tapping the wheel, his nerves vibrating. How'd he let someone get the jump on him? He clasped the steering wheel, his knuckles surely white, though it was too dark to see. He looked over at Harper. "You okay?"

She gave a slight nod, holding two fingers gingerly to her temple. "I took a good one."

"What happened?" he asked.

"You stepped out and dropped to the ground. I was already stepping out behind you and the guy caught me on the side of the head. That's the last thing I remember."

"Third guy."

"Yeah," she said.

"Did you see anything about him?" he asked, glancing in the rear-view mirror. Relief filled him when he saw no headlights. They'd take the back way up the winding roads to Jeopardy Falls and on to their ranch.

"It all happened so fast. He was dressed in dark clothes. Pale skin from what I could see in the dim light, but it was like a flash and now a blur."

He reached over and clasped her knee. "We'll be to safety soon."

"No police?" she asked.

"The priority is safe territory." He tapped the wheel. "Besides, we can't tell them much other than we had intruders. It goes in some report and that's the end of it. I've gone through this before. We can always report it first thing in the morning when we all go in to see what they may have touched or taken."

"Who do you think they were? Someone from Christian and Andi's case?"

He glanced over at her in the sweep of headlights across her face from a lone oncoming car. "I don't know. Maybe. But I don't know how much is in the office related to their case. Andi keeps her laptop and files with her, according to Christian, and he works more by the seat of his pants with just a notebook. Though Greyson has done some reconnaissance work for them."

She narrowed her eyes. "You don't think we could have triggered this, do you?"

He glanced over at her, then back at the winding road. "I don't know, but if we did, it means we're barking up the right tree." But, given they'd just started with the investigation, if it was their doing, how much more was to come as they dug deeper? How dangerous would it become?

THIRTY-EIGHT

FORTY-FIVE MINUTES LATER with no one following, Deckard guided Harper into his kitchen to the scent of hominy and red chili. "Smells great, Cool Whip," he said, greeting Riley, trying to play it as causually as possible so she didn't worry.

"Hey, Slugger," she said, smiling with a smattering of freckles across her cheeks, and then her smile faded. "What happened to you?" Her gaze tracked to Harper. "Oh no. You too. Let's get that cleaned up."

"It's okay," Deckard said. "I've got her. I'll grab the first aid kit out of the bathroom."

"But first, what happened?" Christian asked.

"There's not a lot to tell. . . ." But he went through it all the same.

"After Deck stepped through the door, I followed, but Deck fell knocked out on the floor in front of me. I barely turned when I was nailed upside my head with the butt of a gun. We saw the two men, as Deckard said, but there was a third man waiting."

Greyson handed Harper and Deckard each a bag of ice.

"Thanks, man," Deckard said as Harper extended her thanks as well.

Greyson nodded. "And you said they were there to gain intelligence."

"That's what we heard."

174

"You think it has to do with the heists?" Christian asked.

Deckard held the bag of ice to the back of his head, which also needed to be cleaned up. They could see to each other unless Riley insisted on fussing over both of them.

"It's possible, but Andi keeps her work with her in her satchel, I think."

"That's correct," Andi said.

"I don't have much at the office," Christian said. "I keep my note-book with me."

"It could be because of things I ran," Greyson said. "I'll have to run a trace on my computer, see what was accessed."

"That's the odd thing. They bypassed your desk, heading straight for the back office."

"Your office." His sat in the back, Riley's nearest the front, and Christian's off the front hall. The only other office in the back was their guest office should they bring someone in to help on some-thing.

"We were out fast; they could have gone through your computer after we were unconscious."

Christian rested his forearms on the table. "But why *your* office?"

Deckard exhaled. "I hate to say this, but I think one of the in-quiries Harp and I made struck a chord with someone. I keep all my files in my office."

"We'll need to go through things with a fine-tooth comb," Grey-son said. "Did you call Santa Fe PD?"

"Not yet. My mission was to get Harper and me to home base. I'll call Gary at Santa Fe PD and let them know."

"I'll head to the office to meet them, scour through everything to note if something is missing or if I can tell what, specifically, they came for."

"I'll go with you," Riley said.

"I can go," Deck said. "You all enjoy dinner."

Riley placed her hands on her hips. "You look like you got hit with a baseball bat. Both of you. Call Gary, give him your report, and let Greyson and me handle the office. Deal?"

It sounded like a question, but it wasn't really. When Riley set her mind to something . . .

"Okay," he said, then looked at Harper. "Let's get that wound cleaned up."

"I'll leave the posole on the stove for when you're done." She glanced at Christian and Andi. "Help yourselves."

"Thanks, Riley," Christian said, "but are you sure you don't—"

"We got this, and you've had enough excitement for one day."

Deckard sighed. Wasn't that the truth.

Ten minutes later, Harper sat on the double sink vanity, swinging her legs while Deckard fished out the supplies, laying each needed item out on the vanity beside her. He reached for the rubbing alcohol. "This is going to sting a little."

"I'll be okay, but thanks."

He soaked a cotton ball with it, and with as much tenderness as he could, cleaned out her wound. Her hands flinched once, but otherwise she held still, nearly unaffected. She was one tough lady.

"I'll put some Neosporin on it and then a bandage."

"I appreciate it, but not sure a bandage is needed," she said.

"I suppose you're right." It was more an impact injury than a big open wound.

"Your turn," she said, hopping down and indicating for Deckard to hop up.

"I'm good, but thanks."

She dipped her chin, her brows arching. "You have blood on the back of your neck. Let me at least clean that up."

Arguing was pointless, and he had no desire to walk around with the now-dried blood on his person. He hopped up, and she reached for the rubbing alcohol.

"Okay, mister," she said, "let's shift you sideways." She rested a hand on his thigh and pushed in indication for him to shift sideways.

He swallowed at the incredible feel of her touch, despite their current circumstances. The woman had a natural way of getting to him . . . in a very good, but very dangerous way.

Three hours later, Riley and Greyson returned.

"How'd it go?" Christian asked.

"The police came in and did a fingerprint sweep, but as you said, the intruders had gloves on, so none showed up on their fingerprint reader but ours," Greyson said.

"Can you tell what they touched?" Deckard asked. "As I told the police, we heard them say not to move anything, just to look."

"At first glance it looked like nothing had been touched," Greyson said.

"But after that?" Harper asked.

Greyson looked at Deckard. "They were in your file cabinets."

"How could you tell?" Deckard asked, definitely not questioning the man's information, but, rather, how he knew.

"The dials were left on a different number sequence than you leave the three on."

He always left them set on specific numbers so he could tell if someone ever got into the safe-style lock on them. "Could you tell which files they looked at?" Deckard leaned forward, and Harper did so in automatic unison.

"There was one lifted higher than the others," Greyson said, his lips grim.

"Let me guess," Deckard said. "Anne Marlowe's file?"

Greyson nodded.

So, it was about them. They really must have ticked off the wrong person, but which of the people they talked to was it? "Hopefully, they did as they said and didn't take anything out of it."

"I know they didn't take these," Greyson said, pulling two files out of his leather messenger bag. He handed them to Deckard and Harper as she sat beside him, her leg inadvertently touching his on the bench seating at the table.

"What are these?" Deck asked, flipping the first folder open.

"Copies of the full police report and the autopsy report on Anne Marlowe."

Harper's jaw slackened. "How did you get those?"

Greyson took a long sip of his iced tea.

"Greyson has his ways of making things happen," Riley said. "But he prefers to remain a man of mystery. Even from us," she said, lifting her glass before taking a sip.

Neither looked at the other, but something was passing between his sister and Greyson. Deckard shook it off as a big brother and younger sister taunting, just in playful and often silent ways. "This will be a huge help. Beyond huge," he said. "Thanks, Grey."

Greyson dipped his head.

Harper looked over. "I know how we'll spend our ride to Albuquerque."

"Albuquerque?" Riley said.

"We're going to interview people at the lab tomorrow," Harper said. "So we figured we'd spend the night at my place in town."

"You sure you don't want to wait until the morning?" Riley said.

"You know I'm a night owl, not a rooster. I'd rather make the drive tonight," Deckard said. Besides, he liked driving on the nearly abandoned roads—at least as far as he could go until he hit the highway, but even then, the lights of Albuquerque were spectacular. Much like the woman sitting beside him.

"If, and I completely believe it is," Christian said. "If this is about you digging where someone wants to leave things untouched, you could be in danger at Harper's." He looked to Harper. "No offense to your place, but the ranch is probably safer."

"I've got a good alarm and close neighbors," she said.

"We'll be fine," Deck said.

"I sure hope so," Riley said.

So did he. He'd feel much better when he knew who his adversary was. Going against an unknown was always harder, like chasing shadows.

THIRTY-NINE

AFTER THEY'D ALL talked through the day they'd had and the investigations, Harper and Andi—both armed, just to be safe after the intruders today—headed out for the firepit while Deckard went to pack a bag for the trip.

Stars blanketed the sky like a thousand fireflies overhead.

"So," Harper said, taking a seat on one end of the sofa, a cup of tea in hand.

"So," Andi said, taking a seat on the other end. She set her Mexican hot chocolate on the side table, then lifted one of the toss pillows and cuddled it. For whatever stupid reason, it made her feel secure. Not as secure as when in Christian's sight, but she didn't want to acknowledge that sentiment. She did not need a man to feel secure, but he made her feel safe all the same. And not to be cliché, but she really did have butterflies looping inside her and the sensation of the flutter of their wings along her skin. He made her tingle, and that was dangerous. Though, in retrospect, Jeremy had never made her tingle. Not once.

"So . . ." Harper nudged.

Andi exhaled. Here it came. "Now's probably not the time," she said, trying to buy herself some time before admitting what she knew was coming.

"We've covered the cases, at least for the night. I don't know about you, but I'm ready to shift topics. I could use something fun."

"And, I'm fun?" She shook her head with a smile.

"The thing you got going between you and Christian is."

Andi cocked her head, ready to say there was no thing, but Harper would see right through her.

Harper propped her elbow on the back of the couch and rested her head on her hand. "So, let's dish. He's cute."

The man was beyond handsome. Andi tried to remain impassive as his gorgeous face flashed before her mind, but a smile broke on her lips despite herself.

"See . . ." Harper smiled in triumph. "I knew it."

Andi leaned over and retrieved her drink, the silky smell of dark chocolate and the warming scent of vanilla wafting from the cup. "Gloating is not becoming on you." She smirked, then took a sip, whipped cream tickling her nose.

"Oh, please, I see the way you look at him."

She swiped the cream from the tip of her nose. "You're being ridiculous."

"All right." Harper sat back. "But he looks at you the same way."

Andi pulled her legs up on the cushioned patio couch and tucked them beneath her. "He does?" she asked, unable to help herself.

"Oh yeah," Harper said.

The butterflies swirled.

"But I know what you're going to say," Harper continued before she had a chance to speak. "It's ridiculous. I just met the man. I couldn't have feelings for him. He certainly couldn't have feelings for me. Blah. Blah. Blah."

"All valid points. Thank you for saying them."

Harper rolled her eyes. "Honey, one of these days you're going to have to take another chance at life. I know you were hurt, but Christian isn't Jeremy."

"How do I know that? I thought Jeremy was a good guy. Good enough to marry."

"There you go." Harper waggled her finger at her, and she clutched the pillow tighter.

"What?"

"Good enough. You thought Jeremy was good enough. He was exactly what your stupid parents—sorry about that, but I call them like I see them—wanted. Someone handsome and intelligent and driven. What they didn't care about is how he treated you or made you feel, especially after you were engaged."

His behavior had shifted after the engagement. Subtle at first, then growing. Snapping at her for little things. Running late for their dates. Distant at times.

"You know what I think," Harper said.

"Am I going to be able to stop you from sharing?"

"No. And I'm ignoring that slight. I think Jeremy already had Stepford wife number two picked out, and he just used what went down as an excuse to do a cruddy thing."

"What makes you think that? If he was cheating, why wait until the fallout to dump me?"

"Because people's admiration drove him. He was the hot new agent with the smart and beautiful fiancée, and he wasn't going to risk people's disapproval if he could help it. Heck, I think if that hadn't happened, you two would be married now, and he'd have Miss Cupcake on the side."

Andi opened her mouth to argue, then shut it. As much as she hated to admit it, she'd harbored the same thoughts. "Fine. You want me to admit it? Jeremy wasn't who I thought he was."

"Exactly. He wasn't who anyone thought he was. He fooled us all—so dump that guilt over not seeing through him from your mind." She stirred her spoon in the tea mug, clanging against the ceramic a time or two. "You clearly have feelings for Christian. He's not Jeremy, so lose the reservations."

"I just met him."

"Sometimes things happen fast."

Andi scrunched the pillow tighter, playing with the tassels along the edge—running the threads through her fingers. "But, what if . . ."

Harper leaned forward. "Honey, what did I tell you about what-ifs?"

"That God's in control, and there's no use trying to figure out a future we can't know."

"Right." Harper took a sip of her tea while Andi swallowed a sip of the yummy, spicy chocolate drink.

"So, just admit it," Harper began, no doubt ready to press her until she admitted her feelings for Christian.

"Admit what?" Deckard said behind Andi, and she about jumped out of her skin.

"Sorry." He made a little kid "sorry" face with puppy dog eyes and an exaggerated grin.

"All good," Andi said.

Harper set her cup down. "Are you ready?"

He lifted a backpack. "Yep."

"You don't think this might take a few days?" Harper asked.

"Oh, I'm sure it will. Probably a week."

"Then why just a backpack?" Harper angled her head to look over the couch at his hands. "No other bag?"

"Nope." He clutched the green nylon pack against his chest and patted it. "Got everything I need."

"Okay, then let's head out." Harper stood, grabbed her cup, and gave Andi a one-armed hug. "Be safe."

"You too," Andi said, looking between her and Deckard. "You guys are clearly digging up stuff those involved want to keep hidden."

Deckard cocked his head. "The question is, how far are they willing to go to keep it hidden?"

FORTY

"MIND IF I JOIN YOU?" Christian asked Andi before Harper and Deckard had vanished around the main house.

"Please," she said.

To her surprise, he sat on the couch with her rather than in one of the myriad of chairs.

Her heart thumped. Her traitorous heart. It was all Harper's fault. She'd put the notion in Andi's head. Okay, she hadn't put it there, but she'd exacerbated it.

Christian reclined against the sofa, draping his arm along the back of the cushions.

He'd showered while Deckard packed, and she and Harper talked. But he hadn't shaved. The five o'clock shadow covering his rugged jawline and blanketing parts of his cheeks was extremely attractive. *Great.* Just what she needed. Thinking him even more handsome. Was that really possible?

"You seem lost in thought," he said, the firelight dancing across his chiseled features.

Danger. Danger, Will Robinson. Tread easy, girl.

"You're very perceptive," he said.

She cocked her head. Where had that come from?

"Your earlier observation . . ."

"Oh, I didn't mean—"

"No. You were right." He stood and strode to the stone counter by the kiva fireplace.

"Oh?" she said, not pushing this time.

Christian took a seat on the edge of the counter, took a deep inhale, then streamed it out. "Uncomfortably perceptive," he said with a humorless laugh.

She stiffened. Shoot. She'd pushed too much. "I'm sorry, I shouldn't have—"

"No," he said. Was that a catch in his voice? "It's good you did."

"Oh?" She scooted closer to the edge of the couch.

He rubbed the back of his neck. "There's something I need to tell you."

"Oh" It was taking everything inside her not to press. But how many times could she say *oh*.

He swallowed, his Adam's apple bobbing in the shadows and the flickering firelight. "I don't . . ." He cleared his throat.

She waited, forcing her jumbling self to be patient, not to heed the ridiculous urge to wrap him in her arms and tell him that, whatever it was, it'd be okay.

"I guess it's best to start from the beginning." He took a stiff inhale, his shoulders hiking up, then released it, his shoulders easing back down.

Her stomach swished. How bad was what he had to share? A swift uneasiness raked through her.

"I . . . Deck, Riley, our older sister, Bristol, and I grew up in a world of illusion," he began.

Another sibling? She wanted to ask about Bristol but forced herself to remain still, to just listen.

"My parents," he continued, pain etching hard across his face, "were famous . . . or . . ." He shook his head. "Or rather, infamous illusionists in Vegas when I was young."

"Really?" That didn't sound so bad, though she doubted Vegas had been fun to grow up in. They were probably exposed to a lot. Maybe that's why they all struggled in some way.

184

"I know it sounds sort of glamorous, but believe me, it was far from it."

She could imagine . . . well, could fathom.

"My par—" He swallowed. "*They* were an illusionist duo on the stage, but no one knew that beneath all the magic, they were nothing more than world-class cons."

"What?" She hadn't seen that coming.

"They were conmen . . . well, a conman and woman. But that's just a more sophisticated word for *thieves*. And that's what my . . . what *they* were. Thieves and scammers."

"Is that why you all do what you do?" she asked, unable to keep silent. Were they trying to catch people like their parents?

"Yes and no," he said, and she forced herself to be quiet, to focus on him and not all the theories and ideas stirring through her mind.

He exhaled, his shoulders drooping deeper. "They used us."

Her gaze narrowed. Surely, he wasn't suggesting . . . "When you say they used you . . ."

He looked down, his jaw shifting. "They used us in their cons."

Her heart dropped.

"They used us as pawns to help them steal, swindle, cheat—you name it."

"Oh, Christian." She stood and moved to sit against the counter beside him. "I'm so sorry. I can't imagine . . ." What kind of awful parents would do such a thing?

"The thing is, greed is never satisfied. They kept going for the next big score, pulling off bigger and bigger cons until they conned the wrong guy. A very powerful man in Vegas." His knee bounced faster.

She reached down, took his hand in hers, interlocking their fingers. "How old were you then?"

"Ten."

She gaped at him. "*Ten*? They used you in cons before you were ten?"

"They used me as far back as my earliest memory. There's not a time I can remember growing up where I wasn't being used . . . or left on my own," he said.

Tears beaded in her eyes. "They left you guys alone?"

"Bristol split after we left Vegas, but yeah—Deck, me, and Riley were left in sleazy motel rooms for days on end while they worked cons they didn't need us for or went on benders. . . ."

He shrugged, trying to fight back the nearly all-consuming memories. To speak of them without feeling as if he were right back in those desperate moments.

Andi squeezed his hand tighter, tears filling her eyes.

He didn't want her to feel sorry for him. He just wanted her to know the truth—the full truth—before *their* feelings . . . He inhaled, reveling in the feel of her hand in his. Before their *actions* went any further. The feelings were already there.

"We moved from town to town . . ." he continued.

"While you and Riley played your pun games in the back of the car?" She offered a soft smile, but sadness filled it.

He nodded. "We worked whatever they made us do, even stealing food a couple times when money was tight." His gut seized, but he continued on, before he lost the courage. "That man, the wrong one they conned, eventually found us and took revenge on my parents. My dad died in a fiery car explosion."

"Oh, Christian." She squeezed his hand. "I'm so sorry."

"My mom, he let live but made sure she was caught and imprisoned. She's still there." And he hadn't seen her since. A small voice kept prodding him to go, to give her a second chance like he'd received, but he'd ignored it thus far. Maybe he should listen, but that decision wasn't getting made tonight.

"I'm afraid to ask, but what happened to you guys?"

"Deck and I took off, but first we made sure Riley was in a good children's home. We kept tabs on her, and she went on to a good foster home."

"How old were you guys?"

"Thirteen and fifteen."

"You were on your own at *thirteen*?"

"I was always on my own. Well, Deck and I were." Deckard had always been there for him through good and bad, and he always would be.

"I'm so sorry," she whispered, leaning her head against his shoulder.

Man, he wanted to leave things there. To stay like this, but she needed to know what he'd done.

FORTY-ONE

RUBBING HIS THIGHS, his muscles rigid, he swallowed and said, "You might want to sit back for this next part."

"What?" Confusion echoed in her green eyes.

"I need to tell you something." He clutched her hand, knowing as soon as he told her, she'd pull it back.

"Okay?" Hesitance hung in her tone.

He wished with all his being he could just put a pin in it like he had thus far, but it was time for that pin to come out. She was worth it, even if it meant nothing continued to grow between them. She'd been betrayed by so many, he couldn't betray her trust too.

He swallowed again. "Deck—" He cleared his throat.

"What is it?" Her fingers caressed his.

He looked her in the eye and exhaled. He owed her this. "Deck ended up in juvie for a con."

She straightened. "But I thought . . ."

"He got saved by a guy who spoke on Sundays at the juvie center and led Bible studies, but that's Deck's story to tell. Mine . . . the reason I'm so good at beating heists is because . . ." He cleared his throat. "Because I used to pull them off."

She stiffened in his hold. "I'm sorry. What?"

Pain raked through him as she pulled back.

"I don't understand."

"After Deck went into juvie, I met a guy, and we ended up getting a run-down place together. And after working crummy jobs that we got 'off the books,' we came up with the idea to plan the perfect heist. I'd . . ." He shifted his jaw, the muscle inside quivering. "Stuff my parents had me do, people we interacted with . . . it all gave me skills at pulling off a heist."

"Wait." She pulled back as far as she could go. "You're saying you actually pulled off a heist?"

"Two, actually. Out in Cali. Two art galleries."

She didn't need to say anything, the turmoil brewing in her eyes said it all. He'd lost any chance with her. But he needed to finish it all. He wouldn't leave anything on the table.

"We got caught and went to juvie. At first my buddy and I started planning another set of heists for when we got out, but Deck came to see me. Every week. Bringing his Bible. Witnessing to me."

She shifted to face him better.

"When we got out, I told Ethan I couldn't do it, that Christ got ahold of me and I couldn't turn my back on Him. I tried sharing Jesus with him, but he wanted nothing to do with Him. I tried to warn him off the heist. He was good, but not good enough. He couldn't do it without me. I warned him he'd get caught."

"And?"

On a sharp swallow, he nodded. "He did. I tried to visit him afterward. Knowing how Jesus transformed me, I thought . . . I prayed . . . But he refused to see me. After a while I gave up."

"And Ethan?"

"Still serving time."

"And you?" she asked, her voice quivering.

"Deckard had been waiting for me all along. After getting out of juvie, he'd started working at Greyson's PI firm in Tucson, then bought it from him after he moved it to Santa Fe, and then bought the ranch here in Jeopardy Falls. I went to school in Albuquerque. Got my degree and came to work for Deckard. Trying to . . ." He shrugged at how stupid it probably sounded.

"Trying to make up for what you did by stopping or solving other heists?" she asked.

"Yeah." He raked a hand through his hair, the heat from the fire warm on his skin—a stark contrast to the chill he felt inside, the fear she'd never look at him the same.

Her eyes softened. "I'm so glad you found Jesus."

"Me too." A hollowness tore at his gut. He wanted so desperately to pull her into his arms, but he had to respect her space, her timing. And the fact she may not ever want to pick back up on the feelings growing between them.

"I . . ." she started.

Trill. Trill. Trill.

She looked down and pulled her phone out of her pocket. "It's Harper. I better take it."

He nodded.

"Hey, Harp. What's up? Uh-huh. Okay." She held her hand over the receiver. "I'm going to take this in the house, if that's okay."

"Of course."

He watched her walk away.

■ ■

"So what's up with the *uh-huh*?" Harper asked as Andi entered Christian's bedroom where she'd slept and shut the door behind her.

"Shhh. Hold on."

"Oooh. So this is going to be something good," Harper said, keen interest echoing in her tone.

Try very bad. Her chest squeezed. She never saw that coming, and her flight instinct was screaming *run*. She exhaled, wondering what *he* was feeling as how she reacted raced through her mind.

"Are you there?" Harper said.

"Yeah." She sat on the bed, her knees bent, clutching a pillow tight to her chest.

"For goodness' sake," Harper said. "What happened? Are you okay?"

"Yes. No. I don't know."

"What's going on?"

"Christian told me something, and I don't know how to handle it." She raked a hand through her hair, the smell of the fire from the pit clinging to it.

"Okay . . ."

"I want to tell you, but . . . I also want to respect his privacy." He'd opened up to her in confidence.

"So leave out the details. Just go big picture."

How did she do that? "I . . ."

"You?" Harper said, before taking a sip of something.

Andi exhaled. "Okay," she said, trying to think big picture only and not get lost in the weeds. "He did something in his past. Let's just say he . . ."

"Wore Mickey ears?" Harper proposed.

"What?" She laughed in spite of herself. Leave it to Harper to defuse a tense situation with something so out of the blue.

"Will that work?" Harper asked, then crunching sounded over the line.

"What are you eating?"

"Cracker Jacks. Sorry. I'll wait until we're done."

"No. It's fine, but you only eat those when you're stressed. So what's up?"

"Just trying to find the right line with Deckard," she admitted.

"What do you mean?" Andi leaned into her legs, resting against the weight of them. "Do you *like* Deckard?" There was something in her tone. Something that bespoke of interest.

"Sure I like him. He's fun to be around, but I don't *like, like* him."

Andi arched a brow. "You sure about that?" Her friend's tone said otherwise.

"I couldn't possibly," Harp said. "I just met the man."

She'd just met Christian, but she knew how she felt for him. Or had before . . . *No.* She still did, but that didn't mean things wouldn't change between them. "Sometimes things move fast," she finally muttered. Their feelings had happened fast. Fast and hard. He dizzied her in a way no one else ever had.

"No," Harper said. "It's just . . . I caught myself thinking I might not be ready to go on my ICRC stint."

"Really?"

"Don't sound excited. That's not a good thing."

"Why isn't that a good thing?" Harper hadn't dated anyone in a while. Always keeping her distance for her love of travel, her love of volunteering with humanitarian organizations like ICRC. She always said she couldn't get attached, so her dates never went past the fourth one.

"Because that's my priority," Harper said. "God's my priority, and He's put it on my heart to go. The fact I wavered for even a moment says I need to keep a strong boundary there."

"Or maybe it means His will for you is changing."

"Don't be ridiculous."

"God's will for our lives is a constant, but it doesn't mean He keeps us on a straight line. It's a walk of many hills and valleys." She knew the valleys well. "And often He moves us right when we get comfortable with something."

Harper exhaled.

Good. She was pondering that.

"Okay, we were talking about you," she shifted the conversation. "So what's up?"

Andi debated on pushing it with Harper, but the weight of what just happened with her and Christian was mounting. She needed to get it out. "Okay, so they had a rough childhood. I can't express how rough." But *rough* didn't cover it.

"I'm sorry to hear that. But that explains the pain Deckard wears."

"You see it too?"

"Oh yeah."

"So . . . in his teens Christian wore Mickey ears. And it wasn't good, but he's taken them off and put on Christ."

"So . . . ?"

She frowned. "So . . . ?"

"So what's the problem?"

"He wore Mickey ears."

"But he doesn't anymore, and it sounds to me like whatever he did is behind him and he's a new creation in Christ, or am I reading that wrong?"

"No. You just about nailed it, as usual." Harper was such a pain in her rear—always nailing things, which left little room for hiding.

"So, if that's the case, then what's the problem?"

Andi kicked her feet out in front of her. "I thought I knew Jeremy, but I didn't."

"You're comparing Christian to Jeremy again?"

"No. I'm just saying I don't exactly have the best track record when it comes to picking the right guy."

"Jeremy fooled everyone, and correct me if I'm wrong, but you and Christian aren't even an item yet, and he already felt compelled to tell you about Mickey ears in his closet. Sounds like strong integrity to me."

Huh. She hadn't thought of it that way. She needed to go back and talk to him.

Please, Father, my head is swirling. Help me know what to do, what to say. He's hurting, and I hate it. I beg your guidance and direction. Please see me through whatever this is. Wherever it's going. Let it be from Your hand.

FORTY-TWO

"WHO WAS THAT?" Deckard asked, returning to the car after going in the Jiffy Mart to pay for gas and grab a snack.

"Andi," Harper said.

He handed her the white plastic bag. "I didn't know what you liked, so I grabbed something salty and something sweet."

"Ah, thanks."

"The Ho Hos are mine." He smiled, and she laughed. "So everything okay back at the ranch?" he asked.

"I think so."

He arched a brow. "That doesn't sound convincing."

"Just a lot to take in."

"I hear that." He opened his Ho Hos and pulled back out on the road to Albuquerque.

Harper shifted in the passenger seat to face Deckard better. Since they were going to be working the case together, they didn't need two cars, so they decided to use hers. But already feeling a bout of sleepiness coming on, she'd asked Deckard if he'd mind driving, and he seemed more than happy to do so.

She was glad he took the back way—down 14 South. She liked it so much better than I-25. It possessed far more character and reminded her of a lazy river, just floating down, easily gliding around the turns. It was lulling.

She riffled through the bag. "Sweet tea?"

"That's for you," he said.

"Thanks." She twisted the top off and took a sip, then set it in the cupholder. "So . . ." she said, shifting to recline against the locked passenger door so she could face him better—read what she could of his expressions on the dark, winding road, though the almost-full moon overhead added some illumination. Making herself comfortable, she grabbed the autopsy report Greyson had provided and began again. "So where should we start?"

He glanced over, then back at the road. "Start?"

"We've got about an hour. I thought we could talk through the case file and autopsy report Greyson dug up."

He darted a glance over with an arched brow, then focused his attention back on the road. "I thought you were tired."

"So did I." She scanned the report. "But I think I got a second wind."

"Okay." He chuckled. "Where would you like to start?"

"Well, the autopsy report shows no defensive wounds on the victim. How is that possible, unless we go with my theory of her being hit from behind first?"

"Fair enough assumption."

"And the depth of the wound to the back of her head shows a strong impact. I'm holding by my theory."

He glanced over. "We'll have to see how it plays out, but I'm starting to think it's not good to bet against you."

She smiled, then shifted. She needed to ask him . . . but how to approach it. She shifted again.

"What's up, squirmy?"

"Sorry . . ." Her mind was diverted, and if she didn't ask, it appeared it would stay that way. "I have something to ask you. Well, more of a thought to express, but it brings things into question, so I'm . . ." She was hesitant to ask, given the ramifications if she was right. How Deckard would feel if it was true.

He released a chuckle beside her.

"What?" she asked, narrowing her eyes.

He chuckled again. "Do you always ramble like that?"

"No . . . yes." She gave a sheepish smile.

"Don't get me wrong." He smiled back. "I think it's adorable, but not something I've encountered before."

"Really? Riley never goes around and around like that?"

"No. As peppy as Riley is, she keeps most of her thoughts to herself."

Much like him, she imagined. "That's one way to go," she said, slipping her shoes off and dropping them on the floorboard—always more comfortable without them on.

"I think I'm afraid to ask what's in that mind of yours." A smile curled on his lips, headlights bouncing across his handsome face.

Too bad she couldn't have a relationship. Not while serving like she did with ICRC for two months every year, and a mission trip nearly every vacation week she got. Her attention and devotion needed to remain where God had called her—protecting the dignified treatment of the dead after conflict, disasters, or situations of violence, and helping to identify lost loved ones. It crushed her spirit seeing such death, such hurt, but God kept telling her to go, so she did, fully dependent on Him to carry her through and make her helpful.

Andi argued she could at least give a relationship a try, but what was the point? She didn't date just to date. She wanted to eventually find someone she could build a lasting relationship with, but given her work with ICRC, now was most definitely not the time. She couldn't have divided devotion. And why was she going there? It wasn't like Deckard had shown that type of interest in her. *Great.* Now her thoughts were rambling too.

"I lose you there?" he asked.

"Sorry. Woolgathering."

"Haven't heard that word in a while."

"No?"

"Nope. Riley calls it daydreaming, and boy, does that girl daydream."

"I think daydreams are nice." It was easy enough to slip into them while soaking up the sun on her patio, just letting her thoughts fly free.

"I suppose." He tapped the wheel.

She narrowed her eyes. "You don't think so?"

"Just never done it."

She sat forward. "You've seriously never daydreamed?"

"Nope."

"Well, that stinks."

He arched a brow, shooting a quick glance at her. "How do you figure that?"

"It's a great way to let your thoughts run free, to have dreams while you're awake and can remember them."

He drummed the wheel. "I'll take your word for it."

She reclined against the passenger door. Wisps of clouds slipped over the moon, casting an eerie atmosphere. Night held inky black around them. She shifted her gaze, focusing on the stars blanketing the sky.

Deckard shot her a smile, the movement crinkling the corners of his deep blue eyes, eyes that lit with the passing of a lone car—its headlights sweeping across his face. "You really shouldn't sit like that," he said. "It's not safe."

She tilted her head, confusion anchoring inside.

"If we were hit," he continued, "the airbag would jam your knees into your chest. I've lectured Riley on the same thing. Granted, as kids we never buckled. For goodness' sake, we'd sit on the floor of the backseat playing games or Riley—always the sun seeker—would lie up on the slim space by the rear window of the car, reading her book."

"I remember those days," she said, enjoying the slice of his childhood he'd just shared with her. "Okay," she said, lowering her knees and sliding them at an angle.

"Let's see, where were we?" she said. Or rather, where were her thoughts? "Okay, so we've run through what Andi did the night of Anne's murder in the lab. What I did and saw at the crime scene. Simmons's alibi and the fact his shirt went missing from the cleaners, which explains why none of his epithelial cells were in it—a seeming mistake on the killer's part in trying to set Simmons up."

"Very true. I hadn't considered that angle before, but valid point. And remind me what epithelial cells are?"

"Epithelial just means the thin tissue forming the outer layer of a body's surface."

"Right. Thanks."

"No problem. I know it is a scientific niche, and a lot of people don't understand what all we do."

"It sounds fascinating. Not my thing." He smiled. "But fascinating."

"It definitely can be."

"So your earlier question . . . ?" he asked.

"Right." She just needed to say it. "I've been wondering . . . what if the person or people who set Andi up . . . probably the same people in your office tonight or those working for them . . . What if they did so to intentionally get Mitch Abrams off?"

FORTY-THREE

HE HADN'T SEEN that one coming. "Are you saying you think Mitch is guilty?"

"I'm saying it's a possibility. Whoever set Andi up did so with the evidence that convicted Mitch Abrams. Discrediting her, destroying the DNA sample, and losing the shirt . . . or rather someone having stolen it is my guess. All of it exonerated Mitch . . . or at the very least, vacated his sentence."

"And if Andi made a mistake?" If he was considering her supposition, she needed to at least consider his.

"You still think she botched the job?" Disappointment filled her eyes and tone, which made him feel like a heel—questioning her friend. But they both had to stay open to the possibilities until definitive proof was found either way. After working for Mitch, he'd thought it had already been found. And it still might turn out that way, but given those in Andi's life, given how his brother looked at her, given the smart, enjoyable woman Andi turned out to be, for the first time, he prayed he was wrong.

"Not botched on purpose," he added, trying to cushion the blow. Why did Harper's disappointment hit him so? "*If* she botched the job, I believe it wasn't on purpose, but her results and testimony were the evidence that convicted Mitch." Even now, out of jail, Mitch had to live with that weight of stigma around his neck. Last time he saw Mitch, he'd split with his wife, was living in a rental place, and was focusing on rebuilding his company. He was a shadow of a man.

"So, you're saying you think Andi was negligent?" Harper pushed as they wove their way along the twisting road.

"No. I'm not. She has asked me to investigate whether or not she was set up. I can't have any opinion until I thoroughly investigate. Which means, I need to come at this as neutral as possible." And he was torn. If he proved Andi was set up, then the question became who'd done so and why. Which meant reevaluating everything he thought he knew.

"When you find Andi's innocent—and I have full faith you will—you'll have to ask yourself who stood to gain from setting her up. But even more so, why was she set up in the first place?"

That was a hard one to swallow, but Harper wasn't wrong. He no longer worked for Mitch. He worked for Andi, and more so for his brother, who'd pleaded with him to take the case. He needed to shift his mindset. Start the entire investigation from scratch—for Andi's sake and, even more importantly, to find the truth. "Good questions to ask, but remember Mitch had an alibi that night."

"And his alibi . . ." she said. "We should run through it."

"Right." He tapped the wheel, collecting his thoughts. "Mitch was down in Las Cruces at a conference when Anne was killed."

"Okay. What kind of conference?" she asked.

"He's a real estate developer, and the conference was about the development of public works and new planned communities."

"And did anyone vouch for him being there?" she asked.

"Everyone. It was a small conference. Maybe fifty people at most."

"So he was seen at the time of Anne's murder?"

"No, he said he had an awful headache and went to his room at about eight thirty."

"And you didn't find that suspicious?"

Granted, it was odd timing, but . . . "People get headaches."

"So at the time Anne was murdered, Mitch was alone in his room?" she said, skepticism rich in her soothing voice. He'd never had a voice calm him before, but hers oddly did, despite the topic of their discussion.

"Yes," he continued. "Mitch said he called Anne to say good night a little after ten and went to sleep."

"So there's a call between them that night?" She shifted, sitting with her back fully against the seat.

They rounded the last bend, and the brilliant lights of Albuquerque and expansive metro areas shone like a thousand candles in the midst of a dark desert.

He looked over, and she was smiling—a wide one that lit her face in the hazy moonlight.

She glanced over. "Beautiful, aren't they?" she said. "I never tire of entering the city at night."

"Beautiful," he said, more of her than the lights, but she was right.

"So back to the phone call . . ." It didn't take her long to refocus.

"Right. It lasted roughly five minutes." The case details were cemented in his head.

"Did Anne receive any other calls that night?"

"According to her phone records, which Mitch's defense attorney let me see, no. Mitch's was the only call that night, but Simmons had called the night before, and they had a twenty-minute conversation. Mitch said Anne told him about the call—that Simmons said how desperately he wanted to be back with her, but she'd told him she'd found someone new. According to Mitch, he did not take it well."

"According to Mitch, huh? I'm assuming the police asked Simmons about the nature of the call?"

"Yes, according to my sources, Simmons claimed he only called to say he missed her, and noted that she sounded 'off.'"

They rolled into the city, lights surrounding them. "Take a right on Tramway. I'm up in Sandia Heights."

"So you've got a great view," he said.

She nodded. "A breathtaking one." She inhaled, then streamed it out, raking a hand through her golden hair.

"Oh, you're going to want to take a right up here onto San Rafael. You'll see O'Beans Coffee just before the corner."

"Got it." He flipped on his blinker and made the right.

"Head straight back. It's the second-to-last driveway on your right before you hit Honeysuckle Drive."

"Wow. You live *way* back here." He looked to the foothills the community nestled against.

"I love it. You can hear coyotes at night, see the lights of Albuquerque almost as good as when you enter on 40."

Deckard followed the road, and she waited to point her driveway out. "One more question before we get home . . . my home . . . You know what I mean."

Home. He was just starting to get the concept with his ranch. But it still didn't feel permanent . . . *settled.* The fear it could be ripped away still lingered, and he hated his parents for that.

"Is it possible Mitch drove back or was already on the way back toward Albuquerque when he placed the call?" she asked. "He met her, killed her, and headed back to his hotel in Cruces well before morning?"

"It's a three-hour drive each way," he said.

"Next driveway." She pointed.

He turned onto her drive and pulled to a stop in front of her condo's two-car garage. "Nice place," he said.

"It's home." She smiled.

Home. There was that notion again.

"What do you think?" she said, her hand on the door handle. "Is it possible?"

"That Mitch drove there and back? It's possible." He exhaled. "But we really should focus on Andi's situation—work the facts to figure out whether or not she was set up. That's the job."

"Job? That sounds so . . ."

"Sorry." He shrugged. "It's easy to get pulled in too deep. I've found I need to keep a level of distance between me and the case. That's why I worry about you working it. It's hard to remain neutral when a person cares so much."

She climbed out, and he did the same, grabbing his backpack from the backseat.

"I appreciate your concern," she said, leading him up the shale stone pathway around to the front door, which sat on what looked like the side of her house. "But I'm good." She held out her hand, and he dropped the keys into her palm. "Thanks for driving."

"No worries. But seriously, what if the investigation proves Andi botched the job?" He wasn't trying to be harsh. He just wanted her to be prepared if it came out that way.

"We won't find that because she didn't," she said, continuing before he could get another word in. "Now, back to Mitch." She unlocked the door and shoved it open with a push of her shoulder. "It sticks," she said with a shrug.

He stepped in after her. "You really should leave at least one interior light on while you're away. It's not safe to come home to a dark house." He looked around, the front door still open behind him. "Especially being so far out here."

"You're probably right. Andi gets on me all the time."

"You two are close."

"Very," she said. "She's my bestie."

He smiled at the term. Riley had a few friends, but none she'd label as a bestie. She, like her brothers, kept her emotional distance, never relying on anyone outside of one another.

Harper flipped on a light. "Grab the door, would you?"

"Sure." He shut it behind them, locked it, and put the chain in place. He turned to find her standing there, hands on her hips.

"Look," she said, "we're coming at this case from opposing perspectives, so for now I say we agree to disagree."

"Sounds fair."

"But just for the record, I believe the two cases are intertwined—Mitch and Andi's. Intertwined so deeply that if we only pull one thread, we'll miss the full picture."

FORTY-FOUR

ANDI PADDED in bare feet toward the bedroom door. She'd waited so long to make a decision, to know it was the right thing to do, she feared Christian was already crashed out on the couch, but she had to see, had to try, or she'd never sleep.

She eased the door open, having heard him enter the house a while ago. A small light was on in the front room, but he could have fallen asleep with it on. She tiptoed out and peeked around the corner but found the couch empty.

Huh. Her shoulders dropped. She looked toward the dark kitchen and back to the bathroom with the open door.

Had he slipped back out to the firepit?

She wrapped her arms around her waist and stepped out back. The chill of night dipped low, and she wished she'd grabbed a jacket or a blanket, but he caught sight of her, and she wasn't turning back.

"Hey," he said, straightening on the sofa, one arm draped across the back of it.

She took a seat beside him.

"Here," he said, offering her the throw blanket he had across his lap.

"Oh, I don't want to—" Before she could fully protest, he'd draped it across her shoulders. "Thanks," she said, "but won't you be cold?"

"Nah, the fire is still pretty hot."

She bit her bottom lip. "We could share."

His heady gaze fixed on hers. "We can?"

She nodded and slipped the throw from her shoulders and laid it across their laps, scooting closer so it covered them both.

Knowing what she wanted to say but needing to gather her courage, she bit her bottom lip. How did the man make her feel at ease and at the same time so discombobulated? "I . . ." She cleared her throat. "I'm sorry I rushed off."

He shifted to face her head-on, his shoulder brushing hers in the process.

She warmed at his touch. He wasn't making this any easier, dizzying her thoughts so. "I—"

"I know it's a lot to take in," he said. "I understand if you want to . . . if you need to . . ."

"What I need is to tell you . . ." She took a deep inhale and released it, gathering her boldness. "I'm so glad you found Jesus." She reached out and took his hand.

He interlocked his fingers with hers.

"I'm so happy that He helped you become the man you are." There, she'd said it. Part of it anyway, but now she knew God was carrying the words out of her. "We're both a new creation in Christ. And I'm so glad you trusted me enough to tell me about your past."

He gave a soft nod, his deep brown eyes searching hers.

"What you shared . . . the fact that you shared . . . only makes me want what is happening between . . ." She bit her bottom lip, emotions wobbling like a Tilt-A-Whirl inside her. Her thoughts dizzied.

He scooted closer still, the warmth of his leg rubbing hers. "Between?"

She fiddled with their fingers interlaced together, then looked up at him. "Between us."

"So . . ." He swallowed, his Adam's apple bobbing. "There's still a chance for us to pursue an *us*?"

She nodded, heat flushing her cheeks.

Reaching up, he cupped her face, caressing her cheek with the pad of his thumb.

Butterflies pinged through her.

"I'm so glad," he whispered, his lips inching closer to hers, their breath mingling.

"Me too," she whispered back. The words had barely crossed her lips when he pressed his to hers. Ever-so-slow and tender at first, their kiss deepened. Emotion whiplashed through her as she clung tighter to him, pulling him close.

He slipped his strong arm around her, his sturdy hand splaying across the center of her back.

Heat infused her as his scent enveloped her—wild and free.

She kissed him back with all she had, never wanting the kiss to end. Time faded, the minutes swirling together.

Trill. Trill. Trill.

Noooo.

Christian pulled back ever-so-softly, his breathing hard. "That . . . we . . . that was . . ." he murmured, his forehead pressed to hers as the ringing of his cell stopped.

She nodded, her breath taken away. *That kiss.*

His phone rang again, his hand still resting on the small of her back.

No.

He sighed and peeled himself away. "I better . . ."

She nodded. Given everything going on, no matter how much she wanted them to ignore it, he needed to answer.

He looked at his phone. "It's Joel."

At this point, she feared what news might come.

FORTY-FIVE

HARPER FLIPPED A SWITCH on the hallway wall, and light flooded her home.

"Come on in," she said, leading him down the short foyer hall and into what could only be described as a greenhouse with potted plants lining the perimeter of the space. Windows, two stories high, surrounded them. His gaze followed them up to the vaulted ceiling and a loft overhead. A jungle's worth of flowering plants sat on the loft's wide ledge, vines spiraling down.

A U-shaped sectional sofa sat flanked by two armchairs with those fluff-ball ottomans Riley loved. An area rug covered the tile floor, and a cool old trunk sat in the center of the seating arrangement. He smiled. Harper Grace hadn't ceased to surprise him. She was one cool chick, and if things were different, if *he* were different, he'd definitely pursue getting to know her on a deeper level. "Nice place," he said, following her in as she turned on more lights, strategically placed throughout the living space.

She looked up at him, her blonde hair spilling over her shoulder. "Thanks. I moved in a couple years ago, and I love it. You'll see it in the morning, but I have the best view of the sunrise. If you're up that early."

"I'm always up for the sunrise. I don't need much sleep." It'd come from never really being able to securely fall asleep at night—always needing to be somewhat alert for what might come. A last-minute dash to a "safer" motel. A drive to a middle-of-nowhere town to hide from the last man they should have conned. It'd cost his dad's life, landed his mom in jail, but thankfully hadn't touched them. Though that fear always weighed in the back of his mind—that someone would harm his siblings.

"Cool," Harper said, thankfully having no idea of the hardened memories streaking through his mind. "I'll set the coffeemaker to go off at five."

He chuckled. How did she manage that? To bring light into his darkness so easily. "I'm not up quite *that* early." He rolled out of bed just before daybreak.

"Gotcha. Well, coffee will be waiting when you get up."

"Thanks. Where should I put my pack?" he asked. Packing light was a safety measure he'd held on to since childhood. *Be packed and on the road in under two minutes.*

"Come on," she said, moving for the back hall. "I'll show you to the guest bedroom." She opened the first door on the left and flipped on the light switch. "Here we are."

A queen-sized bed with pink flowers across the comforter and white pillows that looked like shag carpeting covered the bed. He arched a brow and looked back at her.

"Sorry for the girly decoration. My niece comes to stay with me for a while in the summer, so I let her decorate the room."

"Nice aunt."

"I've got to be the favorite one, you know." She winked.

He smiled. "Do you have a big family?"

"Five of us. Four girls and one poor guy who has to put up with all of us." She chuckled. "Well . . ." She remained standing close to him, fiddling with a strand of her hair. "I guess I should let you get settled. It's late."

He swallowed, attraction sifting through him. "Sounds good," he managed, not wanting her to leave. "I'll see you at 0600."

She nodded. "Sleep tight."

A smile tugged at his lips at the expression. "Thanks. You too."

It took her a moment, but she turned and headed back for the living room.

Entering the bedroom, he set his pack on the frilly bed and chuckled. If Riley saw where he was sleeping, she'd never stop razzing him.

He pulled his lounge pants out of the pack and set the bag aside.

Sliding his shirt over his head, he took the sniff test. It smelled like the firepit. He glanced to the adjacent bathroom. Best wash it out and save his second T-shirt for another day as he imagined they'd be hunkered here a while.

He pulled the sink plug, turned the water on, and pumped some of the hand soap in. Once it filled halfway, he shut off the warm water spewing in and stuck his shirt in, scrunching it about.

A knock sounded on the door.

"Come in," he called over his shoulder.

"I forgot to give you some towels for the morn—" She stopped short.

He pushed the stopper bar down, and the water drained.

She cocked her head, a ripe blush on her cheeks. "What are you doing?"

"Washing my shirt." He rinsed it out.

"I have a washing machine . . ." she said as he wrung the shirt out and hung it over the shower bar. He reached for the stack of towels in her hands.

"Right," she said, passing them over.

He set them on the counter and used the small towel to dry his hands.

"Just routine when I travel," he said. "I'm usually in motels without washing machines."

"Very Jack Reacher." She smiled.

As much as he loved the first *Jack Reacher* movie, he'd learned how to live on the road years before it released. Learned how to run and how to stay off-grid. It was no wonder Riley excelled as a skip tracer. She'd learned from a young age how to get lost and the tactics used to do so. All she did was think like the person she was tracking, and she caught them every single time.

"Well . . ." Harper murmured, backing up. "I better head to bed. Night again."

He smiled. "Night, Harper."

———

She closed the guest room door behind her and leaned against it. *Wowza*. She'd never seen a more beautiful man. Not beautiful in a girly way. No, there was nothing girly about Deckard MacLeod. He was all man. If she was interested in pursuing a relationship . . . but she was not. Why did she suddenly have to keep reminding herself of that?

Pressing off the wall, she shook her head. But if she was interested in a relationship, it would be with a man like Deckard MacLeod. He was strong, loyal to his family, intelligent . . . but haunted. By what, she didn't know, and she'd resist the urge to pry. It was clear he was uber-private about his life. Guarded. But she ached to know, ached to see the hurt he wore like a cloak disappear.

She sank down on the couch and bowed her head, unable to rest yet.

Father, I pray for Deckard. For the pain I see etched in his eyes, always lingering there, even when he smiles. I don't know what haunts him, but I can see it runs deep. I pray you'll lift that burden from him. Let him breathe the fresh air of peace in you. In Jesus' name I pray.

——— ■ ■ ———

"Are you there?" Teresa asked.

Cyrus stepped outside, his partner asleep. Of course it would be raining. He stood under the overhang, far happier with their base for this heist. It was a serious upgrade from the trailer.

"Hello?" she said, her pitch rising.

"Yes," he ground out.

"I have to say I don't like this attitude. I think you've forgotten who you're dealing with."

"Oh, I'm sure you'll remind me all about your husband and his thugs. Speaking of thugs, have you settled Enrique down to observe and restrain?"

"Perhaps."

He clenched his teeth. "I've told you I need Casey, and that's his condition. The guy and the girl stay alive. For now." Though he was far more interested in the girl. If Enrique hurt her, he'd kill him. What happened to her was his choice, not the thug's and certainly not Teresa's. She'd already stolen a woman from his life once, he would not let it happen again. Andi Forester was his to do with as he liked.

"I don't like it," she said, her nails tapping incessantly on the other end. Always tapping one surface or another.

"Neither do I." He loathed being dependent on someone, but he needed Casey's skills. All of them played a role for now—even Andi and Christian. In the end, it would be him holding all the goods and Teresa with the fakes she'd never see coming. Mostly fakes. He'd researched the items for years, had fakes made and stashed in each location near the true stashes. But with the recent collection at Tad's Albuquerque gallery being added to the list by Teresa, he didn't have time for his guy to fashion replicas, so those artifacts would be real, but it didn't matter. He'd have more money to sail away into the sunset with than he could use in a lifetime.

The thought of one-upping Teresa heated his limbs. Finally, he'd pay her back for her cruelty, her mocking, and her killing Mandy. After what his girlfriend had done to him—leaving him holding the proverbial bag and landing him in the slammer—he'd plotted revenge but learned Teresa had already seen to it. But she was also his to do with as he willed. It wasn't Teresa's place. It was time she learned it.

"Are you still there?" she asked with an air of impatience.

"Yes. What do you want, Teresa?"

"Just checking on my investment."

"I told you we're set."

"And you're not taking too much heat? You can pull this off?"

So little faith in him. "I've got this."

"We'll see." A blip interrupted their call. "I've got to go. Enrique is on the other line."

He stiffened, wondering what the thug was up to now.

"By the way," she said before cutting off their call, "that witch shot him."

He erupted in laughter. "What?"

"They saw him watching, and there was some sort of chase, and she shot him in the shoulder, but I fail to see the humor in it."

She would, but he didn't. His feisty girl was even more spirited than he realized, and the thought heated his limbs.

The call dropped, thankfully. He had weightier matters to deal with than Teresa.

The door opened behind him, and Casey stuck his head out. "What are you doing out here?" he asked, rubbing the sleep from his eyes.

"Grabbing a smoke."

"I thought I heard laughter . . . talking."

"Nope. Just me and a smoke." He pulled one from his pocket and, cupping his hands over it in the rain, lit it.

Casey frowned. He wasn't buying it.

Cyrus winced. He needed to be more careful. The last thing he needed was the pawn catching on to the real plan.

FORTY-SIX

HE'D KISSED ANDI, and it had been like no other kiss he'd experienced, though the list wasn't long. Given his past, he'd always kept impenetrable boundaries in place with the two girls he'd dated, and neither of them lasted beyond a month.

Lord, you know I've prayed for you to bring the woman you created for me into my life in your timing. The way I feel about Andi . . . you know. You know my heart and my hurts, and I need you to lead me by your Holy Spirit. Give me wisdom and discernment. The thought of being vulnerable terrifies me, and after the attempts on our lives, the case terrifies me too, especially for Andi's safety. The notes have been left for her, and she's garnered enemies in the course of her career.

They needed to research all the men and women she'd busted, whether in jail or out on community service. One of them could be back at it, pulling her into this nasty game.

Help me protect her. I just found hope with Andi. Please don't let it be dashed. And let my full hope rest in you, in your sufficiency to keep us safe and to guide us. To walk beside us and never leave us. Thank you, Lord.

He prayed he'd be able to protect her. Protect them for what was coming next, because his gut said the stakes were going to continue to increase. This game was far from over, and only growing more deadly.

The motel room reeked of smoke and rotting fruit. Deckard shifted through what was left of their food supply. He could go without food, but Riley was clutching her stomach, her unspoken sign of hunger. He reached for the bread bag, but only a moldy crust remained. Maybe he could cut that part off and still make her a sandwich. It'd been four days this time, and every time they left, he feared—and hoped—they wouldn't return.

He shook his head, hating what he was going to do, but what choice did he have? He pulled out the few measly dollars he'd stashed under the top sheet of his mattress on the floor. He'd given Riley one of the beds. His parents claimed the other. Christian took the meager sofa, his long legs sprawled out over the edge. Good. He was asleep. His little brother wouldn't know what he was about to do.

Heading out into the dark, solemn night and locking the door behind him, he took off on foot for the Jiffy Mart, his plan firmly in place, despite how much he hated the thought of it. Riley needed food.

Entering the Jiffy Mart, he lifted his chin at the cashier—a teen reading a magazine, clearly bored in the wee hours of the night.

He made his rounds. Grabbed the couple items he could afford. A candy bar and a soda. But it wasn't enough, given they had no idea when or if their parents would return.

While the cashier wasn't watching, he noted the cameras and moved around them, slipping more food into his bag. Once finished, he headed for the register. Paid for the two items and headed back out into the night.

Guilt shrouded him as he walked back to the seedy motel in the Middle of Nowhere, USA. Overwhelming shame gripped him, his limbs tightening. The pressure on his chest increased until he couldn't breathe. He fought the urge to cry, to scream, but he couldn't hold it in. "Why?" he hollered to the sky, convinced no one was listening. They were on their own, and there was no rescue coming. "When will this stop? Just make it stop."

A knock rapped. Was he back at the motel already? No. He was walking down a dark alley.

The knock rapped again.

"Deckard?"

Harper's voice reached through to him, and he shot up in bed—his skin drenched in sweat, the blankets and sheets completely asunder. He pinched the bridge of his nose. Another stupid nightmare. Would they never cease?

Light streamed in from the hallway as the door cracked. "Can I come in?"

He straightened the blanket over him. "Sure," he said, raking a hand through his hair—damp along the base of his neck.

He swiped his forehead as she opened the door fully and stepped in at a gentle, almost hesitant pace, wearing colorful cacti PJ bottoms and a matching T-shirt with a blooming cactus on it.

"You okay?" He scooched up to sit with his back against the headboard.

"I'm fine, but you didn't sound like it. I heard . . ."

He took a steadying inhale. *Great.* She'd heard him. "It was just a nightmare. They happen."

She moved to the side of his bed, hovering there.

He patted the mattress by his legs. "You can take a seat."

"Thanks," she said, doing so.

"I'm sorry if I woke you." Embarrassment flushed over him. He rarely got embarrassed, but this was flat-out mortification.

"I'm not worried about that. I just wanted to make sure you were okay." Concern filled her beautiful green eyes.

"I'm fine. Just a stupid nightmare. They happen." He repeated the line he used whenever he was in a situation like this. Though, being within earshot of someone else rarely happened. Usually it was just him and his demons.

FORTY-SEVEN

ANDI WOKE to the homey scent of cinnamon. And not just cinnamon but sweet icing too. She sat up. Cinnamon buns. Had Christian made breakfast for her?

Climbing out of bed, she cracked the door, hoping to get to the bathroom without being seen so she could at least brush her hair and teeth.

"Morning," he said, making her jump. "Sorry. Didn't mean to startle you. Was just using the loo."

"All good." Wondering just how much of a mess she looked, she pressed her lips together, remembering the feel of his on hers. "Morning."

"I made breakfast," he said.

"It smells wonderful. I'm just going to duck into the bathroom, and I'll be right out."

"Sounds like a plan."

She stepped inside the bathroom, closed the door, and looked into the mirror. Yikes! Her hair looked like a wookie. She grabbed the hairbrush Riley had lent her along with a new toothbrush and paste. Maybe while they were running around for interviews today, they could grab some items from her house.

Taking care of her hair, teeth, and deodorant—the vital three—she looked back in the mirror. Pale with dark circles. Great. She grabbed the tinted moisturizer and dabbed it under her eyes and across her face, giving her a little shine. She added a swipe of Burt's Bees tinted lip balm, and with a deep breath, wondering what the day would hold, headed for the kitchen.

The scent of cinnamon buns infused the air, mingling with Christian's outdoorsy aftershave. She wasn't sure which smelled better.

"Coffee's ready," he said, gesturing to the pot.

"Thanks." She needed copious amounts after tossing all night.

"You sleep okay?" he asked.

"Not really," she answered honestly.

"Me either. Too much happening."

"Too much?" Was he referring to the case or the kiss?

"We have a target on us. And having to constantly cover our backs makes it hard to focus on the case itself."

"Agreed." She held her mug with both hands, warmth seeping through the ceramic.

"Let me grab you a roll, and we can go over our day."

"Sounds good. They smell yummy."

"They're just the Pillsbury ones, but I like them." He plated one for her and set it at the high-top kitchen table.

She took a seat opposite him and took a bite. "Delicious," she said, licking a streak of icing from her finger. "Where should we start our interviews today?" He knew everyone in town. She knew no one. Best to let him pick the order.

"I think our first interview should be with Sarah Basinger."

"Okay. Why? I'm good with whatever you think, but just curious why her?"

"Because she was the town librarian for nearly four decades."

"The town librarian." She wasn't tracking the connection. "I'm guessing she was at the gala?"

"Oh yes. She attends every function in town. Knows everyone and everything."

That explained it. "So she's the town gossip?"

"In a way, yes," he said, taking a sip of his coffee.

"In a way?"

"Sarah knows all, and I mean all, but she's judicious about who she shares the snippets of knowledge with. She doesn't gossip just to gossip. She's more like a news cable dispensing critical information to those who need it."

"She sounds interesting," Andi said before taking another bite of her roll. It melted in her mouth. "These are seriously amazing."

He smiled. "I'm glad you like them."

"Sorry for getting off topic. You were telling me about Sarah."

"She's a fascinating lady and has done so much. She rafted the Grand Canyon while camping out along the way, hiked the Appalachian Trail—the full trail by herself—and even went skydiving not so long ago."

"That's amazing. So if she was the librarian for four decades, how old is she?"

"Eighty-three. She retired about ten years back."

"Wow, and she still attends every town function?"

"And walks three miles every day. I see her every morning when I'm headed to the office."

"Since you live so close to Jeopardy Falls and it's such a cool town, why is your office in Santa Fe? More people, more traffic going by it?"

"Greyson moved the office from Tucson to Santa Fe, and when he sold it to Deckard, he decided he wanted to keep it out of our town, away from our ranch. Some of the people we work for are . . ."

He couldn't be about to say "less than savory," as she couldn't picture any of them taking on those types of clients. Not now that she had spent time with them—even Deckard MacLeod, of all people. Funny the difference a day or two could make.

"Sometimes," he continued, "the people we work with have others who want to harm them or keep something hidden, even come to the office to threaten us to back off."

"I imagine that doesn't go over well."

"Nah. Riley gives them heck."

She laughed. "I can see that." She speared a forkful of cinnamon roll. "She and Greyson are funny together."

"Yeah." He shook his head and smiled. "It's like an older, refined brother and a wild, barrel-racing younger sister. Polar-opposite personalities. They're usually the ones running the office, when she's not skip tracing."

"I wouldn't have called Riley being a skip tracer."

"Yeah," he said, setting his coffee cup down. "It comes from us hiding as kids. She knows how those who are hiding think, and she's super talented at tracking them down."

"Sounds like it."

"She also helps people get lost," he added, pushing his empty plate to the side.

"Like WITSEC?"

"More like abused women, women escaping sex trafficking, that type of thing."

"Wow. That's so cool. You all are uniquely talented, but the one I'm curious about is Greyson. I just got this mysterious vibe from him at dinner last night."

"Greyson is the most generous man I know, and he excels at everything he does. He took Deckard on when he was just starting out, gave him a job, taught him everything . . . Well, probably not everything, knowing Greyson. Then he decided he wanted to slow things down, so he sold the firm to Deckard."

"And stayed on in the support role."

He nodded.

"Intriguing."

"That's a good word for him." Christian chuckled.

"I best go get ready," she said, hopping down and carrying her plate to the sink.

"I'll take care of the dishes. You get ready, and I'll run you through the rest of the interviews on our list for today."

"Sounds like a plan."

Andi settled in the passenger seat, smiling at the quaint town of Jeopardy Falls as they drove through it.

"Sarah lives just a few minutes away," Christian said, "but would you like to grab some fuel for the day? Java Joe's is right around the corner, and they have the best nitro brew."

"Yum. Yes, please."

His cell rang as he pulled up. "Deckard," he said, glancing at the phone screen.

"Why don't I run in and grab our drinks while you talk?" she offered.

"Great. I'll take a nitro cold brew black. Thanks," he said.

"You got it."

Ten minutes later, she exited the shop, the burgeoning wind whipping the hair about her face.

Christian hopped out and opened the door for her. "Thanks."

She climbed inside, and he followed suit.

"How's everything with Harper and Deckard?"

"Good, they're heading out for their first interview."

The thought of Deckard MacLeod on her case still seemed so surreal.

Christian looked over and gave her hand a squeeze before pulling out. "If anyone can find the truth, it's Deck. You're in good hands."

She prayed he was right.

He arched a brow. "You don't look convinced."

"It's just new to me, and . . ."

"And?"

"My DNA testing put Mitch Abrams at the crime. Deckard believed him innocent and got him off. I don't see how the two can both be right."

"That's a good point," Christian said, finally having a clear opening to reverse out of the lot. He shifted into drive and headed back up the hill they'd come down. "Shortcut to Sarah's." He then slowed to wait for kids riding their bikes on the neighborhood roads to move to the side.

"I always loved riding my bike. Just something freeing about it."

"Yeah, I never learned."

She dipped her head, feeling awful she'd brought up something that made perfect sense he wouldn't have been able to do. "I'm sorry. I . . ."

"All good." He shrugged. "Just never took the opportunity. I can ride a motorcycle and a horse. Just never tried a bike," he said as he pulled in the driveway of a caramel-colored adobe home. He shifted the Equinox into park and cut the ignition.

"We have to rectify that when this case is over," she said, sliding closer to him. "I know the perfect place, and we can take a picnic with us."

He squeezed her hand again. "That sounds perfect." He tilted his head and cupped her face.

Without thinking, she leaned into him, and he placed a soft, lingering kiss to her lips. "I've been wanting to do that all morning," he whispered, kissing her again. She got lost in the feel of his lips on hers, his breath mingling with hers.

He pulled back just enough to break the kiss.

Come back.

"I wasn't sure . . . if . . . how . . ." he murmured.

She slipped her hair behind her ear. "How things would be this morning? If we were . . ." she said, nudging him along.

"Moving forward?" he said.

"Yeah." She held her breath. *Please say yes.*

He caressed her cheek. "I hope so with all my being." He leaned back in, his hand slipping behind her neck, his fingers running through her hair.

"Are you two going to sit and canoodle all day in my driveway?" a woman said.

Andi flung back, her eyes opening wide. She looked over at the elderly woman standing in front of the car, one hand on her hip, a smirk on her lips.

Oh sheesh. She'd been so caught up in Christian, she'd forgotten they were in someone else's driveway.

He gave a we-got-caught smile and hopped out of the car. "Sorry, Mrs. Basinger."

He moved around to open Andi's door.

"No need to say sorry. Come on inside. I've made tea."

Andi tilted her head. "How'd you know we were coming?"

"When you get this age, you know everything, Miss Forester."

Andi looked at Christian. Apparently, she did know everything. Andi smiled. She had a good feeling they just might get a nugget of a clue they desperately needed to move the case forward.

FORTY-EIGHT

CHRISTIAN FOLLOWED MRS. BASINGER around her front walk, Andi beside him.

Mrs. Basinger opened her bright blue door front door that she'd painted with bright red and yellow tulips.

"Come in, dears." She moved to offer them passage. "Have a seat in the front room and I'll get us some tea."

"That's kind but not necessary, Mrs. Basinger," Christian said.

She turned on him, her face pinched in an expression of scolding. "What do I keep telling you, young man?"

"Sarah," he said with a nod.

"Better." She smiled, then turned toward her kitchen, her multicolored yoga pants and bright purple shirt bringing a smile to his lips. So full of life and character.

Andi sat on the loveseat facing the front window, sunlight spilling through the upper panes as the still-cool wind danced through the open lower screen.

He strode over and took a seat beside her.

"Now," Sarah said, carrying a wobbling tray toward the coffee table in front of them.

He hopped to his feet.

"Don't you dare," she said before he could take a step.

"I was just going to help."

"And I appreciate it," Sarah said, "but I'm perfectly capable."

He hesitated as the tray shook in her hands.

Sarah arched her narrow brows higher, and without another word he sat.

Andi smothered a giggle beside him, and it brought a smile to his face.

"Now," Sarah said, finally setting the tray on the table. She lifted a sloshing pitcher of tea. "Who would like a glass?"

"I'd love one. Thank you," Andi said, and Christian followed suit.

Once they both had a drink and a biscochito cookie in hand, Sarah took a seat in the armchair across from them.

"How can I be of help?" she asked. "I heard you two are investigating the heist sprees going on."

"Yes, ma'am." Christian cleared his throat at Sarah's disapproving glance. "Sarah."

"Could you tell us about the gala?" Andi asked.

"What about the gala, specifically?"

"She likes questions to be specific and concise," he whispered under his breath to Andi.

Andi nodded and redirected her attention to Sarah. "What time did you arrive?"

"At half past eleven."

"So a half hour before it ended?" Andi said.

"Yes, dear." Sarah lifted a biscochito to her mouth painted rose with lipstick and took a delicate bite, then swallowed and wiped her mouth with one of the navy cocktail napkins she'd brought on the gold serving tray. "Let me guess, dear. You were assuming I arrived at the start and left early?"

Andi's lashes fluttered again. "I . . ."

"Oh, no harm, dear." Sarah smiled. "It's only natural to assume a woman of my maturity would be home early and off to bed, but I think the end of the party is when the real party begins." She lifted her hand to her chest. "Oh, I don't participate." She laughed. "The look on your face . . ."

Andi's cheeks flushed pink.

"I don't go in for all that carrying on, but at that late hour of a gala—or let's just call it what it was at that hour, a party—that's when you see who's really who."

"I hadn't thought of it like that," Andi said. "But it does make sense."

"It's like having the best seats to a show. It's how I know so much." She winked at Christian.

He mushed his lips together to hide a smile. Sarah Basinger was such a character.

"And did you see anything noteworthy?" Andi asked.

"Now you're asking the right questions, dear," Sarah said, sitting back and crossing her legs. Her bright floral yoga pants against the geometric upholstery made for one funky pattern. Sarah had been a renowned painter before rheumatoid arthritis had stolen her delicate painting skills, but she'd taken to bigger projects like the front door or the mural on the back of her house. She had the best attitude—one he greatly admired.

"I don't know if it's noteworthy in the truest sense of the term, but . . ." Sarah leaned forward as if about to impart a secret just between her and Andi. "I did see a woman I didn't recognize get out of a black sedan. Well, it was dark . . . so a dark sedan."

Right about the time their mystery woman showed up on camera.

"Did she have long, dark hair?" Andi asked, leaning forward too.

"No . . . and then yes." Sarah smiled.

Christian blinked.

"I don't follow," Andi said.

"I saw a woman with spiky blonde hair step out of the passenger seat of the car. Then whoever was driving yelled at her and threw a wig out the window. She put it on. A long, dark one."

Andi looked at him, her eyes alight. If he didn't know better, he'd say with mischief. "Our mystery woman."

"Were you able to see her face?" Andi asked, excitement bubbling in her voice.

Christian held his breath until Sarah answered. This could be the break they needed.

"Oh my. Yes. But I didn't expect such excitement over it."

"Thus far, you're the only one to remember seeing her face," Andi explained.

"Well, I suppose I was the only sober one at that hour. Most were walking around in a haze or laughing stupor," she said.

"Could we take you to the station to work with the sketch artist?"

"No," Sarah said.

"No?" Christian frowned.

"Oh, I'll go and do it, but there's no need for you two to take me. You have plenty on your hands, and I'm sure more people to interview. I can see myself down the handful of blocks just fine."

Christian looked to Andi. Might the danger spill over to Sarah? Andi nodded. "Sarah, I think we—"

"Don't say it again, young man. Thugs don't scare me." Andi's eyes widened as the sweet lady continued. "If there comes a day I can't walk the streets of this town on my own, it may as well be my last."

"Okay then. Well, thank you," Christian said, as Sarah got to her feet.

"It's no trouble. Would it also help to know the license plate of the car she arrived in?"

After an unhelpful stop at the home of two gala attendees who reluctantly admitted they didn't remember anything after the first hour of the gala, Christian and Andi planned their next step parked back outside of Java Joe's over a second nitro and a couple of glazed doughnuts.

Once again, Christian's cell rang. "O'Brady." It was good that information was coming in, but he was hoping for a few quiet moments with Andi, and perhaps another world-shaking kiss.

"It's Joel," his friend said on the other line.

"Hey, Joel. Let me put you on speaker so Andi can hear, if that's all right?"

"Of course," Joel said.

Christian switched the call to speaker and turned the volume fully up for the sheriff. "You're a go," Christian said.

Joel cleared his throat. "I just wanted to let you know that Sarah was able to give us a full description that led to a detailed sketch. We've got it running on the news now."

"And the license plate number she remembered?" Andi asked.

"We traced it to a car stolen out of a parking garage downtown. Owner reported it missing that same night, and a patrol car found it abandoned across town. We've asked Santa Fe CSI to run it for prints. I doubt we'll get anything useful, but I'll keep you posted."

"Thanks, Joel."

"You two have any luck?"

"Beyond Sarah's help, no. But we're heading to Brad Melling's house. Maybe we'll garner some interesting information there. There's certainly no love lost between him and Gaiman."

"You think he could have been involved?" Joel asked.

"He's one of the top suspects," Andi said.

"Oh?" Joel asked.

"He had a strong motive for wanting to get back at Gaiman, which puts him near the top of my list," Andi answered.

"Who else is up there?" Joel asked. "Curious if we're on the same wavelength."

"Brad Melling, Veronica Gaiman, and Tad, of course."

"You think he robbed his own gallery? I mean, I know that happens, but Tad seems so squirmish."

"I don't trust Tad as far as I can throw him. I can't explain it, but there's something unsettling there," she said.

"Well, keep me posted," Joel said. "And I'll return the courtesy."

"Of course," Christian said, then ended the call. He glanced over at Andi and smiled.

"What?" She furrowed her brow.

"Nah. It's just the first time I've heard you go by your gut."

"I don't trust it very often."

"Maybe you should trust it more," he said, running the back of his fingers along her neck, wishing they had more time. The look in her eyes said she was wishing it too, then something shifted.

He cocked his head. "What's wrong?"

She pursed her lips.

"What's that face for?" He chuckled. "Looks like you ate something sour."

"It's just . . ." She shifted to face him better. "I wholeheartedly believe someone set me up, but what if I was wrong?"

He frowned. "About being set up?" He didn't believe that for a second. She was too good and meticulous to botch a job, and that wasn't just the amazing way she made him feel, how she made him want to be a better man just for her. His gut said she was innocent of all the claims.

She fiddled with the black tassel on her blouse. "No." She shifted, pulling her knee up on the seat.

"Then what?" he asked, resting his hand on it.

"What if I was wrong about Mitch?" she said, her voice quiet.

"What do you mean?"

"What if he was innocent and what I said sent an innocent man to jail?"

"You reported what you found."

"A partial match to Mitch Abrams. Though *partial* in this case means a rare chance it wasn't him." She hesitated, biting her lip. "But a chance still existed."

"You testified it was a partial match. You did the work and told the truth."

"But how can we both be right?"

"You and . . ."

Her shoulders drooped. "Your brother."

"Deck is working for you now."

"Yes, but that doesn't mean he suddenly believes me."

"Deck's a good enough investigator, he'll start from zero and work your case from there."

"But he got evidence to prove Mitch's innocence. How can he be innocent and me still set up . . . if that makes any sense."

Christian slumped back against the seat and exhaled, soaking in what she was saying. Their case was twisty enough by itself, but weave in Deckard and Harper working her case, and it was a tangled mess. He exhaled. "I know it won't be easy, but let's allow Deck and Harper to handle your case and us focus on ours."

She nodded.

"Hey." He tipped her chin up with a crooked finger. "I don't for one second believe you did anything wrong."

"You just met me, despite how deeply . . ." She cleared her throat. "The fact is you haven't known me long. How can you be so certain?"

"Because my gut never lies." A flash of movement caught his attention. He rapidly shifted his gaze. A man slipped behind the brick building.

"What's wrong?" She scanned the parking lot.

"Hang on a sec." He shifted the car in reverse. It was probably nothing, but his gut was telling him otherwise, and as he'd just told Andi, it never lied.

Pulling around the rear of the building, he scanned the area . . . nobody walking, all rear establishment doors shut. He shifted his gaze to the parked car. No white SUV. A total of ten cars were parked. Was the man sitting there in one of them? No way he had time to disappear from sight that quickly. He had to be somewhere.

"Start scanning the cars," he said.

"They all look still, and from this vantage point, empty to me."

"You're right. We need to get up close to each. See inside." He pulled the Equinox into an open slot and cut the engine. "You go left. I'll go right, starting with the purple Dodge Dart."

"I didn't know those even existed anymore," she said, stepping out of the vehicle and rounding it to meet Christian before he had a chance to open her door.

Her hand by her gun, ready to pull it if necessary, Andi strode for the first car on the left while he moved to the relic of a car, his hand ready to pull his weapon as well. He glanced in the car, both the front and rear seats, his gaze casting on the floor of it. Nada.

Andi indicated the cars she'd cleared, but she had two to go while he still had three. He moved for the silver pickup truck, but before he reached it, the engine roared and it reversed out of the slot, the same man Andi had shot driving.

"Get down," he hollered as the truck passed by her position. She did so, and the truck squealed on, its tires leaving a burning smell as it peeled out.

They raced back to the Equinox, and within a minute were flying out on the road after the truck with only a vanity plate that said CrissY.

FORTY-NINE

"THERE IT IS," Andi said after a minute of thinking they'd lost what, given the vanity license plate, had to be a stolen truck. "Six cars ahead on the right . . . now left."

"I got him," he said. The truck was swerving in and out of traffic.

Christian pressed the accelerator, speeding ahead, weaving safely in and out of traffic, then speeding up even more once they hit an open stretch of road. He had a short distance to catch the man before they ended up in the heart of downtown Santa Fe where Christian could easily lose him in the Sunfest crowd. The three-day-long festival packed the sidewalks, overwhelming the streets with traffic.

The truck pulled ahead and increased its speed. No one else was on the stretch. Now was his chance. They started to gain on him, pulling closer.

The man rolled down the window and . . .

"Duck!"

A bullet ricocheted off the hood, then thankfully deflected into the mesa.

Another one whizzed by the window just before a blue minivan swerved out into the road from a side street, cutting them off.

Christian hit the brakes, his tires squealing, the odor of burnt rubber filling his nostrils. He moved into the other lane, trying to wave the minivan back, fearful the man would fire again, but the truck had pulled far away.

They were headed for the center of downtown.

"What's all this?" Andi asked as they came to an abrupt stop with a line of cars at the light with no sign of the truck. He must have made it through the light.

"The Sunfest festival," he said, tapping his fingers along the wheel. *Come on. Turn green.*

Finally, the light switched, and the three cars in front of him moved forward painfully slowly. He tapped the wheel harder.

Andi scanned the area. "There!" she said, pointing a good block ahead to the truck parked along the sidewalk.

Great. He was no doubt on foot.

"I'll double-park. You stay in the vehicle, and I'll check his, but I'm sure he's blended into the crowd by now."

"You're in the driver's seat. I'll hop out." And she did so before he could argue. Hand ready to pull her weapon, she moved along the truck. Then shook her head after clearing it.

She hopped back in the car. "We find a place to park and go after him."

Christian surveyed the mass of people spreading far and wide before them. They'd get on foot, but they'd already lost him.

· · ·

After stopping at Urban Outfitters to grab fitting clothes for their investigation, Deckard followed Harper into the FBI building in Albuquerque, swiping through to the crime lab with special permission for him to visit by Harper's boss, Greg Dunkirk, the forensic director.

"You okay?" she asked as they made it through security and headed for the elevator.

"Just don't like the danger surrounding my brother and Andi. Too many close calls."

"I agree. I didn't like leaving them any more than you did, but they want us here. This is most important to Andi."

"More than her life?" Deckard arched a brow.

"This is a big part of her life. The part that was stolen."

"We'll work the case, work on clearing her name if the facts back up what she says happened."

"Clear her name. Huh," Harper said, swiping her keycard to enter the main crime lab facility.

"Huh, what?" He frowned.

"Just sounded like you're actually starting to believe Andi's innocent, that she didn't make any mistakes."

He mulled that over. "I think it's possible." Miranda—Andi— wasn't what he'd expected. Spending time with her, short as it was, showed a different side.

"Wow. That's progress," Harper said.

"Let's not get ahead of ourselves. We need to look at the evidence, gather the facts." That's what he'd base his determination on.

"The evidence is gone," Harper said.

"That's not the evidence I'm talking about."

"Oh? Then what evidence are you talking about?" She lowered her voice as they passed a group of people.

"I am looking for evidence of *how* the DNA got corrupted and the shirt 'misplaced.' And if it wasn't by Andi, as you and my brother wholeheartedly believe, then the question is who did it, and why?"

"Well, Greg runs the lab, so he's the best place to start. Oh, and Andi went by Miranda as an FBI agent. Some people have probably heard her called Andi, but it might be easiest if you use Miranda."

Deckard smiled. He'd just gotten used to Andi and now it was back to Miranda. "Got it. Thanks. And I remember Greg. When I started my investigation, Mitch's defense attorney got his approval for us to get a guided tour of the lab. The forensic analyst who gave us the tour and explained what had gone wrong was working the same night as Andi."

"Pamela Whitmore?" Harper asked as they pushed through another set of doors. "That was the only other woman working that night, and me, of course, but I was primarily out in the field."

"Right. I'm pretty sure that was her name. I'd recognize her if I saw her."

"We'll talk with her, too, if she's on shift. If not, we can track her down," Harper said, leading the way down a long hall and then through a myriad of them. White tile floors and brown office doors with rectangular windows framed in the center by the wood lined the corridors. Finally, she stopped in front of an open office door. "Knock, knock."

The man looked up from his desk and smiled. "Harper." Tall, with silver hair and a matching beard, he stood and moved around the desk to greet her. Gold wire-rimmed glasses sat halfway down his nose. He patted her on the shoulder. "I thought you were leaving for your Red Cross mission today."

"It got delayed for a week, so I went to visit Andi."

Greg nodded as his gaze shifted over her shoulder.

"This is Deckard MacLeod. I don't know if you remember him. . . ."

"Sure. The PI investigating for Mitch Abrams. You came with his defense attorney."

"Right." Deckard nodded.

"Nice to see you again," Greg said, shaking his hand.

"Same."

"But I'm confused. Mitch is already out, and Harper said she was investigating Miranda's claims. So . . . who exactly are you working for?"

Deckard swallowed. "I'm working on behalf of Andi . . . Miranda."

"Well . . ." Grey said, moving back around to take a seat in one of the old-fashioned wooden swivel chairs with spindled backs. His lab coat had his name stitched in blue, he wore a matching blue button-up shirt underneath, and the top of his yellow tie showed where the top two buttons were open. He sat back and steepled his hands. "This is an interesting turn of events," he said with a glimmer of a smile.

Deckard tilted his head. "You could say that." He still struggled with wrapping his head around the change of events a year could bring.

"Please," Greg said, indicating the two wooden chairs opposite him. "Have a seat."

Deckard pulled out a chair for Harper, then sank down in the one beside her and leaned forward. "Harper tells me you were the only person besides her that remained kind to And—Miranda."

"It never quite sat right with me," he said. "What went down."

"So you believe Miranda is innocent of the claims against her?"

"Innocence and guilt . . ." Greg said. "It's hard to make a definitive claim of innocence when the evidence indicates you."

"But what if she's right and someone set her up?" Harper said, straightening.

"I suppose the question in that case would be, Who set her up and why?"

"That's exactly what we're trying to find out," Harper said. "The only way Deckard can help is if he can see the lab and the evidence locker."

"Oh?" Greg's inquisitive gaze fixed on Deckard. "Is that true?"

"Yes, sir," he said, shifting in the hardwood chair, trying not to adjust the Dockers pants Harper said he should wear, not to tug at the tie or loosen the button-down shirt.

She said he'd get further dressed this way, but it felt foreign and awkward. He was a jeans, boots, T-shirt, and Stetson kind of guy.

"And why is that?" Greg asked, pinning his gaze on Deckard.

"Because it happened here," he said with a respectful tone. "If what Miranda believes is true, the sample was corrupted in the lab after she correctly stored it, and the missing shirt was taken from the evidence locker after she brought in the box to be catalogued."

Greg silenced an incoming call and kept his full attention on them. "And what do you think you'll discover? Particularly, after all this time?"

"I would like Harper to show me the process the DNA went through. Where the sample was tested. The data or record of it.

The proper way to store DNA. What the evidence locker looks like. Who was on shift the day the shirt disappeared . . ."

"My," Greg said, "it appears there's a lot to be learned."

"We need your permission to get Deckard in the lab and evidence locker," Harper said.

"Yes, you do." Greg swiveled in his chair, and they waited. After a moment, he sighed. "Very well. You have my permission, as long as you don't interfere with the work anyone is doing. And other than the data Miranda had on Mitch Abrams, no forensic information is to be shared from any other cases being processed both now and from before."

"Yes, sir," Harper said.

"So you both agree. You'll limit your exposure to these afore-mentioned items?"

"Yes, sir," Deckard said, and Harper nodded.

"All right." Greg gave a single nod of permission.

"Thank you, sir," Harper said.

"Yes, thank you," Deckard said.

"One more thing," Greg said.

"Sure," Deckard said.

"I want to know what you find," he said. "As the forensics director, I want to know what's happening in my lab."

"Do you mind if I ask you about that?" Deckard said.

Greg dipped his head. "About . . . ?"

"About the hierarchy of positions here. I don't really understand what roles they fill."

"Oh, certainly. Ask away," Greg said, silencing another call. "I'd be answering that all day if I picked up every time it rang. I'm a scientist. Not a phone operator. So," he said, redirecting his attention, "I'm the forensic director. I am responsible for the overall daily operation of the laboratory, as well as reviewing and coordinating the work activities of the full staff."

"So you run the place," Deckard said.

Greg smiled. "Basically."

"And the forensics manager?"

"He oversees the forensics lab, the lab supervisor, and the evidence division."

"Harper said you have a new forensics manager?" Deckard said, trying to poke deeper while not insulting the man who had been passed over by Todd Phillips for a job, which, given the plethora of degrees and awards hanging on Greg's wall, he was far more qualified for, as Harper indicated.

"Yes, Kevin Gaines was promoted after Todd Phillips left the FBI."

"We both know you should have been given that position," Harper said. "You're entirely more qualified, and a nice person to boot."

"Well, thank you, Harper. But clearly someone, or more than one person on the hiring committee, didn't think so."

"We don't think that was by accident," Deckard said.

Greg held up a finger, stood, strode to the door, and looked up and down the hallway. Then he shut the door and returned to his seat. "I'm not saying it should have been me, but it definitely shouldn't have been him. He's not qualified, disciplined, or frankly intelligent enough for that position. I was already looking for a replacement for him as well as keeping an eye out for someone for my position. I certainly wouldn't have recommended Todd for it."

"If you were looking for your replacement, had you been offered the job?" Deckard asked.

"Not quite, but it looked very favorable. I'd made it to the last round of interviews and was told by the head of the hiring committee that they were impressed by my credentials and they would be in touch soon. Next thing I knew, Todd had the job, just like that. I didn't even know he'd applied for the position. I thought he had his eyes on mine."

"I don't suppose they said why they went with Todd?" Deckard asked.

"Actually, they didn't even call me. I found it very strange. I learned Todd had the job, and I called to thank them for their consideration and time, rather hoping they'd say something, but he just mumbled a 'You're welcome' and wished me the best in my endeavors."

"Any idea what kind of job Todd's doing over there? I can't imagine well," Harper said.

"I've heard lots of complaints from the academy members, but it doesn't seem to have any effect on those in charge. He's still there."

"Do you know who on the hiring committee might be willing to speak with us?" Deckard asked.

Greg rocked back in his chair—it creaked with the motion. "I'm not sure anyone will, but if it was going to be someone, it would be Ms. Cavet."

"Ms. Cavet. Great. Thank you."

"You're welcome. If you get anything out of her, please let me know. I just don't understand."

"Of course," Harper said.

"So what prompted Kevin Gaines's move into Todd Phillips's role?"

"That was my appointment. He deserved the job. That's who I was going to move into Todd's role when I fired him."

"Did he know you were going to fire him?"

"I told him he should consider looking for another position."

"And how did he take that?"

"Like his ever-cocky self. Said it would be my loss."

Deckard looked at Harper, and she nodded. A man who knew he was going to lose his job would be an easy mark for someone's bidding if promised a massive promotion in place of the boss who was firing him.

Finishing up their interview with Greg, Deckard followed Harper down the hall, adjusting the Dockers and tugging at the infernal tie.

She looked over her shoulder. "You're ridiculous."

"I look and feel ridiculous," he said.

"I think you look handsome," she said, adjusting his tie. "Oh . . ."

She straightened. "Here comes Pam. The other analyst on shift that night."

"Great."

"Hi, Pam," Harper said. "We were just coming to see you."

"Me?"

"Yes. We need to talk with you."

Pam's gaze darted between them, then landed on Deckard. Her skin paled. "I recognize you."

FIFTY

DECKARD AND HARPER SAT DOWN in the lounge with Pam Whitmore.

"I left you a message yesterday," Deckard said.

Pam pulled her lab coat tighter about her. "It was a busy day. I didn't have time to return the call. Besides, why do you need to talk to me again?"

It'd been a bit, but he'd recognized the severe angle of her haircut and thin brown eyes.

"We're looking at the night of Anne Marlowe's murder again," he began. "Can you tell me what you recall about that night?"

"Wait." Pam's gaze narrowed, her brown eyes fixed on Harper. "Why are *you* looking into Anne's murder? Oh . . ." She leaned her head back with a knowing smile—thin as her lips were. "You're trying to prove Miranda didn't mess up, aren't you."

"Yes."

"Does Greg know you're doing this?" Pam asked.

"Yes. He gave us permission to investigate here."

"Well, I don't have anything to say." She moved to get up.

"That's rather harsh, considering you worked with Miranda for several years," Harper said.

"I'm sorry." Pam stood, wrapping her arms tightly about herself. "I just don't want to get involved, and I don't understand why he"—

she stared at Deckard—"is working with you. He works for Mitch Abrams."

"Worked," Deckard clarified. "I'm now working for Miranda."

Pam squeezed her arms tighter about her waist. "That's an interesting turn of events."

Deckard gave a nod. "You could say so."

Pam hesitated.

"Please, Pam," Harper said, her voice strained. "What if the roles were reversed? You really think Miranda wouldn't try to help you?"

Pam's jaw shifted, her leg bouncing so much Deckard feared her heel would fly off and nail him in the face.

"Just a couple questions," he said.

"All right." Pam retook her seat, her gaze darting about the space. "But just a couple. I need to get back to work."

"Thank you," Harper said. "Okay. Can you run through what you remember about that night?"

"Fine." Her voice held a chill, but at least they'd gotten her talking. "We were working two murder cases. Miranda took Anne Marlowe's, and I worked Mr. Woodward's evidence as it came in."

"Did you witness Miranda running the trace evidence test?" Harper asked.

"Of course. We were running DNA at side-by-side stations."

"Any chance you saw her store the DNA sample?" Deckard asked, leaning forward.

Pam looked down and swallowed.

"Did you see her do it correctly?" Harper asked, her questioning gaze pinned on the lady.

Pam hesitated.

"Pam, she lost her job and reputation over this. If you saw her storing the sample correctly, please tell us," Harper said, her tone and eyes pleading.

Pam's gaze darted to the closed door, then back to them. "I can't lose my job too. I'm a single mom, and I have a family to support."

Harper's shoulders stiffened. "Are you saying you saw her do it correctly?"

Pam swallowed and nodded.

"All this time you knew, and you lied about it?" Harper asked, disbelief in her wide eyes.

"I didn't *lie* about anything." Pam's voice turned short. "No one ever asked me."

"But you could have spoken up," Harper said.

"Look, Harper, you don't have kids. You're carefree. Traveling all over the place for months at a time on some special leave you arranged with the Bureau, which I still don't understand. But the fact is, some of us need our jobs, need to support our families. Now." She stood. "If you'll excuse me."

"Just one last question," Deckard said.

Pam shook her head. "This conversation is over."

■ ■

The trek around the town had turned into nothing but a dead end, as Christian and she had unfortunately expected. But he'd definitely been there, watching them again. The thought of being in a killer's crosshairs sent a shiver down her spine. But more than the fear trying to erode her peace, she was flat-out mad. She'd lost him again.

"Here we are," Christian said, pulling her from her thoughts and redirecting her gaze to Brad Melling's home in Santa Fe. It was, in a word, ostentatious. The only three-story house Andi had ever seen in the area. Large columns held up sprawling balconies across each level. But it was the ornate lawn ornaments and the Greco-Roman columns that gave it that over-the-top feel.

"So this is Tad's ex-partner's place?" Andi asked. "Somehow I can see that." She chuckled.

"Right," Christian said, raking a hand through his hair.

The warmth of the day sunk into her bones, making her feel like finding a lounge chair poolside and just enjoying the day with Christian. She wondered what things would be like with them when the case was over, which she prayed was soon.

Following him up the winding path, she noted the stone garden.

Different shades of rocks mimicked the rippling of waves, with cacti in sections looking like coral. She had to admit, that aspect of the grounds was pretty cool.

Reaching the front door, Christian used the large lion knocker to signal their presence. A few moments later, a woman in her late fifties answered the door.

"Kathlyn," Christian said. "How are you today?"

"Hi, Mr. Christian. I can't complain."

"How many times must I ask you to just call me Christian? By the way," he said, "I'm digging the new haircut."

"Oh." Kathlyn touched her dark brown hair as a small blush spotted her cheeks. "It's nothing." She shrugged a delicate shoulder.

"No, it really frames your face well. You look ten years younger."

"Oh, Mr. Christian." She giggled.

"This is my colleague, Andi Forester," he said.

She supposed it was the proper investigative term, but she wondered how he'd introduce her outside of the case. As his friend? His girlfriend? Neither had discussed what their kisses meant, other than they wanted to move forward. But what that entailed, exactly, she wasn't sure. At least not on his end.

"Nice to meet you," Kathlyn said, holding out her hand.

"Pleasure," Andi said, shaking her hand.

"We're here to see Brad," Christian said.

"I'm afraid Mr. Melling isn't here."

"When do you expect him back?" Andi asked.

Kathlyn leaned in as if imparting a secret. "He's at Miss Veronica's, so it could be tomorrow before he's back . . . if you know what I mean."

Andi's brows shot up. "I'm sorry," she said. "Did you just say Miss Veronica's, as in Veronica Gaiman?"

Kathlyn put a finger to her lips but smiled.

"How long has that been going on?" Andi asked.

"About six months."

Christian's eyes widened. "Six *months*?"

Kathlyn nodded and moved to shut the door.

"Thanks," he said.

"Yes, thank you," Andi said, more questions to ask running through her mind, but Kathlyn was done talking. Andi could read it on her face, and shutting the door sealed the deal.

"Well, that was helpful and surprising," Christian said as they walked down the drive for their car, a cool breeze floating in the hot air. The chill of night had faded, and the sun was beaming its heat down in flames.

"Kathlyn seems like a sweet lady," she said.

"She is. She deserves so much better than working for Brad."

The drive to Veronica Gaiman's was a short one, fifteen minutes through a slew of neighborhoods with only a handful of house styles that just repeated.

They made their way to the door, and Christian rang the bell. It chimed in a series of irritating high notes.

After a moment, a woman in her thirties with beautiful caramel skin and dark hair answered the door.

"Hi, Rosario," Christian said.

"Hello, Christian. Nice to see you."

"Always nice to see you. This is my colleague, Andi Forester."

"Nice to meet you," she said.

Rosario nodded with a smile. "Miss Veronica is out by the pool. This way."

They followed Rosario through the large terracotta-tiled foyer, the walls a rich, textured rust. A large chandelier hung in the center of the space.

Continuing on, they passed through the living room, a dark leather sectional fixed in the expansive room's center.

Rosario opened the French doors on the other side, and Andi shifted her gaze to the crystal blue pool, then the figures of two people locked in an amorous embrace next to it. *Bingo*. They couldn't try and claim their relationship was platonic after that display.

"Thanks," Christian said, and Rosario nodded.

They stepped out onto the beautiful cobalt-and-white tile spanning the full patio and, from this angle, the pool. A white fountain spurted water on the far edge, flowing down into the pool.

Still locked in an embrace, neither noticed their presence.

Christian cleared his throat.

They froze, then eased their gazes over.

Veronica paled. "I—"

"Yeah. Looks like you shot any 'we're just friends' excuse in the foot," Christian said.

Brad took a deep inhale, his bare, hairy chest rising, then falling. "Then you might as well come sit."

"We don't have to tell you anything," Veronica sputtered. Her red swimsuit dipped low in the front and the back.

"No," Christian said, "you don't, but then we'll just assume the worst. You prefer to go that route?"

Andi smiled. *Well played.*

"There's no need to go there," Brad said, his cigar robe—which she had no idea they even still made—hanging wide open, the silk straps hanging down, swishing across his swimsuit. Interesting attire didn't come close. "Would you two care for a drink?" he asked, moving for the crystal decanter on the white rolling cart.

"No, thank you." Andi sat on one of the chaise lounges, seated upright, her feet planted on the ground. Christian, on the other hand, reclined on his.

The sun reflected off the pool, dancing along its clear blue surface. Bubbling directed her attention to the hot tub at the west end of the property. Perfect for watching sunsets, she bet. Another fountain fed into it. The backyard was gorgeous. Veronica Gaiman did well for herself, unless this had been her and Tad's home.

"Veronica," she started. "Your home is lovely."

"Thank you." Veronica lit a cigarette, inhaled, the tip glowing orange, then exhaled with a sigh as smoke ringed out of her mouth.

Andi did her best to ignore the smoke flowing in her direction and started with her first question. "Is this where you and Tad lived?"

Veronica's face soured. "Yes, but it's mine now . . . or soon will be in the divorce."

Andi smoothed her skirt, wondering how that would work if her and Brad's affair ever came to light.

"Does Tad know?" Christian asked, getting straight to it.

Veronica took the martini glass from Brad's hand. "Thank you, love." She took a sip, two green olives jiggling as she lifted it to her mouth. Swallowing, she lowered the glass and turned her gaze on Christian. A gaze that appeared a little too friendly for Andi's taste.

Brad rested a hand on Veronica's shoulder, taking a stance behind her, a martini glass of his own in the other hand. "Yes. He knows."

"Is that why he cut you out of the business?" Christian asked, again straight to the point.

Andi smiled. She liked his style.

"No," Brad said. "His hostile takeover came first."

"And the divorce?" Andi asked.

"My idea," Veronica said, popping an olive in her mouth.

"That came before he found out as well," Brad said. "That's how this happened."

Andi frowned. "I beg your pardon?"

"After I found Tad cheating for the second time in our marriage—though I'm sure there were more—I told him to get out and that I was divorcing him. But it doesn't mean it didn't hurt to discover his affairs. Then, he cut poor Brad out of the galleries on some technicality he'd—and I say this lightly—masterminded in the contract they'd signed. He ripped the rug right out from under him."

"Okay," Christian said, shielding his eyes from the blaring sun. "So what does this have to do with you two?"

"I heard what he'd done to Brad, so I went to comfort him," Veronica said.

Andi's brows arched. She wondered exactly what *comfort* meant in this instance.

Brad squeezed Veronica's shoulder. "Roni and I have been friends for years. Ever since I started the Jeopardy Falls gallery with Tad."

Christian glanced at the white rolling cart. "I wouldn't mind a lemonade after all," he said, sitting up and lifting the back of the chaise up on the rungs until it met his back.

"No problem," Brad said. He looked at Andi, and his gaze ran up and down her. *Ewww.* The distinct need for a shower washed over her. "Would you care for one too?"

"Yes, please." The day was really heating up.

After a glass of lemonade and a half hour explanation of how exactly Tad cut Brad from the contract, Veronica took over the conversation.

"I started all three galleries with him," she said, "and being the slimeball that he is, he's trying to weasel me out of them, and I'm not going to let that happen."

Christian swung his legs over the side of the chaise, shifting to sit as Andi was.

"I'm working with my lawyer on that. Proprietary details," Veronica said before popping another olive in her mouth, her cigarette burning down in the marble ashtray.

Brad finally moved around from standing behind Veronica to sitting beside her. "Tad's a weasel, as Roni said. He stole my shares in the galleries in a totally underhanded but legal way. Ronnie isn't going to let him do the same to her, and her lawyer feels she can beat him."

Christian arched a brow. "Beat him?"

"Yes. To gain control of the galleries," Veronica said like it was completely obvious.

"I mean this in the politest way," Andi said, "but do you have a right to the galleries?"

A deep scowl fixed on Veronica's face.

"I mean, are you on the legal documents?" She hadn't seen Veronica's name on anything that she could recall.

"As I said, I was with him when we started the galleries, but no, my name is not on the business papers. That's what I'm trying to get around with my lawyer. To prove I have a claim to them."

If Veronica was telling the truth and she wanted the galleries, it made no sense for her to have them heisted. But was she telling the truth?

"And if you win," Christian asked, leaning forward, "will you bring Brad back on as a partner?"

She looked up at Brad with a smile. "Of course."

Andi reached for her glass of lemonade, condensation drizzling down the tall glass. Why didn't she believe her?

"And you, my dear," Veronica said, smiling at Andi, "are going to be the one who will set things right."

Andi frowned. "Excuse me?"

"Tad had our galleries robbed, and when you prove it, he'll rot behind bars where he belongs, and the galleries will be mine. *Ours,*" she sputtered out, looking at Brad with what must be the closest she could manage to a tender smile.

"Do you have proof that he set up the heists?" Andi asked, praying Veronica did.

"I know he met with that lady we just saw on TV," Veronica said with a cocky tilt of her head and a wave toward a large-screen TV.

Christian arched a brow. "The mystery woman?"

"Yes." Veronica handed her empty glass to Brad, and he scooted to fill it straightaway.

"Are you sure?" Christian asked, leaning forward and resting his hands on his knees.

Veronica looked at Brad, then back to them. "Positive. Brad and I were at this inn in Angel Fire. It was late, and the inn was basically shut down."

"I decided to run out and grab us more wine," Brad said, jumping in. "When I got back, Roni and I decided to enjoy it on our balcony."

"It was a beautiful evening," she said. "While we were enjoying our wine, a man strode out to one of the patio tables. His gait looked extremely familiar, but I shook off the thought. Tad doesn't exactly stay in quaint inns. He's a Ritz-Carlton kind of guy. Anyway . . ." She redirected herself. "Soon a woman appeared."

Andi scooted forward, hanging on Veronica's words.

"They sat in the shadows and talked, but . . ." Before Andi could pose the question on the tip of her tongue, Veronica added, "They stood and passed by the line of patio lamp poles, bathing them in light. It was most definitely Tad and the woman from that sketch they are showing on TV."

"You're certain?" Christian said.

"Positive." Veronica nodded.

Andi looked at Christian and smiled. They'd just connected their mystery woman to Tad well before the heists.

Seemed Tad had some explaining to do.

FIFTY-ONE

ANDI OFFERED to drive next, and Christian gladly let her. He sat back against the passenger seat of the Equinox as they waited at Sonic for their food to come out. Andi, of course, had wanted to bypass lunch and keep going, but she . . . *they* both needed to eat.

The server skated out with their tray, spinning in a circle before reaching the vehicle. She handed Andi the food and wished them a good day.

"Okay, two cheeseburgers and tater tots for you," Andi said, digging in the brown paper bag and handing the items to Christian. "And one cherry limeade."

"Thanks," he said.

"Onion ring?" she asked, holding one of hers up.

"Thanks," he said. "Tot?" He held the paper container bursting with tots over for her.

"Thanks." She popped one in her mouth, then took a sip of limeade. "So what do you think? You believe Veronica and Brad? If so, it doesn't make sense she'd conspire to have the galleries robbed, but there's always the possibility they are just covering their backs."

"Meaning?" He popped a tot in his mouth.

"They didn't personally rob it. I think we can be certain on that from the video footage of the heist. It was two men and neither resembled Brad's physique. But that doesn't mean that they didn't hire someone."

"Yeah." Christian sighed. "I'm not feeling it, but we can't ignore the fact that they have motive with Tad cutting Brad out and trying to do the same with Veronica."

"Rolling with the hypothetical possibility . . ." Andi said. "The question becomes, are they in it for the insurance money or for the money the fenced items bring in?"

"I suspect they are fine for money, but, then again, even when everything on the surface indicates wealth, you just never know. Not until you start digging. Let me call Greyson, see if he can check into their financials. Determine if it was worth the risk in their minds to set this up."

"Sounds like a plan. I'm not feeling it either, but it's always better to dig than just brush stuff off."

Christian placed the call to Greyson, and after a handful of minutes, hung up.

"We set?" she asked.

"Yep. Greyson's on the financials. And Riley is going to take a ride out to the inn where Veronica and Brad said they saw Tad and our mystery woman to see if any of the staff recognize her. If she was a guest. Anything about her would be more than we have." So far no hits were coming back from her picture on the news.

"Agreed."

He blew a strand of hair from his forehead, but it just fell back in place. He tried again, and she chuckled.

"Here, let me," she said. She scooted toward him and brushed the unruly hair from his forehead, then ran her fingers through his hair to help it blend back in.

An unexpected wave of tingling shot through him from the gentle touch of her hand.

Their eyes held a moment, and she pulled her hand back, biting her bottom lip. "I'm so glad . . ." She cleared the emotion bubbling up her throat and tried again. "I'm so glad Sarah saw the woman and was able to do the sketch. I think it's the key that's going to open the first door we need to walk through."

"Agreed, and Riley's good. She'll get the information we need."

Christian's cell trilled. "I hope it's Deckard and Harper with an update," he said, retrieving his phone and putting it on speaker at the sight of Joel's name. "Hey, Joel. Andi's here with me. Okay to put you on speaker? We've got interesting news for you."

"Of course. Hey, Andi," Joel said. "So before I get to my news, tell me about yours?"

Christian raked a hand through his hair, wishing it was Andi doing so. He longed for her touch, but now was not the time to be focusing on how wonderful she felt. He cleared his throat and attempted to clear his mind. "Did you know Brad and Veronica are having an affair?"

"Seriously?"

"Yep. Witnessed it ourselves."

"Uh," Joel said, letting the word hang in the air a moment before continuing, "that couldn't have been pretty."

"Yeah . . ." Andi said. "Most definitely not."

"What's your news?" Christian asked.

"Unfortunately, not good," Joel said.

"Oh?" Christian stiffened, wondering what more could be coming.

"The sketch we've been showing on the news. We got a hit."

Christian frowned. That wasn't bad news unless . . .

"The sketch matches a Jane Doe found in Pecos."

"Our mystery woman?"

"I'm afraid so," Joel said.

Another murder victim. He feared how many more there would be before this case was over and the killer behind bars.

"I'm so glad Christian sent Cara someplace safe," Andi said, "or I fear the same would have happened to her."

"Agreed," Joel said. "The cops in Pecos that found her took the mystery woman's prints. . . ."

Please let there have been a hit.

"Her name is Julia Brown. Last known address was in L.A."

Christian arched a brow. "L.A.?"

"Yes. But speaking to her former landlord, she left Cali about six months back."

"No idea how she got here, why she was here, or where she was staying?"

"No on the first two. On the third . . . given the seedy motel her body was found in, I'm going with her being a transient."

"You think she came for the score?" Christian asked, his gut saying that was precisely it.

"That seems to fit what we know, but it's not enough to make a formal declaration. I'm going to follow up with Tad regarding this new evidence. I'm sure you both want to talk to him too. I'll find out his current location, let you know, and we can meet up there."

"Thanks, Joel. We won't step on your toes," Christian said.

"I never worry about that. See you two there."

Christian looked over at Andi after he and Joel hung up. She had an impish smile on her face.

He reached over and cupped her cheek, running the pad of his thumb along her bottom lip. "What's that mischievous smile for?"

Her smile widened as she leaned into his hold. "It's time to trap Tad in a web of his own making."

FIFTY-TWO

DECKARD HELD THE DOOR for Harper as they entered the Arizona Forensic Science Academy's office headquarters on Lake Drive. The woman at the front desk looked up at them. Mid- to late-forties, brown hair in a braid, elegant in carriage.

"Hi," Harper said, striding to her.

"Hello. How may I help you today?"

"We need to speak with Todd Phillips," she said as Deckard placed himself behind her and a little to the right.

The woman scanned a calendar on her desk. "I'm sorry. I'm not showing any appointments for him today."

"Oh, we don't have an appointment."

The woman lowered her glasses down on her nose, looking up at them through the upper part of the lens. "I'm afraid Mr. Phillips only takes visitors by appointment."

"I used to work with Mr. Phillips," Harper said with a smile. "I'm sure he'll be okay with it. I'm Harper, by the way."

"Temperance," the woman said. "Pleasure."

Not a name heard often. "And this," Harper said, turning toward him, "is Deckard MacLeod."

"Ma'am." He dipped his chin.

"You called here yesterday," she said. "I took the message."

"Unfortunately, Todd never returned our call, but Deckard here is a private investigator," Harper explained, easing into a casual vibe

254

with Temperance. Much better than the aloof detachment when they'd first walked in. Harper had a way of putting people at ease.

"A private investigator?" Temperance's penciled-in brown brows arched.

"Yes, ma'am. We're investigating a murder case," he said. "We really need to speak with Mr. Phillips."

Temperance leaned forward, rising up from her desk to lean against the front counter separating them from her. "Is he in some sort of trouble?" she whispered, pushing her glasses back up on her nose.

"Possibly," Deckard said. "That's what we're here to determine."

She smiled. "I'll go get him. Y'all wait here."

"Well, she changed her tune when she heard Todd could be in trouble," Deckard said.

"He's certainly not a pleasant man to work for," Harper said.

"Sounds like it." Deckard slipped his hands into his Dockers pockets and walked the length of the lobby, praying they'd get answers or at least a feel for whether the man had any involvement in setting Andi up. *Setting Andi up.* When exactly had he started believing her? He was getting ahead of himself. There were more facts to examine, but he couldn't ignore what he'd learned thus far, and for the first time since he was hired by Mitch Abrams's family, he was questioning the man's innocence. What if he'd been wrong? What if he'd gotten a guilty man out of prison? His shoulders tensed as he stared out the glass wall overlooking a picnic area. Andi being innocent and Mitch being innocent didn't have to be mutually exclusive. Did they?

A tall man with curly brown hair, green eyes, and a hard-set jaw walked into the lobby.

"Harper," the man said with a frown. "What are you doing here?"

"We need to talk to you," she said, indicating Deckard.

"Who's this?" Todd flicked his chin at him.

His tight muscles coiled more. "Private Investigator Deckard MacLeod," he said.

Todd's carriage stiffened. "What's this about?"

"We need to talk to you about Anne Marlowe's murder," he said, not pulling any punches.

"Oh," Todd said, an odd relief crossing his face. "This is about Miranda, isn't it."

"Yes," Harper said, straightening.

Todd looked at Deckard, a smug expression on his face. "She dragged you into this, didn't she."

He rocked back on his heels. "I offered to take the case."

Todd rolled his head back on a humorless laugh. "What case? She botched the job. End of story." His small eyes narrowed nearly to slits. "I knew you looked familiar. You're the one that questioned us at the lab. You and Mitch's lawyer."

"Mitch's? Sounds like you knew him."

"No." Todd shook his head. "Why would you say that?"

"Using a first name so casually usually denotes familiarity."

"It was a big case and a big turnover. I read about it in the news. Wait a minute. You were the one who proved Miranda botched the job and misplaced evidence, so why are you here about her now?"

"I'm working for her," he said.

Todd chuckled, the sound grating on his nerves. "Playing both sides . . ." Todd said. "Interesting. You must just take whatever case comes along."

Deckard's jaw clenched. "Hardly."

"Well, I'm afraid you're wasting your time on this one." Todd looked at Harper. Was he implying the case or the lady?

"I don't think so." In either case.

"Really." Todd linked his arms over his chest. "I can wager you haven't found a shred of evidence showing Miranda didn't screw up."

"Actually, we have." Anticipation shot through Deckard, awaiting Todd's reaction.

The man's cocky grin faded. "What?"

"Yeah." He'd unsettled Todd. Time to turn up the heat. "It's turning out to be a really interesting case."

Todd tugged the lobe of his right ear. "How . . . how so?"

"Don't you worry about the particulars." Deckard smiled. He had Todd right where he wanted him. "However, we, of course, want to hear your side."

"My *side*?" Todd tugged his earlobe harder.

Interesting tell.

Todd shifted his stance. "I don't have a side in this."

"Your input," Deckard said. Todd was going to shut down on them if he pushed like this, so he switched tactics. "I'd like your insight on the matter."

"Oh." Todd's stiff shoulders eased a smidge. He glanced at his watch. "I suppose I can do that, but we'll have to be quick. I've got a meeting in five."

"Five minutes it is," Deckard said.

"Let's head out to the picnic tables," Todd said, gesturing to the back glass door. "It's more private out there."

"After you," Deckard said. He glanced back at Harper and winked. They'd get what they needed from Todd.

She smiled.

Settling around one of the round red picnic tables, Deckard leaned forward, not wasting any time. "Let's go back to the night of Anne Marlowe's murder."

Todd shifted. "What about it?"

"My understanding is that the supervisor, Kevin Gaines, was out sick."

"Yes." Todd's tone shifted to curt.

"You covered for him," Deckard said, as Harper indicated with a soft nod for him to continue to run with it.

"Yes," Todd clipped again.

"And is it correct that you'd never covered for a supervisor before?"

"Who told you that?" Todd's piercing gaze landed on Harper. "Her?"

"Among other people." Andi counted, and Greg had chimed in as well.

"So?" Todd shrugged a flippant shoulder. "I didn't see any sense calling someone else in when I was already there."

"How'd the night go?" he asked, resting his forearms on the metal table.

"Fine."

It was amazing, the man was stiffening more by the second.

"Can you elaborate?" Deckard said. "Anything out of the ordinary happen?"

"Not that I noticed."

Todd looked ready to flee, so he turned up the heat. "Did you work any of the evidence that night?"

Todd looked at Harper, irritation etched on his face. He knew she could call him out if he lied, if it occurred while Andi was there or when Harper returned to the lab after being at Anne's crime scene.

Todd tapped the table. "Yes." His voice twitched. "I helped out."

"There were two murder cases that night. Which one did you work?"

"Why does that matter?"

"It's a simple question," Deckard said.

"I helped Pam work the Woodward case." The man was losing patience. He needed to hurry. Switch back and forth between topics or he'd lose him now.

"Did you happen to notice Miranda doing anything incorrectly?"

Todd hesitated, then said, "No, but she obviously did. Now, I believe our time is up."

"Sure. Thanks for your time," Deckard said, standing as Todd did. Harper followed suit. "Great job you got here," he added. "Impressive." Butter him up a little.

The hint of a proud smile curled on Todd's thin lips. "Thank you."

He strolled beside Todd as they made their way toward the building. Might as well poke the bear now that their time was up. "Interesting you beat Greg out of the promotion, given his credentials and all."

"Clearly the hiring committee was impressed with *my* credentials and offered me the job." The same line they'd heard from Ms. Cavet during their call on the way over.

"I've always heard references can make all the difference," Deckard said. "You must have received some great ones." He forced a smile.

Todd rested a hand against his chest. "I'm humbled to say I did."

"From whom?" he asked point-blank.

Todd's jaw flickered, or at least the muscle in it. "That's none of your business."

"Why? You got something to hide?" he pushed.

Todd laughed, but it was cold, awkward. "What would *I* possibly have to hide?"

"Hmm," Deckard said as they filed back into the lobby. "That's the question now, isn't it."

"This meeting is over." Without a good-bye, Todd turned heel and disappeared through the door he'd initially come out of.

After thanking Temperance, Deckard and Harper stepped out into the warm afternoon sun.

"Well, he was none too happy," Harper said as they made the way to his vehicle.

"Which, to me, indicates his probable guilt," Deckard said.

"You think Todd was the one who corrupted the DNA sample?"

He pulled his keys from his pocket and clicked the doors open. "I'd bet money on him."

"I agree," Harper said as Deckard opened the car door for her. "We really shook him up."

Deckard smiled wide.

"What's the smile for?" she asked with a curious one of her own.

"It means we're rattling the right cages."

FIFTY-THREE

CHRISTIAN AND ANDI ENTERED Tad's Jeopardy Falls gallery following Joel's call to meet him there. Moving through the gallery, they located Tad and Joel in the back office.

"What are they doing here?" Tad asked as soon as they entered the room.

"I think Andi should be here to hear your confession," Joel said, resting one boot on the bottom chair rail where he sat.

"My confession?" Tad chuckled, then, at their silence, his laughter died. "What confession?"

"The one you're going to give us," Joel said.

"I'm not going to give you anything, because I didn't do anything."

"We know you met with her three months ago," Joel said.

"Her, who?"

Joel slid the picture of the woman, as she was found murdered, in front of Tad.

Tad gagged and covered his mouth.

"And here's Alex." Joel slid the picture of the poor girl toward him.

Tad gagged harder and bolted to the bathroom.

After Christian overheard far more than he ever wanted to, Tad returned, pale as a ghost.

Tad retook his seat, and Joel didn't give him a moment's rest. "Tell us about the mystery woman, as you called her."

"I don't know anything about that woman," Tad said, shifting in his seat and dabbing his perspiring forehead with a silk handkerchief he pulled from his shirt pocket.

"You don't know her?" Joel pointed at her crime-scene photo.

Tad gagged and turned his head. "Please take that away before I get sick again. I don't know her!"

"Then maybe you need another look." Joel leaned forward with the picture.

"Fine." Tad huffed. "Take the picture away and I'll tell you what you want to know."

Joel sat back, steepling his fingers, indicating with a dip of his chin for Tad to proceed.

Tad grunted out an exhale. "She was the woman from the gala. But that's all I know."

Joel looked up at Christian and then Andi and indicated with a slight move of his head for them to jump in anytime.

Christian pulled out a chair for Andi, and she slid into it. "Thank you."

He nodded, then flipped a chair around, straddling it. He rested his hands against the chair back and interlaced his fingers. "We know you're lying."

Tad blanched. "Nice tactic."

Christian arched a brow. "Tactic?"

"Yes. To get me to talk. I don't have anything to say."

"That's fine. You don't have to help us, but you're next," he said.

Tad swallowed. "Wh-what do you mean?" His pitch was high enough for dogs to hear.

"Whoever these guys pulling off the heists are," Joel began, "they clearly don't like loose ends. And like it or not, you're a loose end."

"Why . . . why would you say that?" Tad's voice quivered, despite his poised posture.

"Because," Joel continued, "you know both of the other victims, and you know who's behind the heists. You can either give them up or become their next victim."

Tad swallowed, then wiped his brow. "I can't." He shook his head. "I've never even seen them. I don't know who they are."

"Oh?" Joel sat back and shifted, crossing one booted foot over the opposite knee. "You do know them."

"I just said . . ." Color rose up Tad's neck.

"We know you hired them," Andi bluffed.

"We know you needed the insurance money," Christian added, courtesy of Greyson's digging into Tad's financials. "You've got a hefty gambling debt, and you needed a way to pay up before they . . ." Christian drew a line across his neck.

Tad sat back, arms crossed. "I don't know what you're talking about."

"How about this," Andi said, leaning forward. "We know you met with your mystery woman months before the heist. We have eyewitnesses."

Tad's gaze darted from them to the door, then back again.

"You lied to us about when you met her," Joel said. "And you know what else you're lying about? Hiring two men to rob your galleries." Joel straightened. "And here's the thing. They murdered people, which makes you an accomplice."

What minuscule color remained in Tad's pale face drained. "I had nothing to do with any of that."

"Then tell us what you did, and maybe we can keep you safe," Joel said.

Tad shifted. "You don't really think . . . I mean, you're just bluffing about me being next, aren't you?"

"They've murdered two women. Why not you?" Christian said.

"I'm not lying. I've never seen them. I have no idea who they are. I only worked through Julia."

"Ah." Christian cocked his head. "So you do know her name."

Tad gripped his shirt, running his fidgety fingers along the row of buttons.

"We know it too," Joel said. "Julia Brown."

"How did you communicate?" Christian asked.

"She called to set up our first meeting."

"And then?" Joel pressed.

"Then we used a PO box."

Joel scooched forward. "Where would that be?"

"In Santa Fe." Tad's fingers fixed on a single button, squeezing it between his forefinger and thumb.

"Great," Joel said. "You're going to take me."

"No way." Tad shook his head. "They'll know I talked."

"Who will?" Joel asked with a lift of his chin.

"The men . . . the thieves." Tad swallowed.

"Ah," Andi said. "So you did hire them?" She looked at Christian and smiled. Ambrose Global wouldn't be paying out a dime.

"No." Tad cleared his throat, crossing one leg over the other and smoothing a wrinkle from his white linen pants with his hand. "They approached me."

"Start from the beginning," Joel said, setting a tape recorder on the table and pressing Record.

"I never met the men. The ones in the heist video. That's the first I ever saw them, and that's the truth. I only met with Julia. She was the middleman, if you will. She told me she had two clients who wanted to help me out with my gambling debt and make me rich."

"And you jumped on it without thinking of the consequences," Joel said.

"How was I supposed to know it would get deadly?"

"How could you bring Alex into it?" Christian asked. "She was just a kid."

Tad ran a hand over his head and exhaled. "I didn't pull Alex into anything. She must have seen something, done something that made them mad. It had nothing to do with me."

"Made who mad, Tad?" Joel pushed.

"The . . . the men in the video footage of the heist."

"So they killed her for it?" Christian asked.

"I don't know anything about her death," Tad said. "I swear."

"What about Julia?"

"Again, I don't know." His voice hiccupped.

"Where are they going to hit next?" Andi asked.

"I have no idea."

"So they have no further use for you," Joel said, then looked at Christian. "That's a tenuous place to be."

"I never saw them. I have no idea who they are. There's no reason to kill me!" Tad's rushed speech bordered on a holler.

Christian leaned forward, his gaze fixed on Tad. "You're assuming they need a reason."

FIFTY-FOUR

DECKARD FOLLOWED HARPER back to the lab. They were waiting until the officer working the evidence locker on the day Andi supposedly pulled the shirt out of the locker was on shift. Arriving nearly a half hour early, Harper took the time to run Deckard through every step of processing the DNA Andi had performed that night, along with showing him the storage facility. The data from that night showed that Andi had extracted and identified the partial match to Mitch.

"If only it'd been a complete match one way or another," he said as they wrapped up and headed out for the evidence locker.

"Andi was only one skin cell shy of a full match," Harper said, walking beside him.

"One cell?" His step hitched. "That's it?"

"Yep."

"You're saying one more cell and it would have been considered a complete match to Mitch?"

"Exactly."

When she put it that way, it made the identification even stronger in his mind. But Mitch? Could Deckard really have misjudged him so? Could Mitch really have played him that well? His chest tightened as they scanned into the evidence building. If Mitch was

Anne's killer, he'd find a way to prove it, but with Mitch's conviction being vacated, there was no way to charge him with the crime again.

His muscles coiled. What if he'd put a guilty man back on the streets?

"Hey, Mack," Harper said, greeting the man in the cage. "How you doing today?"

"Hey, kiddo," he said. "Can't complain."

Kiddo? Deckard arched a brow.

"I'm the youngest on the team. Still a newbie," she said. "You don't make 'full rank' until it's been a year. But we're well past that," she said playfully. "It's been over two years. I've earned my stripes."

Mack chuckled, his whole diaphragm moving. "I suppose you have, but *kiddo* just fits."

"Great." She smirked.

Mack smiled, lifting his chin. "Who's this?" he asked, his gaze fixed past Harper onto him.

"This is my friend Deckard MacLeod. He's really interested in how all this works."

"Deckard Macleod . . ." Mack tapped his pen on the counter. "MacLeod." He frowned. "Are you the one that busted Miranda Forester?" he asked, his voice hard and questioning.

"Oh, come on, Mack. You knew her as Andi too."

"Fine. He worked for that Abrams guy and busted Andi."

"You don't sound pleased," Deckard said.

"I'm not."

Deckard looked at Harper. "I thought no one else here believed Andi was innocent."

"In the lab. And I didn't know until right now that Mack did."

"No one ever asked my opinion," Mack said.

What was it with people copping out because no one asked? *Step up, people.*

Mack leaned forward, resting his arms on the counter. "You're one of those private detectives, right?"

"Yes." Was this it? Had Mack seen what happened with the shirt?

Mack looked around. Deckard followed his gaze. No one else was present, thankfully.

Mack leaned his whole torso on the counter, his mouth nearly flush with the cage. "I'm not proud of this, and this has to remain between us. Detective-client privilege and all that."

Not exactly how that worked.

Mack took a sharp inhale, then released it in a nasally stream. "I think my wife is cheating on me."

Okay, not at all what he was expecting.

"Can you help me out?"

"I'd be happy to help when this investigation is complete."

"Great. And the money? I don't have a lot. That's why I haven't hired a PI yet."

"I'm sure we can work something out." Deckard didn't do cheating spouse cases. His expertise centered on cons and scams, but for Mack—if the man was going to be helpful—he'd make an exception.

"Okay. All I can tell you is what I know."

"Which is?"

Mack shifted his head, the overhead light hitting the gray in his dark hair cropped short. Once convinced they were still alone, he sat back, linking his arms over his robust stomach. "You ask. I'll answer."

"Were you working when Andi brought in the evidence from Anne Marlowe's case?"

"Yes."

"And did you go through the contents of the box?"

"No. That's up to the analyst to properly pack it up and store it. Andi was the last on the chain of custody. She signed it in the logbook, stored it, and then headed out. Nothing unusual there."

"And the day she was accused of taking an item from the box?"

"I wasn't on shift. Randy Fox was."

Harper frowned. "But the schedule sheet said it was you."

"Then it's wrong."

Great. Someone on the inside had altered it. The question was, who was responsible for it all? His money was on Todd.

"Can we see the logbook from that day?" Harper asked.

"Oh . . ." Mack sat back. "I'm not supposed to show those."

"Just a quick look," Deckard said, hoping the promise he'd look into Mack's cheating wife would work in their favor.

Mack looked around yet again. Nobody. "Okay," he said, "but I never gave you this." He stood and moved to a row of cabinets. It took a minute, but he fished it out.

"Here," he said, flipping to the page in question.

Deckard skimmed the page, looking for Andi's name. Harper watched over his shoulder.

"There she is," Harper said.

Deckard scanned the line. It had Andi's name, date, time, and an item number. "I'm assuming this number correlates to the evidence box from Anne Marlowe's case?"

"I can look it up just to be certain." Mack typed it in. *Click. Click. Click.* "Yes, that's correct," he said.

"Thanks," Deckard said, then shifted his attention to Harper. "Does it look like Andi's handwriting?"

"Yes . . . but the item numbers are different from those of the time and date."

Both he and Mack leaned forward, looking.

"You sure about that?" Deckard asked, not noting a difference.

"She crosses her sevens," Harper said.

"Okay . . . oh . . ." All the sevens were crossed, but the ones in the item number were all up higher on the stick part of the numeral. "Excellent job," he said.

Mack furrowed his brow. "What am I missing?"

"They're crossed in different places," Deckard said.

"Are you sure she just didn't get sloppy?" Mack asked.

Harper arched a brow. "Andi, sloppy?"

"Fair enough." Mack's cell rang. "Hang on," he said before answering, then stood to take the call, shifting his back to them.

Deckard took the opportunity to jot down all of Andi's information, along with who else was in and out of the evidence locker that day.

"Sorry about that," Mack said, lifting the logbook, closing it, and returning it to the cabinet.

"Thanks for all your help," Deckard said. "One more thing. Do you know when Randy will be in or how we can get ahold of him?" He could find it, but it would go faster if Mack just handed it to them.

"He moved," Mack said.

"Moved to a new job?"

"In a way. He moved back to Boston, but you didn't hear that from me. He didn't tell anyone else where he was going. Just left."

"When was this?" Deckard asked.

"Oh, I don't know. I'd say about a week after everything happened with Andi."

"Meaning, after I started digging into things?" Had Randy been spooked by it? Did he have something to hide?

"No." Mack shook his head. "I'm pretty sure he'd left before you and that defense lawyer realized the shirt was gone."

Ten minutes and a finished conversation with Mack later, Deckard followed Harper down the long rows of the storage facility, evidence containers piled high on the shelves, nearly reaching the ceiling.

"Wow," Deckard said. "This is a lot of cases. A lot of crimes."

"Sad, isn't it," she said.

"Very." Crime was pervasive. It always had been in his world. But at least he was on the right side of the law now.

Harper moved to the section the evidence from Anne's murder was in, and they searched the aisle, reading the victims' names.

"Ah. There it is," Harper said, pointing up. She moved for the sliding ladder and pulled it over.

"I can get it," Deckard offered.

"It's okay," she said, already climbing the ladder steps. "Got it." She pulled, lost her balance, and came tumbling down, clutching the box. "Whoa!"

"Got ya," Deckard said, catching her, the box and all. His arms wrapped around her, holding her. The skin where her shirt was askew was warm and soft. It was the most innocent of touches, but something sparked through him all the same. "I should put you down," he said.

She nodded.

"Right," he said, moving his bottom arm first, and not releasing her until both her feet were firmly on the ground.

"Okay," she said, setting the box down, then lowering to the cold concrete floor beside it.

He followed her lead, sitting beside her.

"Let's see what we've got." She pulled out a sling backpack and opened it. She fished out two plastic wine glasses.

"Looks like a rendezvous to me," Deckard said. No one took wine hiking.

She pulled out an unopened bottle of wine. "I'd have to agree." She set it aside and fished a little deeper. "Wine opener," she said. Lastly, she pulled a neatly folded lightweight blanket. "The register also says there was bread, cheese, and chocolates. Food items get disposed of after being tested."

"Tested?"

"For poison, date rape drugs, et cetera."

"And none were found, if I remember correctly."

"Correct."

She pulled out Anne's clothes, the bloodstains visible through the plastic evidence bag. Next came the shoes . . . with zero blood on them.

"That's odd," he said.

"What is?" she asked.

"If you're stabbed, blood is going to splatter. You'd think it would be on her shoes, at least some of it."

"Not if she was lying down while stabbed, like I surmised. Think about it. If he knocked her out, which I strongly believe he did, then he could have laid her in the rock pile, straddled her, and stabbed away," Harper said.

Deckard rubbed the back of his neck, playing the scenario through his mind. "Why not just stab her on the bench?"

"I'm guessing so it would look like Simmons went into a passion-fueled rage. The killer put the rock in the pile with the rest to make it look like she'd fallen back on them."

"Then he what . . ." Deckard said. "Straddled her and stabbed away? No, then there'd be other cloth traces. He knelt beside her and stabbed away? I swear. It's the weirdest murder I've ever seen."

Harper shook her head. "I'm sorry to say, I've seen weirder."

He arched a brow.

"Trust me." Harper shook her head. "You don't want to know."

"I'll take your word for it."

"Why not just stab her standing up?" Harper said. "If the killer was setting up Simmons, why go through the trouble of knocking her out?"

"He probably didn't want her to scream. Kids party back in those woods. He wanted to silence her before he killed her."

"A fair scenario. But why leave the shirt?"

"So Simmons would be blamed, and I'm sure the killer didn't want to risk carrying any evidence with him."

"Again, makes sense," she said, then pulled out Anne's purse, which was found in the trunk of her car. "Keys . . ." she said, jangling them. She continued, pulling out a miscellany of items, and last came Anne's work badge for Councilman David Markowitz's office. "He's the councilman with that new sprawling condo complex coming downtown."

"Yeah. He's been lobbying for it big time," Deckard said. "I spoke with him while investigating Mitch's case."

"And?"

Deckard shrugged. "Your typical politician, but surprisingly helpful at the same time."

"How so?"

"Markowitz said Anne had been skittish lately. Not herself. He heard her talking in hushed tones on the phone several times. Said she seemed scared."

"Of what?"

"He thought maybe it was boyfriend or ex-boyfriend trouble. He asked if she was okay, she said yes, and he let it go."

"If he'd said something more, told somebody, maybe she wouldn't be dead."

"I doubt he could have done much. There wasn't anything other than suppositions to tell. If she was scared, she should have gone to the police."

"If it was about Simmons, she was probably scared. He's a powerful man," Harper said. "And Mitch?"

"A real estate developer. Nice home. Pretty wife . . ."

"That he cheated on."

"Yep. And who divorced him when he was found guilty," Deckard added.

"She believed he did it?" Harper said.

"Yeah."

"Did she say why?"

"Kim said he liked getting his way. If Anne had broken things off with him, he would have become angry."

"And she thought angry enough to kill?" Harper asked.

"That's when she stopped talking to me. Said she was finished with Mitch and the better off for it." And she never looked back. With a cheating husband, he couldn't blame her.

"I'd say she's right."

After finishing up with the evidence and returning it to the shelf, they thanked Mack and headed out of the facility.

"What now?" she asked.

"Boston." Deckard smiled.

"Boston?"

"We're going to talk with Randy Fox in person."

"Not over the phone?"

"I need to see body language, facial expressions to tell if he's lying. We'll probably get a lot more out of him in person."

"Because you're intimidating?" She smirked.

He arched a brow. "You think I'm intimidating?"

"Not to me, but you have that presence when on a case."

"Let's hope it works on Randy and Todd, because I think one of them holds the answers we need."

FIFTY-FIVE

CHRISTIAN HELD THE DOOR to MIS open for Andi.

"Andi," Greyson said, standing. "A pleasure to see you again."

"Thanks. You too."

"Andi." Riley smiled as she rounded the corner into the lobby of the office. "I didn't know you guys would be in today."

"We've got so much going," Christian said. "We could use a round table."

"I'll make the drinks," Greyson said.

Ten minutes later, they all congregated around the round table in the conference room. Greyson took his usual seat by the glass panels, his espresso on the ledge beside him, a black dry erase marker in hand. "So catch us up," he said.

Christian looked at Andi. "Where to begin?"

"Tad," she said.

"Right. Tad cracked."

"He confessed?" Riley said. "I knew it. Such a little weasel."

"Run us through it," Greyson said.

Christian gestured for Andi to proceed, and she relayed the entire conversation with Tad.

"Joel is escorting Tad to the PO box he made drops at with Julia," Christian added when Andi wrapped up. "He said he'd keep us posted."

"Unfortunately, I doubt anything will be found at this point, given Tad owns no more galleries to rob," Andi said.

"You think Tad's safe," Riley asked, "considering what they did to Alex and Julia?"

Christian exhaled. "As long as he's in police custody."

Riley crossed her legs. "And if he's released on bail?"

"I sure wouldn't want to be him," Andi said.

"Do you think Julia Brown was the woman's real name?" Greyson asked.

"Hard to say. Her prints are linked to it—that's how Joel's search found her. They're still running the sketch on the news, so hopefully someone that knows more will see it. If we find out more about her, maybe we can find a tie to our two robbers," Christian said before taking a sip of his double espresso.

"And where they're going to hit next. Assuming this isn't over," Greyson said.

"You think it isn't?" Riley asked.

"No," he said with a shake of his head.

"Agreed," Riley said, then looked at Andi. "Any ideas?"

"Nothing certain, but I have a theory."

Christian arched a brow.

"It just came to me on the way over," she continued. "Think of the specific items that have been taken." She pulled her notebook and a catalog from her satchel. "My boss sent the catalog of Tad's collections over when the case started." She flipped the catalog open. "All of the pieces taken are either Aztec in origin or were from Mexico. His are rare collections, even the wine he's amassed—some of the rarest in the world, but that's gone thanks to the fire. So they got nothing from the Taos gallery."

Greyson draped one hand over his knee. "But you think they're amassing a collection for a particular collector. Someone with lots of money and a taste for the finer things?"

"Exactly," she said.

Christian loved to watch Greyson's mind work.

"So . . . the question is," Riley said, "if they are planning to hit another gallery, which ones contain an Aztec or Mexican heritage collection?"

"Exactly," Andi said.

Christian looked at Andi. "Let's start researching."

She nodded. "And it would be a good idea to cross-reference any that you installed the security system at, along with any that my company insures."

Christian sat back and stretched out his legs, crossed his ankles. "Excellent idea." He shifted his gaze to Greyson. "There's one thing we need to do first."

Greyson arched a brow. "Oh?"

"Confirm that Ethan Poppin is still in jail."

Riley's brow pinched. "Ethan Poppin? Where did that come from?"

Christian exhaled. "It's a huge long shot, but he was livid I didn't go through with the heist. He blamed me for him getting caught, and it wouldn't surprise me if he tried to get some revenge . . . if he were out of prison."

"Do you really think he could pull off this level of heists?" Greyson asked.

Christian sat forward, propping his elbow on the table. "His being involved doesn't make sense for three reasons. First, he should still be in jail. He has years left on his sentence. Second, to answer your question, no. He was never that good, which is why he got caught. And third, all the notes have been directed at Andi and written in a woman's handwriting—I'm assuming Julia did them before she was killed. So, to me, it makes far more sense that it's someone Andi busted, if revenge is our thieves' motivator. However . . ." He linked his fingers together. "I want to cover all my bases."

"Grant has gone through the list of those I had a hand in convicting," Andi said. "They are accounted for. Two are under house arrest and the two on parole are where they're supposed to be. None seem to have the funds to hire someone either. But . . ."

"I can do some financial digging," Greyson offered.

"That'd be great," Andi said. "You just never know."

276

"Which is why I want to rule Ethan out," Christian said. "Rule out all possibilities, no matter how remote."

Greyson smiled at the saying he'd always impressed upon the team. "The other factor to consider is whether Ethan might be pulling the strings from behind bars. Sadly, it happens more often than we'd like to think."

"Agreed." Christian nodded.

"I'll place a call to the warden while you guys research potential galleries," Greyson said.

Christian took a sharp inhale and streamed it out. He needed to relax. It was probably a fool's errand to even check. Ethan had never been that good, but something wove its way inside him this morning, whispering Ethan's name. And it wouldn't let go.

FIFTY-SIX

CHRISTIAN LOOKED to the door the minute Greyson returned from his desk, a legal pad in hand. "What's the word?"

"They kept me on hold forever and then told me the warden would have to call me back. No one would answer my questions. They said I had to wait for the warden." He looked to the glass panels. "So I see you've made progress."

"Riley has been a huge help," Andi said. "And she's fast."

"Andi's additions were off the top of her head," Riley said. "Impressive memory."

"I just studied heists of the past, the catalogs of the galleries my company insures." Andi shrugged. "My only recollection of back-to-back heists were two heists that two teens pulled off. Two teens who ended up in juvie." Her quizzical gaze shifted to Christian.

He gave her an I'm-busted smile.

"I remember they were masterful heists. The thieves—you and Ethan—only got caught because of trying to move a stolen piece too fast and public."

"That was Ethan."

"I hate to say impressive, but the execution of them was."

"But we deserved jail for what we did," he said.

"And you served your time."

Riley's gaze bounced between the two of them. "And it's in the past," she said, always standing up for her big brothers.

"Exactly." Andi nodded. "But it's no wonder you're so good at busting them."

"I wish I was in this case."

"We'll get them," she said with assurance, then cast her gaze at Greyson. Christian's followed. Grey still stood by the glass columns with writing in black scrolled across them.

"What are the two columns for?" he asked.

"The list on the left are galleries where I've consulted on or upgraded their security system," Christian said. "The right column are galleries in New Mexico, Arizona, California, and Utah with collections that might interest our thieves. They have the most Aztec and Mesoamerican collections in the country."

"What's with the underlined ones?" Greyson asked, moving to take a seat at the table.

Riley popped a butterscotch into her mouth and tossed the wrapper on the table.

Greyson stared at it, then her.

Christian smirked. He gave it thirty seconds.

Twenty seconds in, Greyson reached for the wrapper and tossed it in the trash.

"I would have gotten it," Riley said.

"Sure you would have," Greyson said. "That's why I find wrappers all over the place. I sat on one in my chair today."

"Oops," Riley said.

"What were you doing at my desk, anyway?"

"I needed a stapler and couldn't find mine."

Greyson smiled—that half smile of his. "That's why everything was out of place."

"I put things back," Riley insisted.

Andi leaned over, her mouth by Christian's ear, her breath warm and tickling. "Are they always like this?" she whispered.

"Usually worse," he said, fighting the urge to forget the Bickersons were in the room and pull Andi into his arms and—

"Not where they belong," Greyson countered, yanking Christian from his thoughts.

"Show me," Riley said, tapping her pen on her notepad.

"I already straightened them."

Riley shook her head. "Of course you did."

Greyson opened his mouth for a rebuttal, then realized Christian and Andi were staring at them. "Sorry about that. Where were we?"

"You were asking about the underlined locations," Andi said.

"Right," Greyson said, straightening his tie. "They are . . . ?"

"Locations that overlap." Christian stood and moved toward them. "These three are locations I installed the security systems upgrades."

"And Ambrose Global insures them," Andi added.

"And the circled one?" Riley asked.

"Hunter Gallery in Phoenix," Christian said. "Has all three. I installed the security system, Andi's company insures them, and they have one of the biggest Mesoamerican collections in the region. Primarily Aztec."

"I'll ask my boss to give them a warning call," Andi said.

"Good idea," Christian said.

"Feel free to use the phone at my desk," Greyson said, nodding at Andi.

"Thanks," she said, standing and excusing herself from the room.

Greyson looked to Riley. "Her I trust to keep things in order."

Riley glared at him, and Christian smothered a chuckle.

"Are you and Andi going to stake out the Phoenix gallery?" Riley asked.

"I think as long as they have security in place, we're good. Besides, there are others to consider."

"Three others are in Arizona," Riley pointed out.

"And three in California," Greyson said.

"It's a crapshoot to try and pick the right one," Christian said, his limbs tightening. Talk about a frustrating dilemma.

Andi returned to the room. "Grant is calling all the listed galleries he insures."

"Great. Hopefully that will be a big deterrent," Greyson said.

Christian exhaled. "I just pray no one else gets hurt."

"I'm leaning toward the Caldwell or Jensen galleries," Andi said.

"Why is that?" Greyson asked, steepling his fingers.

"Thus far, the thieves have taken small objects, easy for transport. The other collections have a lot of larger pieces," Andi said, crossing her legs.

"Small," Christian said, "but highly valuable."

"So they did their homework," Riley said.

"Most definitely." Andi tapped her notepad with her pen.

"And the heists look like art in themselves," Christian said. "You should have seen how flawlessly things went until the camera feeds were cut."

Andi cleared her throat. "Christian has an appreciation for their work I don't share."

"I don't appreciate their robbing the place, but their execution was stellar. These are no average robbers."

"Yes, but sooner or later, they'll trip up," Andi said.

"I hope you're right," Christian said, finishing off his espresso.

"One thing I'm curious about," Riley said.

"What's that?" Christian asked.

"Why those collections? Is there a high demand for those objects?" Riley asked.

"I can make a call. Check to see if they are in demand on the black market," Greyson said.

"Or . . ." Andi said. "They already have a buyer lined up."

"Another strong possibility," Christian said.

"I'll reach out to my black-market contacts. See if we can discover who that buyer might be," Greyson said.

Andi's eyes widened. "You have contacts on the black market?"

"He's got contacts everywhere," Riley said with a swish of her hand.

"It's always good to have something up your proverbial sleeve," Greyson said. "To be one step ahead."

"Go on the offense, not the defense," Christian said.

Greyson smiled. "Always strike first."

"You should see this guy in a fight," Riley said, poking her pen in his direction.

"Fight?" Andi said. "But you're so dignified. I mean, not to assume . . ." She blushed.

"It's all right." Greyson smiled. "I only engage when it's necessary."

"It's not really an engagement," Christian said.

Andi crinkled her nose. "What do you mean?"

"He strikes first," Riley said. "One swift shot to the jugular and it's over."

"Strike first," Andi said.

Greyson nodded. "Yes, ma'am."

FIFTY-SEVEN

THE FIRST AVAILABLE FLIGHT to Boston didn't leave until five o'clock the next morning, so they headed back to Harper's for the night, though Deckard doubted they'd get much rest. His head was spinning, trying to compartmentalize all the information they'd been flooded with.

The final interview with Kevin Gaines had been the quickest. The man, compared to the others, took a different tactic. He went on the offensive, barraging Harper for blaming others for her friend's mistake. When asked a direct question, he either deflected or gave a one-word answer with a grunt. The conversation, or lack thereof, convinced Deckard he knew more than he was saying, and Harper concurred.

Harper opened her door, and they beelined for the couch. Both flopping down. It'd been a long, frustrating day. Harper kicked her shoes off. "Feel free to kick your boots off. Make yourself comfortable."

"Thanks." He did just that.

"I don't know about you," she said, "but my head is spinning. I'm running all the conversations over and over. I feel like I'm missing something."

"I feel the same. Any of the people we talked to today could either be involved in setting Andi up directly or they simply looked the other way."

"Either way, they're despicable," she said with a deep exhale.

"Agreed." He feared he fell into the latter category. He hadn't looked the other way in the same sense, but he had sent her away when she came to him for help.

"You okay?" Harper asked, tucking her feet under her.

"Yeah." He raked a hand through his hair.

"I'm not buying it."

He chuckled. "No one could accuse you of being timid."

"Nope. I've never seen the point of tiptoeing around something. So what's up? Something is clearly bothering you."

He'd ask why she thought that, but in the end it didn't matter. She was right. He raked his hand through his hair again, then exhaled. He wasn't one for sharing, but something about Harper Grace weakened his defenses. "I should have listened to Andi when she came to me. If I had, she wouldn't have had to go through all she did, and I might have caught the killer."

"You worked for Mitch. It would have been a conflict of interest, but yes, it probably would have been wise to at least listen."

"You don't sugarcoat things, do you." While her response didn't make him feel better, he admired her honesty.

"Nope. I've learned honest and upfront works the best. It takes all the minutiae out of things."

He chuckled. "That's one way to look at it."

"I don't think we're too dissimilar in that regard," she said, then stretched her neck and winced.

"You okay?"

"Yeah." She rubbed her neck and winced again. "Just a knot."

"Here," he said, standing and moving to sit beside her. "Let me give it a try."

She blinked.

"I've got good hands."

She chuckled. "That didn't sound at all like a line."

"I know, but ask Riley. She gets all knotted up barrel racing, and these," he said, waggling his hands, "get the kinks out." He dipped his chin. "Trust me."

"Okay." She scooted her back up against him and slipped her hair over her shoulder.

He cracked his knuckles, and she cringed. "That sounded awful."

"All good." He cupped the back of his right hand on her neck, feeling around for the knot.

"Ouch."

"Sorry. Had to find it. I'm just going to put a little pressure on it to start."

"Okay."

He rubbed and gently applied pressure. Then with soothing brushes of his hand, he massaged it. Kneading with a bit more pressure, the knot started to ease beneath his fingers. "Better?" he asked.

"Much. Thank you."

"You're welcome." He sat back, trying to ignore the pulsing sensation in his chest, the warmth in his limbs. A first in a long, long time.

"Dinner was great," Andi said as Christian cleared the plates. "Thank you."

"You're welcome."

"I love chicken parm," she said, standing and moving to the sink to help him. "You wash, and I'll dry."

"I've got it," he said, thunder crackling in the distance.

The swiftly moving clouds, dark and thick, passed by the window in the blustering wind.

"That came on fast," she said. It'd still been a blue sky when they reached the ranch. They'd been hoping to have a fire in the firepit, but the now dousing rain ruled that out.

Lightning illuminated the sky with a striking flash, followed by a loud grumble of thunder.

"I better go check on the horses," he said. "You good?"

"Of course." She finished the last plate and set it in the drying rack.

Lightning struck again. A massive, thundering boom shook the window. The fastened-back shutters rattled on their hinges.

Drying her hands on the towel, Andi hung it over the oven door handle. Another strike of lightning and the lights flickered.

She looked about the kitchen. Best find a flashlight in case the lights went out. Before she could move, thunder boomed and the electricity died. She patted her pocket for her phone. Nada. *Great.* Where had she set it? The living room? The bedroom? No. The bathroom. She'd set it on the sink when she pulled her hair out of its bun.

She moved with caution, trying not to bump into anything in the near pitch-black engulfing her. Her chest tightened. *It's just a thunderstorm.* Moving tentatively toward the center of the house, she stared at the pouring rain, drops pelting off the central courtyard's glass walls. She followed the courtyard around. Lightning struck, illuminating the space, followed by thunder. She'd barely taken a second breath when it struck again, illuminating a man with a gun across the courtyard from her. Her heart seized, and she ducked behind the recliner, praying he hadn't seen her. Her back against the chair, she swallowed, wishing the thunder away so she could hear if he was coming.

Her heart thumping in her chest, she peeked around the chair, but it was too dark to see anything. She couldn't stay there. She needed her gun from the bedroom, her phone from the bathroom. Needed to warn Christian so he didn't walk in unaware and get shot.

Lightning struck again. The burst of light showed the man moving around the courtyard.

She needed to move. Taking a steeling breath, she moved in a low crawl, weaving around furniture she could duck behind when lightning flashed through the house.

The man switched directions, moving her way.

No. No. No.

At a bang from outside, he turned toward it, his back to her, and she took the opportunity to hurry as quietly as possible to the bathroom.

Once inside, she grabbed her phone and slid behind the door. Afraid the man would hear her call, she texted Christian.

> Man in house. I'm in bathroom. Don't have gun.
> Hurry.

She peeked through the slit in the door. The next strike of lightning showed him moving back around her side of the courtyard, putting himself between her and her gun in the bedroom.

Her phone vibrated. Her chest squeezed the breath from her lungs. *No. No. No.* She switched it to Do Not Disturb. *Stupid.* She should have done that in the first place. She pressed her back to the wall and looked at her phone for Christian's response.

> Get in tub.

She looked through the slit in the door and listened. Footsteps moving her way.

Darkness engulfing the space, she crawled for the tub and eased herself in. The ceramic cold against her body, she lay flat. *Please, Lord.*

You can do this. Go for his eyes.

Unless he came in shooting.

Footsteps sounded. Thunder roared before she could peg their direction, but they were close.

Gooseflesh rippled up her arms—adrenaline searing through her limbs.

The door squeaked on its hinges as it opened fully.

She held her breath. Heavy footfalls. One. Two.

Pop. Pop. Pop.

A curse echoed in the room followed by a slam.

Someone was down.

Please. Please. Don't let it be Christian.

Her breath ceased.

"It's okay," Christian said, and she gulped in air. *Thank you, Lord.*

She raised up on her elbows. He stood at an angle, his gun aimed at the floor.

She peered over the edge of the tub. The man lay on the floor, blood oozing from his chest, Christian's muzzle aimed at his head.

Exhaling, her body relaxed with relief and filled with anticipation. They had him, and finally they could get some answers, or so she prayed.

FIFTY-EIGHT

CHRISTIAN HANDED ANDI the gun while he zip-tied the man's hands. He'd called Joel and anticipated the cavalry and an ambulance to arrive soon. Not a moment later, the front door opened.

"Guys?" Riley called out.

"In the bathroom," Christian said. He'd gotten a good shot off, and they didn't want to risk moving the attacker until the paramedics arrived.

Riley raced around the corner and stopped short in the doorway. "Oh, my goodness, I'm so glad you're okay. I heard shots and thought my heart was going to stop." She clutched her chest.

"Trust me, I felt the same," Andi said.

Moments later, surprisingly not unanticipated in her mind, Greyson arrived, followed shortly by Joel and an ambulance.

The paramedics rushed in, tending to the man who moved in and out of consciousness until he was hauled away.

"I'm following him to the hospital in Santa Fe," Joel said. "I want to be there when he fully comes to."

"Thanks, Joel."

The sheriff nodded and tipped the brim of his hat before heading for the door. "Y'all stay safe."

Everyone nodded, but how could they be certain? Hits were coming from every angle. The question wasn't would another one come, but rather, when. Even with their thug, for lack of a name, in the hospital, there were more players in the game. A game she doubted was even close to over.

A half hour later, Christian handed Andi a lemonade before sitting on the couch beside her, rubbing the shoulder she kept rolling and stretching.

Greyson continued to pace the length of the family room, his hand fixed on his chin.

Riley's gaze tracked him. "Please sit down. You're making me nervous."

"Sorry," he said.

She scooched over, and he took a seat next to her. "I've got some bad news," Greyson said. "I wanted to make sure Andi was okay before I shared, but you need to know."

Andi reached out and took Christian's hand, slipping her fingers between his.

Christian straightened. If Greyson said it was bad news, it was bad.

Greyson cleared his throat. "I heard back from the warden."

Christian stiffened, his limbs taut. It couldn't be.

"Ethan Poppin got out early on parole."

Christian exhaled. Somehow, he'd known this was coming since he'd brought it up at the office. Despite all his reasonings for why it couldn't be Ethan, something anchored in his gut told him it was. He just hadn't wanted to admit it to himself. "How long ago did he get out?"

"A year," Greyson said, draping his arm across the back of the sofa.

Christian rubbed the back of his neck. Plenty of time to plan the heists. At least they knew their opponent now.

"He's supposed to stay in state . . . in California, where he was caught and served time. He checks in regularly with his parole officer over the phone, but as we all know, he could be anywhere, as long as he makes that weekly call."

"All right, that means . . ." Christian said, trying to wrap his head around the facts. *Focus on the facts, not the emotion coursing through you.* Just the thought of Ethan being out brought back a rush of bad memories—of who he used to be.

"You going to finish that sentence?" Riley arched a brow.

"Yeah." He raked a hand through his hair. "We're going to need to think about this differently. Andi isn't the motive. I am."

"Agreed," Greyson said.

Riley sat back, her shoulder resting against his arm.

"Sorry," he said, going to move it.

"Greyson, you're fine," she said, and he remained, but stiffness overtook him.

Christian bypassed wondering about Greyson's reaction and carried on. "Ethan and I planned our heists in juvie. Maybe . . . I mean, it stands to reason he could have met his new partner in prison. And, if so, they probably spent their time planning this all out. You can do far more from the inside than you'd imagine—it's quite frightening."

"I'll find out the identity of the man in the ambulance," Greyson said. "If we're lucky, he's Ethan's partner in crime, and we're well on our way to breaking this case. But maybe he's just another player. One sent to keep an eye on you too. If he was one of Ethan's cellmates or ties to him another way, I'll find out."

"Great." Christian looked to Andi, her hand still clutched in his. They needed to get Ethan back behind bars. He was no longer the man Christian had known all those years ago. He'd shifted to working with deadly partners. That wasn't the Ethan he knew.

"Well." Greyson stood and smoothed his dress shirt. "I imagine we should leave and let these two get some sleep." He looked to Riley.

"Agreed." She stood beside him.

"Ri," Christian said. "I know we got the guy, but I worry about you in your house alone. We can all bunk up in the main house."

"No need," Greyson said.

Christian arched a brow.

"I'll stay with Riley," Greyson said, straight to the point as always.

"I don't need anyone to stay with me. I've got my gun, and I'm a good shot."

"Humor me. Let these two get some rest," Greyson said, clearly trying to give them space.

"Very well," Riley said. "But only because you'll harangue me to death if I don't agree."

"Perfect." Greyson smiled.

"We'll grab you some of Deckard's clothes, so you don't have to sleep in your suit."

"I'll be fine."

"I can harangue you too."

Greyson's lips twitched into a smile. "Very well."

Riley smiled, then turned her attention on Andi, giving her a big good-night hug. Then, she tousled her brother's hair. "You keep this lady safe."

"Yes, ma'am."

Within a moment, she and Greyson filed out the door.

"Call us if you need anything," Greyson said over his shoulder before Riley shut the door behind them.

"Those two are quite the mix," Andi said.

Christian exhaled. "Funniest dynamic, right?"

"Greyson is so reserved and Riley's . . ."

"All over the place," Christian supplied.

"I was going to say vivacious."

He smiled. "I suppose that works too."

A half hour of cuddling on the couch later, Christian rolled his head to the side, looking at her eyes blinking in and out of slumber. "I think you better get some sleep."

"But I'm so comfy," she murmured, pulling the blanket tight about her.

"It'll be better if you can lay down in bed." Not that he wasn't treasuring holding her in his arms, but sleeping sitting up couldn't be best for her.

"Just a few more minutes," she murmured, snuggling deeper into his hold.

"Okay. Then off to bed with you." He kissed the top of her head and settled back in.

Cyrus's phone rang.

Casey looked over.

"It's nobody." Cyrus clicked it off. He'd have to call Teresa at a more private time.

It rang again.

Casey looked at the phone mounted on the dash. "Nobody is calling again."

He once again silenced the call. *Get the idea.* He grunted. How thick-headed could she be?

Finally, after a third try that ended the same, she stopped calling.

He pulled into their new home base, the heist not far away—the pulsing energy that always coursed through him before a hit burned his limbs.

He tapped the wheel as he pulled into the garage. They were on their third commandeered vehicle no one was looking for.

After double-checking the supplies they'd need, Casey moved for the house. "You coming?"

"I'm going to enjoy a smoke."

"Why do you always smoke outside?"

"I like the fresh air."

Casey laughed. "Fresh air and smoke, that's an interesting combination."

He was not amused. "I'll be in shortly." Once his simple-minded partner went inside, he lit a cigarette and made the call.

"It's about time," Teresa said when she answered.

"I told you. I can't talk in front of him, or he'll get wise to what we're doing."

"Fine, but I've got a huge problem."

At least she said *she* had a problem, because her problems weren't his. Not any longer.

"Enrique's been arrested."

He narrowed his eyes. "How do you know that?"

"He used his call to reach out to one of José's men in California. He relayed the info to José. All I know is he better not talk or *él está muerto*. And the same goes for you too if you fail me."

FIFTY-NINE

DECKARD ROLLED OVER and looked at the alarm clock. He stretched and clicked the light button so he could read the black numbers on the dull gray background. 2:15.

Time to get up. They needed to get ready, make the drive to the airport, and be there an hour and a half before their flight to Boston.

He sat up, placing his socked feet on the floor. The storm had whisked in cold, damp weather. Rubbing his neck, he gave himself a moment to rouse, then stood, stretched, and headed into the hall.

Rounding the corner, he bumped straight into Harper, knocking her off her feet.

"Oh, geez." He offered his hand. "I'm so sorry."

"All good," she said, taking hold of his hand.

He pulled her easily to her feet.

"Thanks." She ran her hand through her tousled hair.

He smiled. She looked adorable.

Adorable? He didn't use words like *adorable.* His brain was going haywire around Harper Grace. It was like he was falling for the lady, but he couldn't be. He didn't fall. "Ladies first," he finally said, gesturing toward the bathroom. "I'll go make some coffee."

"You're a lifesaver," she said, rubbing her eyes. "Thank you."

"You're welcome." He stood there, smiling at her like a fool. *Get your head on straight.* "I'll go now."

She stepped inside the bathroom, and the shower spray sounded as he moved for the galley kitchen. He stepped to the coffeemaker, assuming the coffee was kept nearby. He probably should have asked. He started looking in the cupboards.

Glass shattered behind him, and a bullet hit the island.

He dropped to the ground.

Glass shattered again and again, bullets slamming into different objects.

He crouched low, grabbed a knife off the counter, and moved. Waiting at the end of the island, he took a solid breath and bolted around the corner, flying back to his room for his gun. He slammed into Harper, both tumbling to the floor.

"Was that . . . ?" she asked, scrambling to her feet in her robe.

He yanked her back down. "Gunfire."

The shattering ceased. The echoing stilled.

He took the opportunity to bolt to his room and grab his Glock. Rushing back to the door, he held at the frame. Harper had wisely moved back around the corner.

"Call 911," he said before he crouched down and moved for the front room.

"What are you doing?" she asked in a rushed whisper.

"Going after them." He moved to the front door, stood to the side, gun raised, and cracked the door open.

After a moment, he moved outside. The air was thick and heavy from the storm.

Moving erratically, he positioned himself with a full view of where the shots had come from, but no one was there.

A car revved in the distance.

He raced toward the next condo, still moving erratically in case someone lingered behind. Leaning out from behind the neighbor's condo, he caught sight of two red taillights disappearing in the distance.

A knock yanked Christian from sleep. He pulled his gun and slipped his arm out from under Andi's back. She stirred and blinked up at him.

He held his finger to his lips as another knock sounded. He moved for the door and stood to the side, reaching for the handle.

"It's Greyson."

Greyson? He frowned.

What time was it? He opened the door.

Greyson stood there, his expression tight. "Sorry to wake you, but there's something you need to hear."

Christian stepped back so Greyson could enter. "What time is it?"

Greyson looked at his watch. "0530. Miss Andi," he said, nodding at her on the couch as he strode inside.

"Greyson." Andi nodded, pulling to a fully upright position.

"What's happening?" Riley asked from the doorway before Christian had a chance to close it.

"What are you doing up?" he asked. Why was everyone else wide awake?

"I heard Greyson leave the house and saw him walking toward your place."

"So naturally you followed." Of course his sister did.

"Sorry I woke you," Greyson said, resuming his pacing from earlier.

"Please sit down," Riley said. "It's too early in the morning for your pacing."

He took a seat on the smaller sofa, and Riley plopped down beside him—her in a relaxed position, him ramrod straight.

Christian shut and locked the door, half expecting someone else to come walking in. He returned to the sofa where he and Andi had fallen asleep, shockingly sitting up. Though, given the little sleep they'd been functioning on, it wasn't that surprising.

"What's up?" he asked, curious what Greyson had found. The man could find one M&M in a two-hundred-pound tub of Skittles.

Greyson cleared his throat. "Ethan Poppin shared his cell with only two men during his incarceration."

A surge of expectancy shot through Christian's limbs.

"The first," Greyson said, "was a Camden Hunter. He shared a cell with Ethan the first two years of his incarceration."

"And then?" Christian asked, anticipation pinging through his bouncing leg. His gaze flashed over to Andi, now fully awake, her attention rapt on Greyson.

"He served the remainder of his years with a Cyrus Timal. Ethan was released three months before Cyrus."

"What was Cyrus in for?" Riley asked.

"Armed robbery and assault. Seems he robbed two armored cars and got rough with the drivers before he was captured." Greyson shifted, still sitting perfectly straight, but his limbs not quite as stiff.

"Armored cars aren't easy to rob, and he managed two of them," Christian said.

"And he's clearly violent," Riley chimed in. "What else did you find out?" she asked Greyson, shifting to sit sideways to face him better.

He looked over, his gaze slipping over her, and he smiled. No doubt at her *Goonies Never Say Die* PJs.

"Greyson?" she asked.

"Right." He cleared his throat. "He was also tied to a missing-person's-turned-murder case."

They all waited silently for him to continue.

"He was living with a young woman. Police records indicate she was a thief too, knocking off a couple jewelry stores. The detective I spoke with said he figured Cyrus and her for a couple."

"Very romantic . . . two thieves." Riley rolled her eyes.

"When she got busted attempting a third robbery, police booked her. But the judge at her arraignment let her out on a ten-thousand-dollar bail."

"Cheap change for a jewel thief," Christian said. "A good one, at least."

Greyson released a streaming exhale. "Not long after, she went missing. A year later, what remained of her body was found by two kids swimming in a lake. Someone had strapped two concrete blocks around her waist. Whoever did it knew their knots—they were still in place. Local police divers had to cut the rope to retrieve the corpse."

"And they know it was her?"

"Any possibility of fingerprints was long gone, but they were able to match her dental records."

"You think Cyrus killed her for getting caught?"

"The detective on the case, Jax Johnson, said it looked like a professional hit."

"And he didn't peg Cyrus as the murderer?" Whether it was Cyrus or not, the man who'd tried to take out Andi had no qualms about murder—and likely had been the one to kill Alex and Julia.

"No. He certainly could have put out a contract, but he was in jail at the time. Detective Johnson said Cyrus was distraught, mumbled something about a woman named Teresa. Once he got out, that's the last they saw of Cyrus until his arrest eight years ago for the armored car heists."

"Any idea who Teresa is?" Andi asked, taking notes at this point.

"Yup. Here comes the frightening part," Greyson said, his voice strained.

"That wasn't the frightening part?" Riley asked, her already big blue eyes growing wider still.

"I'm afraid not." Greyson shifted forward.

"Then what is?" Christian asked, his muscles taut, his pulse thwacking through his ears.

"Cyrus Timal's sister is Teresa Gutierrez. She's the wife of drug kingpin José Gutierrez."

"Cyrus's brother-in-law is a drug lord?"

"I'm afraid so," Greyson said.

"What if she's the collector?" Andi said. "Maybe she's amassing a heritage collection of her own. The items came from Mesoamerica."

"Could very well be, and if that's the case, it stands to reason,"

Greyson said, getting to his feet, "they'll flee to Mexico when this is all over."

"If we don't stop them first," Christian said.

"No pressure there," Andi said.

"What else do we know about Cyrus and Teresa?" Christian asked.

"They grew up in New Mexico. In Lordsburg," Greyson said. "Teresa got started in crime earlier. I can't see her juvie records, but she was arrested three times before she was nineteen."

"Seriously?" Andi said. "Drugs?"

Greyson nodded. "The first time with her boyfriend . . . a Tomas Nelson." Greyson set her mug shot on the table.

"Great," Riley said.

"Then twice with a guy named Leo Hernandez." Greyson showed them another mug shot of Teresa, along with a news article he'd found with a picture of the two. "So, as you can see, her affection for drugs started early."

"Crazy," Riley said.

"And there's one more thing," Greyson said.

"Of course there is," Christian said. "And at this rate, I'm guessing it's worse news still?"

Greyson inclined his head.

"Worse than a drug lord?" Riley said.

"Given the information I received, I placed a call to my friend in the DEA."

Christian sat against the back of the couch, the stiff pillow propping him up. The man had connections everywhere. "And?" he asked.

"He said one of Gutierrez's men, Enrique Chavez, entered the States a few days ago."

"The man in our bathroom," Christian said.

"Highly likely, but I'm sure we'll have confirmation soon."

"Whoever he is, at least one guy's out of the picture," Andi said, shifting to sit closer to Christian, her arm against his.

Greyson rubbed a hand across his head. "Yes, but there's likely more."

Christian narrowed his eyes, studying Greyson's expression. For the first time since working with Greyson, he heard worry thick in his voice, could see it creased along his brow.

"You're worried," Christian said before thinking better of it in front of Andi and his sister. But it had caught him off-guard. They'd been through some serious and very dangerous cases, and Greyson had held calm and firm through them all—until now.

"Concerned," he said. "For your and Miss Andi's well-being."

"Miss Andi?" Riley said. "You're not that much older than us."

"A decade more than you," he said.

Riley pulled her knee to her chest. "In the grand scheme of things, it's not a lot."

Christian exhaled, trying to still his thudding heart. He'd been away from Ethan nearly a decade, but clearly his ex-partner's anger burned on. The image of Ethan's face the last night he'd seen him flashed through his mind. Ethan was furious at getting caught and blamed him, going so far as to tell the police he'd robbed the gallery with him. Thankfully, he'd had an ironclad alibi, or given his past and Ethan's false word, it could have gone south. The fact it didn't angered Ethan all the more.

Handcuffed and being escorted out of one of the Bureau's interrogation rooms, Ethan's warning he'd get Christian back all those years ago reverberated through his mind. Apparently, Ethan was holding true to his threat, but just how far was he going to take it?

SIXTY

DECKARD BUCKLED IN for their delayed trip to Boston, thanks to the shootout at Harper's place and all that involved. Six anxious hours aboard, knowing Randy might be the one who held the information they needed, gnawed at his gut. If they were wrong about Randy, they'd have to regroup and reassess.

Please, Lord, let Randy have the answers we need. Let him be honest with us. Help us to know who is behind this, and I pray it's not Mitch. If it is, how could I have been so wrong?

When asked who stood to gain the most from what happened in the lab, he'd been thinking promotion-wise, but when his brain stilled enough and he spent silent time in prayer, it came to him. Mitch obviously stood to gain the most from what happened in the lab that night. He stood to gain his freedom. But how? How would he have managed it all? And if it wasn't Mitch, who was the real killer?

"You okay?" Harper asked, looking over as the plane began its taxi toward the runway.

"Yeah. Just thinking it through."

"Yeah. I can't get it to stop racing through my head either. I'm praying Randy has answers and is willing to tell us. Or he at least points us in the next direction to go."

"I prayed the same except for the new direction. I should have prayed that rather than just thinking we'd be at a loss."

She reached over and squeezed his hand. "Let's take it one step at a time, like you said you always work your cases."

Normally he did, but this one had gotten personal.

"Do you think the police will have any luck finding whoever shot at us?"

"I wish I could say yes. . . ." They had nothing to go on except the casings found from their shooting position and the bullets found lodged in different places of her home.

"Yeah. That was my thought, but we can pray."

True. God could do abundantly more than they could even ask or think. He prayed with all his soul that God would open the door they needed to walk through and that they'd survive whatever was waiting for them on the other end.

Christian rolled his aching shoulders under the hot water streaming over him. He rested his hands against the tile wall.

There'd been no point in trying to go back to sleep. Everyone was on edge after last night's intruder.

Frustration seared through him, the hot water only serving to heat him more. Was no place safe? What had they all walked into?

A knock rapped on the door. "Christian," Andi said, her voice rushed.

He jumped out of the shower, threw on a towel, and opened the door. "What's wrong?" He stood there dripping.

Beet red consumed her cheeks. "Sorry. I didn't stop to think. I . . ."

"What's wrong?"

She swallowed, casting her gaze away, then back up to his face. "A gallery in Phoenix was hit last night."

"Okay, I'll get dressed and see how fast we can catch a flight."

"Greyson's already on it. There's one leaving in two hours."

Right now, two hours felt like forever. "We better pack bags. We don't know how long we'll be based there."

"I was thinking the same thing. They hit a string here. They could do the same in Arizona."

SIXTY-ONE

HARPER AND DECKARD STOOD OUTSIDE Randy Fox's door. They'd stay all night if they had to. Sooner or later, he had to come home. They'd hoped to catch him at his work, but thanks to a very friendly receptionist, they'd learned he'd already left for the day.

"I still say she was flirting," Harper said with a smirk as they sank to the floor.

Might as well get comfortable—who knew how long of a wait they had.

He shrugged "Ah . . ." he said, lifting his hand flat and tilting it back and forth, "maybe a little."

"Please," she said, rolling her eyes. "I can see that smug grin peeking to come out. You nearly had the poor woman simpering."

"Poor woman? Please, she was the one flirting. I was just being—"

"Charming," she said.

So Harper thought he was charming. He smiled.

"See. There's that grin." She was having a good time ribbing him.

"What grin?" he said, trying to force his lips to stay still, neutral, but he was doing a terrible job at it. He liked that Harper viewed him as charming, but he honestly hadn't been flirting with the woman. She had handled that all on her own. He'd simply remained polite and professional.

"That smile," she said, her expression and tone jovial.

Down the hall and around the corner the elevator dinged.

They looked at each other and said, "Randy," in unison.

Deck prayed it was him. He got to his feet, then offered Harper a hand and helped her up.

A man about their age with brown hair came walking down the hall juggling two brown paper grocery bags in his arms.

He glanced up, his gaze landing on Harper, and then did a double take.

He froze.

"Hey, Randy," she said.

Randy dropped the bags and bolted.

"Come on, man. Don't make me chase you," Deckard hollered after him as he took up pursuit.

Randy sprinted around the corner and frantically pressed the elevator buttons. He looked up, saw Deckard coming for him, and dodged into the stairwell. Deckard followed. Randy rounded the first set of stairs and nearly bowled into an elderly woman wearing a leotard, leggings, and legwarmers. Trying not to take her out, Randy shifted sideways, lost his balance, and tumbled down the remaining few steps, landing in a pile on the platform.

Deckard jumped down. "Love the legwarmers," he said to the lady, and then looked to Randy. "Look, dude. We just want to ask you a few questions. We mean you absolutely no harm."

"That's why you're wearing a gun." Randy lifted his chin.

"I'm a PI," he said. "Required for my occupation." He offered Randy his hand and helped him to his feet.

Randy brushed his hands off on his jeans. "A PI?" he said. "Who are you working for?"

"I'm working for Miranda Forester. Just trying to prove she wasn't the one who botched the evidence."

"Look, man. I'm sorry about what happened to Miranda, but I can't go there. I talk to you and I could end up dead."

"Dead?" Deckard frowned. "Look, whatever you say is safe with us. I won't tie anything back to you. You obviously know Harper, so I'm going to assume you know Miranda as well."

"Yeah, I do."

"What happened to her wasn't right." She was innocent, and there was something far more sinister at play than he'd expected. He wouldn't rest until he figured it out, and it was starting to look like Randy was the key to opening the next door of this crazy maze. "Please just talk with us. I'll keep it in full confidence."

"You really have no idea what you're dealing with," Randy said.

"Then tell us. Please."

Randy released a shaky exhale. "Come on in the apartment, but what we discuss stays in the apartment. Deal?"

"Deal," Deckard said. "Unless someone is in immediate danger from what you tell me. That I can't ignore."

"The only ones in danger are you guys if you keep at it," Randy said in a hushed whisper, even though they were the only ones there. "The powers that be will take you out."

Deckard arched his brows. "The powers that be?"

"In the apartment," Randy said, leading him up the stairs.

Fifteen minutes later, Deckard and Harper sipped on cups of coffee while they waited for Randy to clean up the broken-egg mess from dropping the grocery bag and put away his perishables.

"How long have you lived here?" Deckard asked, looking about the sparsely furnished apartment.

"Awhile," Randy said. Grabbing a cup of coffee of his own, he took a seat in the armchair facing Deckard and Harper on the couch. He took a sip, then set his mug on the windowsill beside him. "You want to know about the shirt."

Harper lurched forward. "Yes."

"Whoa there," Deckard said. "Don't want to spook the poor guy," he said out of the corner of his mouth.

"Right," she whispered, easing back.

"Dude." Randy rubbed his hands on his jeans, his knee bouncing up and down as his leg shook. "I've been spooked ever since."

Deckard scooted forward on the couch, inching to the edge. "Ever since?"

"Ever since I got that call," Randy said, lifting his mug in his wobbly hold and taking another sip. "Does anyone else know you're here?" He looked at Harper. "Anyone from the Bureau?"

"No." She shook her head.

"The only people who know we are here are part of our investigative agency, and no one there will utter a word." Deckard lifted his coffee mug, the hot ceramic heating his hands that refused to warm. Boston in October was colder than he'd anticipated. "We pride ourselves on discretion. It's a necessity in our business." He took a sip, the warm liquid sliding down his throat.

"Please," Harper said, fidgeting with the hem of her green blouse—the same emerald of her beautiful eyes. "We know something is very wrong, but we don't know where to go next."

"Not *where*," Randy said, setting his mug down. "*Who*."

Harper frowned. "Who?"

Randy stood and strode to the back hall. "I have something you'll want to see. Wait here. I'll be right back."

"No problem," Deckard said.

"Thank you," Harper added.

She scooted closer to Deckard. "I think this might finally be the information we need," she whispered as she reached over and clutched his free hand.

"You're cold," she said.

"It's cold in this place."

She rubbed his hand, trying to warm him. It only took a second with her soft hand caressing his.

Randy shlepped back in, clutching a folder to his chest.

Harper kept holding his hand, and the hint of a smile touched Deckard's lips.

"Look, you two might wish you hadn't gone here." Randy tapped the folder. "I'll give them to you, but you can't tell anyone where you got them." Desperation settled in his dull gray eyes. "You give me your word?"

"Yes, sir," Deckard said, letting go of Harper's hand momentarily to shake Randy's hand.

Randy seemed taken aback by the gesture, but he shook Deckard's hand in return, then cleared his throat. "Before we get to these . . ." He crossed his legs and tapped the folder against his knee. "I have to tell you what led up to it."

"The shirt," Harper said, leaning forward.

"Yes. I was working the locker when Miranda came in that day."

"What did she sign out?" Deckard asked, taking another sip of his coffee, praying this was it—that Randy held the piece that would put the scattered puzzle together.

"I don't know." Randy's knee bounced. "The item numbers are too many to memorize."

"Did you see what it was?" Harper asked.

"Not clearly, but . . ." Randy paused, rubbing his chin, and Deckard prayed he wasn't backing off. "It wasn't the shirt," he finally said.

"How can you be certain?" he asked, needing to make sure Randy was positive.

"Because I took the shirt," Randy said.

Deckard nearly choked on his coffee. "I'm sorry," he said, wiping his mouth.

"You took the shirt?" Harper said. "Why? I don't understand."

"I got a call," Randy said, his hand trembling, the coffee in his mug almost sloshing over the rim.

Who had called, and who had this guy so flipping scared? "From who?" Deckard asked.

"He didn't say."

"What did he say?" Harper asked, tightening her hold on Deckard's hand, anticipation fixed on her face.

"He told me I had to listen very carefully." Randy set his mug down and shifted in his seat. He swallowed, his Adam's apple bobbing in his lanky neck. "I had two things to do."

"And you just listened to him?" Harper asked, irritation building in her voice.

"You don't understand," Randy said, perspiration slithering down his temple.

Deckard narrowed his eyes. "What don't we understand?"

Randy swallowed again, a memory shifting across his gaze. "They had my sister."

"Who's they?" Deckard asked. "I thought you said *him*. . . ."

Randy rubbed his arm. "There was one man on the phone, but he sent . . ." His voice cracked. "He sent me a video of my sister." Tears beaded in his eyes. "She was gagged, bound, and blindfolded. The man on the phone took the video. Another one had a gun to her head."

"Could you see anything about them? Any physical features?" Deckard asked.

Randy rocked back and forth on his chair. "Nothing in the video. The one holding the phone stayed off camera except for his hand, the other wore a black mask."

"Was there anything to identify them?"

"The one on the phone had a signet ring on his finger. Gold, some engraving on it."

"Could you see what was on it?" Harper asked, straining forward and tugging Deckard's hand with her.

"No. It was too fast."

"Anything else?" Deckard asked, hoping for something, anything, to get who was behind this.

"His voice was gravelly," Randy said, "which applies to hundreds of guys out there, but the one with the gun to my sister's head told her to shut up when she whimpered. His voice was different."

"Can you describe how it was different?" Harper asked, her tone back to her gentle, soothing self.

"He had a hint of an accent." Randy rubbed his arm faster.

Sheesh, this guy looked like he was going to jump out of his skin. But if someone had Riley . . . Rage boiled hot in Deckard's chest.

"What kind of accent?" Deckard asked, simmering his flaring temper. "Was it regional like Boston or Georgia? That type of thing?"

"I think it was Eastern European."

"Okay, so two men. One with a gold ring and gravelly voice, which is a great detail," Deckard said. Randy had been FBI. The level of fear in his eyes indicated how dangerous what they were about to learn was. "I'm guessing they returned your sister safely?"

Randy nodded.

"Did she recall anything about them?" he asked.

Randy straightened, his voice rising in pitch. "Nothing. She was terrorized by the experience."

"Did you alert the Bureau?"

"No way." Randy shook his head. "The men made it crystal clear they'd kill her if I did." His face paled. "You have no idea what it's like seeing your baby sister . . ." He hiccupped on a sob but contained it.

"And after she was safe?" Harper asked. "Why didn't you tell anyone?"

"I got her out of there. As far across the country as I could."

"She lives here too?"

"No. She lives in an undisclosed location."

"I understand." If it were Riley, that would be the extent of his answer as well. "Okay," he said. "And there's nothing else you remember about the men?"

"No." Randy shook his head. "Not from then."

Deckard narrowed his eyes. "What do you mean, not from then?"

Randy raked a hand through his hair. "I'll get to that, but first you have to understand . . . to know . . . how it started."

"Explain it to us," Harper said, compassion brimming in her eyes.

So empathetic. Sometimes he wished he were like that, but it wasn't in his makeup.

Finally, Randy cleared his throat. "They told me to take the shirt or they'd kill her. I . . ."

Deckard shifted, working to make his body language nonthreatening. Who were these people?

"So I took the shirt out of the evidence box and slid it into my messenger bag. I have a back flap where I keep personal items, and I left at the end of my shift."

Randy looked at Harper. "I'm so sorry, but I changed the evidence bag number in the logbook. I know that hurt Miranda, and I didn't mean for it to, but these men . . . I feared they'd come after Debbie again if I said anything. Their threats weren't empty."

"Debbie's your sister?" Deckard said, clarifying, and Randy nodded.

Harper's jaw clamped, clearly holding back what she truly wanted to say.

"Then?" Deckard said, before Harper lost her restraint and reamed out the guy for hurting her best friend.

Randy stood. "I need more coffee," he said, moving around the island to the kitchen space.

As jittery as he was, the last thing the dude needed was more caffeine.

Harper looked over at him.

He nodded. They had this.

Randy retook his seat, and Deckard waited for him to start. And waited . . . "Okay. I'm guessing they had you destroy the shirt," Deckard said, when he could wait no longer.

"No." Randy shook his head. "They had me deliver it."

Deliver it? Deckard took a steadying breath. Was it possible Randy had seen the men . . . seen something? "Who did you deliver it to?"

Randy took a sip of coffee, and they waited again.

Anticipation tingled through Deckard's limbs, his knee bouncing.

"They told me to drive to Elephant Butte."

"Okay . . ." Deckard nudged.

"They had me go to Rock Canyon Marina alone. They said if I'd told the Bureau, if they saw anyone else there, they'd kill Debbie, and they would take their time. I won't go into the details of what they said they'd do to her." He looked at Harper. "Not in front of you." She nodded her thanks. "But it was brutal, and I believed them."

"So you took the shirt," Deckard said, trying to keep Randy on track, not let him get stuck in the weeds.

"They told me there was a life-preserver box on the main dock leading to the slips, to put the shirt in it and drive away. Don't look back, they said. Don't say a word or they'd come for my sister and me both. I didn't care about me, but I couldn't let them harm Debbie."

"So you did as they said?" Deckard said, understanding the man's love and concern for his sister.

"No," Randy said.

Deckard pulled his chin in. He hadn't expected that.

"I drove away, but I went up to the hill overlooking the marina, parked a ways back, crawled in, and watched, looking through my telephoto camera lens. I needed insurance. A bargaining chip if they ever threatened my family again."

"So you saw who retrieved the shirt?" Harper asked. Hope drenched her voice.

Please, let this be it, Lord.

"Better yet," Randy said, holding up a photograph. "I got his picture."

SIXTY-TWO

THANK YOU, JESUS. Finally, a lead. Deckard reached for the photo.

He narrowed his eyes. He'd seen the man in the photograph before, but where? His brain tracked back, trying to place him. He noted the signet ring on his finger. "Masonic lodge," he said, holding up the photo and pointing at the ring.

Randy nodded, the muscle in his jaw flickering. "He grabbed the shirt and looked around the parking lot. I guess to be sure I'd gone. Then he strode down the dock to a boat. Another man met him there and took the shirt." Randy pulled out a second picture and handed it to Deckard.

He looked down, his eyes widening. It was quite a bit farther away, but the image was clear enough. "That's Councilman Markowitz." Wearing what appeared to be the same signet ring. "Anne Marlowe worked for Markowitz," Deckard said.

"You think he killed her?" Harper asked.

"No. Well, he probably had a hand in it, but . . ." Deckard sat back as the puzzle finally fell in place—at least the big pieces. He raked a shaky hand through his hair. It couldn't be.

"Deckard," Harper said. "You all right? You just went white."

"I know who killed Anne." He had a picture in his house of him, the councilman, and the man who'd retrieved the shirt at a charity dinner. Deckard gripped the photo tighter. And all three wore the same Masonic signet ring.

"Who?" Harper asked, her voice echoing through his thoughts.

"Andi was right," Deckard said, the air gut-punched from his lungs. How had he not seen it?

"Deck, who killed Anne?" Harper asked, jarring him from his thoughts.

"Mitch Abrams killed Anne."

Randy sat back. "Do you understand now? If they're powerful enough to get Mitch Abrams out of prison, who knows what they can—" He stopped short, his jaw tightening. "Wait a minute." His skin flushed. "I thought you looked familiar. You worked for Mitch. I saw an article in the news about how your detective work got him off." Randy stood. "You have to go now."

"But he's working for Miranda now," Harper said. "He didn't know—"

"No." Randy paced, shaking his head. "I'm not sharing any more. You're the one who got Mitch off."

"I had no idea," Deckard said. "I swear." He stood, trying to corral Randy. "Look, man, if there's any way I can right this wrong, I'll do it."

"You can't re-try him for Anne's murder," Randy said. "Double jeopardy. He's gotten away with it for good."

Deckard tried taking a deep breath, but it wouldn't come. "I didn't know," he choked out. "How could I not know?" He sank back down, letting the couch hold him up. Mitch Abrams had played him.

Randy studied him. "You really didn't know?"

"I had no idea." Shock riddled his limbs—cold and penetrating. He sank back against the cushions, trying to run everything from the case through his head. "I helped a guilty man get out of jail," he said, swallowing. "And I can't do a dang thing about it."

"Maybe not about Anne's murder, but there's something else . . ." Randy looked at Harper. "You trust this guy?"

"One hundred percent," she said.

Randy dipped his head, arching his brow. "You're sure?"

314

"Positive," she said.

"I'll be right back." Randy stood, moving for the apartment door.

"Where are you going?" Harper asked.

"Across the hall." Randy stepped into the hall, leaving the door open wide behind him.

"Deck," she said, clutching his hand again. "I'm so sorry. I can't imagine . . ."

"I got a guilty man out of jail," he said again, his brain a fog of disbelief. How was he going to live with that?

A knock sounded in the hall, and he directed his attention back to Randy. The neighbor's door opened, and Randy talked to the guy—their voices too low to hear. The man disappeared, and a few minutes later, returned with a lockbox.

"Thanks," Randy said, loud enough for them to hear. He strode back in the apartment and kicked the door shut behind him. He paused, balanced the lockbox against his body, and managed to lock the door. "It took me a bit to figure it out," he said, "but I got it. After I got Debbie settled here . . ." He cleared his throat. "Somewhere safe."

Which was a matter of minutes away, he'd bet.

"I went back, laid low, and did surveillance. I needed to be on site, but out of sight."

He was well trained for it from his years with the Bureau. At least Deckard was guessing it'd been years, based on the guy's age.

"Then I was able to do a good amount of research and compile evidence from here."

"Why didn't you take what you learned to the Bureau?" Harper asked, the frustration and annoyance back in her voice.

Deckard rubbed his chin, letting it all sift through. He didn't blame Harper for being irritated with the man. He'd hung her best friend out to dry, but they had to keep him talking.

"Because the men who did this were powerful enough to corrupt a Bureau crime lab. I had no idea who I could trust, who all had been corrupted. And, bottom line, I wasn't willing to do anything to jeopardize my sister's life."

Deckard sat forward, straightening his shoulders. He understood the man's deep concern for his sister. But sitting on evidence that could burn the men responsible . . . He struggled with the thought of suppressing it as Randy had done.

Randy studied Deckard long and hard. "I'm sharing this because I trust Harper, and she obviously trusts you."

"Thank you," Deckard said. "Truly."

"You're sure you want to see this?" Randy said, tapping the lockbox. "The responsibility will shift to you—to do something with the information. You have to promise you'll leave me out of it."

"I promise," Deckard said, and he'd hold true to his word.

"Don't think I'm handing away the only copies. I kept this set close in case I had to run in a hurry, but I have two more sets hidden throughout the city."

"Wise man," Deckard said.

"And you swear you'll do the right thing with the information?"

"I promise." Deckard nodded.

Randy took a deep breath, then looked to Harper.

"He will." She nodded. "Whatever the right thing is, Deckard will do it. I promise."

He warmed at the steadfast belief she had in him. Now, if Randy would just believe him. They needed to see what was in that box.

"All right," Randy said, inputting the combination to the lockbox. A click sounded, and he lifted the lid. "I have proof that Mitch Abrams and Councilman Markowitz have been working together on a big land deal to build new condos, stores, an entire planned community."

"Okay," Deckard said, unsure where this was going. "That alone is not illegal." Though Mitch, a real estate developer, working with the councilman who lobbied for the land deal was unethical.

"It might not be, but I bet the fraud department at the Bureau might feel differently. However, what *is* illegal is the fact that they've never built it."

"What?" Harper frowned.

"They got big money from investors and money from people, families that bought houses and plots of land."

Deckard slumped back. That was the last thing he'd expected. "Mitch is running a Ponzi scheme, and the councilman must be getting kickbacks by lobbying for the projects."

"Oh, he's getting kickbacks, all right. I have a friend . . . a hacker," he said. "I'm not proud of going that way, but I didn't know who else I could trust."

"And?" Deckard prodded as all the pieces shifted into place. A murderous place. Anne must have seen or overheard something. She probably confronted them or tried to break things off with Mitch, and he'd killed her for it—trying to set Judge Simmons up in the process. If Simmons hadn't had last-minute company, he might have gone down. A wife's alibi was always questioned.

"Markowitz's kickbacks are hidden deep in his offshore financials but they're there. Wire transfers, the whole nine yards. And the man who retrieved the shirt is William Richards. He has loose ties to the mob."

Deckard dipped his chin, arching his brows. "Are you serious?"

"There's dirty money involved from the backers. It's no wonder they wanted Mitch out of jail. They needed him. He held the land rights to the whole complex in his name. They stood to lose millions if their plans didn't go through."

"What plans?" Harper asked.

"It's an elaborate scheme my friend explained. They pay the first lien of investors with the newest investors' money, pretend they're moving forward. . . ."

"They probably have a trailer and some equipment on site. Give the impression they're just waiting on whatever issue they make up. Then it's one thing after another," Deckard said.

"Exactly." Randy nodded.

"So they expected Judge Simmons would be convicted for Anne's murder and Mitch would be home free. And he probably would have been if it weren't for Andi being so good at her job and finding his skin cells," Harper said. "They probably had Todd there that night to watch her results, and when the only DNA came back as Mitch's, they freaked. He couldn't do anything about her results, but I bet he corrupted the sample that very night. And Andi took the fall." Red flared in her cheeks.

"I owe Andi a huge apology," Deckard said.

"You were going up against a lot of evidence pointing to her."

And he fell for it. Rage burned through his limbs. How could he have been so duped? Mitch had played it so well. Like those people who are so twisted they lie like it's the truth. Like Satan in the Garden of Eden. He swallowed. "What do you have for me to take to the Bureau?"

"The contents of this box will do it. Special Agent Glen Tiller is who I'd go to. I'm assuming no one has corrupted the fraud department, but at this rate, who knows."

They spent the next hour going through the evidence Randy had brilliantly amassed. They'd be able to nail all three men, but Deckard was personally going to pay Mitch a visit.

SIXTY-THREE

CHRISTIAN AND ANDI EXITED the Trent Gallery in Phoenix.

"Well, that felt like a waste of time," she said.

"At least they were polite, but given the circumstances, I can't see them keeping us in the loop. I'm an out-of-state PI, and your company doesn't insure the gallery."

"I know. It wasn't on our list, which makes me nervous," she said as they made their way across the large parking lot to their rental car.

"We don't know how to track them now that they aren't falling into any of the categories we made."

"True, but I'd say we're still playing a game," he said, his muscles stiffening as he scanned the parking lot.

"What?"

He gestured to the car—to the note made out to Andi on the dash.

"You locked the car, right?" she asked.

He nodded. "A car lock isn't much of a deterrent to art thieves."

"True," she said. "You have gloves?"

"Not in the rental car. I better grab one of the officers. They'll need to take the letter as evidence anyway."

"Agreed."

"Actually, why don't you head in. I'll keep watch out here."

She scanned the area. "You think they're watching?"

"Given the hairs on the nape of my neck standing up, as cliché as that sounds, I'd say yes." There were two office buildings across the way. They could be in either one of them. "Let's both go in."

"Okay." She nodded.

He rested his hand on her lower back, and they reentered the building. Grabbing Officer Trujillo, they headed back outside.

Officer Trujillo slipped on his gloves, lifted and then opened the letter. He stepped back so both Andi and Christian could read what it said.

> *It Can Be Cruel, Poetic, Or Blind. But When It's Denied, It's Violence You May Find.*

"The answer is justice," Christian said.

"What sense does that make?" the officer said with a shake of his head as he folded up the note. He slipped it into the envelope and then slid the envelope into an evidence bag. "You two be careful. Safe travels home."

"Oh, we're basing here for a few days."

Trujillo's brow arched. "Oh?"

"They hit multiple galleries in New Mexico." It would have been three if they hadn't staked out Tad's Taos gallery. It just hit him—Tad must have tipped them off. That weasel.

"We have a theory they'll do the same here," Andi said.

"That would be a bold move," Trujillo said. "Bold, but stupid. We'll have extra coverage on all the galleries in the area. Well, we'll drive by each on patrol. There are too many in the area to have an officer stationed at each."

"I think that's what they're counting on," Christian said. Once the officer left, he turned to Andi. "It's a Riddler riddle."

She arched a brow. "Like *Batman* Riddler?"

"Yeah. Ethan and I used to read them when we were in juvie."

"What do you think it means?"

"He views what he's doing as getting justice for himself. And by trying to harm me, in his mind, I'm getting the justice I deserve."

"He's crazy."

"Or so warped by revenge, he doesn't see the magnitude of what he's doing."

Climbing into their rental car, he pulled out of the lot. "I'll update Greyson on the way to the hotel."

"Good idea," she said.

"Hey, Greyson," he said when Greyson answered the call.

"How'd it go?"

"We didn't get much information from the cops, but we couldn't expect much more, given the circumstances. We're going to stay put in case they hit any other galleries. Headed to the hotel now."

"Makes sense."

"Have you heard from Deckard and Harper today?" he asked.

"Yes, have you? Did he tell you what happened?"

Christian frowned. "No, I haven't had the chance. What happened?"

Greyson hesitated.

"Tell them," Riley said in the background. "Or I will."

Greyson exhaled. "They were fired on at Harper's condo."

Andi lurched forward. "What?"

"They're fine. Still went to Boston, a little later than planned, and should make it back tonight."

"But they won't go back to her place, will they?"

"No. They are coming to stay at my place, as is Riley."

"Under duress," Riley said in the background.

"Thanks, Greyson. I wouldn't want her alone out on the ranch."

"Don't worry. Go get settled in your hotel and keep us posted."

"Will do."

Hanging up, he and Andi looked at each other. How much crazier could things possibly get?

A half hour later, they'd checked into their hotel for the night, getting adjacent rooms.

They'd just entered their rooms when Christian's cell rang. He glanced at the screen. "It's Deckard."

She sat on the edge of the bed as he answered.

He listened for a bit, and then said, "You're kidding. Sure." He handed her the phone. "He wants to talk to you."

He sat beside her on the bed, his heart leaping in his chest for her and the news.

"What? Really?" Tears streamed down her face. "I appreciate it. Thank you, Deckard." She disconnected the call and hung her head as more tears fell.

"He did it. He proved you were right. There was a setup."

She looked up at him, tears flowing down her face. "I was starting to think it would never happen."

He rubbed her back. "It's not over quite yet. They're going to get Mitch to confess."

"How on earth does he plan to do that?"

"Deckard's furious Mitch conned him. He'll find a way."

"But he can't go back to jail. Double jeopardy."

"Deck said they've got another way."

"How?" She furrowed her brow.

"He didn't say, but if Deck's got a way, they'll get him."

She shook her head. "I just can't believe they proved the setup. That I'm innocent."

"Well, I can, but this calls for some celebrating."

She looked up at him and blinked.

He swiped her tears with the pad of his thumb. "I saw some dresses in the lobby shop that would look beautiful on you. Go pick one out and charge it to the room. We're going to have our first date."

"What?" She laughed.

"I'm serious. I'll see you back here in an hour?"

"Okay." She nodded with a smile.

"Just don't leave the hotel." Ethan was off his rocker. Christian feared what he'd do if he got his hands on Andi or any of his loved ones.

SIXTY-FOUR

WAITING TO SEE where Ethan and Cyrus would strike next, knowing it was coming but not being able to stop it, was excruciating. Greyson and Riley had alerted all the galleries on their list, and Christian prayed that would help, but the galleries were, in reality, sitting ducks—even with beefed-up security. Police were on alert, and an APB had gone out on both Cyrus Timal and Ethan Poppin. Maybe they'd be lucky and a squad car would pick them up before they could strike, but he doubted this was over.

He slid his shirt on and buttoned it up. It seemed wrong in one sense to be having a date with Andi while Ethan and Cyrus were out there, but short of literally combing all the streets and searching every building in town, there wasn't any more that they could do. And she deserved one good night in the midst of all this mess. She deserved the best.

He'd always believed—or hoped—he'd fall in love one day. But he could never picture it, couldn't imagine what it would be like, after having grown up in a home without love. Now he had a loving family with Deck and Riley—Greyson too—a solid profession, and a home with roots. All that had been missing was meeting a wonderful woman he'd fall for. Now she was getting ready in the next room. It was new and just at the beginning, but falling he most definitely was.

I pray, Lord, that you'll bless us with a wonderful night and that you'd prevent Ethan and Cyrus from striking again. Let them be caught before they can do any more damage. I love you, Lord. Amen.

He moved through his room, grabbing the flowers he'd had brought up, and strode to the connecting door. Taking a steadying breath—it was amazing how she set him tingling with anticipation when it'd been less than an hour since he'd seen her—he smoothed his shirt, cleared his throat, and knocked on the door.

———————————————— ■ ■ ————————————————

Andi moved for the door at the sound of the knock, taking a moment to adjust the dress she'd bought. Excitement shot through her, sparking in her limbs as she strode to the door, the soft blue A-line dress with layered skirt swishing about her legs.

"Just a sec," she said, pausing to put on the gold heels and then smoothing the gold sash across her waist.

She opened the door and her mouth dropped—or at least she feared it had. "You clean up nice." A warm smile curled on her lips. Christian always looked *good*, but dressed up in black trousers, a white button-down shirt, his forearms rippling with toned muscles, his broad chest . . . *Wow. Just wow.*

"Thanks," he said, handing her the bouquet of flowers.

"Aww. Thanks." She sniffed them. "I'll set them over here and call the front desk for a vase." She laid them on the desk, then turned back to Christian.

"You're gorgeous," he said. "You always are."

Gorgeous? No one had ever called her that before.

"I have reservations at the hotel restaurant, but you know what I really want to do?" he said, brushing her hair back and placing a kiss on her forehead.

Her limbs tingled from his tender touch, and a delighted smile curled on her lips. "I have a feeling I do."

"And?"

"I want to too," she said.

"You sure?"

"Don't even have to think about it." She smiled.

An hour later, shoes were kicked across the floor and they were on it. Room service trays laden with yummy food waited on the coffee table, but they'd been too competitive in an albeit friendly way to stop and eat.

"Uno," he said, flipping down the green three.

They'd been talking about how much they both loved the game since they'd started working with one another. It was the only card game she was good at, but apparently she'd met her match. He was decimating her.

"Oh, come on." She threw her cards down. "No way! Not again."

He arched a sexy brow. "Want to go again?"

"You bet. We're playing until I beat you, mister."

"Mister, huh?"

She smirked. "Yes. Now shuffle the cards in that fancy way of yours."

"Fancy?" He smiled, fine lines creasing at the corners of his beautiful brown, honey-tinged eyes.

"Where you lift them up in a way that defies gravity."

"Like this," he said, lifting the cards in a long, streaming line.

"Exactly," she said.

"Want me to teach you?" he asked.

"Yes, please." She couldn't even shuffle the basic way, having to just jumble the cards by mixing them sideways in her hands over and over.

"Okay." He raised up on his knees. "Come here."

She didn't have to be asked twice. Getting on her knees, she scooted over on them. "Here," he said, positioning her in front of him, her back against his strong, chiseled chest.

She swallowed.

"Now," he said, wrapping his arms around her. "Take these in your hand," he said, placing them in her right palm, "and if you pull up with purpose, they'll fly in your hand."

She tried and tried, then finally did it. "I got it!"

"Very good," he said. "Now . . ." He smirked. "If only you were that good at UNO."

"Oh, you did not."

"Pretty sure I just did." His grin widened.

"All right, let's go," she said, rolling her shoulders and stretching out her arms. "We're going as long as it takes for me to win."

"Ooh. I don't know if I have all night in me." He chuckled.

"You just wait."

The sun up and his stomach growling for another round of room service—this time breakfast—he laid down his last card. "Uno," he said with an I'm-sorry smile.

She grunted and shoved his shoulder. It was playful, but from the glimmer in his eyes, something was coming. Before she could blink, he snaked his arms around her, tackling her—more like laying her down with gentleness—to the floor.

She laughed.

"You give up yet?"

"Never."

He smiled. "I had a feeling you'd say that." He brushed the hair from her forehead, his smile shifting to one of tenderness. He tipped her chin up to press his lips to hers.

Andi's phone trilled.

No! She didn't release her hold but knew it was inevitable. What was it with ringing phones at the worst possible moment?

They both looked over at her cell vibrating across the coffee table.

"I'll get it," she said, fumbling up and over to the coffee table. "It's Greyson," she said, staring at the screen.

Christian patted his trouser pockets. "I must have left mine in my room," he said, lying back, his weight propped on his elbows, his long legs stretched out.

"Hello," she answered, putting it on speaker.

"Hello, Andi," Greyson said.

"Hey, man," Christian said. "Sorry, left my phone in the other room."

"It's fine," Greyson said, his voice tense.

"It doesn't sound fine," Christian said. "What's up?"

Greyson exhaled. "Christie's Auction House in L.A. got hit in the wee hours of the morning—it looks like our guys."

It was a six-hour drive from Phoenix to L.A. If Ethan and Cyrus had been watching them at the Trent Gallery, they had to have had everything set up pre-heist. How far out had these heists been planned and in play?

"Christie's wasn't on our list," Andi said.

"It was on Ethan's." Christian sunk onto the edge of the bed.

Andi frowned at the same time she and Greyson said, "What?"

"I just didn't think . . ." He raked a hand through his hair. "Christie's was the heist that got Ethan arrested. I should have realized he might return to the scene of his crime." What kind of game was Ethan playing?

"And . . ." He released a stream of pent-up breath.

"And?" Greyson said.

"I think they're going to hit again in Cali, and I might know where, sort of."

"Oh?" Greyson asked.

"Yeah." Christian paced the plush carpet. "Ethan picked Christie's, and while we were researching it, before I walked away, he got all gung-ho about hitting an art collection on a yacht."

"A yacht?" Andi said. "That's unique."

"Yeah." Christian stopped pacing. "We did some preliminary research on a handful of them, so he could be hitting anyone on that list. I've got to stop and think like Ethan would."

"Okay, so why go back to Christie's?" Greyson asked. "Especially after he was busted there."

Christian exhaled, the reason behind it now clear. "In addition to money, of course, he's attempting to prove to me that he's now the better thief."

"So he really did have this all planned out? First hitting places with your security systems so you'd be called in," Greyson said.

"And put on the suspect list," he said.

"Then nearly killed." Andi paced the room, her hands clasped.

"I don't think that was Ethan's plan," Christian said. "I think it was all Enrique. Ethan is playing the game, and he clearly didn't want it to stop back there. I bet it was Cyrus's sister who sent Enrique to kill us. She didn't care about a game. Only the artifacts, if I'm guessing right."

"They left a message at Christie's," Greyson said.

"What did it say this time?" Andi asked.

"It was actually made out to Christian and in a man's handwriting."

"Why the change?" Andi asked. "Why were the notes made out to me in the first place if this was all about you? And why in a woman's handwriting?"

"I'm guessing so that it wasn't obvious it was him straightaway. It would make sense why they used a woman's handwriting to start," Christian said, cracking his knuckles from the hours of shuffling cards.

"Julia's handwriting, you think?" Andi asked.

"That'd be my bet. I'm guessing they had her write them before this all kicked off. Certainly before she was murdered. They probably figured a woman's handwriting would throw us off."

"And now?" Andi asked.

"Ethan knows we're on to him, so he's communicating directly with me. What does the message say, Grey?"

"'They try to beat me. They try in vain. And when I win, I end in pain.'"

"Death," Christian said.

"Was Ethan violent before?" Andi asked. "I mean, when you knew him?"

"No." Christian shook his head. "Not at all. I feel certain Enrique is the one who's been after us, and he also matches the description of the man seen with Alex in the white SUV, so I'm guessing he killed her too."

"And Julia?" Greyson asked.

"Could have been Enrique or it could have been Cyrus. He's got to be the violent one in the theft partnership. Ethan never was."

"Maybe he's changed," Andi said.

It was possible, but just didn't fit with the man he knew, though that man might not even exist anymore. Jail changed people. Bitterness rotted the bones.

"Well, one of them is certainly violent," Greyson said. "One or possibly both of them severely beat two security guards at Christie's. They're being seen to now and thankfully will be all right."

"They're taking bigger risks," Christian said. "Hitting a place with guards." This was getting more dangerous by the second.

"Sounds like they're determined to see their plan through, no matter the cost," Andi said.

"That's what I fear," Christian said, looking at Andi. She could hold her own, but he'd protect her with his life.

"What do we do now?" Andi asked, rocking back on the soles of her bare feet.

"Now we catch them," he said, moving for his gun, slipping it into his waist holder.

"How?" she asked.

"Just to be safe, we go through the list of all the places in California he and I researched."

"Including the yachts?" Greyson asked.

"They are my highest priority. Ethan was really hyped up about the possibility. I'll text you a list of the ones I remember researching. See if you can find what marinas they're currently in—if any are in Cali and still operational. If I was planning a double heist, I'd hit a yacht next. No one would expect it in domestic waters, plus easy getaway by boat."

"Consider it done," Greyson said. "I'll get you two on a flight into L.A. and text you the info. Call when you're on the ground."

"Will do."

"And, Christian . . ."

"Yeah?"

"Be careful. If Teresa Gutierrez sent one man to take you guys out, I doubt she'll hesitate to send another."

SIXTY-FIVE

THE FOLLOWING MORNING, Deckard rang Mitch's doorbell. Thanks to Greyson's call, everything was in place, but how was he going to deal with the fact he'd helped set a murderer free? Righteous anger burned through his limbs. Anger for all Mitch had done to Anne, to Andi, and for pulling a brilliant con on him. How hadn't he seen that? Maybe he needed to rethink things? Take some time off to clear his head? But all that had to wait until Mitch was where he belonged, even if it was for a different reason.

Mitch opened the door, then smiled. "Deckard. I've been expecting you."

"Oh?"

"I've been keeping tabs on you."

"Really. What for?"

"Just interested in the man who set me free."

Deckard swallowed the bile that rose in his throat. He had to remain calm, level, and keep his focus on the bigger picture or he'd lose it on Mitch. "Can we come in? I've got something I need to run by you."

"Sure, okay." Mitch's gaze fixed on Harper.

The thought of Mitch even looking at Harper, especially the way he was right now—with a mix of interest and curiosity—turned Deckard's stomach. Made him want to yank Harper away from the

330

evil man as fast as he could. What Mitch had done was flat-out evil. He was a wolf in sheep's clothing.

"I'm Harper Grace," she said, pulling Deckard back to the moment.

"Harper." Mitch took her hand and placed his other one over their clasped ones. "So nice to meet you. You're Deckard's friend?"

Deckard clamped his jaw. He wasn't asking. He knew exactly who she was. He knew about everything—sending someone to try to take them out. It was him. Deckard took a stiff inhale.

Harper looked at Deckard. "Yes." She nodded. "And partner," she added.

Good answer. They were partners on the case, but Mitch could naturally assume romantic partners, given the way it was phrased. Which equated to—"let go of her hand before I bust your lip." It took all the restraint he had to keep from lunging at Mitch for all he'd done, for all the pain and sorrow he'd inflicted.

"Ah. I see," Mitch said, releasing her hand. "Then I'd say he's a lucky man."

She looked at Deckard with a smile. Mitch had taken it the way they'd hoped. Whatever kept the creep from leering at Harper. He would be a lucky man indeed if Harper were his, but they were hardly there yet. And with her leaving for her mission with the International Committee for the Red Cross, their chance, his chance to . . . to . . . He rubbed his neck. He needed to shift his focus.

"Right," he said. "So can we come in for a couple of minutes?"

"Sure." Mitch stepped back, allowing them passage in. "Would you like a beer?"

"Soda would be great, if you have it," Deckard said, buying them time. He'd drink the soda nice and slow.

"Harper, how about you?" Mitch asked.

"I'm good, but thanks."

He smiled, then led them through the oversized foyer, down a short hall, and out into the open kitchen and living space.

Clearly, Mitch was faring far better than the tiny apartment he stayed in right after his conviction was vacated. Deckard took a sharp inhale, trying to simmer the anger coursing through him. It'd all been an act. The tears shed over the loss of Anne, the disappointment over his wife leaving him, the poor man starting over from scratch with his reputation shot. He'd probably moved into this house shortly after they officially parted ways.

He scanned the space while Mitch rummaged in the fridge. His gaze centered on the photographs lining the bookshelf. He took a step closer, one in particular catching his eye. One taken of Mitch, Councilman Markowitz, and the man Randy had identified as taking the bloody shirt from the life-preserver box.

Mitch turned around and handed Deckard his soda. "You like the pictures?"

"I just noticed this one. I think I had seen it before when I was working your case."

"Right," Mitch said, strolling toward it.

"Are those Masonic rings?" Deckard asked.

"Yep. One of the oldest societies in our country, founded long before our country began," Mitch explained.

"Right. I recognize the councilman, but this guy I can't place."

"Just another lodge member."

"Ah." Mitch could blow off telling him about the third man. It didn't matter. They knew who he was, and if the picture was taken before Mitch went to prison, it meant the three knew each other before, and regardless of how Mitch played it off, the three were tight. Tight enough for the man to kidnap Randy's sister and hold her hostage until Randy pulled the shirt from evidence and handed it over to him on Mitch's behalf.

"You should drink your soda before it gets warm," Mitch said.

"Sure," Deckard said, opening the can. "So are you back to running your real estate development company?" he asked.

"Yep." Mitch twisted the cap off his beer.

"You must be doing well. I mean, look at this place."

"The company is doing well. We're building a brand-new community off Taylor Avenue," he said, leading them to a round table in the corner with a large diorama on it. "Here's the design."

"Impressive," Deckard said. "But wasn't this supposed to have been built a while ago? I think right around the time you went to jail."

Mitch rubbed the back of his neck. "We're running behind schedule because of my time in jail, but it's coming." He shifted his gaze from Deckard to Harper. "What do you think, Harper?"

"Very nice. In fact," she said, "I believe I read about this planned community in the news."

Mitch smiled. "Oh yeah?"

"Yeah. Your friend, Councilman Markowitz. Isn't he the one who did all that lobbying for it?"

"I believe so," Mitch said, stepping away from the diorama.

"How many other communities have you planned with him?" Deckard asked.

"What?" Mitch swiped his nose. "I haven't built anything with the councilman."

"Really?" Deckard said. "Then I wonder why he and your backers helped get you out of prison?"

"Excuse me?" Mitch said, his gaze cold, piercing. "I don't know what you're talking about."

Deckard pulled the envelope from his jacket and dropped the pictures of Markowitz taking the bloody shirt from William Richards. "Looks like your two buddies had a vested interest in getting you out of prison."

Mitch's jaw tightened as he walked toward the pictures. "What are these?"

"See for yourself," Deckard said.

Mitch picked the one of Markowitz holding the bloody shirt in the evidence bag.

"He got you out of prison, right?" Deckard prodded.

"No." Mitch's voice grew as cold as his stare. "*I* got me out of prison. I had what they all needed, and I certainly wasn't going to give it up unless they got me out."

"What'd you have that was so valuable they'd go through all they did?" Deckard asked.

"The land rights. They'd have been out millions without me," Mitch said, picking up the picture of him with Richards and Markowitz.

"And Anne . . ." Deckard said, his chest squeezing. "She discovered something, and you killed her for it."

A wicked grin spread on his lips. "So you finally figured it out." Mitch chuckled. "Took you long enough. And the great thing is"—Mitch dropped the picture back on the table—"thanks to you and a little thing called double jeopardy, you can't do a thing about it."

"So what was it? She figured out you and Markowitz were duping investors in the real estate development projects, cheating families who bought homes you were never going to build?"

"Stupid . . ." Mitch rambled on with a string of curse words describing the woman he'd killed in cold blood. "She was listening when she shouldn't have been, looking for things she shouldn't have."

"So you and the councilman are running a Ponzi scheme, and Anne discovered it. Maybe even found evidence against you."

"I admit no such thing. I barely know the councilman."

"Really? Sure sounded like you knew him well. And there's this . . ." Deckard pulled out the last picture Randy had given them. The one of Mitch and Markowitz exchanging an envelope.

"There's no harm in knowing a councilman," Mitch said. His lies were so clear now, but he was no longer playing a part.

"I wonder what you two were exchanging. I'm assuming not the money we located in your and Markowitz's offshore accounts."

The muscle in Mitch's lip twitched. "I don't know what you're talking about."

"Well, the FBI fraud unit is digging into it. I'm sure they'll figure it out. I have a feeling we'll be seeing you back behind bars." Deckard clapped Mitch on the shoulder. "Thanks for the soda." He set it down. "We'll see ourselves out."

"You have nothing," Mitch hollered. "These pictures prove nothing."

"Feel free to keep them. The FBI has all they need," Deckard called over his shoulder.

Deckard let Harper head out first as they strode to the front door, his hand on the grip of his gun just in case Mitch's fury got the better of him and he tried anything stupid.

Mitch stalked after them. "You can't do this."

"That's the thing, Mitch, I already did." Deckard stepped outside in the warmth of the sun and smiled at the FBI vehicle in the driveway.

SIXTY-SIX

CHRISTIAN HELD THE DOOR of Christie's Auction House in Los Angeles open for Andi. Agents still moved around, crime scene tape cordoning off an open door to their right.

Once on the ground, they'd checked in with Greyson. He'd located all five yachts Christian had texted to him. One was dry-docked, and four were in various marinas, stretching from San Diego all the way to a marina near Rosewood. He didn't recall any of the yachts they cased having a Mesoamerican collection, so what were they after?

They decided Greyson would do a little more research, and they'd call back once they were finished at Christie's. Perhaps one had acquired an Aztec or Mesoamerican heritage collection since they'd first researched them in what seemed a lifetime ago. For him it was. He had a new life in Christ. He prayed the same for Ethan, that his bitterness would leave him, that he'd stop the course he was on that would only end badly—possibly in death, given his violent partner. He prayed Ethan hadn't crossed that line, prayed God would open his eyes to the new life he could have in Him.

Christian released a pent-up exhale as they took in the lobby and followed voices down a hall.

Once again, they were stuck in a holding position, and he hated it. But there was no sense driving randomly up and down the coast until they had at least some confidence in where they were headed.

If they chose the wrong yacht, they could be hours away from the right one. Over seven hundred miles stretched between San Diego and Rosewood. They had to hold firm until they figured out the target, and then they'd have to pray they made it in time.

The hall exited into a wide room with rows of white chairs lined up to face a stage with a podium. His gaze fixed on the wooden door with crime-scene tape across it, then to a distraught woman who stood talking with a man. Definitely FBI.

"We should talk with her." He inclined his head. "When she's done with the agent."

"That won't be happening," a man behind him said.

A man whose voice he knew all too well. He closed his eyes on a breath, then turned to face his past. "Agent Hopkins," he said.

"Christian O'Brady," Hopkins said, looking past his shoulder at Andi. "And who is this?"

"Andi Forester," she said, fishing a card from her bag and handing it to Hopkins.

"An insurance investigator." His black brows arched. "We've already worked with one. He left maybe twenty minutes ago."

"My company doesn't insure Christie's."

He handed her card back to her. "Then what are you doing here?" He looked between the two of them and laughed. "I see. You've hooked up with an insurance investigator. All part of the con, O'Brady?"

His jaw tensed. "I'm not pulling a con." And he wasn't "hooking up."

"So I suppose you had nothing to do with this." Hopkins indicated the area with the crime-scene tape with a sweep of his arm.

"I told you, that's not me anymore."

"In my experience, people don't change, which is why I wasn't surprised to find this here." Hopkins pulled an evidence bag from his jacket pocket with a cream envelope like all the rest. This one with his name scrolled across. "Looks like your partner left you a message."

"He's not my partner, and I'm not involved."

"Then what are you doing here, and why was this"—he wagged the envelope—"left for you?"

"I'm working the case."

Hopkins chuckled, hard. "Ah, that's rich. Working the heist investigation." After a moment, he stilled. "Oh, you're serious."

"Yes. I'm a PI." He showed his badge. "Miss Forester and I have been investigating the robberies from the start—in New Mexico. That's why we're here."

"Sure you are."

Christian took a steadying breath and prayed for composure. "Can we see what's in the envelope?"

"Oh, I don't think that's necessary." Hopkins slid it back into his pocket.

"He's been leaving us clues," Andi said. "We need to see the next one."

"So you're saying your partner is leaving you breadcrumbs?" Hopkins rocked back on his heels.

Christian pumped his hands in and out of fists, then shook his fingers out. He would not lose his temper, no matter how obtuse Agent Hopkins chose to be.

"So far he has been," Andi said.

"If you call Sheriff Brunswick of the Jeopardy Falls, New Mexico, sheriff's department, he can vouch for us on this."

"I'll do just that. You two take a seat while I make the call." Hopkins gestured to the rows of chairs already set up for the auction that was to take place tonight.

Ten minutes later, he returned. "All right. I'll read the note to you, and you let me know where we"—he indicated his teammates with a sweep of his hand—"need to go next."

"It's not always about a place," Christian said. "Sometimes it's a more general message."

"Like the last one hinted at death," Andi said.

Hopkins rocked forward onto the balls of his feet. "As in, they're going to kill someone?"

"This isn't just a heist case," Christian said. "It's far more deadly.

Two women have been killed, but I think he was implying my death in the last note he left."

"Why? Because you got away with the last heist while he got incarcerated?"

"I told you, I didn't get away with anything. I walked away before it started."

"Right." Hopkins slipped his fingers in his belt loops. "You're still selling that story."

Christian bit back the reply he wanted to express. "Because it's the truth. Now can we please hear the letter. We're losing time."

He pulled the envelope out of the bag, took his sweet time opening it, and cleared his voice before reading it. "'Every time you lose something, you always find it—'"

Christian groaned. "'The last place you look.'"

Hopkins held his hands up in a please-explain gesture.

"Because once you find it you don't need to look again," he explained.

"So they're headed to the last place you'd look," Andi said.

"Or . . ." Christian weighed what he knew about Ethan. "Or it's the best place I'd look, and he's trying to throw me off."

"So this . . ." Hopkins said, waving the letter, "didn't help us at all."

Christian tilted his head. "Maybe not you." He turned to Andi. "Let's go." He really had no idea but couldn't pass up the chance to raise Hopkins's blood pressure.

"If you find anything, you better call the Bureau," Hopkins called after him.

"Dude, this is getting out of hand," Casey said.

Cyrus's muscles coiled. How he longed to snap Casey's neck, but to his great frustration, he needed the man for one last heist and then he was dead.

"You didn't have to beat the guards."

"What I do is my business," he seethed out.

"Last time I looked, we were in this together."

So the pawn was getting some boldness.

"Oh, we're in this together, right up to the end." Or his end.

Contrary to what Casey thought, or Teresa for that matter, this was *his* game and he'd see it through to the end, no matter who he had to take out in the process.

SIXTY-SEVEN

"HOW DID IT GO at Christie's?" Greyson asked over the phone. It'd been hours, and Christian feared they may not have the answer they sought, but he prayed for God to reveal a definitive location to pursue. After the FBI left, they'd spent a little over an hour with the woman at Christie's. She was kind, answered all their questions, and graciously let them assess the crime scene. She said the more people trying to catch the thieves, the better.

"After the FBI, including Hopkins, left, we were able to see how the heist was pulled off and the specific items taken."

"Agent Hopkins?"

"Yeah."

"Eh. That couldn't have been pleasant."

"Not even close."

"Garner any helpful information?"

"Yes. Two things," he said, switching the phone to speaker so Andi could hear and chime in if she wanted. "I'm putting you on speaker."

"Hi, Miss Andi."

"Greyson." She smiled.

"What two things?" Greyson asked, frustration in his voice, which was something they rarely saw in the man. He was always "on" things, not frustrated by them.

"Ethan's skills have seriously grown," he said. "The safe lock he beat took exceptional skill." Christian would have cracked it as well, but it wouldn't have been easy.

"That's not comforting," Greyson said. "And the second thing?"

"We got our next message."

"What did it say?" Riley asked.

"Hey, Ri. I didn't know you were there."

"Yep. Staying to help Greyson."

"I told her to get some rest," Greyson said. "She's been here since Christie's was hit."

"I'm fine," she said, dismissing his suggestion. "So what was the message?" she asked again.

"It was another riddle. 'Every time you lose something, you always find it . . .'"

"'The last place you look,'" Riley said.

"Very good." His sister loved riddles as much as he did. Or had. This string of riddles was definitely changing his affection for them.

"So where is the last place you would look?" Riley asked.

"Great question." He paced, and Andi tapped her finger against her lips with a pensive expression on her face.

She looked adorable when she was thinking. The way her nose scrunched up. But her nose was not what he should be focusing on.

He raked a hand through his hair and prayed for guidance.

"Okay," he finally said. "Let's go through where the yachts are based."

Papers riffled on the other end. "The *Fisher of the Sea* is based in Marina del Rey," Greyson said.

"*Beach Hair, Don't Care* and the *Grecian Palace* are docked in a marina in San Diego."

"*Wasting Time* is dry-docked up in Santa Barbara, and the *Mr. Beaumont* is up north in a marina by Rosewood."

Christian snapped his fingers. "That's it."

"Rosewood?" Riley asked. "But it's in Northern California. You really think they'd drive umpteen hours in the opposite direction of the Mexican border, where he's no doubt taking the loot to . . .

Okay," she said with an exuberant exhale. "I got it. It's the last place that makes sense."

"They've got a serious head start on us. They'll probably be gone before we get there."

"No, they won't," Greyson said. "Head to the Southland airstrip. I have a friend with an Airbus H175. He'll get you there."

"In the meantime, call the *Mr. Beaumont*. Warn them."

◼ ◼

"Okay, I'm going to sit you down in that parking lot ahead," Bart, the pilot, said over the loud swoosh of the propellers. "It's about a half mile from the marina, but it's the closest I can land."

"That'll be great," Christian said, then pulled his phone from his pants pocket. "I'm going to check in with Greyson," he said to Andi.

She nodded.

"Greyson," he said, pinching his other ear shut with his hand to drown out the noise. "Any luck?"

"I think you've got the right yacht. It's a long story, but the owner has amassed a museum-quality collection of Mayan and Aztec artifacts according to one of the gallery owners who sold him several of the pieces."

"Great news," he said. "Were you able to get ahold of the ship or the dockmaster?"

"Dockmaster, yes," Riley said. "Yacht, no."

"That's not good."

"He said the yacht pushed out to sea about a half hour ago," Riley said.

"Can you tell him we're en route and ask if there's a boat we can use?"

"Already done," Greyson said. "It's waiting for you. Coast Guard is sending a boat out too."

"Great," Christian said.

"What's your ETA?" Riley asked.

"We're landing now. I've got to go."

"Be safe."

Despite all the years he'd known Greyson, how the man worked his magic was still a mystery.

"Good luck," Bart said.

"Thanks, and thanks for the ride."

Shutting the door behind them and ducking from the propellers, despite them being too high to reach—it was a gut reaction—they bolted out of the way and waved as the helicopter rose back up in the sky.

He looked at Andi. "Ready?" he asked.

"Ready." She nodded and took his hand, and they ran.

SIXTY-EIGHT

FEAR FOR THE *MR. BEAUMONT'S* OWNER and crew-members surged through Christian as adrenaline seared his limbs, his body warming with each stride.

Five anxious minutes later, they entered the LightPoint Marina.

The dockmaster met them at the ramp leading down to the slips, his hat clutched in his hands. "You Christian?" he asked.

"Yes, and this is Andi Forester." He gestured at her, standing beside him.

"Harvey," he said. "Your colleague Greyson arranged a fast raft for you. Follow me this way. The yacht isn't answering my radio calls."

"Any idea where it's at?"

"It was headed due west. I could see its lights about a dozen miles out, but then they disappeared. Your fast raft is this way." They followed him down the ramp. The sea breeze was warm, the marina silent other than the soothing lap of the water.

"Do you know how many crewmembers are aboard?" They needed to know what they were walking into. How many to expect and how Cyrus might have subdued them.

"This departure was not expected. Mr. Beaumont said they would be in port several days. He gave all the crew, except a couple, time off."

"When you say a couple?"

"The chef and head steward were the only ones I've seen around all day."

Christian prayed Cyrus hadn't harmed them like he had the security guards, or—his chest squeezed—taken it to the next level.

His heart thudding in his chest, adrenaline burning in his arms, Christian climbed into the black fast raft and held a hand out to Andi. She kicked her shoes off and set them on the dock. "I'll be back for these."

They would be back. Hopefully with Cyrus and Ethan in tow.

"You've got a floodlight and sea anchor there. Is there anything else I can get for you?"

"We should be good—and thank you."

Harvey nodded. "Shouldn't be too many boats out there at this hour. Hope you find them fast. I'm worried about Mr. Beaumont. He's got a heart condition."

Christian prayed that Mr. Beaumont, and everyone else aboard, were okay. Prayed he and Andi would reach the yacht before anyone got hurt, but he feared they were already too late. He started the engine.

Harvey untied the raft from the pylon. "Be safe," he said as they pushed off.

Christian looked over his shoulder as they moved to sea, the lights of the marina fading into the distance. The floodlight would have been helpful, but it'd give away their position. They needed the element of surprise, needed to let the hazy moon be their light.

The raft bounced over the water. "Hang on," he said to Andi. "Serious stretch of waves." Christian steered straight for the closest one. He rode it up and over, catching air, then slapping down on the back side of it.

Andi held the handle on the side.

"You good?" he called over the roar of the fast raft.

She nodded.

A few minutes later he caught sight of lights to the west, and as the moon peeked a bit more fully through the clouds, he spotted a vessel bobbing in the ocean's wake. "I got a yacht four hundred yards due west. That has to be it. I'm going to cut the engine, glide in two hundred yards, and then we'll swim for it."

"You seem to really know what you're doing," she said.

"Knowledge from a previous case."

346

"I'm going to want to hear about that one when this is over."

"You got it." He prayed it ended soon, with Cyrus and Ethan behind bars where they belonged.

"Glad I changed into jeans for this one," she said as they eased toward the yacht. "A skirt could have been awkward."

"I wish we both had wetsuits." But it'd be trousers for him. He studied the yacht.

The *Mr. Beaumont* rose and fell on the waves. The top deck was silent. Dark. But lights shone on the next deck down. "I'm trying to remember the layout, but we cased five yachts, and it's been years." Though potential heists he'd plotted out never fully left his mind. "I believe that's the main cabin level. There's a big living space there, if I recall correctly."

"Most likely where the collection is," she said, pulling her outer shirt off so just her tank top remained.

He followed suit, taking his shirt off—less cumbersome in the water. "We'll enter off the dive platform on the stern. Move along the port side." He indicated the path they'd take with his hand. "With all the lights out above deck, we should have the element of surprise." He just prayed that didn't backfire on them, that Cyrus wouldn't start shooting when they appeared—or hurt the owner or what crew members were aboard.

Reaching a good anchoring point two hundred yards out, he eased the sea anchor into the dark water, then turned to look at Andi. "Okay," he said. "We're going to have to swim the rest of the way in. We need the element of surprise, and we need to be as silent as possible, so breaststroke."

She nodded and adjusted her waist holster.

He did the same, then secured the knife he had strapped to his calf. "Ready?" he asked.

"Ready," she said.

"Follow my lead."

Slipping off the side of the raft into the cool, dark water, they swam toward the boat in nearly silent strokes, their noses just above the water.

When she reached the dive platform, Andi rested her hand on the metal surface.

Christian raised himself out of the water and onto the platform. He assessed their surroundings. No sign of anyone on deck. He turned to offer Andi his hand, but she was already up and getting to her feet.

Moving along the port side, with guns ready to fire, they worked their way onto the bridge, clearing it as they moved. Christian waved two fingers aft, and they moved for the cabin door leading to the stairs, if he remembered correctly.

Please, Father, keep us safe. Protect us and the crew.

Muffled noise came from down a level. They climbed down the steps, and Christian saw two people—a man and a woman, bound to two chairs, duct tape over their mouth, tears streaming down the woman's face. She whimpered, but then her eyes widened. She'd seen them.

Christian held a finger to his mouth, trying to indicate they were there to help. He longed to unbind them, tell them to run for safety, but safety was miles away, and they needed to move, to subdue Cyrus and Ethan.

The man's gaze moved to him too, and he nodded. He understood.

Christian pointed toward the bow of the ship. No reaction from either of them. He pointed to the stern. The woman nodded. He pointed up, though it appeared dark and silent above deck. She didn't respond. He pointed down. The man nodded.

So another level down. He mouthed *Thank you* and signaled for Andi to follow him. She positioned herself at his six, and they moved for the stairs. Several steps down, voices carried up.

"Look at this loot," Ethan said.

Christian released a controlled stream of air. It'd been years since he'd heard Ethan's voice, and it brought a flood of memories rushing back, but he shoved them aside. He signaled for Andi to hold. If he listened well, he could place where each man was in the room.

"This vulture vessel is worth a hundred grand alone," another man said.

Cyrus.

"And this ugly stone frog will bring in forty grand," Ethan said. "Look at this."

"Not that," Cyrus said at something Ethan must have picked up or pointed to.

"Why not?" Ethan questioned.

"Too big to transport," Cyrus said.

"Okay." Something hit the floor.

"You broke it," a third man said.

That had to be Mr. Beaumont.

Christian took a stiff inhale, and Andi's assertive gaze said she was ready for this.

Placing his left hand palm up, he used the fingers of his right hand to indicate where he believed Cyrus and Ethan were in the room.

She nodded.

He pointed to Cyrus's position based on the sound of his voice and movement, then to himself. She nodded. Then he did the same with Ethan's position and pointed to her. Again, she nodded.

Please, Lord, keep us safe. Protect us from evil men.

He held up three fingers, and again she nodded.

One. One finger up. *Two.* He steeled himself as he held two fingers up. *Three.* They moved.

Moving down the remaining steps, Christian rounded the stairwell, his gun aimed at Cyrus. Andi followed suit, her gun aimed at Ethan.

Cyrus dove behind Mr. Beaumont. Bound to a chair, the elderly man looked terrible. His face was bruised, and a wound on his head bled down his cheek. Cyrus held the muzzle of the gun to his temple. "Gun on the girl, Casey."

Casey? So Ethan was still going by his old nickname—after his favorite MotorGP rider, Casey Stoner. Some things hadn't changed, but Ethan certainly had, and not for the better.

"With pleasure," Ethan said, fixing his gun on Andi, but his mocking smile stayed on Christian. "Took you long enough to show up, but I knew this meeting would be inevitable."

"What are you doing, Ethan?" He gestured to the beaten Mr. Beaumont. "This isn't you."

"How would you know who I am?" Ethan roared.

"The Ethan I knew never harmed people or took a hostage."

"Shut up!" Cyrus said, crouching behind Mr. Beaumont, his gun pressing hard into the man's temple.

Mr. Beaumont winced at the pressure.

His gun still aimed at Cyrus, Christian's chest squeezed. He still didn't have a clean shot, and he couldn't risk hitting Mr. Beaumont.

"Hello, Andi," Cyrus said, his voice dropping an unsettling octave. "I'd say nice to meet you, but I already know you."

"You don't know me," she said, keeping her gun aimed at Ethan as he kept his on her—pointed at center mass.

Christian's throat squeezed shut. *Please, Lord, don't let him hurt her.*

"I've been watching you." His voice crawled along Christian's skin. "I know you *well*. The perfume you wear, the silk sheets on your bed, the way you shave your legs."

Andi's face paled, her jaw stiffening.

"We just haven't met face-to-face until now." He smiled.

Smiled? Christian stiffened. The violent man's creepy affinity for Andi was beyond disturbing. Fear for her safety gripped his mind.

Ethan's brow furrowed. Confusion and a bit of alarm awakened in his wide-eyed expression as he stared at Cyrus.

"Now, this is going to go one of two ways," Cyrus said. "We shoot one another . . . or we're going to walk out with Mr. Beaumont here. You will not follow, or we'll shoot him. Understood?"

Christian didn't move, didn't respond to his ultimatum.

"Understood?" Cyrus roared, wrapping one arm around Beaumont's neck. "Or maybe I'll just shoot her." He aimed his gun at Andi's head. "I'm a heck of a shot."

Christian's muscles coiled. Cyrus was not bluffing.

Andi stood her ground, her gun aimed at Ethan.

"Cyrus," Ethan said. "This is getting extreme."

"This is what we're going to do, unless you want to die too."

Ethan's face slackened. "You'd shoot me?"

"Get in my way and I will. Just try me."

Ethan continued to aim his gun at Andi, not saying a word.

"Smart choice," Cyrus said.

Christian prayed the man would move just a little so he'd have a shot, but Cyrus held behind Mr. Beaumont just right.

"Now," Cyrus said. "Toss me your guns."

"Not happening," Christian said. They released their weapons and they were dead.

"I'll kill him," Cyrus said, still jabbing the muzzle of his gun into Mr. Beaumont's temple.

He wasn't bluffing. It was only a matter of *when* he would kill Mr. Beaumont, not *if*. Christian stilled his racing heart, focusing, zeroing in on Cyrus and his twitchy movements. He needed to play this right, so they bought more time to save Beaumont.

"Go ahead," Christian said. "You'll be dead as soon as you drop him."

Andi's face stayed fierce in his peripheral vision.

"Now!" Cyrus's face strained, the veins along his forehead turning a nasty shade of purple.

"Not happening." Christian's aim remained steady.

"Up the stairs, Casey," Cyrus ordered Ethan with a tilt of his head.

Ethan nodded and backed up the stairs, his gun on Andi until he disappeared out of sight.

"Okay, old man," Cyrus said, keeping the muzzle of his gun aimed at Beaumont with one hand while he easily loosed the sailor's knots binding the elderly man in place. He yanked Beaumont to his feet and positioned himself so there still was no shot. They backed up the stairs.

Andi looked at Christian, her brows pinched. "What are we waiting for?"

"We're giving them time to get in the yacht's raft. That way Cyrus doesn't feel cornered, and then we give chase."

SIXTY-NINE

"NOW," CHRISTIAN SAID, and they flew up the steps.

They stopped just long enough to untie the two crewmembers from their bonds.

The woman bent forward from the waist, sobbing and clutching her stomach.

"The Coast Guard should be here any moment," he said. "Apprise them of the situation. We're going after Mr. Beaumont." He wished he could promise them the elderly gentleman would be okay, but with Cyrus, he couldn't be sure.

"Something's not right with the one," the man said. "Be careful."

"Agreed, and we will." He'd protect Andi with his own life if need be.

An outboard motor sounded. "We've got to go," he said.

They raced for the platform and dove into the dark waters, swimming for the fast raft. Reaching it, they both rolled in over the side. Andi pulled up the sea anchor, and Christian started the engine and directed the raft toward land. Cyrus had to be heading back in.

"Here," he said, racing forward, bouncing and jarring over wave after wave. "Take this." He handed the floodlight to her. "Sweep it in front of us."

"Will we catch them?" she asked. "That poor man."

"We'll get them." They had to. "Hold on tight," he said as they swept over another wave.

She gripped one of the handles with her free hand, still sweeping the light over the surface and the crashing waves.

They flew over the water, soaring above it as they came over the curl of the waves.

"There," she said, the light landing on the yacht's Zodiac raft. Cyrus steered the craft, Ethan up front, and it looked like Mr. Beaumont lay on the raft's floor.

"We've got them," Christian said as they gained on them.

Cyrus looked back—the floodlight fixed on him. He fired, and they dove to the hard rubber floor of the raft.

Christian pulled his gun from his holster. "Lay low, but steer the boat and keep the light on them, if you can."

"I've got it," she said.

He raised up enough to fire over the raft's bow, aiming for Cyrus. *Bang. Bang. Bang.*

Cyrus ducked. He yelled something at Ethan, who then crouched low, moving for the aft.

Cyrus's head raised just above the raft's edge, and Christian fired again.

Again, Cyrus ducked. Then he grabbed Mr. Beaumont, hauling him to his feet—the two swaying as rippling waves bobbed their raft. Once again, he held Mr. Beaumont in front of him so Christian didn't have a clear shot.

Cyrus smiled in the floodlight and fired into Beaumont's side.

The man cried out in pain.

Cyrus threw him overboard, Ethan gunned the engine, and the Zodiac streaked away.

Christian's muscles hardened to the point of pain. Cyrus knew they'd stop to help, and they would lose them, but there was nothing else they could do. They steered straight for Mr. Beaumont.

Reaching the sputtering man, Christian reached over the edge and brought the man close to the raft's side. "I'm sorry. This is going to hurt," he said, slipping his arms under Beaumont's armpits. "Here we go." He hauled the elderly man up and in. The man screamed and writhed in pain.

"It's going to be all right," Andi said, kneeling over the man and applying pressure to his wound. "Coast Guard is on the way. We've got you."

But they'd lost Cyrus and Ethan in the night.

■ ■

"What are we going to do now?" Andi asked after they'd passed Mr. Beaumont over to the Coast Guard—who sent another boat out to search for Cyrus and Ethan, though her gut said they wouldn't find the men.

"Figure out where they're going to make the trade with Teresa," Christian said, toweling off on shore, thanks to the Coast Guard's provision, though puddles still formed around their feet.

"You think the heists are done?"

"Yeah. I think Ethan gave us a strong clue to lead us here because he knew this was their last job. And it stands to reason Teresa will be coming to the States or sending men to collect her goods."

Andi exhaled. "The question is where."

"Let's head back home and see what we can figure out," he said.

"You don't think the swap could happen near the Cali-Mexico border?"

"It might, but Teresa and her drug-lord husband live in Chihuahua, Mexico. My bet is it's going to be around the New Mexico or Texas borders. It'll take them time to make the drive back. They can't risk flying with stolen objects. We should be able to reach MIS headquarters within five or six hours if we take a commercial flight, but maybe we—"

"How else would we . . . Oh, Greyson," she said. "Seriously, how does he do it?"

"I wasn't joking when I called him our Lucius-slash-Alfred. He's always there to help, and he provides us with just what we need when we need it."

"But how?" She didn't like being out of the "know."

"He's a private man with a lot of connections we don't understand, and I imagine a good deal of money, but we respect his privacy on all of that."

"Gotcha. Doesn't it make you wonder, though?"

"Of course, but Deck and I have chalked it up to him just being a man of mystery." He chuckled.

"And Riley?"

"She can't let it rest." He shook his head with a slight smile. "Those two are a mess."

"I'd say in the best possible way."

"Now's not the time to unpack that, but we will later," he said. "I just can't see it."

She shrugged a shoulder. "I hate to say it, but most men are oblivious when it comes to that kind of stuff."

He tugged her to him. "I'd hardly say I'm oblivious to you."

"Mmm." She smiled. "And I'm glad of that."

He pressed his lips to hers. This wasn't the time, but he couldn't help himself. Just a short kiss now that they were out of danger. At least for the moment.

As anticipated, Greyson arranged a private jet for their trip home, landing them in Santa Fe less than two hours later. If Cyrus and Ethan were headed back to New Mexico, they had nearly a full day's drive.

"We've got a very short window to figure out where they're headed for the exchange," Christian said as the gang all sat around the round table, Harper included.

"We've got some help in that area," Greyson said.

Riley hopped off the stool and moved to stand beside Greyson at the glass panels, a marker in hand. "Flynn Josephs with Border Patrol responded to the picture of Teresa Gutierrez I put out. She crossed the border under the alias of Rebecca Martinez. He said Feds are looking for her too."

"I don't care who finds and stops them—Border Patrol, the Feds, or us," Christian said. "As long as they're caught."

"Agreed," Deckard said, kicking back in his chair. He propped his boot against one of the table legs, balancing himself at an inclined angle.

Christian did the exact opposite, leaning forward. "Where did she come over the border?"

"Antelope Wells port of entry."

"She came up through New Mexico and in the bootheel area?" Christian said. "I expected Juarez-El Paso."

"Agreed," Greyson said. "The key is finding out why there."

Riley crossed her legs. "She could have just wanted to go through a less populated entry. Sort of sneaking in, if you will."

"But it's easier to blend in with a larger group of people," Deck said.

"Good point."

Christian exhaled. "All right, let's review what we know about Teresa Gutierrez. We want to find someplace on this side of the border she'd wait at until Cyrus and Ethan make the drive back."

"And we should find out if where she's staying is the same place they'll make the drop or if there's a second location we need to figure out," Andi said.

Christian reached over and gave her hand a squeeze. Everyone noticed, but he didn't care. "So what do we know?"

"She and Cyrus were born in Lordsburg, New Mexico. Both American citizens. She now has dual citizenship."

"That's a fairly small town. . . ." Christian said, running that through his mind.

"It's the county seat of Hidalgo County," Riley said, scanning the pages. "Population now around four thousand. Back when they were kids growing up there . . . I can't imagine how small it was."

"Let's see if there's any property in her name," Christian said.

"Or her alias," Riley added.

"Or her maiden name, Timal," Andi said.

"I'll go do the search," Greyson said, tucking a legal pad under his arm and heading for his desk.

Christian sat back. "If we're lucky, there's still property in one of her names."

"Or Cyrus's name," Riley added.

"Excellent point," Christian said.

"I'll go ask Greyson to run Cyrus's name as well," Riley said, bouncing from the room.

Christian shook his head. Always so much energy.

Andi had a knowing smirk on her face.

"No," he said. "Not possible."

Deckard frowned. "What isn't?"

Christian sighed. "Andi's got this theory about Greyson and Riley."

Deckard's brow pinched. "How they drive each other crazy?"

"No. That there's . . . *interest* there," he said, tapping his pen against the table as he tried to erase the notion from his mind.

Deckard laughed. "That's hysterical."

Andi and Harper exchanged a knowing glance.

"Not you too?" Christian said, looking at Harper.

She shrugged. "I'm with Andi on this one."

"You both are off," Deckard said, setting his front chair legs back on the floor.

Time slithered by like oozing tar—slow and engulfing.

Greyson finally returned. "Okay. I found a property in the last name Timal."

"In Lordsburg?" Andi asked.

"Just outside of town. Riley's digging through more records, but I'm going to guess it was their childhood home since it was in her maiden name."

"Got it," Riley said, rushing through the doorway. "The property belonged to Luis and Margaretta Timal. The 1990 census shows them having two children. A boy and a girl. Ages one year old and ten."

"Cyrus and Teresa."

"Correct."

"Great job, as always," Christian said. "We've got a five-hour drive ahead, but we'll still easily beat them there."

357

"I'll be here if you need anything looked into or found," Greyson said.

Christian nodded.

"I'll go," Riley said.

Greyson looked over at her, concern in his eyes.

Christian narrowed his eyes. Was Andi right? *No way*.

Deckard looked at Harper, and she nodded. "We'll go too."

After a little more conversation regarding logistics, they decided Deckard, Harper, and Riley would ride together in case they needed to divide and conquer.

Christian glanced at the building in the rearview mirror as he pulled out of the lot. Greyson stood looking out the window, a worried expression on his face. Greyson never looked worried. . . .

Pulling out onto the main road, he prayed Lordsburg was the right location and that they would beat them to it. And most importantly, that no one died at Cyrus's or Teresa's hands. She had a reputation for making people disappear. Cyrus had possibly killed two women, had nearly killed Mr. Beaumont. If cornered, neither of them would hesitate to pull the trigger.

The drive to Lordsburg was a half hour shorter than the GPS indicated. Probably because he flew down the road at the top speed limit all the way. He followed Google Maps's direction, and when they made the final turn, his heart dropped. Instead of the Timal home, they were looking at a strip mall and a dead end.

SEVENTY

"YOU'VE GOT TO BE KIDDING," Christian said, banging the wheel.

Andi reached over and squeezed his hand.

"Sorry. I thought we had them. Now we have to start over."

The fear of losing them, of not finding them before Teresa, Cyrus, and Ethan disappeared across the border, ate at him. The bootheel of New Mexico, which sat barely south of them, was known as a drug runner's highway, a way to slip from New Mexico into Mexico unseen. Given Teresa's husband's drug empire, as well as her having grown up in the area, she must know the routes very well.

While small in comparison to other areas of the state, it still was a lot of ground to cover, with no-man's-land to the west of Antelope Wells and to the east until the Columbus Border Patrol Entry Station. They needed something to focus their search. Greyson had alerted Border Patrol of the situation, and they'd be sweeping the border, but again, there was a fair amount of no-man's-land to cover.

His cell rang. "Yeah, Deck. I see."

"What do we do now?" he asked.

Christian pinched the bridge of his nose. "Let me think."

"She's in this area for a reason. She's from here, so she's got to be holed up someplace she views as safe."

"We can canvass the area," Deckard said. "See if anyone has seen Teresa or might know where she'd be."

"Good plan." He swallowed, praying for direction.

"Why don't you and I go look through property records," Andi said.

"Maybe there's another place that belonged in their family," he said.

"Agreed," Deckard said. "Let's check back in on the half-hour mark."

"Sounds good. But let me know if you find anything sooner, and I'll do the same."

"Roger that." Deckard disconnected the call.

"Property records would be kept in the courthouse," he said, looking over at Andi. Man, they worked well together. He was going to miss this time with her when the case was solved. But, of course, he wanted it solved.

Locating the courthouse in town, Mrs. Applegate—a kind lady in charge of public records—showed them down to the dusty room on the bottom level of the courthouse. Basically, a room where records had gone to die. "Let's start searching for Timal," he said. "I think any other property that would tie to them would be under that name."

"But I'll also check under her married name and the alias she used when she came over the border," Andi said.

They pulled boxes down by initial—they were assuming it indicated the letter the surnames in each box started with.

Armed with the *T*, *G*, and *M* boxes, they sat on the floor and started digging in.

"Anything?" Andi asked after an hour.

Christian shook his head. Were they on a wild-goose chase? Were they in the wrong area? What if they got away?

"Hang on . . ." Andi said, clutching a piece of paper in her hand from the *T* box. "There was a house owned by Jorge Timal back in the fifties."

"He must have been the grandfather or uncle or something of the sort." Having found nothing, he started packing the *G* box back up. "Where is it?"

"Hang on," she said, flipping through the rest of the papers in the file she'd pulled it from. "It's been sold three times in the last thirty years."

"Is the last owner Teresa or Cyrus by any chance?" *Please, Lord. Don't let this be another dead end.*

Andi shook her head, clutching the file. "The current owner is Maria Nelson." Her shoulders dropped as his heart did.

Another dead end. The clock was ticking, and they were going to run out of time if they didn't figure it out fast. But where to look next? Were they even on the right path? Had they taken a diversion that led nowhere?

She set the file down and braced her weight by planting her palms on the floor behind her. She blew a stray hair off her face while he dusted off his hands.

Please, Father, show us the way.

Moments passed in silence. Then Andi looked up with a tilt of her head.

"What is it?"

She reached for the folder and riffled through the papers. "That name . . . Why is it familiar?"

He furrowed his brow. "What name?"

"Nelson," she said, pulling out the paper in question. "I've heard that before when we were discussing the case." She clutched the paper, dust smeared across her cheek, and sneezed.

"God bless you."

"Thanks." She looked up at him, fire alight in her eyes. "Do you remember us talking about it?"

He racked his brain, feeling it simmering somewhere in the back of his mind. He ran the case through his mind. All the craziness of it. All the people they talked to. Everything they knew about Teresa . . . "That's it!" He scrambled over to her.

"You remember?"

"Teresa was arrested three times between age eighteen and nineteen."

"That's it. The first guy she got busted with was something Nelson."

"Tomas," he said.

"Right." She beamed.

"But we saw Maria somewhere too . . ." Where was it? He closed his eyes and tried to picture where he'd seen it spelled out. "Hang on. I'm calling Greyson."

"Okay."

"Hey, Grey."

"Christian, did you find something?"

"Yeah. I think so, but I'm not positive. I need you to do me a favor. Look for Teresa's mug shot. From her first arrest. Let me know when you've got it." He tapped his foot, his gaze holding Andi's. Anticipation and worry swirled inside. *Please, let me be on to something.*

"Okay. I've got it in front of me," Greyson said.

"Does it have her middle name on it?"

"No."

"Check the other two. I think one did." *Please, Lord, let me be right.*

"Yes!" Andi said.

"Yep. The second one has it," Greyson said while Andi beamed with a smile. "Teresa Maria Timal."

"That's it. We got it." He prayed that's where Teresa was holed up and that they weren't too late.

SEVENTY-ONE

THE ADOBE HOUSE stood a half mile outside of town. Assessing the area through binoculars, west of the run-down dwelling, Christian shook his head. It was a logistical nightmare. Flat. No coverage other than a few trees. Fortunately, they'd come prepared.

"Okay," he said to Deckard over the comm system they'd brought.

"We'll have to get our rifles and set up." If only they had natural-colored camo to blend in. At least they were properly armed.

"Roger that," Deckard said, then paused. "I'm not keen on the women being out here alone, but no way they're going to stay in a group."

"We both know Riley can more than hold her own, and Andi and Harper are trained FBI." He was trying to convince himself as much as his brother.

"You're right," Deck said.

It was the truth, and they were all strong, formidable women, but he still worried. Andi had burrowed into his heart, and he cared deeply about the lady. When this was over, he was taking her on a real date.

"It'll be good," Deckard said in a reassuring tone.

Christian prayed so.

Fifteen minutes later, they were set—Christian positioned on the west, Deckard on the east, Harper to the north, and Riley to the south. Andi had pulled the proverbial short straw and was parked behind a copse of trees with a heightened view of the road leading to the house. One road in and one road out.

The Peloncillo Mountains rose in the background. Why couldn't the house be there? So much cover.

Settling flat on his belly, Christian worked to make himself fade into the mesa as much as possible. The house was still through his scope. No sign of movement through the shut curtains. No car in the drive. He gripped his rifle.

Please, Father, don't let this be another dead end.

An hour later, he repeated the prayer with all his heart. *Please, Lord.* Time was ticking away. If they'd chosen poorly, Cyrus and Ethan could be in the wind by now.

Yet another hour of no movement, and he was tempted to call no joy. But approaching the house directly, not knowing who was inside, how many there were, or how they were armed would have been beyond foolish. And if Cyrus and Ethan approached while they were in the open, he had zero doubt it would turn deadly. He didn't want anyone dying today. He wanted to bring them in, have them back behind bars where they belonged.

Another hour of the same, and he fought the urge to punch the ground. Had they made the wrong call? Had *he* made the wrong call?

He prayed with everything inside of him that he hadn't.

"Any sign?" he murmured low to the other four.

A round of noes came back.

He squeezed his eyes shut. "One more hour and we reassess."

"Roger that," Deckard said.

"Don't give up hope," Andi said. "I have a feeling about this."

A rock wedging into his side, he prayed she was right.

A handful of minutes later, the curtain swished in the front right window.

Thank you, Lord. Relief and a new surge of energy coursed through him. It took extra restraint to remain still.

The curtain pulled to the side, revealing a petite woman with dark hair. She gazed out, scanning the area. He keyed in on her face. It was Teresa Gutierrez.

Thank you, Lord. Relief swarmed in his belly, but he held perfectly still. "I've got eyes on her. Front window. Right of the door. It's Teresa."

"Roger that," Deckard said. "I've got the rear covered."

Both Riley and Harper confirmed their positions.

Teresa's gaze swept over his general position, but he was six hundred yards out. Far enough out of eyesight if he remained still. The flat mesa stretched for miles with no impediments between her and him except the few rocks surrounding him, so movement could draw her attention. But still—no way at this distance. He kept his gaze fixed on her through his long-range scope.

A handful of turkey buzzards dipped from the sky overhead, landing off to his right. Something must have died, but he kept his gaze trained on the window.

A tall man with dark hair strode up behind Teresa, taking a scan of the land over her shoulder. It wasn't her husband. He'd seen his picture. Perhaps another one of her thugs to replace Enrique, whom Joel had arraigned and now was behind bars awaiting trial. One down. Four, including the unknown man, to go.

The man's gaze swept the area again.

Christian remained still, only the breath passing through his lungs making the smallest movement in his diaphragm.

After a moment, the man rested his hands on Teresa's shoulders and guided her back. He took one more sweep of the land and closed the curtain. They had a minimum of two in the house, and he was betting no Cyrus or Ethan. The pair was scanning the area, no doubt waiting for them to arrive. Given the loot they'd be delivering, they'd need to arrive by car—at least to unload. The question was, Where was Teresa's vehicle, and was someone waiting in it for her when she needed it?

"We've got two unfriendlies confirmed in the house," he said over comms. "There could be more, but at least we know we have Teresa."

He kept his breath even, his heartbeat level.

They'd notified the Bureau's art theft team of the potential drop site since it was their case, but it would take several hours to arrive from Albuquerque, and that was if they were able to leave straightaway.

"Andi, you can confirm with the Bureau that Teresa is on site. You should probably alert DEA as well."

"Will do. Oh . . ." She had a swift intake of air. "We've got a black Dodge Sprinter approaching from the west, heading your way."

"Deck, hold very still."

"On it."

"All right, team," Christian said. "I'll fire as soon as Cyrus and Ethan exit the car. If they make it into the house, we're looking at a shootout. I'll take them fast in a nonlethal area."

"And Teresa?" Deckard asked.

"She'll be a sitting duck in the house. I think she and the man will come out low and head for the van. Then we move in once they are visible."

"Hel—" Andi's voice went silent as scuffling and thumping sounded. "He—"

Fear squeezed Christian's throat. "Andi?"

A car door slammed.

His heart stilled. "Andi?"

No response.

Adrenaline surged through him. "Does anyone have eyes on the van?"

"Not yet," Harper said, followed by Riley.

The way they were positioned, they didn't have eyes on Andi.

"Andi!" he hollered, begging God for her to answer.

"Already on it," Deckard said, closest to Andi's position. "I've got the van. It's heading down the road for the house now. In sixty seconds, you'll see it."

He swallowed, praying the answer was no before he asked the question. "Do you see Andi in the van?"

SEVENTY-TWO

"NEGATIVE EYES ON ANDI," Deckard replied. "The only one I see is Ethan driving."

"No Cyrus?"

"Not up front."

His chest squeezed, cutting off his breath. He could be in the back with Andi.

"Everyone hold still," Deckard said as the van came into view.

Deckard was right. Only Ethan sat up front.

Christian's heart thumped.

Ethan pulled the van parallel to the house, cutting off his line of sight to the door.

This was not good. "They know we're here. This is"—he squeezed his eyes shut, the words sticking in his narrowing throat—"a hostage situation. I just need eyes on Andi to confirm."

"I see her," Riley said. "Through the windshield. She's wrestling with the man in back."

Cyrus. "Do you have a clear shot at Cyrus?" he asked.

"No," Riley said. "Their heads keep coming in and out of view. But it looks like she's giving him heck."

That's my girl.

He took a steadying inhale. Their objective had changed. Andi was the priority. He'd get her back no matter what it took.

Ethan turned, looking over his shoulder, talking toward the back of the van, his motions frenzied. After what looked like a freak-out moment, Ethan turned back around and cut the ignition. He un-buckled and shifted to exit from the passenger side.

He'd left Christian with no choice and only the briefest of win-dows. Waiting for the natural pause between breaths, Christian squeezed the trigger and held the recoil firm.

The van window shattered, and a loud pop echoed in the air as Ethan flailed forward. The turkey buzzards, hissing that awful suck-ing sound, flew up with large flaps of wings as Christian shot out the van tires on his side of it. Harper blew the back rear, and Riley took the front one on the house-side of the van. They were grounded.

"Any eyes on Cyrus?"

"Yes," Riley said.

"You have a shot?"

"No. He's holding Andi in front of him. He opened the rear van door and is moving for the house. The front door is opening."

"Do you have a shot?" *Please let Riley have a shot.* If Andi got pulled into the house . . . His breath caught. He wouldn't even let his mind go there.

"No. Not the way he's holding—" She sucked in a breath.

"Riley? What's wrong?"

"Andi just elbowed him in the nose. He's pulled back. She just shoved her finger in his eye, and he . . ."

His pulse whooshed through his ears so loud it was hard to hear Riley. "And he?"

"She dropped to the ground and is rolling under the van."

Smart lady. "You have a shot on Cyrus now?" he asked Riley.

"He's opened the passenger door and is using it as a shield. Hang on . . . I might . . . if he just . . ."

Andi popped up on Christian's side of the van and positioned herself against the wheel well.

Brilliant girl.

Pop. Pop. Pop.

His heart stopped.

Andi curled up tighter behind the wheel well.

Crack. Crack. Crack.

Glass exploded in shattering shards.

His heart leapt in his throat until he realized Riley was taking shots at Cyrus through the passenger door window.

Crack. Crack. Crack.

Those shots came from the north. *Harper.*

"She got him," Riley said.

Thank you, Lord.

"He made it into the house, and the door's shut, but he's hit."

"Cover me. I'm going for Andi," he said.

"I'm closer," Riley said. "I can reach her faster. Cover me."

Argumentative words were ready to leave his mouth when he spotted Riley running in a low crouch, ducking behind the three lone trees.

Shots rang out of the house's side window toward Riley.

Andi crawled over to the back wheel well.

"Riley, hold," Deckard said. "I'm coming around. I'll have better coverage. And there are no windows or back door on the house. I'm safe until I round by you."

Pop. Pop. Pop.

Three shots hit the van's side opposite the wheel well Andi had been leaning against.

Christian fired high over the hood of the van. *Pop. Pop. Pop.*

Fire retorted back.

Then fire riddled from what had been Riley's position. It was now Deckard, moving in place as Riley shifted out.

Riley bolted in a crouch for Andi, gunfire volleying back and forth.

His pulse whooshed louder in his ears, drumming out all noise except the rapid fire.

Riley landed by the first wheel well, gun in hand. She spoke to Andi, and she nodded.

His sister looked in his direction, pointed directly toward him, and held up one, two, three fingers. On three, the two ladies bolted in zigzag patterns for him.

He kept his gun aimed and his scope fixed on the van.

"Come on. Come on. Come on," he muttered. *Please let them reach me, Lord.*

Boom. Boom.

Deckard's gun.

Pop. Pop. Pop.

To his nine.

Someone had come out of the house.

Gunfire exchanged, his heart racing for Andi and Riley.

The ladies slid on the ground beside him, and he uttered a prayer of thanks. Relief swirled inside like a wave rocking nausea through his gut. That was too close.

But this wasn't over yet. They still had Cyrus, Teresa, and an unknown in the house, and a van no doubt full of treasure.

Cyrus, Teresa, and the third unfriendly had two choices. Hole up in the house or move. The answer was always move. They were going to breach the door and come out firing. He doubted, in all the commotion, they realized the tires were flat. They wouldn't be going anywhere unless they had another vehicle stashed somewhere, but they'd have to come out to reach it.

"They're moving!" Harper barked. "Out front."

Christian fired.

Boom. Boom.

A man hollered.

"Cyrus is down," Deckard said.

One down. Two to go.

Christian aimed his scope under the van. Two feet from the ankles down appeared, and he fired. A woman's voice swore and hollered as she fell over, crashing to the ground.

Pop. Pop.

At his three. *Harper.*

Teresa's bloody ankles drenched the white of her shoes crimson.

"She's down. Two shot ankles, one shoulder. Her weapon fell out of reach unless she moves."

"The man is still inside," Deckard said. "I can see him moving in and out of a slit in the curtain. If he just stills."

Crack. Crack. Crack.

Adrenaline surged in Christian's limbs. Not his brother's gun. The man was firing from the side of the house.

Silence.

Fear churned in his gut. *Please let Deckard be okay.*

Boom. Boom. Boom.

Thank you, Lord.

"He's down," Deckard said after a moment.

"Access to weapon, or unknown?" Christian asked, needing to know before he gave the order to move in.

"He won't be reaching for anything," Deckard said as black Tahoes rolled down the road, dust kicking up behind them.

The cavalry had arrived.

SEVENTY-THREE

DECKARD LEANED against the doorjamb of his kitchen.

"Are you sure you don't want me to take you to the airport?" Andi asked Harper.

"You go to the rodeo and watch Riley win," she said with a smile.

"Okay." Andi nodded. "I know there's no arguing with you."

"It's about time." Harper chuckled. She wrapped her arms around Andi and gave her a giant hug.

Then everyone else got in line.

Deckard leaned tighter against the doorjamb, ignoring the feelings sifting through him. He didn't do emotional. Everything was fine. He'd drive Harper to her place in Albuquerque, wait while she packed, and see her to the airport. He'd be fine.

"Thanks for taking her to the airport," Andi said, a slight smirk on her lips.

"My pleasure," he said as casually as he could muster. Everyone could think what they wanted. He and Harper were just friends. Yes, he greatly enjoyed her company. Yes, if he let himself think about it, he'd miss her. That's why he wasn't going to think about it. She was leaving for the Middle East to serve with the International Committee of the Red Cross for two months. His fear for

372

her safety would drown him if he let it. He cleared his throat. "We should get going."

"Right," Harper said. "Well . . ." She looked at the gang one last time. "I can say it's definitely been an adventure."

"Be safe on your next one," Andi said.

"Will do."

"Keep in touch as you're able," Andi said.

"Will do."

He wondered if he'd hear from her at all while she was overseas. If she'd think of him. He shook off the thoughts, annoyed he kept tracking back to her. He liked her, probably far more than he was willing to admit. But he couldn't spend the next two months pining over her when they hadn't even had a date. Hadn't even discussed the fact that something was brewing between them. Or brewing in him, at least.

She strode to his side.

"Ready?" he asked.

She nodded with a smile.

The ride to her condo was filled with the normal chatting they'd spent the last couple weeks doing, and after she packed, the ride to Albuquerque International Airport went far too fast.

"You can just drop me at Departures," she said as they approached.

Shaking his head, he pulled into the parking ramp. "I'm walking you in."

"Okay, thanks."

"I can't believe this all you're taking," Deckard said as he pulled the rolling duffel from the Equinox while she slipped her backpack on.

"I'm on the move a lot. I can't afford to have heavy baggage to trek everywhere. Besides, it's a war zone. I don't need to look nice."

He gripped the duffel straps harder. "I hate the thought of you in that environment. It's not safe." For anyone.

"I know, but the organization advocates for the protection and dignified treatment of the dead after conflict and violence.

I primarily work clarifying the fate and whereabouts of missing persons and identifying human remains. It's important work and where God's called me." She paused. "Part of where He's called me."

He wanted to ask where else God was calling her, but he didn't want to push her. She'd share if she wanted to, and she didn't. But something other than excitement shone in her beautiful eyes. Hesitance. Maybe. Just maybe she was feeling something too.

He raked a hand through his hair. "Should we go?" He gestured toward the sliding doors at the end of the parking aisle.

She held his gaze a moment, then nodded. "Yep. It's time."

When they reached the security line, he shoved his hands into his pockets and rocked back on his heels. "Well, I guess this is it. It's been . . . unusual."

She chuckled. "That's one word for it." She slipped her hair over her shoulders. "Maybe when I get back—"

An overhead announcement cut her off.

"Maybe?" he asked as soon as the announcement ceased.

"Maybe we could do something less intense," she said with a soft smile.

"I'd like that."

They stood in silence a moment until she said, "I better go."

"Right." He moved forward and wrapped her in his arms. It felt . . . *right*. Placing a kiss on her cheek, he stepped back.

She stared at him, eyes blinking, a flush of pink on her cheeks.

"Stay safe."

She nodded and headed into the TSA PreCheck line through security.

He knew he should leave, but he couldn't make his feet move. He watched as she passed through the security scanner and grabbed her backpack off the conveyer belt on the other side. She stood still a moment, then turned. Her gaze fixed on his, and something he couldn't put into words passed between them, and then, with a wave, she was gone.

Leaving Harper at the airport, Deckard crossed town and drove through the Hillsdale Cemetery. The police had arrested Mitch Abrams, Councilman Markowitz, and William Richards, and all were headed for trial.

Gratitude filled his heart. He'd be there for it all, attend the trial and see Mitch back behind bars where he belonged, even if it was for different reasons.

He turned right at the first crossroad, parked, and got out. Grabbing the flowers he'd bought, he turned to find the gravestone he sought. The man in the cemetery office had given him the general direction, but it took him a moment before he found Anne Marlowe's grave.

He knelt down, brushing a few leaves away, and replaced them with the flowers. "They got them," he said, looking around to make sure he was alone. He'd never spoken at a graveside before—let alone been to one. Not even when his dad was killed. There'd been dangerous extenuating reasons behind that decision, but he wondered if he wouldn't have made the same decision regardless.

He shifted his attention back to Anne's gravestone, which read *Beloved daughter. Rest in peace, my love.*

No matter what life she lived or poor decisions she'd made, Anne was loved, and she didn't deserve to be butchered.

"He's going back to jail. I just wish it was for what he did to you." He raked a hand through his hair. "I'm so sorry I bought his lies, so sorry he conned you too. But he will soon be behind bars, and now you can rest in peace."

Standing, he felt a combination of relief and fury, the weight off his shoulders now that they were going to jail mixed with the fury of being conned. Mitch had played him well, and it wouldn't happen again. He'd go back to Greyson and walk through where he went wrong.

But that conversation would have to wait. Today was Riley's rodeo, and the whole gang was going. Even Greyson. Deckard half expected him to show up in a suit. He and Christian had made a wager. He'd said suit, and Christian went with jeans. The loser had to muck out the stalls tonight.

He turned on his Spotify, and first up was one of his favorite songs— "Amarillo by Morning." He sat back and gazed at the winding mountains, enjoying the solitude, the lost-in-time feel as he passed the old mining town of Madrid. This was home, but while it brought him comfort, he still longed for a peace he feared he'd never find.

SEVENTY-FOUR

"THAT WAS SO MUCH FUN," Andi said, following the rodeo. The brewing wind had made it especially entertaining with tumbleweeds rolling by and getting stuck under the bleachers where they sat and cheered Riley on. Riley had taken first place in barrel racing and won a cute heart-shaped buckle with gold engraving.

"I still can't believe that was your first time attending a rodeo," Christian said.

"If I'd known it was this much fun, I would have started attending years ago."

"But," he said as they walked down Main Street in Jeopardy Falls, "it's not your first fair, is it?"

"I've been to the state fair, but that's a . . ."

"Whole 'nother ball game," he said. "This is one of those small-town fairs where the proceeds benefit the fire department."

"That's cool," she said, taking in the heart of downtown. It had been transformed. There were rows of games to play, food stands that smelled amazing, and stalls of artwork of varying kinds—from turquoise-and-silver jewelry to slate paintings and everything in between.

"This is awesome," she said, twirling around to take it all in.

He took her hand and spun her.

"Nice move," she said. "You'll have to twirl me on the dance floor later."

"You assume I can dance."

She rested her hands on her hips. "I guarantee you can dance. Deckard . . . maybe not."

Christian looked over at Deckard sitting on a picnic table, his boots on the bench, eating a funnel cake.

"He can dance, but . . ."

"He rarely does. I bet if Harper were here, he would," she said, slipping her hand in his.

"You know, I think you're probably right."

After playing games and eating far too much food, they moved to look through the artist's stalls.

"The turquoise is gorgeous," she said, scanning every piece. She looked up at Christian. "I never noticed it before."

"What's that?"

"They're all unique. Their patterns, color, texture."

"Yep," he said, tugging her close as they exited the first stall.

She smiled up at him.

"Unique . . . just like you." He leaned down and pressed a lingering kiss to her lips.

Her head swam. He thought her unique. She liked that.

They continued walking, his warm hand in hers as they entered the next stall.

She perused all the turquoise jewelry. "Look at this one," she said, tugging him over. "Look how blue this bracelet is. I've never seen turquoise this clear blue."

"It's Sleeping Beauty," the woman running the stall said.

"I beg your pardon?" Andi asked.

"It's Sleeping Beauty turquoise," the woman explained.

"It's beautiful." Andi smiled. "Did you make the jewelry?"

The woman nodded.

"You're very talented," she said, and the woman nodded with a sweet smile.

"Try it on," Christian said.

"What?"

"Try it on. Here," he said, taking the bracelet and sliding it onto her arm, then he pressed a tender kiss to the inside of her wrist before letting go. Gooseflesh rippled over her from head to toe.

"What do you think?"

"Hmm?" She was still reeling from the kiss.

"Do you like the bracelet?"

She looked in the mirror at the Sleeping Beauty turquoise bracelet in the shape of flowers all around her wrist. "It's gorgeous." And something she'd love to wear. Something that was actually *her*. Not the plain professional she'd been playing for the last year. It was time to return to just being her.

"Then it's yours," Christian said, taking out his wallet.

"What? You don't have to do that."

"I know, but I want to." He smiled, then paid the woman.

"Thank you," she said.

They both thanked her as they headed out of the stall.

"What now?"

He smiled. "Dancing." He gestured down the string light–lined Main Street to the dance floor on the other end in the center of the large downtown park. "Can I spin you around the dance floor?"

She grimaced.

He chuckled. "What was that face for?"

"Your twirling me got me excited about the idea, but I don't know how to dance," she said, embarrassment flushing her cheeks.

A curious grin tugged at Christian's lips. "You really don't?"

"Nope," she said. "Zero rhythm, and I can't keep time to save my life."

He took her hand in his. "I'll teach you."

"Okay, but no complaining if I step on your feet. Deal?"

"Deal." He nodded.

They made their way to the park and stepped on the dance floor as "Blessed the Broken Road" began to play.

She followed Christian's gaze toward the band and cocked her head. Had the singer just winked at Christian? "What was that about?"

"What was what about?"

"Never mind. Okay, what do I do?"

"You place one hand here on my shoulder."

She did.

"Good. Now, take my hand," he said, holding his arm up to her shoulder height. "We're going to go two steps right. One left. In time with the music."

She arched her brows. "I wasn't joking when I said I can't keep time."

"No worries," he said, his hand holding hers, tight and warm. "I'll keep time. You just follow my lead. Ready?"

"I sure hope so." She exhaled, wondering just how embarrassing this was going to get.

"Left foot back first," he said. He took a step, and she fumbled.

She released a nervous laugh. "Sorry," she said. "I told you I wasn't joking."

"All good." He smiled. "Let's try again. Same thing. Ready, and one step back on the left. Good," he said. "Two on the right. Good."

Before she knew it, he was leading her around the dance floor. It took a while for her to stop counting each step and just relax into his lead, but she finally did. Being on the dance floor with Christian, caught up in the words of the Rascal Flatts song, she realized God truly had blessed the broken road she'd been on with restoration and love. She was so grateful.

She glanced over to spot Greyson asking Riley to dance.

Surprise filled Riley's face, but she said yes.

"Look," she said, nudging Christian's hand that way.

"Well, that's a first. So is him wearing jeans. Looks like Deckard will be mucking out the stalls tonight."

She frowned.

"Deckard and I bet what Greyson would wear, and I called jeans. You know, it's the first time I've seen him wear them."

"Really." She smiled over at Greyson and Riley. Whether the brothers wanted to admit it or not, there was definitely something brewing there.

"You know, you never told us why you call Riley 'Cool Whip.'"

"It's a cowboy nickname for someone who is formidable and never gives up on their passion."

"I like that," she said while he twirled her.

"Good, because I have one picked out for you."

She arched a brow. "Oh?"

"Moonflower."

She liked it, but . . . "It's a cool nickname, but why moonflower?"

"It means amazing fighter, and that's what you are."

She smiled up at him. "You really think so?"

He pressed his forehead to hers. "I know so." He lowered his face so his lips brushed hers. "Know what else I know?"

She shook her head.

"I'm falling in love with you," he whispered against her lips as "To Make You Feel My Love" by Garth Brooks began to play.

"That's good," she murmured back.

"Oh?" His breath tickled her mouth.

"Because I'm falling too."

He pressed his lips achingly slow to hers.

She wrapped her arms around his neck as he deepened the kiss. Everything else faded away until all she felt was him—his secure arms holding her tight, his skin warm against hers—and she prayed this moment would never end.

At some point, the band really did stop, but they remained, moving to music only they could hear.

If you enjoyed *One Wrong Move*,
read on for an excerpt from

The Killing Tide.

Available now wherever books are sold.

ONE

FIRE RIPPED THROUGH Finn's right shoulder, ricocheting down his arm. Battling the eight-foot swells, he struggled to get his charge to the swaying basket and up into the Coast Guard helicopter.

Gritting his teeth, he swam backward. His right arm encircled her waist, but his grip kept slipping. "We're almost there," he hollered over the rumble of crashing waves.

She squirmed and flailed forward. "Stan!" she sobbed, lunging for the listing boat Finn had just dragged her from.

"I need you to be still, so I can get you to safety. I'll go back for your husband. You're going to be all right." He tightened his grip, ignoring the lancing pain.

Light faded to darkness. The storm was moving swifter than anticipated. The team would insist they go, but he wasn't leaving without the husband.

Finding strength he didn't think he possessed, Finn rolled the woman into the basket.

Tears streamed down her cheeks. Sloshing whitecaps slapped them away.

Gripping the edge of the basket, he strapped her in, the clips pinching his finger. Once she was secure, he circled his throbbing finger. Tony retracted the cable.

385

Buffeting winds rattled the basket as it swung up into the air.

Please, Father, let her reach safety.

"We've gotta go," Tony yelled down. "Storm's moving in."

"Three minutes." *Please.* He'd never left anyone behind.

Lifting the basket into the bay, Tony hollered to the pilot, then turned his gaze back to Finn. "You got two."

Finn headed for the sinking boat as Tony lowered the basket.

The wind at Finn's back carried his failing strokes through the water. *Just one more, God,* he prayed. *Let me save one more.*

Spots clouded his vision, his right arm refusing to rotate. A torn rotator cuff?

Time ticking away, he dug in with his left arm but was barely crawling forward.

The man, according to his wife, was trapped belowdecks, his left leg broken and pinned beneath debris. The wife had tried to get him out but wasn't strong enough.

The wave-lashed boat listed nearly full to port. He had to swim faster, harder . . . ignore the pain.

The copter's blades swooshed almost silently over the ocean's roar as it rose higher above the heightening waves. The basket swung over the raging surface.

A fierce wave pummeled over him, dragging him under. He breached the surface only to be lashed by another wave.

Rising above the surface, he watched as the boat sank mere yards away.

The wife's piercing shriek echoed over the reckless, churning sea.

Tony hoisted the basket up and lowered the cable for him.

"No!" Finn hollered, shaking his head. He'd never left a man behind.

"Time," Tony insisted, "or you'll get us all killed."

His entire being sinking inside, Finn clipped in and rose above the angry sea.

TWO

GABBY ROWLEY DROVE THROUGH the nearly deserted downtown streets. The press-awards banquet had been a success, according to her boss at the *Raleigh Gazette*, but the local event was nothing like the press galas she'd attended before Asim Noren destroyed her international journalism career and nearly ended her life.

She glanced at the moonlight glinting off the faux crystal trophy she'd been awarded for excellence in journalism for her exposé on drug dealer Xavier Fuentes.

A shiver tickled her spine at the thought of their last encounter—his dark eyes boring into hers.

She jumped as her cell rang—her Bluetooth signaling a call from Noah.

She exhaled a steadying breath and answered. "Hey, bro."

"Hey, kid."

She glanced at the clock. 11:03. "You're calling a bit later than usual. Everything okay?" In his line of work, she never knew.

"Everything's fine. Just wanted to check in."

Since Fuentes's arrest and the confiscation of millions in cocaine, her brother's protective side had come out in force.

"How's Mom?"

387

"Good. I know she gets lonely at times, but the kiddos are keeping her busy."

Kenzie's son and daughter had brought so much joy to their lives, especially with Owen's birth just three months after Gabby's, Noah's, and Kenzie's dad—affectionately known as Poppy to Kenzie's daughter, Fiona—passed unexpectedly.

She slowed, making sure she was clear for a right turn, and the silver car behind her honked.

"Was that a horn?" Noah asked.

"Yep. Just on my way home from the awards banquet," she said, making a right. The silver sedan sped around her, disappearing into the night.

"How'd it go?" Noah asked.

"Fine. What's new with you?" She stopped at a signal, the red light refracting off her windshield, making an upside-down *L* across her dash.

"Just finishing up some paperwork. The games start tomorrow."

Every year the Coast Guard Investigative Service team went head-to-head with the NCIS unit from Camp Lejeune in a battle of strength, endurance, and all-out fun. "What kicks it off?" she asked, a strange uneasiness seeping through her. Why was the light not changing?

She glanced around as Noah said something that didn't even register. Sunday night in the business district left dark buildings surrounding her. Her sense of isolation heightened, despite being on a call with her brother.

Tapping her two-inch heel against the floorboard, she ticked off the seconds with no cars passing by, and yet the light remained red.

"Gab? Everything okay?"

"Yeah. Sorry. Just waiting for the light to change." And for the uneasiness sloshing inside to dissipate—an uneasiness she hadn't experienced since that day in South Sudan.

The guttural roar of a motorcycle reverberated behind her. Headlights glared across her rearview mirror as a Triumph slowed to a stop beside her. Relief at not being alone filled her until she glanced over at the black bike.

The man shifted toward her, raising his arm. *Is that a . . . ?*

Lunging over, she'd barely collided with the passenger seat when a *thwack* shattered her window.

"Gabby!" Noah said.

Clutching her hands over her head, she stayed low as glass rained over her.

Praying for protection, she scrambled out the passenger door, her hands and knees colliding with the pavement.

She crawled toward the alley only to be yanked back. Her heart racing, she turned to find her hem was caught on the car door. A quick tug tore the sequined fabric loose.

"Gabby!" Noah called.

She couldn't afford to give up her position, so she remained silent, sweat slathering her back.

Heavy footfalls hit the pavement.

He was coming for her.

Sucking in a gulp of air, she kicked off her heels, said a quick prayer, and darted for the alley.

Shots retorted, one pinging off the dumpster to her left.

Her pulse pounding, she dove behind it. The pavement scraped flesh from her flattened palms. Ignoring the stinging, she crouched low and prayed.

Please keep me safe, Jesus.

Footfalls grew closer.

Tears stung her eyes. With a deep breath, she darted for the next dumpster. A bullet whizzed past her, ricocheting off the container with a shrill ping. She flattened her back against the cool metal. The stench of rotting trash violated the air. An acrid taste skittered across her tongue.

Swallowing her upchuck reflex, she scanned the alley for a way out. A dim light shone at the end. The Renaissance Hotel. If she could make it there, surely she'd be safe.

His footfalls nearly upon her, she broke into a flat-out run. Muscles heating, she stumbled into the road, headlights glaring into her eyes. Her heart sank.

What if the man had backup?

The car screeched to a halt.

"What are you—crazy?" the man yelled through the open driver's window.

She broke into a run as the car sped away. Refusing to look back, she flailed forward as fast as her trembling legs would carry her. Another bullet whizzed past her right ear, shattering the glass front of the hotel. She barreled into the revolving door, nearly tumbling into the lobby.

The front desk attendant lifted his radio. "Security!" He rushed to her side. "Are you okay, miss?" His attention darted to the door. Her gaze tracked with his, praying her would-be killer wouldn't be bold enough to enter. Thankfully he wasn't.

She collapsed into the employee's arms, winded and covered with damp, cold sweat.

THREE

FINN WALKER WOKE from the night terror—or at least that's what the shrink the Coast Guard had made him see called them. It'd been six years since he'd last performed a rescue swim—the first and only time he'd lost a life on duty.

Rolling over in bed, he switched on his nightstand lamp.

Lightning jagged in the sky, followed by a thunderous clap.

A swift gust swept through the window screen, rattling the shade.

He stood and arched his aching shoulder. Just like he did every time it rained.

He inhaled, grateful he could still swim and surf, but his shoulder would never regain the range of motion he needed to be a rescue swimmer. Even if it did, he couldn't go back. Not after failing a man and destroying his family. He pinched the bridge of his nose. All because of a stupid torn rotator cuff?

He grabbed the half-full water bottle off the dresser and took a long swig of the room-temperature liquid.

Leaning against the pinewood bureau, he finished off the bottle. Every single storm, pain shot through his shoulder, and every single storm, the night terrors returned. Forever reminding him how he'd failed the man, and how God had failed him.

391

ACKNOWLEDGMENTS

To Jesus—Without you there'd be no stories. Thank you for the gift of them and for holding me up all the way through, not just the writing process but throughout life. You are my Shepherd, Shelter, and Savior.

To Mike—Thirty-one years and counting. It's been a minute, right? The best minute ever. I love you.

To Kayla—For Starbucks on deadline, for daily Instagram laughter, for daily coffee chats, and for all you do and are. I love you.

To Ty—For all the beach vacations, last-minute math help, daily pictures that bring me laughter and joy, and, of course, our Starbucks runs. I love you.

To Dave—For sticking with me on this crazy adventure we call publishing, for believing in me and championing me all these years. I'm truly grateful.

To Janet—What would I do without you? Thank you for your wit, savviness, kind heart, and all your support. I'm truly blessed God brought us together.

To Jill—Thank you for your wonderful friendship all these years.

To Becky—For helping me through the weeds on this one. Thank you so much, friend!

To the Darlings—I love our group, our friendships, and cheering each other on over Zoom even if it's at 5 a.m. during deadline week and I look like I've been hit by a truck. You're always there to support me and I'm grateful.

To Renee, Caitlyn, and Joy—Thank you for reading various drafts of *One Wrong Move*, even when it was still called by the fancy name of *Book One*. LOL! Your insight helped shape Christian and Andi's story, and I'm grateful!

Dani Pettrey is the bestselling author of the COASTAL GUARDIANS series, CHESAPEAKE VALOR series, and the ALASKAN COURAGE series. A two-time Christy Award finalist, Dani has won the National Readers' Choice Award, Daphne du Maurier Award, HOLT Medallion, and Christian Retailing's Best Award for Suspense. She plots murder and mayhem from her home in the Washington, DC, metro area. She can be found online at danipettrey.com.

Sign Up for Dani's Newsletter

Keep up to date with Dani's latest news on book releases and events by signing up for her email list at the link below.

DaniPettrey.com

FOLLOW DANI ON SOCIAL MEDIA

Dani Pettrey   @AuthorDaniPettrey   @DaniPettrey

More from Dani Pettrey

When a Coast Guard officer is found dead and another goes missing, Special Agent Finn Walker faces his most dangerous assignment yet. Complicating matters is the arrival of investigative reporter Gabby Rowley, who's on a mission to discover the truth. Can they ignore the sparks between them and track down this elusive killer?

The Killing Tide
COASTAL GUARDIANS #1

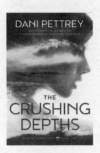

When an accident claims the life of an oil-rig worker off the North Carolina coast, Coast Guard investigators Rissi Dawson and Mason Rogers are sent to take the case. But mounting evidence shows the death may not have been an accident at all, and they find themselves racing to discover the killer's identity before he eliminates the threat they pose.

The Crushing Depths
COASTAL GUARDIANS #2

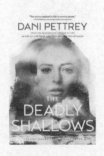

When his Coast Guard base is targeted by an elusive but deadly threat, CGIS agent Noah Rowley is rocked to his core. Desperate for answers, he must team up with medic Brooke Kesler, the only witness who could expose the man responsible. With targets on their backs, can Brooke and Noah find the killer before he strikes again?

The Deadly Shallows
COASTAL GUARDIANS #3

 BETHANYHOUSE

 Bethany House Fiction

 @BethanyHouseFiction

 @Bethany_House

@BethanyHouseFiction

 Free exclusive resources for your book group at BethanyHouseOpenBook.com

 Sign up for our fiction newsletter today at BethanyHouse.com